JILL GU

THAT TIME I LOVED YOU

hope·books

Published by hope*books
2217 Matthews Township Pkwy
Suite D302
Matthews, NC 28105
www.hopebooks.com

hope*books is a division of hope*media

Printed in the United States of America by
hope*books

First edition.
Paperback ISBN: 979-8-89185-021-7
Hardcover ISBN: 979-8-89185-022-4
Ebook ISBN: 979-8-89185-023-1
Library of Congress Number: 2023920886

Boat image by OpenClipart-Vectors from Pixabay

hope*books
hopebooks.com
Because the world needs your hope-filled
words now more than ever

CONTENTS

PROLOGUE

May 25, 1995—Newport Beach, California

He was gone.

Taylor's eyes scanned the waves, her heart beating faster by the minute as she stood frozen in place on her beach towel. She blinked over and over again, looking at the spot James was when he …

When he what? Disappeared? Vanished? What did she just see?

She fixated on the spot he was just moments ago, wondering if her eyes were playing tricks on her. She walked to the edge of the ocean, the water temperature cooler than it was only an hour ago, and she knew he was, in all actuality, not there. Panicked, Taylor ran frantically up and down the beach calling out for him, her voice growing weaker every time she yelled out. Shouting over the relentless roar of the Pacific Ocean seemed impossible, but she tried regardless.

Were the waves too loud? Or was it the hammering of her pulse in her ears?

"James!" Her voice was hoarse now, barely breaking through the wind that seemed to take him only moments before.

As Taylor scoured the beach, she wondered how much time had passed. She looked at her watch lying on her towel. Forty minutes. The longest forty minutes of her life.

Dread overtook her as she waded in the water to look for his body. It was her last resort, even though she knew it couldn't be true.

Drowning didn't make any sense. James was an excellent swimmer—he surfed every weekend he could, was the star water polo player for their high school and taught private swimming lessons at his parents' country club. He wouldn't have gone in the water and simply *not* come out.

It wasn't possible.

She spun in circles searching for the blue-and-white board shorts he was wearing. She felt irrationally angry at him for not wearing his red ones, which would have stood out like fire instead of blending in. But why would either of them think he'd need to today?

She looked at the jagged rocks sticking out in the water and, despite her better judgment, ran over, wondering if he was behind them. Crabs crawled in and out of the holes and crevasses, but James wasn't there.

He wasn't anywhere.

Taylor ended up climbing the steep rock path from the beach back to James's car in the gravel parking lot. *Maybe he ran up to grab something?* It was a fleeting and hopeful thought. Her legs burned as she got to the top, but she didn't care. Her heart sank as she saw his lone, red Honda Accord still parked where they left it almost two hours ago. That already felt like a lifetime ago.

James was nowhere in sight.

Taylor's breath was short when a wave of nausea hit her and she fell to her knees, leaning forward on her hands, not knowing what to do next. Squeezing her eyes shut, she groaned. Breathing became more difficult. Was this a panic attack? She had never had one before.

"Where are you?" she asked shakily into the air to no one, hoping for any answer at all. Her tears began to fall. She used whatever strength she had to try to hold them back. How could she go from elation one minute, to confusion and horror the next?

Still on her knees, she put her head on the dirt, feeling the need to regain control from the anxiety welling up inside her. She tried to slow her breath as she pictured the last moment she'd seen him—James giving her a graduation present; her new necklace in his hand.

Her knees stinging from the rough gravel, she opened her eyes as the wave of nausea passed. She stared at the ground, her skin scratched, droplets of blood forming on her skin. She lifted her head and looked up at the horizon.

He will come back. She was certain.

She steeled herself and stood up, then marched back down to the beach. She packed up their beach towels and picnic food and felt yet another jolt of pain in her chest as she picked up James's flip-flops. With full arms, she headed back up the rocky path without looking back.

"Bye, James!" she called out, now thinking it might be a game. Maybe he would surprise her halfway up the path and this would all be one big misunderstanding. They'd laugh and tell the whole story tonight at the party as she showed off her new necklace, while everyone oohed and aahed over it.

Except, he didn't surprise her on the path.

He didn't show up at all.

Taylor got back to the car, lungs and legs burning from exertion, hands shaking, items dropping from her arms as she fumbled for his keys in the oversized beach bag before clumsily unlocking the door.

She hurled everything into the backseat, but instead of getting into his car to leave, Taylor ran to the edge of the cliff one more time. She stared at the vast ocean, breathing hard. The sun was setting and starting to dip below the ocean's edge. The waves were coming in and breaking on the shore, and the sailboats were still out in the distance. This was supposed to be the most romantic night of their lives. Instead, it was turning into the worst.

"Where are you?" Her breath caught in a cry, and she covered her mouth to stifle her sobs. Taylor replayed the moment in her mind, over and over again, not quite believing it herself—the image of James's back, fading into thin air like a vapor.

He had literally vanished.

Once the sun set, she turned to look at James's car. She dreaded the drive home alone, but she'd have to leave soon. She was cold, her parents were expecting her, and James's parents were waiting for him.

She didn't know what to do about James's parents—Charles and Lydia Brooks. The thought of telling them paralyzed her with fear. They were the stereotypically wealthy and snobby people who thought they were better than everyone else. They were also far too hard on James, their only child. They poured everything they had, including all of their unrealistic expectations, on him. If he got an A on his test, they were mad it wasn't an A plus. If he won a swim meet but didn't beat his personal record, they didn't consider it a win. Nothing was ever good enough for them.

Truthfully, James *was* close to perfection. He was amazing at everything he did. He was kind, thoughtful, a good student, and a good friend. He was honest, loyal, and loved by many people. Plus, James treated Taylor like royalty, and she never had to question his intentions. In Taylor's eyes, he was like a god, but his parents treated him like a fallen angel. It drove her nuts.

Taylor inhaled and closed her eyes. "God," she breathed out, "if you're out there, and you know where he is … can you bring him back to me?" She sighed, and then out of habit from hearing James pray, she finished with, "Amen."

Taylor wasn't religious, but she was running out of options at this point.

She truly needed a miracle, so she quieted herself. She listened, and she waited. But she didn't hear anything back from God. There was no answer from anywhere. Other than the waves below and her heartbeat drumming in her ears, it was silent.

Taylor didn't know what to expect, though.

Despite her hopes, James didn't come running to her. He didn't call out to her. The wind didn't carry his voice to her ears. She didn't hear his footsteps coming up from the beach. Other than the seagulls and sailboats in the distance, there was no evidence of life down there.

A few more tears escaped from her eyes, and she angrily wiped them away.

She turned on her heels, defeated. Her feet felt like lead, not letting her do what she knew she had to, but they eventually took her back to James's car.

Taylor found the door handle through tears and angrily pulled at it. She sat behind the wheel and pulled the seat closer to the pedals so hard that she hit her already stinging and scratched knees on the dash, causing her to cry out in pain.

Putting her head on the steering wheel, she let out a scream that she didn't feel coming and didn't know she had in her. If James were anywhere close, he would have heard it and come running. Her head popped up with hope; maybe her scream had worked.

She waited a minute, but the now-dark parking lot was still empty. He didn't come running at the sound. He wasn't here.

She started the car and wiped her nose with her bare arm. When she heard the song from the cassette tape James had made her, she immediately ejected it, already too pained by the emotions the music evoked. She was tempted to throw it out the window, so that if James were there, he'd see it and know just how angry she was at him, but she thought better of it. She didn't want to be petty at this moment, and she didn't even know if she was actually angry. Instead, she threw the tape in the backseat. She had to throw something.

Maybe she was angry at first, but now a strange combination of anger, fear, and confusion overtook her. She felt lost and alone.

Her mind raced, wondering where he was and what he was *actually* doing right now. She desperately hoped that he was okay. But what if he wasn't? Was he scared? Was he lost? Was he still alive? Should she go to the police?

With questions swirling around her mind and tears streaming down her face, Taylor put the car into drive, and slowly, hesitantly, made her way out of the parking lot.

CHAPTER ONE

Then

May 25, 1995—Newport Beach, California

Taylor had never been happier. She felt light and free, her heart pounding as she ran down the steps and out the front doors of her high school for the last time. The fact that things would soon *drastically* change wasn't even a thought in her mind.

James, her boyfriend of four-and-a-half years, had planned a celebratory beach afternoon just for the two of them and she was running to meet him. Her face hurt from smiling and she felt as if she were floating as she gave a few last-minute waves and hugs goodbye.

Nothing was going to ruin today—she wouldn't let it.

Taylor couldn't suppress her smile as she scanned the front of the school for James. When she didn't see him, she skipped her way over to the flagpole and dropped her thousand-pound backpack that was weighed down with textbooks, all her leftover locker decorations, and old gym clothes that she'd mindlessly stuffed at the bottom. The wafting stale smell caused her to wince, and she had half a mind to throw them away, but then she'd have none of her high school T-shirts left. She wanted to keep at least one, if only for the memory of her and James's love story.

Sitting on the cement wall surrounding the flagpole, she twisted her body and shaded her eyes to look for James's car in the parking lot, but the lot was almost empty already. His brand-new red Honda Accord, that his parents had bought him as a graduation gift, stuck out among the others—and it was definitely not there. She sat on the wall a minute longer, wondering if she should go back into the school and ask the secretary if she could use the phone to call him at home. But then she heard it.

The corners of her mouth turned up as her eyes drifted toward the music, already knowing where it was coming from.

There he was. James, in his new car, windows down, blaring "How Sweet It Is (To Be Loved by You)" which was not a song one blares through car stereos—or any stereo for that matter—but that was James. He lived his life to the fullest, regardless of what other people thought of him. He came cruising down the road, taking a sharp right into the school's parking lot and then a left into the drop-off/pick-up zone, with James Taylor playing at a deafening level.

James Taylor was, for obvious reasons, their forever favorite artist—even though in middle school his music was more like a thorn in their side (sixth graders were seriously cruel).

But now, none of that mattered. Taylor mentally waved off the stares they were attracting, picked up her backpack, and started running to him. James hopped out and ran around to open the door for her, all the while singing along with the song they had dubbed "theirs."

Taylor shook her head, smiling, getting up on her tiptoes to kiss him on his cheek. "You're impossible."

As she got into the car she threw her hefty backpack behind her, which took some force given its weight, and noticed that the back seat was empty. A brief wave of confusion crossed over her as she had assumed that it would be full of their picnic supplies and beach gear. She felt a twinge of disappointment.

Taylor, chill. This is James. It's probably all in the trunk.

Once she was safely seated in the passenger seat, James shut her door, ran back around to the driver's side, and hopped back in. He leaned over the center console to kiss her. To really kiss her—sliding his hand from her cheek and into her hair, pulling her in deeper. Getting lost in the moment, Taylor forgot where she was until she heard someone whistle as he walked past the idling car.

Smirking and breathless, James pulled away. "We only have a few hours left." His voice came out in a gruff whisper. "We aren't going to waste any of it." He winked at her, and heat rose in her face as she assumed what he meant by that, until they both jumped as a driver laid on the horn behind them.

Not at all fazed, James calmly shut his door and looked into the rearview mirror. Then, with a sly smile, he casually put his brand-new car in reverse, slowly backing up toward the car behind them.

Taylor hit his arm. "James! What are you doing?"

She turned around in her seat to see the action unfold, horrified by this new side of James she hadn't seen before. Her worry quickly evaporated when she saw that it was just Mark—James's best friend. Mark scrambled to put his dad's convertible Pontiac Sunfire in reverse so it didn't get hit, screaming profanity the whole time. He was in a fit of panic.

James only started laughing and put his own car into drive, yelling, "See you tonight, bro!" and waving at Mark out his open window. He peeled out of the school's lot and headed toward the beach.

Taylor grabbed his hand and scooted over just enough to rest her head on his arm. James was six-foot-three, and his seat was pushed almost all the way back to make room for his legs. Taylor always hated feeling like she was sitting in front of him when they were in the car together, so her seat was pushed back as far as it could go, too, which meant that she had ample legroom. She really could have put her backpack *plus* their picnic supplies in front of her with room to spare.

Their private beach picnic was the perfect way to end their high school career and enter a new stage of their relationship, and tonight's graduation party at Ashley's house was the best way to finish their perfect day.

Everyone would be there.

After that, they'd leave each other for their summer jobs—James was going to his church's summer camp as Head Lifeguard, and Taylor was staying at home, working for Ashley's dad's pool company. She hoped this summer would pass quickly but knew that being away from James meant it would crawl at a snail's pace. She couldn't wait to start college together that fall and already had a countdown set in her mind.

Thinking of the picnic supplies he'd promised to bring, she casually said, "Hey, where's all the stuff for the beach?" hoping she didn't sound too high maintenance.

James glanced at her sideways, then turned his attention back to the road. "Uh, it's in the trunk?"

Taylor stared at him. "In the trunk?" She raised an eyebrow. "James, is that a question? Or did you forget to bring it?"

She tried not to sound too annoyed, but she'd been looking forward to this for weeks—and while she didn't want to ruin the moment, or their night for that matter, she *did* wonder if James had already ruined it by forgetting. With a small shake of her head, she willed that ugly untruth away. There was no way he would have forgotten. He was just as excited as she was. They'd both been talking about this night nonstop.

"No. I am not asking." James shrugged before continuing slowly. "I know it's not in there, either."

Taylor's head snapped toward him, confused.

He let go of her hand and reached into his center console to grab one of the many cassette tapes he kept in the car.

"I made you a new mixtape," he said, changing the subject and finally turning to look at her. "I called it 'Don't Forget About Me This Summer.'"

Taylor laughed, despite her annoyance, as he smiled his wicked smile that made her swoon all over again.

"Because I don't want you to forget me while I'm saving lives at camp and all."

She hit his arm again. "Like that'll ever happen."

"Like what will ever happen? You forgetting me? Or me saving lives?" James laughed at his own joke, but Taylor quickly opened the case.

He made the best playlists, and she had a whole cassette box at home dedicated to every single one he'd made specifically for her.

With a bright white sticker on a black cassette, it had black and red Sharpie drawn all over it. On the left side, he'd drawn a picture of a tree. It was *their* tree, including the initials they had carved into the tree trunk in front of Taylor's house, surrounded by a heart. On the other side, he'd written, *"Love you always, Tay. TB ♥ JB."* She ran her fingers over the initials, wishing she could freeze this moment, and her feelings, forever.

She slid the tape into his new dual cassette/CD stereo system and held her breath in anticipation while she anxiously waited for the first song. James grabbed her hand again, and unbeknownst to either of them, drove them down Pacific Coast Highway together for the last time.

James already had everything set up at the beach when they'd arrived— leave it to James not to want to waste a single moment of time with her for such a task as tedious as setting up. After an unforgettable afternoon of swimming, laughing, and lots of kissing, they flopped down on their beach towels to soak up a few more rays before sunset.

James took in a deep breath and rolled over to look at Taylor. "I have something for you." Then he sat up and reached into the beach bag.

Taylor sat up, too, taken by surprise. She felt a twinge of guilt. She hadn't gotten anything for him. Was she supposed to?

His hand came out of the bag holding a flat, black rectangular box.

"This is for me?" Her eyes widened and her voice cracked, causing her face to flush with embarrassment.

James laughed at her obvious question.

"Who else would it be for?" He leaned in to kiss her flushed cheek. "Happy graduation, sweetie. This is the start of our forever together."

Taylor didn't move at those words. *This is the start of our forever.* She could only stare at him. He really *was* her forever, wasn't he? But they hadn't said those words out loud before.

"Open it." James's voice was a whisper and Taylor thought that he sounded, dare she think, afraid?

She took the box and slowly opened the lid. A dainty gold chain with a white pearl in the center was sitting on a cloud of white. How did he find something so perfect? Tears stung her eyes—she couldn't wait to wear it.

She would wear it for the rest of her life.

Taylor looked at James, squinting from the setting sun behind him, her throat thick with emotion. "Happy graduation." She smiled and felt a shiver as the wind from the ocean picked up, making goose bumps rise on her arms. She didn't want to take her eyes off the necklace.

He took it from her and stood up, fumbling with the clasp; his hands seemed to be getting cold, too. She took his cue and stood facing him, staring at this gift that she still couldn't believe was hers.

"Turn around," James murmured.

Taylor obliged, lifting her long brown hair out of the way. It was still wet and salty from swimming in the ocean, but she didn't care. Her cheeks were starting to hurt from smiling so much.

"Shoot!" James bent down and Taylor turned to see him pick the necklace up off the sand. "I dropped it. Let me wash it off really quick—I'll be right back." He stood back up, the sandy necklace dangling from his hand, and kissed her on the forehead.

"James, I'm sandy, too! I don't care!" she called after him.

Without turning around, she heard him yell back, "But I do!"

She watched as he ran towards the water, one hand gripping the necklace while the other combed through his dirty-blond hair, streaked with highlights from all the time he spent surfing in the ocean.

Butterflies consumed her stomach. *He's my forever.*

Taylor turned to grab her lip gloss from her bag. A quick swipe wouldn't hurt, not that he wouldn't kiss her without it. But this kiss would be different. This would be *the* kiss that solidified their very first talk of "forever."

Taylor turned around, lips fully glossed, and saw a glimpse of his back running toward the incoming tide before he faded away like a mirage in the desert.

She blinked, unsure of what she saw, but he was already gone.

CHAPTER TWO

Now

June 26, 2016—Myrtle Beach, South Carolina

Taylor was in the kitchen washing dishes when the moving truck pulled up to the Baxters' old house across the street. She didn't know much about the new neighbors other than that they were moving from out of state.

Taylor's three boys, Jacob, Joshua, and Jamie had been playing basketball in their driveway for the majority of the afternoon and stopped to watch. They all had bets with one another as to who was moving in. Jacob and Joshua, her two oldest, hoped that it was a family with a girl their age. Ideally a cute one. Taylor rolled her eyes at them when she'd overheard their conversation. Classic teenagers.

Her youngest son, Jamie, on the other hand, just wanted a friend to play anything *but* basketball with. Their street, Adler Lane, had a lot of kids on it, but none of them had anything in common with Jamie. Most of them were either in high school with his two older brothers, or they were toddlers in strollers.

Her oldest, Jacob (or Jake, as he preferred to be called), was sixteen years old, and much to Taylor's dismay, had just gotten his driver's permit. Jake thought he ruled the city of Myrtle Beach, where he was born and raised. He loved to cruise up and down the main strip, sneaking glances at all the cute summer tourists who came every summer to enjoy the white sandy beaches, concerts on the boardwalk, and a nightlife enjoyable for every age. Despite Myrtle Beach being a tourist town, the locals made it feel small; information traveled easily to everyone who lived there year-round.

Josh was fourteen years old and idolized his older brother Jake, who was, hands down, the coolest kid at school. Jake was the one all the guys wanted to be, and the girls wanted to be with. Taylor called him "Zack Morris," but none of the boys knew what she was talking about, which always made her laugh.

It was Josh, though, who concerned Taylor the most. He was easily swayed by the last person he spoke to about anything, and he was a major people-pleaser. Taylor knew that, at times, this trait was admirable. But most of the time it was his downfall. Josh was often caught in situations he didn't want to be in, or needed help getting out of—all because he wanted to fit in. Taylor wished Josh had a stronger backbone and that he would learn to say "no" and stand up for himself, regardless of what his friends—or his older brother—thought of him.

And then there was her sweet Jamie—their little surprise. Jamie liked to read, solve puzzles, and watch crime documentaries, despite his parents' concerns. His imagination was active. The kids on their street played basketball or rode their skateboards and bikes over jumps that Jamie was always too scared to try. He wasn't an introvert but definitely liked to keep to himself and didn't have a lot of friends. Jamie's best friend was Dylan, and she only came with her parents to their beach house in the summers. Dylan's family had been coming to Myrtle Beach since before the two had been born, so they'd pretty much grown up together. Taylor wished Jamie had a friend at school, preferably a boy, but all the boys at school made fun of him. Taylor was called in for a meeting at least once a month because of a *situation.*

She hated that term. Being bullied was more than just a situation, but the school refused to acknowledge it as such.

Jamie was kind, mild-mannered, and a good kid. He was smart and always won academic awards at the end of the school year. Taylor's husband, Travis, said that out of their three boys, Jamie was the most like him when he was a kid. Taylor loved when he said that, and she also loved that he and Jamie had that in common. Travis never pushed Jamie to be tougher or to play basketball with the boys; he simply encouraged Jamie to be himself.

She admired her husband for that—Travis loved Jamie for who he was, not who others thought he *should* be.

But today was different. Jamie was out in the blazing sun with Jake and Josh, not trying to fit in or even pretend to play. The boys were out there for the sole purpose of making sure they were the first ones to see the new family moving in.

Jake held the basketball under his arm, staring across the street, making it obvious that he was disappointed to see an elderly man slowly make his way from the moving truck and into the house. The old man didn't turn around once.

Taylor just shook her head. Jake was getting to be quite the cocky teen, and Taylor made a mental note to talk to Travis about it later.

Josh was bouncing the basketball by the net, making a shot every so often, acting like he didn't really care. Everyone, including Taylor, saw past the facade. He really *did* care—he just didn't want to be caught staring.

Taylor laughed when she saw Jamie. Her sweet boy, who unashamedly wore his heart on his sleeve, was all the way at the end of the driveway. His hands were clasped in front of him as he waited in anticipation as if a celebrity was about to emerge from a limo at the Oscars.

Taylor felt an urge to be close to her three boys, so she decided to head out to the driveway and meet the new neighbors with them. She turned off the tap, dried her hands, and walked out the side door and into the garage. She pressed the remote to open the garage door. Her eyes did a quick sweep of the space. She was hoping to keep herself busy by picking up the boys' sports equipment, and then maybe have a sudden, *Oh, hey, new neighbor! Didn't know you'd be coming today!* But of course, she knew. The whole street knew. Taylor suddenly realized where Josh got his mannerisms.

As one of the street's original homeowners, the Baxters had been a beloved family on Adler Lane. They were also the family who had started the "Annual Adler BBQ" every Labor Day weekend to celebrate the tourists going home and the locals reclaiming their city. It always started with a family bike ride to the beach while the meat marinated, and then back for a swim in a variety of pools, followed by the best barbequed ribs Taylor had ever tasted—fall-off-the-bone, melt-in-your-mouth sweetness that she could never recreate, no matter how many times she tried. And she *did* try. "It's all in the marinade and then the low, slow heat," Bob Baxter would say. "Then I let God take over and do the rest." His laughter would follow with, "He created the pig, after all!" He delivered this line like clockwork, and Taylor always laughed like it was the first time she'd heard it.

Bob had been the first to pass away. He'd had a heart attack in the middle of the night, and Agnes had woken up to her still, lifeless husband. Taylor couldn't even fathom how Agnes had still wanted to sleep in her bed for the rest of the night. But sometimes love makes you do crazy things.

Taylor knew that more than anyone realized.

Agnes had passed away just short of a year after Bob, and no one knew the exact cause. Taylor always thought it was from a broken heart. The Baxter kids said she'd passed painlessly in her sleep, as if that would help take away the pain of her absence on Earth.

Agnes had always been sweet, but she'd never been the same without her husband. Agnes hadn't known how to live without him, and there had been so many times Taylor had wanted to go over and tell Agnes she knew what she was going through. Taylor knew what it was like to lose the love of your life, but after pushing that memory far out of her mind for so many years, she couldn't summon the words even if she'd tried.

Taylor missed the Baxters, and she knew that the new neighbors could never live up to their standards. But there she was, no better than her boys, trying to hide her gawking as she opened the lid to the dryer to see if there were any clothes in there to fold if only to spend a few more minutes out in the garage.

Taylor let out a sigh when she saw that the dryer was empty and rolled her eyes. With three boys and a husband who changed his clothes more often than a Kardashian on her wedding day, her laundry was endless. And today, of all days, there was no laundry to do.

She looked around the garage, trying to find something—anything to keep her occupied—when she heard a friendly voice.

"Well hi there, boys!"

Taylor's head shot up in the direction of the sound. An older woman, whom Taylor guessed to be in her late sixties, was standing on the step of the moving truck's open door, looking like she was, in fact, a movie star getting out of a limousine at the Oscars. The woman was stunning.

There was also something familiar about her voice which made Taylor stare a beat longer than she should have.

Jamie was the first to greet her, running across the street and fully taking the woman's greeting as an invitation to invade her personal space. Taylor's heart leaped out of her chest every time he bolted like that. The kid seriously did not know how to look for cars before crossing the street and it drove Taylor mad.

She started walking down the driveway after her son.

"Hi!" Her youngest unapologetically shot out his hand. "I'm Jamie and we couldn't wait to see who was moving in here!"

Leave it to Jamie to put it *all* out there. There was certainly no hiding motives now. It was all on the table.

The woman laughed graciously and stepped down from the truck. "Well, I couldn't be more excited to find out about our new neighbors as well." She flashed a white smile at Jamie as she took his hand and shook it. "It's a pleasure to meet you, Jamie. I'm Hazel DeLuca."

"Do you have any kids I can play with?" Jamie got right to the point and Taylor took that as her cue to rescue someone, although she wasn't sure if it was to rescue Jamie from embarrassing himself, Hazel from the awkward and obvious questions from Jamie—or herself before she died of embarrassment from said awkward and obvious questions.

Taylor passed Jacob, who was turning to walk back into the house.

"Where do you think you're going?" Taylor grabbed his arm, but Jake shook it off.

"I saw what I needed to," he grumbled, walking right into the house.

Taylor couldn't believe he was being so rude. He wasn't even going to introduce himself? She'd raised him better than that. She gritted her teeth into a plastered smile that she hoped covered her embarrassment and prayed Hazel hadn't heard him.

Taylor looked at Josh and narrowed her eyes in a you'd-better-not-follow-your-brother-into-the-house stare. Josh, being the people-pleaser that he was, hung his head in resignation and walked with her toward the truck. Taylor hated using his weakness for her own silly and selfish purpose of wanting her family to look like kind and considerate neighbors, but right now she felt no shame playing her "mom card."

Jamie was now telling Hazel about the bet that he and his brothers had about who was moving in, and she heard Hazel say, "Oh, well it looks like nobody won that one, then!"

That's when Taylor interjected.

"Hi, Hazel!" Taylor's hand shot out even faster than her son's had, and Hazel not only took it, but cradled it with both hands, smiling warmly at her, in no hurry to let go. "I'm Taylor." Her voice was small and unsteady as she tried to reclaim her hand, but Hazel had a firm grip.

"Taylor," Hazel repeated slowly, not breaking eye contact, or hand contact, for that matter. "It's such a pleasure to meet you." Hazel gazed deep into Taylor's eyes and at first, Taylor was drawn into it like a trance. She felt a sense of déjà vu, like she'd looked into these eyes before. Taylor couldn't look away and her mind raced as she tried to place Hazel's familiarity.

Taylor imagined the situation from an out-of-body vantage point, as she wondered what her neighbors might think if they saw what was happening. She let out an awkward giggle that seemed to surprise everyone. The stares she received from Jamie and Josh made her feel like she was being chaperoned on a date that she was failing miserably at. She broke away from both Hazel and her out-of-body imaginings, and firmly took her hand back.

"Welcome to the neighborhood," was all she could say, and she nodded her head in a silent bow.

What was wrong with her?

Hazel embraced the gesture and bowed her head in response. "Thank you, dear." Then she turned and pointed to her new house. "I would have loved for you to meet my husband, but he has some health issues, and this cross-country drive has taken a toll on him. I think he'll be sleeping until next Tuesday." She put her hand to her chest and chuckled.

Jamie, Josh, and Taylor all politely laughed along with her, but Taylor couldn't see the humor in it.

"Your boys are so handsome!" Hazel beamed like they were her own. "I didn't get a good look at the one who went inside, but these two ..."

Taylor's eyes went wide, and she smiled to cover up the embarrassment of knowing that Hazel had seen exactly what had happened with Jake.

"These two are the spitting image of their mother." Hazel shook her head in disbelief as if she had just uncovered the meaning of life. "Now, how long have you all lived here?" She crossed her arms, her eyes narrowed, and Taylor was shocked at how fast she could go from sweet grandmother to interrogator.

"My husband and I moved in shortly after we were married."

Taylor grabbed her boys' hands, which she never did, and wondered why she was doing it now. To show unity? Out of discomfort? Either way, the boys were looking at their mother like they didn't know her.

"Is that right?" Hazel put her finger to her temple and closed her eyes in concentration. "So, I'm guessing ..." She bobbed her head back and forth like she was counting, and obviously she was because she shocked Taylor by saying, "roughly eighteen years ago?" Taylor's eyes must have given it away because Hazel put her hand to her chest in triumph.

"Uh …" was all that Taylor managed to get out, brow furrowed at Hazel, wondering if the woman was a psychic.

Are psychics even real? Taylor started questioning everything she'd ever thought about them.

"Oh, I have a gift for these things." Hazel waved her hands in the air, looking pleased with herself, seeming to read Taylor's thoughts.

Like Taylor, Josh looked scared.

Then there was Jamie, who looked like he was in the presence of God Himself.

"And what a gift it is!" Taylor laughed nervously as she gripped her boys' hands even harder, slowly backing up toward the house. "Well," she said with a grin, "we'd better get going and leave you to it. I'm sure you have lots of unpacking to do!"

"Oh, of course!" Hazel waved. "So wonderful to meet you all! I can't wait to meet the rest of your family. Bring them by anytime!" She waved again, then turned and shut the truck door before going around and lifting the back open like it was weightless.

Once back inside the house, Taylor saw Jake sitting at the kitchen table, the chair turned to look out the bay window across the street. "She's weird," Taylor heard him say from behind her before the two youngest erupted in laughter.

"Jacob Hector Perez! *You* are the oldest and you are *supposed* to be a good example to your brothers, and what did you do?" Taylor put her finger to her chin. "Oh, that's right! You *walked away* from our new neighbor and into the house!" She pointed at the ceiling for emphasis.

It didn't work.

Jake just rolled his eyes. "Please, Mom." He stood up and walked up the stairs to his room, adding, "You couldn't get away fast enough, either. I watched you. I just did it first."

Taylor stood in the kitchen, silenced. He was right. Something about Hazel had made Taylor uncomfortable, on top of the fact that she couldn't put her finger on where she'd met her before … if she even had.

Taylor heard Jake's door slam before she let out her breath. She turned to look out the window at Hazel again. The older woman was carrying two huge boxes, stacked on top of one another, into her house all by herself.

"She's Superman's mom." The awe was clear in Jamie's voice.

Taylor laughed. "That's not true."

But still, she turned back to the window to watch her. Hazel was old but didn't act like it. Taylor had a pang of guilt for not asking if the woman needed help, but she couldn't bring herself to go back out there. What was it about Hazel? Her stare, her knowing glances ... It was strange enough to keep Taylor from going back out to help a woman in need, that's for sure.

But was Hazel really in need? She looked like she was doing just fine on her own. There was no hint of her struggling, and it made Taylor stare at her longer.

"Dad's home!" Josh broke her trance as he bounded back out the side door and through the garage, as Taylor watched Travis's car pull into the driveway.

He was home earlier than normal, and Taylor felt instant relief with the knowledge of his close presence. Jamie followed Josh outside, as Taylor went back to the half-full sink, turning the tap back on and waiting for the hot water to make its way through the pipes.

They had a dishwasher, but Taylor washed dishes by hand out of habit. She hadn't grown up with a dishwasher, and her earliest memories were with her mom, washing dishes together—they'd talked and laughed and told stories of their day's events.

But that was in the past, which Taylor never spoke of. It made her heart ache, and she wasn't sure why she still cherished this single memory. She hadn't spoken to her parents since she'd moved to Myrtle Beach. Their relationship had changed after ... well, after they didn't believe her about James. She wished things were different, but it made her cling to Travis and his family.

They were *her* family now.

"Hola, Hermosa!" Travis walked in, the boys close behind him. Taylor smiled, knowing that he only used his Cuban nickname for her when he was up to something. With two bags in each hand, he grinned suspiciously. "I brought dinner."

Taylor threw her dish towel down, flinging her still-wet hands around his neck to kiss him.

"How did you know that I needed this tonight?" She let go of Travis's neck and relieved him of the white bags he was holding. The smell of crab cakes and lobster rolls wafted up and immediately gave her pure joy.

"Well," he said as he loosened his tie and took off his shoes, "it's more like I wanted to celebrate."

Taylor looked at him, confused. "Celebrate what?" The question was flat. She couldn't think of any cause for celebration.

He gave her a sly smile, sat down at the kitchen table, and pointed his thumbs to his chest. "Guess who landed District Manager?"

It took her brain only a second to catch up, but once it did, her heart raced. "No way!" Taylor screamed, jumping up and down before landing on his lap. She took his face in her hands. "What happened?"

Travis waved his hands. "It's honestly not a huge accomplishment."

"How can this *not* be, Trav? You have worked *so* hard for years and now you are *finally* being recognized for it!"

Travis gave her a sad smile. "Diane quit."

"Oh." Taylor breathed out, finally understanding.

Diane had worked for the company only a month longer than Travis had. She'd never married, had no kids, and had thrown everything she had into her work. The truth was, Diane really did deserve the position—but so did Travis. Although they always got along in public, Diane wasn't kind to others in the office. It was as if she was purposefully trying to beat them in a big corporate game, instead of achieving a goal she legitimately wanted. It bothered Taylor, but she didn't want to cause problems between Travis and his coworkers.

"So, she just … quit? No explanation?" That confused Taylor. It seemed so unlike Diane.

"Pretty much." Travis stood up, gently pushing Taylor off his lap. "She sent an email to Stan saying that she was no longer coming into work but thanked him for the past fifteen years."

Taylor's eyes narrowed in confusion. "Do you think she's okay?"

He shrugged. "I'm not sure, but I think we'd know if she wasn't." He started up the stairs, stopping halfway up and calling to Jake who was still in his room. "Hey, Jake! Wanna go shoot?"

Taylor heard the thud of her son's feet running down the hall. Despite being too cool to meet the new neighbor, Jake was still just a little kid at heart, wanting to play basketball with his dad when he got home from work. Her son's excitement stopped Taylor from telling Travis about his rude attitude earlier.

Travis looked at his watch as he started toward the garage. "Hun, give us twenty minutes and we'll be in for dinner. The boys start the summer league tomorrow and I want them to be ready."

"Okay." Taylor glanced at Josh, who was putting his basketball shoes on.

Jamie ran past them in the opposite direction and up the stairs. "I'll be in my room!" he yelled all the way up and around the corner.

Taylor chuckled, wondering what book he was excited to get lost in today. Out of the corner of her eye, she saw Hazel come back out to the truck to grab yet another box. *She might just be Superman's mom after all.*

The thought reminded her of something. "Oh, Trav?" Taylor followed her husband into the garage as he grabbed a basketball and started dribbling it.

"Yeah?"

"The new neighbors moved in today." She paused but he didn't reply. "Her name's Hazel—I'm not sure what her husband's is. He went into the house before I could say hello. So, if she's out there, maybe go introduce yourself?"

Travis stood up straight, smiling. "Yes, dear." After kissing her on the cheek, he winked at Jake who was coming into the garage now, too. "So does that mean that Jake won the bet?" His eyebrows raised in mocked curiosity. "Is Hazel your new girlfriend?"

"Gross, Dad." Jake walked over and stole the ball from him as Travis laughed. "She's like a hundred."

"Jacob!" Taylor scolded.

Josh stepped down into the garage to join them. "Mom, you have to admit," he said as he put his arm around her shoulders, "there was definitely something off with her."

Taylor looked up at Josh, who was already two inches taller than she was, then at Travis with exasperation, but shrugged. "Well, she *was* sweet but ..."

"But nosy," Josh finished for her.

Taylor sighed and scrunched up her face in acknowledgment. "He's not wrong." She dropped her head, resigned to her son's truth.

Travis stole the basketball back, dribbling on the spot with his left hand to his right, then bounce-passed it to Josh, who did the same.

"Okay, so, the moral of the story is?" Travis asked, not taking his eyes off the ball.

"To stay away from them," Jake concluded, stealing the ball from Josh.

"Jacob!" Taylor scolded again.

He stopped dribbling, held the ball, and looked at her. "What? It's true, isn't it?"

They all looked back and forth at one another as Travis tried to make sense of the situation, eyebrows raised, before slowly nodding. "Then maybe staying away is a safe bet until your mom and I get to know them better." He seemed to close the subject, then headed out to the driveway with Jake and Josh following close behind.

Knowing that there was nothing more to say, Taylor turned to head back inside, until a motion across the street caught the corner of her eye. She turned to look in its direction and saw a man standing in the window staring back at them. She was too shocked to look away. The glare from the sun on the window made his face hard to see clearly, but it was unmistakable that he was staring at them.

Taylor pivoted quickly, fearful of being caught staring back. She went into her house and returned to the sink. Although she was still filled with nerves, she glanced up through their kitchen window once more.

But the man was gone.

She pursed her lips together, trying to figure out what to make of what she just saw. While she finished washing the dishes, she replayed the bizarre sight in her mind, over and over.

What was it about Hazel and her husband that made her take notice?

She took plates out of the cupboard and should have been happy to set the table for a dinner that she didn't have to cook, but a shiver ran up her spine as she thought about the encounter.

Taylor decided she agreed with her husband.

They should stay away from their new neighbors.

CHAPTER THREE

Then

May 25, 1995—Newport Beach, California

T aylor drove home in a daze.

Her tears had stopped somewhere between Main Street and Manning Road but returned when she passed by Bob's Burgers. It was her and James's favorite date night spot that had the best burgers in town—not to mention their drool-worthy milkshakes.

Taylor wondered how only two nights ago they were there celebrating their very last high school exam. Her brain couldn't comprehend this reality. It was almost as though now that James was gone, her memories of him should be also.

Her heart lifted when she saw Mark's dad's Pontiac Sunfire in the parking lot, knowing that Mike and Ashley were inside, having dinner before the graduation party. Taylor slowed down, ready to pull in. She needed to tell them, tell *anyone*, about what had happened. She needed a friend, and she needed help—they could help her.

Couldn't they?

Mark would know what to do. Or better yet, he might know where James was. But thinking of the words she'd have to say, how to describe what happened at the beach, what *really* happened—*he disappeared right in front of my eyes*—made her second-guess everything.

Her foot switched from the brake to the gas pedal, and instead of pulling in, she sped up. Taylor loved Ashley, but she also knew that *Ashley* loved Ashley—and would probably roll her eyes at Taylor before telling a story about the time her long-lost boyfriend disappeared, too, thus bringing the conversation right back to herself.

"Ugh!" Taylor cried in frustration as she pounded on the steering wheel. She wanted to talk to someone, to *anyone*, about what had happened. But what would she say and how would she even start to explain it? Could she trust anyone else with what she'd seen? She couldn't let the thought into her mind because it all felt too crazy.

Was it really all that crazy, though?

James was there, until … he wasn't. She didn't even see him go in the water before he … disappeared.

He just … vanished.

Taylor's eyes grew blurry from her tears, and she started talking to James like he was in the seat next to her.

"Seriously, James? How could you just … go? Like, completely vanish into thin air? I mean … is that actually a thing that people *do*?"

She heard her sharp tone and then started laughing like a maniac over her conversation with a phantom James. Just as soon as she started, her laughter stilled. She once again pictured the very moment and her mind spun as she tried to understand it.

It was like the wind blew him away, stealing him like a vapor. There was no other way to describe what she saw, but she couldn't verbalize that to anyone, not even to her best friends.

She continued to step on the gas, solidifying her decision as she looked in the rearview mirror. The bright red-and-yellow neon sign of the burger joint was fading farther behind her. She felt a pang of remorse for not going to confide in her friends then gripped the steering wheel tighter. Her breaths grew shorter, and her heart pounded faster as she turned into her neighborhood.

James only lived two minutes away from her, and she thought about turning around and heading to his house.

Maybe she should talk to his parents first. But if she did, what would she tell them?

Charles and Lydia Brooks were cold toward her, and there was no way they'd believe her anyway, so she decided against it. Taylor shook her head, wondering why she'd thought going there was a good idea in the first place.

Easy. Taylor smiled sadly. *Because James would have gone to see my parents first if I was the one who vanished.*

But she wasn't James, and his parents weren't her parents. The Brooks had never liked Taylor, making it clear that she wasn't remotely close to good enough for their precious son.

Taylor not only knew that they wouldn't comfort her, but they'd also go out of their way to throw out accusations. She knew that they would only be mad and blame her that he wasn't home when they'd asked him to be.

Or worse. Would they blame her for his disappearance? The thought sent chills through her body.

Both Taylor and James were to be at their respective homes by five-thirty p.m. so they could eat dinner with their parents and then get ready for the party at Ashley's tonight. James was going to pick her up at six-thirty p.m., and both of their parents had agreed to give them an extended curfew tonight. This was their last high school party, after all.

Taylor's parents were a lot more relaxed than James's, which surprised Taylor because they'd had a lot of healing to do after Kimberly died. For a few years after the accident, Jerry and Nina had held onto Taylor like she was a life raft, and they were all drowning in their grief. Taylor was only four when her older sister died in a car accident; Kim was sixteen years old. She had just gotten her license but got lost on the way to a friend's house at night. She'd done a three-point turn in the middle of a dark road as another car came speeding down a hill and didn't see her until it was too late.

She died instantly.

Taylor didn't remember much of that time. But through counseling and increased trust in Taylor, her parents started to breathe easier again.

She mourned for the older sister she wished she had known. Her memories were vague, and she sometimes thought she only remembered Kim because of all the pictures and home videos they had of her. Her mother hadn't been the same since. She always stayed close to home, and if she did go out, it was never at night.

Taylor was genuinely surprised when they agreed to let James bring Taylor home so late. But her parents were willing, trusting, and loving.

James's parents, on the other hand, were rigid. They hardly ever let him do anything outside of their church and youth group activities. Taylor sometimes went to James's youth group events and the occasional Sunday service, but she wasn't raised to be religious. She didn't see the point. She was a kind person and made good choices. There wasn't a big need for God in her life.

Or at least she hadn't thought so—until now.

James had grown up in the church, and although Mr. and Mrs. Brooks called themselves "Christians" they weren't very nice. Maybe it was because Taylor didn't believe like they did. She saw how Lydia talked to members of her church and Bible study friends, and it definitely wasn't how she talked to Taylor. To her friends, Lydia was kind and soft-spoken, complimenting them and encouraging them. But with Taylor she was cold and short, barely looking at her during the rare times she did talk to her.

Taylor usually shrugged it off as she and James waved goodbye, walking out the door hand in hand. After dating for almost five years now—with only one break-up in their sophomore year—they really didn't spend much time with the Brooks, and that was just fine with Taylor.

She and James had been dating since eighth grade and had known each other since the beginning of middle school. In sixth grade, they'd been in the same homeroom class and were right beside each other on the class list because of their last names: James Brooks and Taylor Brown.

On their first day of middle school their teacher, Mr. Schmidt, had called out, "James?" And when James hadn't responded, he'd called out, "Taylor?"

Mr. Schmidt's eyes had gone wide, and his face lit up in a goofy grin. "Hey! James Taylor is my favorite singer!" he'd announced. He then proceeded to sing the chorus to "Fire and Rain" to the delight of every immature sixth grader in the class. They'd all erupted in laughter while they'd pointed at James and Taylor, who were both sinking lower in their seats. Their classmates would not let them live it down for two long and embarrassing years.

James and Taylor had avoided each other like the plague for the first few months of school out of sheer humiliation. Middle schoolers could be so cruel, and there was nothing crueler than singling out two new sixth graders who didn't have a chance to defend themselves.

Now, James Taylor (the singer, not the couple) was James and Taylor's favorite artist. Most of the time, they introduced themselves as Taylor and James, not the other way around, but they quickly learned to laugh when their names were pointed out.

Once they'd started dating, they played James Taylor songs every chance they got, embracing their middle school trauma, and finding refuge in the safety of the now-familiar tunes. Although he wasn't at all cool among their peers, they played his songs in the car, at the beach, and at home while study-ing together. They considered him *theirs*.

The September they'd started eighth grade was abnormally hot in California, and a few families had met at the beach one weekend. Although Taylor's parents hadn't gone, she'd gone with her best friend at the time, Kelly, and her family, while James had gone with his best friend, Mark.

Taylor had started majorly crushing on James at the end of sixth grade but hadn't dared tell a soul. In seventh grade, she'd been tormented by the fact that she thought James had a crush on Kelly. Taylor had cried in the bathroom stall during lunch on multiple occasions, especially after seeing James and Kelly laughing together one day after second period.

Kelly had finally figured out what was going on and let Taylor know that she was not interested in James and that Taylor should most definitely go for him. Kelly actually really liked Mark and wanted to get close to James so she could get close to his friend Mark by default.

"Duh," Kelly had laughed. "It's like BFF 101, Tay!"

But after a mix-up at a dance when Taylor went to find James—for no other reason than to stare awkwardly at him—she found him talking to Kelly, who was laughing at something he said, and Taylor swore that her crush on him was over.

For good this time.

In Taylor's mind, Kelly might've had a crush on Mark, but James was most definitely crushing on Kelly.

Then came the infamous Labor Day weekend at the beach when James had the courage to finally approach Taylor. He'd done it as soon as Kelly and Mark had run off to play in the water, leaving Taylor and James alone on their beach towels. Well not *alone*, alone. All the parents were just down the beach. But at least they had not been within earshot of any of them.

"I was looking for you," James swallowed as he finally broke the awkward silence between them, "at the dance," he added, as if he had to clarify.

Taylor, already knowing this after another Kelly intervention but too embarrassed to acknowledge it earlier, played with a loose string on her beach towel, acting dumb. "Oh, really?" Her voice was higher than normal, and she hoped she sounded convincing.

She bent her legs and looked down at her toenails, which she and Kelly had painted the night before at their sleepover. She started to pick at the polish that was still on her skin.

She fidgeted when she was nervous, and right now Taylor was *definitely* nervous.

"Taylor?"

Even though James's voice went quiet, she was aware of every breath he took.

She looked up and stared into his eyes. His beautiful, piercing, bright blue eyes.

"Yes?" Her heart was beating out of her chest, and she hoped he didn't notice.

He hesitated for only a moment, looking out to the ocean, then bringing his eyes back to hers. He took a breath.

"I, uh …" He cleared his throat and Taylor's heart sped up in anticipation of what he might say. "I really like you."

Taylor immediately looked away, trying with all her might to suppress her smile so as not to give too much away, but her heart was doing flips. After all this time, she heard the words she'd longed for.

James liked her. *Her!* Taylor Brown.

Once she couldn't contain her smile anymore, she turned to face him. His face was a mix of confusion and fear, and she burst out laughing.

"So, uh …" He rubbed his hand through his salty blond hair. "That's not exactly the response I was going for." He looked down and started picking the same loose thread on the blue and pink flowered towel Taylor was sitting on.

She shook her head and turned her whole body to face him. She wanted to throw her arms around him, but even after his confession she was still too shy. She was bold enough to put her hand over his, though, and when she did, he looked up expectantly.

Staring into his eyes, she told him what she'd wanted to say for so long.

"I really like you, too."

They both smiled at each other and then looked nervously at the parents as if their parent senses might know exactly what was going on. But they were all in their own adult world, talking and laughing together.

Now, Taylor wiped at her eyes as she recalled the memory—the start of *them*. She wished Kelly had never moved away. She missed their friendship and could really use a friend right now. She sat in James's car outside her house for what seemed like ages, trying to remember anything about the drive over.

But other than seeing the burger joint, she recalled nothing. Muscle memory had taken her home.

Taylor glanced at her house, refusing to let her mind go where it needed to. She had to come clean with her parents. To tell them the truth. She had to tell them *everything.*

Her hands shook as she turned the car off and grabbed her purse, leaving the beach bag in the backseat. She had bigger things on her mind than shaking the sand out of the beach towels.

She shut the car door behind her, her feet slowly taking her up the walkway toward the front door of her house. She felt disconnected from her own body somehow.

Her heart grew heavier with each step, and she wondered how she was going to get through what she knew came next ...

Telling her parents.

She heard something move behind her but didn't register what it was until a man's voice broke through the silence.

"Taylor?"

She inhaled sharply as she jumped, unable to scream due to the adrenaline that coursed through her. There was a man standing at the curb in front of their house by the tree that held her and James's initials. He looked like he was older than her dad—he had thinning, gray hair and wore dark-rimmed glasses, cargo shorts, and a knit black sweater.

She started taking slow steps backward, inching herself closer to her house and farther away from this man.

"I'm not going to hurt you, Taylor ..." His voice was low and calm. He raised his hands in the air, showing her that they were empty. "I didn't mean to scare you ... I just ..."

He reached into his pocket and Taylor let out her breath, whispering, "No. Please ..."

Was he going to shoot her? And how did he know her name?

"My parents are right inside ..." Taylor's voice shook.

Still backing up, her foot hit one of the lights that lined the rock path to her front porch, causing her to fall backward. She let out a gasp, feeling a sting on her elbow from the fall. Getting her bearings without taking her eyes off him, she slowly stood back up, legs shaking.

Out of his pocket he took not a gun, but a piece of paper, and gently laid it on the path in front of him. Standing straight, he backed up into the shadow of the tree.

"If you have James, I—"

He cut her off, shaking his head. "No, I don't have him. Well ... not in that way, I don't."

Taylor wasn't sure if she heard him right.

Not in *that* way? Then in *what* way? She looked at the piece of paper on the path and pointed to it.

"What's that?" Her question fell flat; it was more of a statement.

"I need you to call me. I think I know—" He exhaled and looked down. "No, I *do* know what happened. To James, I mean." He looked back up, his eyes pleading with her, but for what, Taylor wasn't sure. Fear and excitement gripped her all at once.

"You know where he is?"

Taylor let her guard down and was tempted to get closer to him. She took a step forward, wanting to grab him and shake him and demand that he tell her *exactly* where James was.

He shook his head. "I can't tell you *where* he is, but I know ..." He swallowed hard and fixed the glasses on his face. "I know *when* he went to."

"When he ... *what*?" Her voice came out in a whisper as her eyes narrowed in confusion. Nothing he said made sense.

His words came out faster than she could wrap her mind around their meaning.

"He came to me, Taylor ... years ago, telling me this would happen ... telling me all about tonight and that I needed to contact you so you wouldn't worry—"

"Wait." Taylor's voice was now strong, and for some reason, she was angry, but she wasn't sure why. "What exactly are you saying?"

What was this man, who came out of nowhere, trying to tell her?

He rubbed at the stubble on his face. He looked worn out and tired, as though he'd been having an equally rough time to what she was.

He sighed and looked up at her. "James went back ..."

His eyes seemed scared of Taylor and her reaction to what he would say next.

"Went back where?" she demanded, losing patience but not giving him the chance to respond. "Back to the beach?"

She clutched the car keys and wanted to race back to the car, ready to go back to get him. She wanted to throw her arms around James and never let him go. Ever again.

But the man just shook his head again in bewilderment. It was as though he didn't believe what he was about to say or even that he was about to say it. He took a few tentative steps forward, starting to speak, but seemed to think better of it and stayed where he was.

He fixed the glasses on his face and took a breath, looking her square in her eyes.

"Taylor, James didn't go back to the beach. He went back in time."

CHAPTER FOUR

Now

June 27, 2016—Myrtle Beach, South Carolina

Taylor's phone rang and she smiled when she saw the caller ID. It was her best friend, Heather.

She swiped to answer and didn't even have time to say hi before Heather's voice bombarded her ear. "So, did you meet them yet? Tiffany said that Jake told *her* that they're super weird and creepy, and now I'm *dying* to hear what you think."

Taylor rolled her eyes—mostly at her son who was currently sitting at the kitchen table with his laptop. She stared at the back of his head as she replied, "He *would* say that, wouldn't he?"

Jacob turned around and narrowed his eyes at his mom when he heard her tone. He correctly assumed that she was in fact talking about him—but instead of caring, he shrugged it off, and went back to reading whatever sports highlights were on today's news.

Heather's voice interrupted Taylor's frustration with her firstborn: "So, apparently he's sick?"

Heather, always needing to know every bit of information available to her, wouldn't stop until she got all of the answers she needed—and she always needed them yesterday.

"Who's sick? Jake?" Taylor looked at her son again, as he had been the previous topic of conversation.

"No, Tay! The husband!" Heather snapped and Taylor could hear her friend's annoyance through the phone—not only could Taylor not keep up

29

with this conversation, but she could barely keep up with Heather's train of thought on the best of days.

Taylor opened the drawer looking for a pen for her never-ending grocery list. "Well, Hazel said he had health issues, although she didn't elaborate, so I'm not sure what he has."

"You mean you didn't *ask*?" Heather's voice was full of criticism.

Taylor laughed. "No! I didn't just *ask*. Who do you think I am? *Heather Michaels?*"

She heard Heather snort with laughter over the phone. She was probably more delighted that Taylor had used her maiden name after her divorce had been finalized just over a year ago.

Taylor glanced out the kitchen window at the DeLucas' house, as though looking at it would provide any answers.

"Why don't *you* go over there if you need to know so badly?" Taylor huffed, then went back to the drawer, finally finding a pen under her checkbook, and sighed.

Seeing it reminded her that she was late on a payment.

With her phone tucked between her ear and shoulder, Taylor made circles on the notepad, hoping the pen worked. Once satisfied, she opened her checkbook and started writing. The boys' summer basketball league deposit was past due, and she was going to give it to Jake to take to the game today.

"Remind me why we're friends?" Heather's words were so matter-of-fact that Taylor just shook her head, smiling, until she heard, "I'm coming over."

And then Heather hung up on Taylor, ending the conversation just as fast as she'd started it.

Taylor stared at her phone, questioning the entire conversation. Then, after setting it on the counter, she turned to her son.

"Jake, I'm putting this check in the side pocket of your gym bag." She picked up his black-and-white Nike bag and opened it. "Ugh!" Taylor cried as fruit flies flew in her face, and promptly dropped the bag at her feet, swatting the pests in the air in the process.

Jacob looked up, genuinely confused. "What?"

Taylor stood there staring at him, wondering how her son could be so clueless about cleanliness.

"Have you not seen, or *smelled*, the colony that's growing on the half-eaten, rotten banana in there?" She pointed to the bag in case there was any doubt over what bag she was referring to. "Come on, Jake! How long has it been in there?" Taylor walked to the kitchen sink, gagging from the smell. "Do you have another bag you can use today?" She looked back at the gym bag, wondering if she could just throw it in the trash.

"No."

Jake's reply was monotone, and frustration welled up inside of Taylor.

"*No?*" She repeated mockingly, hands on her hips. "Jake! Do you think this is normal?"

Jake wasn't giving her any kind of reaction, which made her blood pressure rise.

"Seriously, do all of your friends walk around with moldy food in their bags, too? Or do you all smell *so bad* that no one even notices?"

Finally, Jake looked up at her. "No."

Taylor knew from the smug expression on his face that Jake knew exactly what he was doing.

Taylor gritted her teeth and wondered if any other mothers felt the urge to throttle their own kids. Lately, she sometimes felt she had to hold herself back.

She looked at the time. Too early for wine o'clock.

A knock on the door was followed by Heather letting herself in, which probably just saved Jake's life because Taylor was ready to pounce. When did her sweet firstborn become so intolerable?

"Okay, so I tried to walk slowly ..." Heather started, then headed over to the counter, picked up the coffee pot and proceeded to pour herself a full mug of the coffee that Taylor had been saving for Travis. "...just in case they were out there so I could say 'Hi' but the house looks like it's locked up tight as a drum!" She took a sip of coffee and closed her eyes. "So good ..." she purred.

Taylor grabbed the now-empty coffee pot, rinsed it out, and then filled it back up to make another pot.

"Morning, all." Travis came in from the garage, sweating from his workout. "It's going to be hot today—I'm already feeling it and it's not even nine." He reached over Taylor to grab a mug out of the cupboard, and she gave him sorrowful eyes because the coffee he was so excited for was already being consumed by Heather. Not that he ever demanded it of her; she just liked to make him feel thought of, not overlooked.

She was thankful that he didn't say anything or show his disappointment. Instead, he smiled warmly at Heather.

"Hey, Heather! Are you and Tiff coming to the game this afternoon?"

Jake stood up so fast that his chair went flying backward, landing with a thud that shocked everyone into silence. Not making eye contact with anyone and without attempting to pick up his chair, he brought his empty cereal bowl to the sink, threw it in, and then marched upstairs.

Taylor's mouth hung open, but if Heather thought anything was amiss, she didn't show it. She just kept on sipping her stolen coffee as if this were a regular Monday. How could Jake not only behave like that, but in front of Heather? And how had Taylor let it happen without reprimand?

Although she knew Heather wouldn't judge the situation, embarrassment still flooded Taylor and she snuck a glance at Travis, whose face was red with anger as he watched his son stomp up the stairs. Travis rarely punished Jake because Jake rarely needed punishment, but this was a side of him they'd never seen before.

"I mean, what is his deal?" Heather sounded disgusted, looking out the window.

Taylor was staring at the top of the stairs where she watched her son walk around the corner and down the hall. "I honestly don't know …" She continued to stare although Jake was long since in his room. "He hasn't been acting like himself lately."

Heather's head whipped around, her long blonde hair following and wrapping around her neck like a snake. "Not Jake, Tay. *Him!*" She pointed out the window and across the street.

Travis's and Taylor's eyes followed Heather's, and Taylor involuntarily shivered.

There was Hazel's husband, standing at the end of his driveway, staring directly at them.

"Can he see us?" Taylor's question seemed silly in the moment as the three of them stared back at the old man who was, without a doubt, staring at them.

"Something is definitely not right." Heather shook her head slowly. "Can I stay a little longer?" She sat down on one of the kitchen chairs without breaking her stare. "I don't think I want to walk home alone after this."

"I'm sure he's harmless." But Taylor wasn't sure she believed her own words. "I mean, he's sick after all, right?"

Heather scoffed. "He's *sick* all right."

"Not like *that*," Taylor rolled her eyes.

She saw that the coffee was ready and poured two more mugs—she needed extra caffeine today. She took one over to Travis, and he thanked her by smacking her butt as she walked away.

"Oh gross, you guys." Heather stuck a finger in her mouth, pretending to gag herself. "You guys have been all over each other since you met."

Travis laughed. "I only wish that were true." He looked at Taylor, giving her a wink. "It took some convincing, but I got her."

He stood up and walked over to Taylor who was washing out the coffee carafe in the sink, and put his arms around her, kissing her neck.

"Travis!" Taylor gasped. "You stink!"

Travis planted a kiss on her neck. "Okay, okay. I'm late for work anyway."

"Besides ..." Taylor turned, giving Travis a long and steady stare, then winked. "I only married you for your mom."

He burst out laughing. "Oh, it's going to be like that is it, mija?" Travis perfectly mimicked his mom's Cuban accent and Taylor laughed along with him. He put his arms around her. "I don't even fault you for that." He smiled and kissed her.

"Hi." Heather fake smiled and started waving at them from the kitchen table that was only four feet away. "My name is Heather and I'd rather be absolutely *anywhere* else."

Taylor broke away from Travis's kiss and snorted from laughing.

"Nice, Tay." Travis laughed, and then pointed at her. "And I only married you for your laugh."

Taylor picked up the dish towel and threw it at Travis, who had already bounded up the stairs. She gave Heather an apologetic look and shrugged.

"I will say, Tay, you definitely ended up with the better Cuban." Heather rolled her eyes.

Taylor fully agreed but felt as though she were walking on thin ice when it came to Heather's divorce. Heather had introduced Taylor to Travis back in 1996 when she was dating Travis's friend, Derek—Heather's now ex-husband.

"So ..." Taylor said, changing the subject as she walked over and sat beside Heather at the kitchen table, "to finish Travis's question—*are* you and Tiff going to the boys' basketball game this afternoon?"

"Well, *I* am." Heather turned back toward the window.

Taylor snuck a glance outside to see Hazel's husband walking up the front path back to his house. He stopped briefly to look at the flowerbed that lined the bricks and Taylor felt something stir in her, although she couldn't put her finger on what it was.

Heather didn't seem to notice Taylor's trance. "I can't say the same about Tiffany, though." She rolled her eyes. "She's meeting a 'friend' at the beach." Heather used air quotes to emphasize *friend*.

"Wait …" Taylor put her hands up in the air. "Tiffany is actually missing one of Jake's games?" She realized her tone sounded a little too much like an interrogation and tried to backtrack. "I mean … she hasn't missed a game their entire high school career."

Heather gave her a look. "I think it's a boy."

Heather stood up and walked to the kitchen island. Sitting on a stool, she raised her eyebrows as if to dare Taylor to challenge her.

Taylor looked back at her, accepting said challenge.

"I'm sure it's not a *boy*," she said, then walked over and sat beside her friend on the stool next to her. "Tiff tells you everything, Heather. *Everything*." Taylor put a hand on Heather's arm. "I think you'd know."

"But what if she doesn't *really* tell me everything? I mean, I *think* she tells me everything, but what teenage girl tells her mom absolutely *all* the things about her life?"

"Fair point," Taylor agreed, frowning.

"Let's list all the things we hid from our parents when we were teenagers. I'll go first." Heather held up her fist, sticking up her index finger. "The first time I tried a cigarette." The next finger went up. "When I went to Dave's party and ended up staying the night, telling my mom I was hanging out with Morgan."

Taylor zoned out as Heather spoke, thinking of the biggest secret she had kept and how nobody knew what it was—not even Travis. This was definitely not a fun game to play. In fact, it was borderline dangerous.

"Okay, okay. I get it!" Taylor stood up abruptly.

She heard herself and cringed. She didn't mean to sound harsh, but she'd definitely come across that way. Even thinking about her past brought out the absolute worst in her, but it wasn't Heather's fault that she didn't know.

Taylor softened her tone. "But you're right. She's probably not telling you everything."

"You okay?" Heather eyed her.

Besides Travis, she was the one who knew Taylor best, despite not knowing *everything*.

Taylor put her hands on the counter and breathed out. "Yes, it's just …" *Don't say his name. Don't say his name*, Taylor urged herself, not knowing what had triggered the memory, exactly. She balled up her fists and blurted out, "It's Jacob!" as she gave Heather a knowing look. It was the safest bet after the little fit her son had just thrown.

Heather threw her hands in the air. "Jacob what? All teenagers are like that." She shrugged.

Taylor had a fleeting thought that maybe Heather really hadn't noticed his attitude from before, and really did think it was just another Monday in the Perez house.

"Listen," Heather continued on a mission, "creepy man is back in his house, so it's safe for me to finish my walk. Let me shower after and then I'll be here at two. Can I ride with you to the game?"

"Of course!" Taylor's voice was higher pitched than she'd intended. She felt like a fraud.

She really did love that Heather came to cheer on her boys, and it was fun when Tiffany did, too. But today, she was excited to have Heather to herself.

This was the third year that the boys had played in this summer basketball league, and as much as Taylor loved watching them play, the crowd was *very* different from the high school games with all the out-of-towners coming to watch. Heather made her feel safe in a crowd full of strangers. She really liked the other families who lived here year-round, but most of them had all grown up here and Taylor was a bit of an outsider herself. She also didn't like getting too many questions about her past, so sticking with Heather was a safe bet.

After the initial "Hi" and generic "How are you?" everyone just left them alone and cheered for their own sons.

Heather gave Taylor an air kiss, then walked out the door, saying goodbye with a flick of her wrist as she walked away.

Taylor smiled after her friend and closed the door.

She spent the rest of the morning and early afternoon reading with Jamie, putting spaghetti sauce in the slow cooker for dinner, and doing two loads of laundry before finally getting herself ready for the game.

By the time Heather came back, Taylor's three boys were already sitting in their black GMC Yukon. Jake and Josh, headphones on, were listening to their game-day playlists on their iPods as Heather stood outside the car trying to get them to tell her what the cool kids listened to these days.

Taylor finished getting a bag packed with water and after-game snacks before heading out the front door.

"Ready?" Taylor smiled at Heather as she locked the door behind her.

Heather smirked. "There'd better be a hot, single dad there today."

Taylor laughed at her friend. Ever since the divorce, Heather was like the teenage girl Taylor had met way back when—always on the prowl, even if they were just at the supermarket.

"Mom, we're going to be late!" Jake's voice was stern from the back of the car, and Taylor wondered who exactly the parent was here.

Jamie talked Heather's ear off in the car the whole five minutes it took to drive to the high school, and Taylor glanced in the rearview mirror at Jake, who was staring out the window in disbelief at the full parking lot of the high school.

Sensing his impatience, Taylor assured him, "I'll drop you boys off before I look for parking." She pulled around to the front of the school and the boys hopped out, Jake saying nothing, only rushing into the school, leaving Josh behind.

"Thanks, Mom." Josh gave her a sweet smile, trying to make up for Jake's bad attitude.

Taylor winked at Josh. "See you in there, buddy. Go get 'em, boys!" she called after them before pulling away, circling the parking lot for a spot.

"There!" Heather pointed to a gray Altima that was backing up. Taylor put her blinker on and waited.

"Why couldn't I go to Dylan's today?" Jamie whined in the back seat, looking at the school as though going to a basketball game were the equivalent of going to jail.

"Because" Taylor said while she turned the wheel, pulling into a spot that was a bit too tight, "we cheer one another on in this family."

Taylor had put the car in reverse to straighten it out when another car stopped and put its blinker on, thinking she was leaving. As she pulled forward, the car sped past them, the horn honking in disapproval and frustration at the lost parking space.

"Find your own spot!" Heather's voice was in Taylor's ear as she turned to yell at the car and catch a glimpse of who was so impatient.

"But, *Mom!*" Jamie's lament only made Taylor grow more frustrated. "They *never* cheer me on in *anything!*"

She got out of the car, slammed her door, and opened up the back one with frustration, knowing he was right but hating his complaints. She grabbed the snack and water bag, ready to tell Jamie *exactly* what she thought of him and his attitude when she heard her.

"Hey, neighbor!"

Taylor froze. Her eyes were wide with shock, and she looked at Heather to gauge her reaction, except Taylor only saw the back of Heather's head—she was already hightailing it out of the situation, weaving her way through cars up to the high school's front doors. Taylor clenched her jaw in annoyance and jealousy at her best friend's getaway.

"Hi, Mrs. DeLuca!" Jamie got out of the car; his bad mood was instantly replaced by cheerfulness upon seeing Hazel.

What was his fascination with her?

"Is Frank with you?" Jamie started tugging on her sleeve and Taylor's eyebrows rose in curiosity.

Frank? Is Hazel's husband's name Frank?

Hazel nodded. "He is with me, Jamie!" Her eyes were smiling bigger than her mouth was. "Although I dropped him off at the front so he'd have less of a walk."

Taylor felt herself relax a little. Hazel couldn't be that bad, could she? Jamie was a good judge of character, and for some reason he was drawn to them both.

Taylor smiled at Hazel and softened her tone, letting Jamie's comfort guide her words. "Are you two here for the basketball game?"

Hazel's laugh was as smooth as melted butter. Taylor found it soothing and intoxicating. She couldn't help but laugh along with her, although she wasn't sure why it was so funny.

Regardless, she was starting to understand why Jamie was drawn to the DeLucas. She was equally curious and, while hesitant, couldn't get enough information about them.

"No, no we're not!" Hazel put her hand on her heart as if that would control her laughter. "Our daughter and grandson moved back to town, and we're here to sign him up for school in the fall." She smiled and held up her purse, patting it and showing a file folder sticking out. "I have all his paperwork, as his mother was not able to be here today—*big* meeting at her new job and all." Hazel wiped her eyes underneath her sunglasses, then got a tissue out of her bag to wipe her nose.

Taylor wondered if she was sick or crying.

"Our grandson isn't the athletic type—he's more into video games and science projects." Hazel winked at Jamie.

"I am too!" Jamie practically yelled at her.

"I know you are! And I can't wait until you meet him—I think you two will be fast friends." Hazel flashed a smile that said way more than she did with her words. "Anyway, Frank is waiting. I'd better be off!" She turned and waved before walking to the sidewalk and up to the office doors.

"Bye, Mrs. DeLuca!" Jamie waved back at Hazel, then looked up at Taylor. "Mom? Can I go with her to meet her grandson?"

His eyes were so full of hope that Taylor felt bad about saying no, but she didn't know the DeLucas well enough to let her son go off alone with them. She didn't even have their phone number.

"Oh, sweetie, there will be another time you can meet him." She saw the disappointment in his eyes and bent down to kiss his perfectly combed side-swept hairline. "Maybe we can ask him to come over for ice cream sundaes after the boys' game?"

"Sundaes?" Jamie was back to his ecstatic self. "Yes, please! Can't I go ask them if he can right now? I know where they are! I bet they'll be in the office! *Right now!*"

He was jumping up and down, his excitement contagious. Taylor laughed and swung the bag over her shoulder, double checking that she had her car keys to lock the car, and then shut the door as they walked to the school together.

Jamie grabbed her hand, and she squeezed it back. She loved that he was still not embarrassed to hold his mom's hand in public. Taylor thought back to when it had changed for the older boys. Jake had been about Jamie's age, and Josh had held her hand until he was about ten, or eleven even. She was thankful that Josh still hugged her and sat close to her on the couch, but Jake thought that physical contact with his mom would give him a disease.

Taylor knew that she shouldn't compare her boys, but it was hard not to some days. She wished that Jake, who already towered over her at sixteen years old, would come up behind her and hug her, or at the very least not be afraid to let others around him know that they were related.

How different they all were.

"Hey, Jamie?" Taylor said, something striking her. "How did you know Hazel's husband's name?" She gave him a sideways glance. "Did you meet him already?"

Jamie nodded. "I did! And I saw his fake leg, too! He lost it when he was in the army."

Taylor let go of Jamie's hand, unsure of what to make of this. When exactly had Jamie met him and why had Frank shown him his fake leg? In what world had she taken her eyes off her youngest son long enough for him to have this crazy conversation with their new neighbor whom Taylor hadn't even met yet?

Like robots, she and Jamie marched up the steps that led to the front doors of the school when they suddenly swung open, missing Taylor and Jamie by an inch.

"I *hate* him!" Josh's anger startled Taylor out of her thoughts, almost getting knocked over by the doors he'd just barreled through.

"Josh, what—"

"I never want to see him again, Mom. *Ever!*" Josh cut her off, then stormed past her and Jamie, who were both staring at him with mouths wide open as he made his way to the parking lot, zigzagging as he scanned for their car.

"Who?" Taylor called as she tried to catch up to him. "*Who* do you hate?"

When Josh turned around, the look he gave her made her take a step back. She had never seen him this angry. Ever. She didn't know he was capable of such rage.

"Your *precious* firstborn, Mom. The one who can do *no* wrong and the one who gets away with *everything.*"

His breathing was steady. His fists were clenched at his sides, and he stared into her eyes with a rage that made Taylor want to back away farther than she was. But she didn't.

She looked right back and took a step closer. "What happened?"

Josh shook his head. "Other than the fact that he's a bully?" He stared at her for a few seconds longer, then turned away from her as tears started to fill his eyes as he started walking into the parking lot. "Ugh! Where's the car?"

Taylor grabbed her keys out of her bag and pushed the panic button. The alarm sounded a few rows over and Josh headed straight for it. She pushed the button again to make it stop, and then hit the unlock button so he could get in and away from the curious eyes that had come out of the school to see the drama they'd clearly watched unfold in the gym.

Heather came up and put her hand on Taylor's shoulder. Jamie's hand was protectively in her other hand as she sighed. "Tay, Jake totally provoked him—I saw the whole thing."

Taylor watched as Josh's lanky body crawled into the car, and then slammed the door behind him. He was the middle child, and the brother that lingered in Jake's shadow. Things needed to change, but how?

"So," Heather continued, "after the provoking, Josh punched him and Coach Chad got in his face, yelling." Heather shook her head. "He was yelling at *Josh*. I mean, *who* yells at Josh? He was probably telling him to keep his hands off his beloved starting player, and then Josh just … stormed out."

A feeling of dread washed over Taylor. There was the weight of Jake's recent actions with little or no consequences at all, and it was catching up to them.

It needed to change.

She took out her phone to call Travis—he was coming from work to meet them. He could stay for the game and watch Jake. Taylor didn't have it in her to stay. She didn't want to give Jake the satisfaction of watching him play. Today, she *was* going to choose a side.

She hopped in the car, waving goodbye to Jamie and Heather. Then, she pulled out of the parking lot just in time to see Frank, standing on the front steps of the school, watching her drive away.

CHAPTER FIVE

Then

May 25, 1995—Newport Beach, California

Taylor opened the front door to her house. Her hands, clutching the piece of paper that man had given her, were still shaking from the encounter with him and what he'd told her. She'd thought she knew what she was going to tell her parents about James—but now? She had no idea.

That man had just changed everything.

She couldn't tell them that James had … time traveled.

That's not even a real thing—right?

Taylor heard the TV in the living room. Her parents were watching *I Love Lucy*. They were *always* watching *I Love Lucy*. They never missed a rerun. She loved her parents for being so unapologetically themselves. But now she was unapologetically afraid of their reactions.

She held her breath as she shut the front door behind her and walked down the hall, still confused by what the man had come to tell her. She wasn't sure if she believed him, but at the same time, she was thankful for some sort of explanation.

Taylor was crazy enough to think that James had just disappeared into thin air, but *time travel*? Her mind went back and forth about what to think and believe about it all, and she wondered what kind of naïve girl he thought she was. Did he already know what had happened? Had he been watching her? Following her? Maybe she needed to tell the police about that man before she told them about James.

Could she even go to the police? She'd have to tell them the *truth*, wouldn't she? Taylor clenched her jaw. *But what is the truth?*

She peered around the corner to where her parents were sitting on their faded hunter green sofa together, a crocheted blanket over their legs and a bowl of popcorn between them. Nina and Jerry were never without TV munchies.

Taylor looked at the clock on the kitchen wall. It was a quarter after six. Right now, most families were finishing up their dinner together, but not the Brown family. Dinner time was always later—usually around seven p.m. Her parents routinely went to bed late, then slept in. Taylor was used to being alone in the mornings before school—making breakfast, eating breakfast, and getting ready in a quiet house. But she didn't mind it at all. Her mom still made her lunch for her the night before, leaving it in the fridge, with a note on the counter with yet another reason why she and her dad loved her so much. They rarely missed a day.

Like today, for instance. Her note read:

> Reason #1,243 why I love Taylor:
> She is the kindest, smartest, and most beautiful girl EVER
> to have a last day of high school.
> Congrats, baby girl! Have the BEST DAY!

Taylor kept them all. Some were funny, some were apologies, but they all showed her just how much she was loved by her parents.

She sniffed just thinking about it, and her dad must have heard her because he smiled when he noticed her lingering in the hallway.

"Hey, Hun!" He took the blanket off his lap as he stood up from the couch and came toward her, wrapping his thick arms around her. "How was the beach?"

"My guess is that it was better than expected considering she's almost forty-five minutes late." Her mom winked at her but didn't get off the couch. Instead, she undid her ponytail and redid her graying brown hair into a bun at the top of her head.

Her mom was so natural and pretty. She wore minimal makeup and chose practical clothes over stylish ones. But she could pull it off. "It's hard being a woman living in California," Nina had said to Taylor one evening as she and her dad were getting ready to go out to a rare work event. "Everyone expects you to dye your hair, wear all the makeup and expensive clothes, and even snip the skin that makes you look old." Taylor hadn't really understood it then, but she did now. The difference between her mom and her friends' moms was stark. But she was proud that Nina stayed true to herself—no matter what anyone else thought about it. Taylor could have been embarrassed by her mom, but she was far from it. Nina stood up to a world with expectations that way. Taylor could see that she was happy and confident in her own skin. Taylor wanted to grow up to be just like her.

Still in her dad's strong embrace, Taylor spoke into his scratchy sweater. "I'm not going to go to Ashley's tonight."

Jerry put her at arm's length and studied Taylor's face. "Who are you and what have you done to my daughter?" His smile was joking but the truth was this really wasn't like her.

She and James went to every party together, usually with Mark and Ashley. They only missed one if there were no parents at the house to chaperone—a strict rule that both James's and Taylor's parents agreed to early on—or, if one of them was sick.

Taylor's heart thumped through her chest, knowing she was about to be found out. "I'll just be in my room," she managed to get out before pulling away from her dad, then all but ran down the hall to hide her face, as her true emotions were written all over it.

"Honey Bear …" Her mom's voice from the couch seemed like an attempt to stop her, but Taylor kept walking, not wanting to look into her mom's eyes and lie. She couldn't tell the truth. "Did you and James break up?"

Once she got to her bedroom door at the end of the hall, Taylor stopped and just shook her head. "No, nothing like that." She teared up, knowing that there was nowhere else to go. "He's just …" Her voice caught in her throat, and she started sobbing.

Jerry and Nina, who were standing at the other end of the hall, looked at each other as concern filled their eyes. They were good at giving their daughter the space she needed, and space was exactly what she needed right now.

"I just—" Taylor wiped her eyes as she put her hand on her bedroom's doorknob, "I just need a minute."

Their one-story, three-bedroom home didn't leave much room for space, but her parents obliged, her dad closing the gap between them and giving her a comforting side hug.

"We'll be here once you're ready to talk, Honey Bear."

Taylor smiled sadly as she opened the door to her room and headed inside. She shut the door behind her and flopped face first onto her bed. In the safety of her room, she let out a quiet sob and let the tears flow freely once again, the day's events swirling through her mind. It had all happened so quickly. She needed time to make sense of it all.

Her mind went back to what the crazy man had said, and she unfolded the paper he gave her to see a phone number scribbled on it. Taylor wondered if she'd actually call him.

She put it in her nightstand just in case, closed her eyes and, for what seemed like the thousandth time, thought about the last moment that she'd seen James.

Was time travel really that crazy after all?

Yes, it is. She decided. *Time travel isn't real. No one just disappears and winds up in a different time.*

Except, James *did* disappear.

True to their word, Taylor's parents gave her space. For a long time. She wasn't sure how much time had passed when Taylor shot up on her bed and stared at her door at the sound of the phone in their kitchen ringing down the hall. She held her breath, hoping that it was James's parents, but also *afraid* that it was his parents. Would they tell her James had made it home and they were dropping him off to pick up his car? Or … she didn't want to think of the alternative, but the alternative seemed like the most obvious answer. Were they calling because he wasn't home, and they needed to know where he was?

"Please no, please no …" she whispered under her breath.

Taylor still had no answers. She needed more time to think, and she needed to give James time to show up again. She *needed* him to reappear.

"Hull-o."

Her dad always answered the phone the same way. Always a statement, never a question. She pictured him leaning against the wall in their yellow kitchen, arms crossed, with the phone resting between his balding head and lifted shoulder.

Between his *uh-huh*'s and *oh really*'s, she knew her suspicions were right.

And then she heard her father say, "Yes, yes. I will let you know once we hear anything. Okay. Bye now."

Taylor let out her breath, grabbing her pillow and putting it over her face as she lay back down. The footsteps coming down the hall following that phone call were as predictable as her parents watching *I Love Lucy*.

She didn't move a muscle when she heard the knock. She thought that maybe she could pretend to be sleeping, but her parents would see right through that.

Although she sat up at the second knock, she still didn't answer.

"Honey Bear?" Her dad's pet name for her came through the door. So soft, so tender.

Taylor closed her eyes as she hugged her knees, starting the sobbing cycle all over again.

The door opened, and then she felt the bed slump to one side as her dad sat down beside her. He put an arm around her and pulled her close. They sat silently for a few minutes as he let her cry. He didn't push her with questions or offer information about the phone call, and she was thankful for that.

Once Taylor caught her breath, she wiped her eyes and looked at her dad. Her mom was also there, leaning against the doorframe, her forehead creased with worry.

Taylor saw the framed picture of her and James at Homecoming on her desk and stared blankly at it.

"He's gone," was all that she could muster after a minute of silence.

"What do you mean, *gone*?" Her dad gently rubbed her back, trying to get more out of her, but there was nothing more to give.

"He's just ... gone." She turned to face him, gaining courage with every word. "One minute he was on the beach with me, and then the next ..." Her mind raced, replaying the moment and trying once again to make sense of it all.

"Did he go into the water?" Her mom took a step closer, wrapping her arms across her chest.

"No," Taylor said and shook her head, "but he was headed to the water ..."

"Then did he run down the beach?" Her mom waved one hand in the air like she could summon an explanation. "Maybe he went behind those rocks you used to catch crabs on?"

"No, Mom." Taylor let out a frustrated sigh. "I looked! *Everywhere*! You think I wouldn't have *looked*?" Taylor was getting angry, and she rarely got angry or upset at her parents.

"Hun, your mom is just trying to make sense of this—"

"And you think I'm *not*?" Taylor raised her voice as she stood up, tearing herself away from her dad, who looked shocked at the outburst. "You don't think that's why I was late?" Her eyes darted between her parents' wide eyes. "I ran up and down that stupid beach, combing every last inch of it trying to find him!"

Nina walked toward her, an arm outstretched to touch her daughter, but Taylor backed up into her nightstand, sending her bedside lamp toward its shattered fate on the old hardwood floors. Taylor didn't bother to look at the ceramic mess by her feet.

She stared defiantly into her mom's hurt eyes, daring her to question her actions.

They stood there, only their breathing audible, the tension thick.

Taylor's voice came out in a raspy whisper. "I did *everything* I could before I knew I had to come home." Taylor's tears started falling again.

Her mom just nodded. "I understand, Hun—"

"But *do* you?" Taylor shot back at her.

"Tay—" her dad started but was interrupted by a distant knock at the front door.

Taylor stopped breathing, then out of fear said, "Don't get it." Taylor's eyes begged her parents. "*Please.*"

She pictured Mr. and Mrs. Brooks on their doorstep and couldn't find any words to tell them about that night. She wanted to have an open conversation with her parents about what had happened—and as crazy as it was, about the man that showed up at their house. She hated that her emotions had gotten the best of her, and she'd blown up at them just now instead of confiding in them.

The knock persisted, only harder this time.

"*Please.*" Taylor's eyes darted between her mom's and dad's eyes, and their eyes were darting between Taylor's, each other's. Then, as if on cue, they all looked toward the bedroom door where the knock echoed from down the hall. "*Please* don't get it."

Jerry stood and wiped a tear off her cheek. "Tay, you know I *have* to get it." He stood up. "James's parents are sick with worry, and they just want answers—"

"But I don't *have* any!" Taylor's shout caused her dad to flinch. She shook her head, squeezing her eyes closed. "Dad ..." She looked up, fighting the tears that would inevitably flow throughout the night. She mustered up the courage to say what she'd actually seen, and the truth that would haunt her. "James, he ... he disappeared."

"Well, he couldn't have just *disappeared*," her mom scoffed and Taylor shot her a look.

"Well, he *did*, Mom. As a matter of fact, he vanished. *Right before my eyes.*" Taylor's chest was heaving as she tried to get breath like she'd just run a marathon. Against her better judgment, she let the next words flow out of her mouth. "What if the universe sucked him in, sending him to a different time, and—"

Her mom laughed. She actually *laughed*, like they were chatting about funny things, not the fact that her boyfriend actually *did* vanish and that she would be emotionally scarred forever. Taylor started to realize that this night would be the night that would completely change the course of her life as she knew it, and it made her sick.

The knock turned into banging as they heard, "This is the police! We need you to open the door."

Taylor froze, unable to look at her parents. Instead, she sidestepped the broken lamp and backed into her bedroom window, slowly sliding down, and hugging her knees as she sat against the wall. She linked her fingers around the back of her head, trying to steady her breath.

She vaguely heard her parents ask her questions, gaining clarity about what Taylor just told them, and what would possess her to think that could happen. And then, in the blink of an eye, her calm, cool, and collected parents fell apart as they proceeded to yell at each other, fighting about what to do next and not agreeing. Taylor put her hands over her ears and slunk down to lie on the floor. She wanted to fall asleep and then wake up from this. Tomorrow would be a new day, and this would all be just a weird and horrible nightmare.

Taylor's heartbeat thudding in her ears made it impossible to guess who was in her room. There ended up being so many footsteps and voices that she couldn't tell whose they were until she heard metal clinking. She turned her head to see handcuffs hanging from one of the officer's hands.

"Taylor?" She heard her name and turned her head to look into the kind eyes of a policeman. "We need you to come with us—to the station—to ask you a few questions."

"By *arresting* her?" Nina was being held back by Jerry, who was equally confused and mad about the situation. "What did she do other than be there when the love of her *life* disappeared?" Nina started to cry, and Jerry put his arm around her.

Taylor stared blankly at the officer and searched his eyes as if they would give something away. Was she safe? If she was, why was she being arrested? Was she even being arrested? Could she trust anyone with the information that wanted to spill out of her?

The officer stopped what he was doing to look at Nina. "Well, ma'am," he said, remaining calm as he put the cuffs back in his holster, "The boy's parents claim that she was the last person to see him. Therefore she, as of right now, is our only suspect."

"Now she's a *suspect*?" It was Jerry's turn to be held back by Nina, and he reached out his arms toward his daughter, who was still on her bedroom floor in shock.

Taylor was unable to move. She was completely incapable of defending herself.

"Sir, please step back and let us do our job." A second officer stood in Jerry's way. "The parents of the missing boy suspect foul play and we—"

The words stung Taylor's ears as she registered what he had said. Everything else faded away around her and she tried to process this information.

James's parents think I ... I did something to him? They think I'm the cause of this? But was it really all that surprising?

The first officer helped Taylor up, and then looked warmly at her. "I'm so sorry this is happening to you. But the more you are able to cooperate with us and the more you tell us, the more we can help you." He smiled and nodded at her.

Taylor didn't feel like anyone was helping her in this situation. Her parents were losing their minds on the other side of the room, and the one officer was starting to lose his patience with them as the other was still kneeling beside Taylor. Did he really think that she was a suspect, or was he just doing his job? His partner was looking at her with accusatory eyes, and Taylor knew that's how James's parents would look at her, too. If they thought she had something to do with this, then she was done for. They had the money, they knew the right people, and they wouldn't stop until they got what they wanted—James, or justice.

Taylor felt alone.

Taylor *was* alone.

Maybe she should have gone to the police first. She should have pulled into Bob's Burgers and asked Mark and Ashley to help her. Maybe she should have done everything differently. But what would it change? James was still gone.

One thing she knew for sure—she alone would have to get to the bottom of where James was. Or, if that man who'd shown up at her house tonight was right, then she would find out *when* James went.

CHAPTER SIX

Now

June 28, 2016—Myrtle Beach, South Carolina

Taylor was sitting on her bed furiously texting Heather about the basketball game the day before.

"Just call her," Travis said as he came up behind her, rubbing her shoulders. "You'll feel better hearing her voice, not reading her words."

Taylor hated when he was right.

"What's all this about anyway?" He let go of her shoulders and disappeared into the closet.

"Travis." Taylor took her eyes off Heather's texts to stare into the closet's opening as if she were looking right at him. "Heather literally thinks that I'm *being dramatic* about the whole incident at the basketball game yesterday. She keeps saying that *boys will be boys*, but it's just not true!" She threw her phone on the bed and stood up, starting to pace the room. "Boys can be good, civilized, kind humans, and being a boy does *not* excuse Jake's behavior!"

Heather's text to Taylor earlier had sparked something in her, and for the first time in years, they were fighting.

There was no answer from the closet, and Taylor took that as a sign to finish her rant.

"I mean, brothers—above all—should treat each other better than they would their own friends, right? So why is Jake being such an—"

"Don't say it," Travis's voice echoed through the closet door, cutting her off.

She was too mad to laugh. Taylor was mad at Jake and Heather, and she was even mad at Josh for who knows what, but she was on an anger spree, and she was just … mad.

"On another note, what should I wear to my work dinner tonight."

Taylor stopped pacing. "Isn't that on Tuesday?" She squinted, as if it would help her hear his voice that was muffled by the distance of the closet and the noise of hangers being shuffled around.

"Today is Tuesday. You're still coming, aren't you? I'm only being recognized for my promotion…" His voice trailed off as she pictured him holding up a shirt, debating its color.

"Oh, right." Taylor shook her head. Summer made all her days blend into one. "It's not that big of a big deal, though. Right? I may just stay home and wash my hair. Maybe knit a scarf."

Travis poked his head out from the closet and stared at her.

"I'm kidding." Taylor walked over to Travis, laughing at his expression. "I'm excited to celebrate your promotion tonight." She kissed him on the cheek before heading down the hall to Josh's bedroom. She wanted to check in on him after last night.

Whether out of guilt or love, she still wanted to check in. He would probably stay cooped up in his room all day, and while Taylor usually didn't let any of her boys do that, today was an exception. She knew that Josh wasn't in a place to venture out and see Jake.

Yesterday, Heather and Jamie had ended up staying to watch the game, then getting a ride home with Travis afterward, while Taylor and Josh had gone for frozen yogurt. Josh had been quiet the whole time and had seemed anxious to get back home.

Their team had ended up winning fifty-six to thirty-four, Jake scoring thirty-two points that game, but Taylor didn't even have it in her to congratulate her own son when he got home. It was the first time Taylor had felt genuine anger toward him, not just disappointment.

Now, Taylor hesitated before knocking on Josh's door. She and Josh didn't have much to say to each other when they were in the car yesterday. Josh had accused her and Travis of letting Jake get away with everything and never disciplining him like they should. Taylor didn't have an argument. She agreed with him but also knew that there hadn't been much reason to discipline Jake until now. Sure, there were things they had to correct in all of her boys, manners to teach, and the odd taking-away-computer-time for saying something they shouldn't have or for pushing a brother a tad too aggressively, but Jake was a good kid at heart. Taylor knew there was something else going on with him and she wanted to find that out first and foremost.

She couldn't tell that to Josh, though; she didn't want to betray Jake's trust and give Josh something to hold over his head.

Not that he would.

Taylor guessed it had something to do with Heather's daughter, Tiffany, but heaven forbid Taylor ever assume that a girl could get his feathers ruffled so easily. She didn't want to poke the bear, so she decided that she'd wait for Jake to tell her, if he even wanted to.

After standing there thinking about the situation for longer than she should have, Taylor knocked on Josh's door. "Hey, bud. Can I come in?"

"Yeah," she heard from inside.

Taylor turned the doorknob and poked her head in. Josh was sitting at his desk reading a book. She smiled. She loved that her boys loved reading. Their personal library was a disaster and they all had way more books shoved in any and all crevices in their bedrooms than she knew what to do with. She made a mental note to go through them and set a pile to keep and a pile to donate.

"How are you feeling?" She wanted to sound gentle, but it came out like he was a toddler in need of mommy's kiss on his booboo.

Josh turned around, glaring back at her to remind her that he was in fact not a toddler and definitely no kisses were needed. Only space.

She nodded. "Can you let me know if you need anything?"

"I will." He turned back to his book, dismissing her.

Taylor shut the door behind her, which she ended up just staring at, wondering if she was doing something wrong.

When she'd pictured having a family, she'd always seen herself being her kids' best friend. They would come running to her, no matter how old, with all their problems and concerns, and she would talk them through it, pretending that they were the ones who had made the good decisions even though it was really her who had put the good idea into their head in the first place. Then they would hug her and tell her how much they loved her, and her kids would go off putting those good decisions into practice while everyone looked on, thinking what a great mom she was and how her kids were the best in all the land.

Her daydream ended when she heard yelling in the kitchen. It was Jamie.

She bounded down the stairs to see Jake sitting at the kitchen island holding up a journal at arm's length while Jamie jumped up, desperately trying to get it back from him.

"Jake, give it back. It's mine!" Jamie jumped up again and again before landing on the side of the kitchen island's barstool, causing him to fall.

Jake started laughing and read from the journal in a mocking tone: *"And then he wielded his sword and drove it into the wizard, who looked at the prince in astonishment over what had just happened ..."*

Seeing Jake act so cruelly toward his brother made something snap in Taylor. She was ready to wield her own sword.

"Jacob Hector Perez!" Her voice boomed loud and harsh and commanded attention. Both boys jumped when they saw their mom standing there, jaw clenched and face red.

Jake slowly put the book down, eyes wide. He had never seen his mom like this before.

Taylor breathed in and out, staring at her oldest son, wondering what to say next. Nothing sufficed. She wanted to strangle him for how he was acting but she didn't want to be arrested—again—and, well, she loved her son. She just didn't *like* him right now.

"Make. It. Right." Taylor spoke slowly, as if he needed to hear every syllable of her words for him to understand them.

Jake nodded, then shut the journal. "I'm ... I'm sorry."

He looked genuinely scared, not taking his eyes off her, and there was something in Taylor that liked that.

"You're sorry for *what*?" Taylor looked into Jake's eyes, demanding he do better.

"For, uh ..." His eyes darted to Jamie, who was sitting on the kitchen floor, hugging his knees to his chest, tears rolling down his red cheeks. Jake's face seemed to soften, and he put the book down and got off the stool to kneel next to his little brother. He looked like he'd just seen Jamie's distress for the first time and a flash of anger crossed his face, as if it were someone else who had been bullying his brother.

Taylor held her breath as she watched her oldest sit on the ground and start to cry, hugging Jamie.

"I'm so sorry, buddy ..." he spoke into Jamie's ear.

Jamie's arms let go of his knees and wrapped around Jake's neck.

"I forgive you," she heard Jamie's small voice.

Taylor let out a breath she didn't know she was holding as her own tears started to fall. Her anger turned to love so quickly that she was confused about how to feel. Was she still angry at Jake, or had her heart turned soft after witnessing this miracle of bonded brotherhood?

Taylor jumped when she felt a hand on her shoulder. She wasn't sure how long Travis had been standing behind her. His smile told her all she needed to know. He'd seen the whole thing. His eyes were misty, too.

"Put me down!" Jamie cried through laughter as Jake picked him up and carried him around the kitchen like a sack of potatoes, pretending to go through his normal morning routine without the knowledge that a brother was on his shoulders.

"Maybe I'll have waffles for breakfast." Jake spun around, making Jamie squeal in excitement as he whipped around in the opposite direction. "Or maybe a banana?" Jake spun around again in a full circle, Jamie's arms flailing. "But where do we keep the bananas?" Jake asked as he kept spinning in circles and Jamie kept laughing.

Taylor and Travis were laughing with them, cherishing the sudden change in Jake's mood. But the moment was cut short when Taylor heard Josh behind them.

"Of course." His voice was full of rage, then he turned and stomped back upstairs. "Jake can literally do *no* wrong." His anger echoed down the hall before they heard his bedroom door slam behind him.

Taylor turned to look at Jake. His face was back to his teenage scowl, and he put Jamie down, acting like the last three minutes of brotherly bliss had never happened. Taylor was pretty sure that Jamie had no idea what was happening because he kept giggling, picking up his book and grabbing a pen to finish his story.

"You should go talk to him." Taylor's face was softer now, her head motioning up the stairs and hinting about Josh, although no hints had to be given.

"Why?" Jake grunted and grabbed his shoes, sitting down at the kitchen table to put them on.

"What do you mean, *why*?" Taylor's voice was rising again, and she was thankful Travis stepped in before she said something she'd regret.

"You know why." Travis's voice was stern but loving.

Jake just looked at his dad and rolled his eyes. "And say what? Sorry you're so weak? Sorry you're not as good as me?"

Taylor drew in a sharp breath. "You don't mean that." Her voice was a whisper, astonished that Jake could think that way toward Josh.

Confusion washed over her as she thought about their relationship. Jake and Josh used to be best friends; they'd done everything together and even demanded that they play on the same team. Josh should have played a level down from Jake, but Coach Chad had let him try out and he'd actually been good enough to play with the older boys. Jake had seemed to be proud of his brother, even more so than Taylor and Travis were of their own son.

So, what happened?

Before Taylor knew what was happening, Jake walked out the front door and got into his friend's car that was waiting at the end of the driveway. Taylor didn't even see Shawn pull up, but she stood there in the kitchen, mouth open, watching the car drive down the street, turn left at the stop sign, and speed toward town.

Travis shook his head. "Is this just a phase? Or do we have to step in and do something?"

Taylor knew that their son was clearly going through something. She couldn't see how this was just a phase.

"We have to do something." Taylor agreed, but her thoughts were too scrambled to comprehend just what that something would be.

Travis gave her a quick kiss on her forehead. "We'll figure it out together, love. Don't worry." Then he walked back upstairs to get ready for his day.

She decided to grab her shoes and go for a quick walk before Travis had to leave for work. She wanted to be alone with her music and her thoughts.

Plugging her earphones into her phone, she searched for a playlist as she left the house and walked down the driveway. Josh had recently made her one with all the songs she knew were "in" right now, but she liked to stick with what was most comfortable to her.

"Taylor!" Hazel waved to Taylor from her front door before speed-walking down her driveway.

"Hey." Taylor sounded exactly how she felt. Annoyed.

Hazel didn't seem to notice, talking like she was on a mission. "I spoke to my grandson, and he would be delighted to spend some time with your

Jamie!" She clapped her hands together and smiled triumphantly, as if this were the single greatest piece of news Taylor would hear all day.

Realizing that Hazel was waiting for a reply, Taylor slapped a smile on her face through gritted teeth.

"He will be so excited to hear that." Taylor's reply was short, hoping to dismiss Hazel gently, but she didn't seem at all fazed.

"He'll be at our house tonight, if Jamie's free?" Hazel continued. "Maybe he can come over for dinner? Or the boys can play a game after dinner if you already have plans?" Her eyebrows raised in question, and Taylor knew she needed to make a decision.

"Actually, Travis and I will be out tonight. It's a … work thing." Taylor gave Hazel an apologetic smile, thankful for an honest excuse. "Plus, I think I'd prefer to be home on a night they get together."

"I totally understand." Hazel smiled. "My daughter is out tonight for a work thing, too. It's why we have Andrew." Hazel gave another laugh and Taylor was confused why this woman laughed at things that weren't funny all the time. "I'd love for you to meet her soon. Our daughter, that is."

Taylor put her phone in her pocket and grabbed her ankle, bringing it up behind her, starting to stretch. She hoped once again that Hazel would get the memo that Taylor was not interested in this conversation.

"Maybe one day …"

Taylor never stretched before going on a walk. This was all such a show, and she wasn't sure if she should be proud or embarrassed of this unnecessary display of dismissiveness.

"Yes, hopefully soon you'll meet our sweet Emily," Hazel repeated, and then, with her arm raised in a wave, she bade Taylor farewell. "Goodbye, dear. Enjoy your run!"

Taylor waved back, and then felt ashamed that she wasn't even going for a brisk walk—let alone a run. She wasn't a runner, only a walker, and not even for the purpose of exercise. She had three boys who weren't getting along. She'd be content sitting at a bus stop with no intent of going anywhere, just for some alone time. This walk was to clear her head and get out of the house.

But now, not knowing what else to do and wanting to keep up the pretense of running, Taylor started jogging down the street. She pictured Travis's face if he saw what she was doing. His big dark eyes would be narrowed, brow furrowed, mouth in a confused smile. The thought made her laugh, and it only took a few strides before her lungs started to hate her. Without a care in the world of being seen, Taylor stopped running, breathing heavily, trying to catch her breath.

She was annoyed that her lungs had betrayed her. Also, she was really out of shape if she couldn't even last through a light jog from one streetlight to the next. Maybe she *should* take up running?

Taylor found her playlist and started walking again when it registered what Hazel had said. Her daughter's name was Emily.

Taylor only knew one Emily and she'd met her when she'd first come to Myrtle Beach searching for answers. It wasn't possible it was the same one with the millions of Emily's in the world, but Taylor reflected back to seeing her for the first time.

Taylor wished that she and the Emily from her past could have been friends, but because of the awkward circumstance surrounding why Emily was there and who her uncle was, it just wasn't possible that they could have had a real friendship.

Taylor started to feel the sadness of what could have been. She sometimes wished she still had her life in California, which felt like a betrayal to her life now. She loved where she was and whom she was with, but she was living under false pretenses that no one knew about. She never felt like she could genuinely be herself here, but she also knew this was for the best.

She kept walking to the beat of Justin Timberlake and let her mind do its best to rid itself of the memories of her past.

She didn't really mean it, did she? If she could go back and change her life, would she?

Taylor let her mind drift back to James. It had been years since she'd let herself go there, but now she felt she needed to know. If she knew she could have James again, would she change her life for him?

She started walking faster, her heartbeat keeping up to the pace of her steps as she thought about her past, the one no one knew about, the one that for years she wouldn't even let her mind remember … until now.

Why was it all coming to the surface now?

It shook her—and despite her burning lungs, she started to run, if for no other reason than to get *him* out of her head.

Again.

CHAPTER SEVEN

Then

May 26, 1995—Newport Beach, California

The sun snuck its way through Taylor's bedroom window, landing directly on her face. She squinted and slowly lifted her heavy eyelids. She was still wearing her bathing suit and coverup that she wore yesterday at the beach, and she felt the grit of the sand between her and the sheets. She was dirty but had no energy to change. She also desperately needed to brush her teeth.

After coming home from the police station last night, she was too emotionally drained to do anything but crawl back into bed and fall asleep.

As she focused on the sunrays that highlighted the dust in the air, the memory of James and yesterday's events set in. If the sand between her toes wasn't a telltale sign, she knew for certain that it was not a dream—it was in fact, her present reality.

Taylor had no motivation left in her to get up, so she rolled over and pulled the covers back over her head, her mind thick with sorrow and confusion over everything that had happened.

Between James disappearing, that random man coming to see her at her house telling her about time travel, the police questioning her at the station, and then James's parents showing up for the sole purpose of accusing her of his disappearance—it was all way too much.

The heaviness weighed on her and she started silently crying again, her mouth open, releasing sobs that only her bed sheets could hear.

There soft knock on her bedroom door brought her back.

"Tay?" Her mom's soft voice followed. "I have breakfast for you."

Taylor stayed silent. She felt as though every muscle and fiber of her being was pushed to its limits yesterday and she physically could not respond.

"Honey Bear? Can I come in?"

Taylor first heard Nina push the door open, then her mom's soft footsteps came closer. Her bed springs creaked to life then sunk to where her mom sat on her mattress's edge. Nina put her hand on her daughter's back and started to rub circles.

Taylor relaxed under her touch and let the thought of sleep wash over her yet again. She didn't want to wake back up to this nightmare.

"I put bananas and peanut butter on your desk for when you're ready to eat." She continued to rub Taylors back. "You probably should, soon. Eat something, I mean."

Taylor couldn't think of eating, even as much as she loved bananas and peanut butter—it was her favorite snack. Not something she'd necessarily have for breakfast, but her mom probably knew better than to come in with a plate of scrambled eggs that could get cold and rubbery fast, not making it appealing to eat if she got out of bed an hour or more later.

She loved the fact that her mom thought about that tiny detail for her, but her heart still hurt over what her mom did.

"Tay?" Her mom stopped rubbing her back and leaned in closer.

Taylor wanted to answer, she really did—but because of her emotional exhaustion, she was on the verge of falling asleep again.

Nina slid the covers off Taylor's head and leaned over to kiss her sweaty forehead. She wiped strands of her thick, tangled, and salty hair off her face. Although she kept her eyes closed, she could picture what her mom's face looked like right now. Deep forehead lines, tight straight lips, and eyes creased with worry.

"Okay. I'll let you be." Nina placed another kiss on the top of her head and whispered, "I love you." before standing back up and walking out of the room, closing the door behind her.

Taylor let out an anxious breath.

She didn't even feel bad for shutting her mom out. Nina knew her better than anyone. But their bond shattered after her mom laughed when Taylor dared to utter the words *time travel* out loud. She knew that if she couldn't trust her mom with that information, she couldn't trust anyone with it, as if she needed another reason to stay silent at the police station. She really did want to tell the truth, but she knew she couldn't say those words again.

Taylor wasn't even sure if she believed it herself.

At the station, she only nodded or shook her head at the officer's questions, then closed her eyes tight when they asked a question that had no explanation other than, "he just disappeared."

But he *did* just disappear, and to Taylor's horror, her parents took it upon themselves to let the police know those were her very words last night.

"All Taylor could tell us about that night was that he disappeared. Right before her eyes!" Taylor's dad had good intentions, but when he told the chief in the hope of trying to spark conversation out of their daughter, it became quite clear that it was definitely the wrong thing to say.

After that, Taylor felt like she was the butt of all the jokes, and if the cold, hard plastic chair wasn't enough to make her feel uncomfortable in the brightly fluorescent lit room, feeling their bewildered stares at her did it. And then the questions coming at her, "Like a magic trick?" or "Into thin air?" made her want to vanish into thin air herself.

She wanted to say yes to all their questions but knew how ridiculous it sounded. Who just disappears into thin air like a magic trick? It doesn't make sense. That doesn't happen in real life. But yet, it did.

Thinking about the embarrassment of last night made Taylor groan and pull the covers back over her head. The sweaty and salty odor embedded in her sheets was enough to make her consider getting up to shower, but she didn't have time to dwell on it because she heard the phone ring and instead, she started to dwell on who was calling.

When her dad answered in a sharp "What now?" and not in his usual "hull-o," she shot up in bed, agonizing over her dad's silence as he listened to the response.

Who was on the phone and what were they saying? Why was he so mad and short with whoever was calling?

"Listen," she finally heard, "we told you all you need to know—"

Taylor wondered if it was the police.

"Yes, I know that." Her dad's voice changed, now sounding sad. Taylor mustered up the energy to get out of bed and tiptoe to the door, trying her hardest to open it without a sound. But she knew that in this old house, the original hinges would give her away.

"No, you can't come today … that's too soon." Her dad was borderline shouting now.

Taylor turned the doorknob not caring what sound it made, she needed to hear this conversation. She opened the door a crack to listen.

"I understand that, but you can't just come and talk to her. She needs time to rest and grieve and—"

Taylor's mind spun, thinking of who was cutting him off and wanted to see her so urgently.

"Please." Jerry pleaded. "*Please* can you just give us a day and come tomorrow?"

Taylor closed her eyes, a tear escaping, and she wiped it away with her long-sleeved coverup that still smelled like the beach and James.

This was a mess. They were just supposed to have a fun beach day before graduation and now she was a suspect in her boyfriend's missing person case. How did things go sideways so fast?

"Okay—yes, I understand. Yep. Bye." Taylor heard the slam of the receiver. Jerry hung up and wasn't happy.

Taylor was about to head down the hall and ask her dad about it but stopped short when she heard her mom.

"So, what now? They just deem her crazy and she gets thrown into a loony bin?"

"Nina—"

"No, Jerry," Nina let out a sob. "She told us something in confidence. I don't care how it sounded, she *trusted* us."

Taylor heard the kitchen chair get pushed back from the table, a cupboard door slam shut, and the kitchen faucet turn on. The dishes in the sink were getting shuffled around with so much fury that she expected one to break in the process. Nina cleaned when she was upset.

"Nina, please listen." Jerry sounded adamant. "This is *all* out of our control. *All of it.* The only thing we can do going forward is get the best help for her that we can. If that's a consultation with a psychiatrist, then it's a consultation with a psychiatrist."

A psychiatrist? Why do they think I need a—?

"The best help?" Taylor heard the faucet turn off. Nina never raised her voice, ever. Being the hippy flower child Taylor knew her to be, she was always love, flowers, and rainbows with an "everything will work out as it was meant to so why worry" type of mentality. But Nina sounded *very* worried right now and Taylor had rarely heard this side of her.

"Jerry, our daughter is *not* crazy, and I will *not* lose another daughter because of this."

A bang caused Taylor to jump, and she wondered what her mom threw. Then, there was silence. Taylor imagined them looking at each other with their daring eyes, maybe her dad's wide with surprise over Nina's outburst.

Her dad sighed. "We are *not* going to lose our daughter, Nina. But what she *does* need is answers … and she doesn't seem to have any." There was another silence, and Taylor was about to shut her bedroom door before she heard him finish. "Maybe she just needs help finding them."

Nina let out a groan. "Maybe? Maybe she needs help? I have a better idea. Maybe we should move. Let's take her somewhere and just … start over!"

"Nina, we can't run from this. They'll find us and it will definitely make her look guilty."

"But what if she *is* guilty, Jer?"

That question lingered in the air for what seemed like an eternity. Taylor put her hand to her mouth to stifle the cries that threatened the very silence she was working so hard to maintain.

This situation was horrible for obvious reasons, but never, *ever*, did she think of the toll it would take on her parents.

Never did she think they would also assume her guilt.

"What are you saying, Nina?" The question was soft and tentative but needed to be asked.

"I'm saying …"

Taylor held her breath waiting for her mom to finish. What did her mom really think? There were so many questions being asked of Taylor, but she didn't think to ask her parents what they thought of the situation. She assumed they'd believe her.

"I'm saying that maybe Taylor stayed silent last night because she didn't want to say anything to incriminate herself. Maybe a psychiatric hospital is better than jail."

And there it was.

Taylor grabbed the wooden door frame to steady herself. She felt light-headed.

Last night, James's parents accused her, the police called her a suspect, apparently there was a mental doctor coming to talk to her, and now her mom thought she might be guilty and wanted to run from the law.

Her heart plummeted as she closed her door again and a shiver ran its way through her. Taylor crawled back into bed, defeated. She was too stunned to even think about crying. She just laid there, her mind blank, and stared out the window at the palm tree swaying in the backyard. She watched the few scattered clouds slowly make their way across the blue sky. She let her mind wander to the party at Ashley's last night and what could have been, daydreaming about showing up in James's new car, wearing her new red tube top and flowered skirt she bought solely for that party. She would have curled her hair and tied it up on one side so that everyone could see the necklace he had bought her. She would have walked in holding James's hand as they relished in starting their new adult life in college and, eventually, their future together.

She must have dozed off because the next thing she knew, she was startled awake in a much darker room by a loud knock. The sky was turning a light purple and she could see that one star that always shone the brightest. Maybe it was a planet?

"Taylor?" Her dad asked before he knocked again, his voice loud but kind. Taylor didn't respond. That was starting to be a pattern.

She felt anger swell inside of her.

He didn't defend Taylor when her mom suggested that she might be guilty. They both must feel that way.

She felt betrayed.

"There's a doctor here to see you, Tay. Can we come in?"

A doctor? *Must be the psychiatrist. Well, better the loony bin than jail, right mom?*

The door opened but Taylor stayed facing the window. She was not in a mood to appease anyone, especially her parents. In fact, she would stay silent for the rest of her life if she had to.

Her dad didn't seem to care that Taylor didn't answer—he was coming in regardless of any answer from her. He turned her light on, causing Taylor to squint with its sudden brightness. "This is Dr. Carter—he's from St. Peter's Hospital." He paused and Taylor questioned if it was because he was letting it sink in what that really meant. But she had no time to think about it, she wanted to get this over with but still didn't want to face her dad. Not after what she heard.

"Tay? He just wants to ask you a few questions."

When she still didn't respond, she heard the doctor's voice in a whisper. "Maybe you could give Taylor and I some time. Alone."

Taylor's breath caught. She knew that voice. But it couldn't be, could it?

"I don't know." Her dad sounded tentative.

Oh sure, Dad, Taylor mentally rolled her eyes but squeezed them tighter out of frustration. *Now's the time to stick up for me, is it?*

Still in a whispered voice, the doctor pushed forward. "I find that patients are far more open and honest when they're not in the presence of a friend or family member that they don't want to hurt, embarrass, or try to please. It will be better for all of us. I assure you."

Her dad must have conceded because her door closed and only one set of footsteps retreated down the hall.

Taylor held her breath, listening. She wondered if Dr. Carter was in her bedroom with her but didn't want to turn around to find out. She didn't even want to let out her breath for fear of him noticing her—which was silly, given that she was an obvious sad lump in her bed and the reason why he was here.

"Taylor, I—"

She heard his shaky voice stop and couldn't take it anymore. She turned her head toward him and there he was. The same man who stood in front of her house behind the trees last night claiming that James had time traveled.

Her puffy and red eyes, full of both wonder and skepticism, stared into his equally wide eyes, searching hers.

"What are you doing here?" She managed to get out, quiet and hoarse.

He stared at her with a look of pity, then looked down at his shoes, wringing a white coat in his hands.

Taylor's voice came out stronger and louder this time. "Are you really a doctor?"

When his eyes met hers again they were softer. He looked sad when he shook his head. "Well, technically yes, I am. But, not like that. I'm a—"

They both looked at each other, breathing heavily not knowing where to go from here.

You're a what? A serial killer? A stalker? A lunatic?

Should she be scared? Call for help? Ask more about his theory?

He cleared his throat before continuing. "My name is really Dr. Callum Decker—but please, call me Callum." He fiddled with his jacket again, breaking eye contact. "I'm a physicist and I came to—" He looked back up at Taylor, "—well, when you didn't call, I wanted to clear up what I said yesterday."

Taylor continued to stare, giving him the space and time to say what he needed to. She didn't know what she wanted to hear, or even what she *needed* to hear, but she waited.

She didn't seem to have a choice.

"There's something I feel you should know." He took a tentative step closer. "I have been visited in the past," he looked at Taylor, pleading with her to understand. "visited by others, just like James, who also traveled back in time."

Taylor clenched her jaw at the sound of his name. Nothing made sense anymore. She had the floating sensation of being in a dream.

This isn't real. She told herself over and over as she squeezed her eyes shut. *This isn't real. It can't be. When I open my eyes, Callum will be gone.*

Taylor did her best to convince herself, but when she opened her eyes, there he was. Tears filled her eyes, but she refused to let them drop. She opened her mouth to say something, but nothing came out.

As if reading her mind, Callum nodded in agreement. "I know this is a lot to take in, Taylor, but James came to see me too …"

A new sense of energy overtook her, and she sat up at this thought. *Why Callum?* Was the obvious question, but she couldn't bring herself to ask it. Why would he go and see this random man instead of coming to see her? Hurt, shame, and confusion washed over her and one by one, the tears escaped, betraying her strength.

"What do you mean he came to see you? Why *you*? And when?" She realized the harshness of her tone and regretted it instantly, but she couldn't be calm about any of this. The more he talked, the more confused she was. How did James even know him?

Callum walked over and sat on her bed. Reaching out, he put his hand on hers, seeming to know what was racing through her head.

Taylor didn't flinch. She probably should be scared by the fact that a stranger was sitting on her bed, touching her hand. But was he really a stranger if he knew James? If all of this was true, and James really went back in time—which in and of itself she had yet to process—and James knew him, then he was here to help her. Wasn't he? He was a safe person, and he was here to help them find each other again.

The corners of her mouth turned up in a smile thinking of the prospect that Callum was here to reunite them.

Taylor found herself bold enough to study him. He had kind eyes behind his dark glasses, graying hair combed neatly, graying eyebrows to match, and laugh lines. He had cleaned up, looking more professional than he had the night before. Taylor looked down in embarrassment, seeing herself through Callum's eyes. She felt gross, and knew she looked and smelled it, too.

Despite her newfound self-awareness, Taylor started breathing steadily again. For the first time since James disappeared, she felt a sense of hope.

She put her other hand on top of his and squeezed it gently, as if to apologize for her words before, and tried again. "Why did he come to see you? And when? Do you know where he is now? Will I see him again?"

Her excitement got the best of her as her questions poured out of her mouth in rapid succession, but she was not accusatory this time. She genuinely wanted to know. If he knew *when* he went back, he'd surely know where he was now and how to get him back, right?

"Well, it's not that easy, Taylor." Callum pulled his hand away from hers and fixed his glasses. "We can't bring him back. I actually don't know how to."

Taylor's eyes narrowed as time, once again, stood still. She was processing what that meant. "So, he's gone?"

Callum stood up and started pacing. Swallowing hard, he hesitated before continuing. "No, not gone, but just not … here. And to answer your question, he came to see me a while ago. Years ago, actually. The first time was in 1967." Callum put his hands in his pockets only to take them back out to run one hand through his thinning hair.

Taylor stared at Callum blankly. Thinking she misheard him, she slowly shook her head, unable to look away. She needed to process the year he said. When she spoke, it was slowly and calmly, reiterating what he said as if this would help her understand. "So, he's not gone, but he went back to 1967."

Callum just shook his head. "No. He——" Callum sighed. "Well, he only came to see me then. He actually went back to 1965." He searched Taylor's face for a reaction, but Taylor's expression was left unchanged. Once again, Taylor heard his words, but questioned their meaning. It couldn't be right.

Callum started using his hands, as if that would help explain. "James was never able to get back to now ... I mean, he's here, but not here as he was when you knew him." He took a step forward, imploring her to look at him. "Ugh, I'm not explaining this well at all, am I?" He ran his hand underneath his glasses, rubbing his eyes. "He's not the eighteen-year-old that he was yesterday. To you, anyway. Do you understand what I'm trying to tell you?"

All Taylor could do was continue to shake her head. She couldn't wrap her mind around what he was saying. If James went back to 1965 and never came back, then—

Taylor's mouth dropped open once she realized.

"How old is he?" She heard her voice, demanding, wanting to know but equally not wanting to know.

Callum looked pained. She could tell that he didn't want to tell her. He didn't want to be the one to shatter her dreams of one day being reunited with her love. But Taylor gave him no choice.

"Callum. How. Old?" Her voice was strong, her urgent need for information coming through her tone as her jaw tightened. She needed to know.

Now.

Callum looked defeated, resigned, knowing that he had to tell her. He looked down at the floor, pursed his lips, his forehead creased with worry, and he rubbed the back of his neck before answering.

"Well, right now? James is forty-eight years old."

CHAPTER EIGHT

Now

July 2, 2016—Myrtle Beach, South Carolina

T aylor woke up Saturday morning with an uneasy feeling in her stomach. Hazel had been on her mind all night and she couldn't stop feeling bad about avoiding her all week. She also felt guilt that she wasn't mentally present for Travis at his dinner. She saw him talk to the new employee, from across the room, but didn't go up to introduce herself. She wasn't even in the room when they announced the new hire—Jamie called about Jake's unfairness toward him, and she spent twenty minutes calming her son down in the foyer rather than applauding her husband.

She rolled over to see that Travis was already out of bed, probably in the garage working out.

Taylor swung her legs out from under the covers, her feet finding her slippers, and put on her old black hoodie before heading downstairs to get coffee. She could already smell the rich aroma before she reached the top of the stairs and her heart lightened.

Travis was usually up before Taylor, and he put the first pot of coffee on in the morning; Taylor made the second. Despite Taylor not being a morning person, knowing that the coffee was already brewing made it easier for her to get out of bed.

As she grabbed a mug and poured her coffee, her eyes wandered across the street to Hazel's house. Travis still hadn't met them. After Taylor had told him about her and the boys' meeting, and then seeing Hazel's husband in the window, Travis was wary of them and didn't make himself as available as he might have otherwise. It was totally out of character for him. He was the one who, like Jamie, was the first to meet anyone new, instantly making them feel welcomed.

Taylor, hands around her hot mug, sat at the kitchen table and looked out the bay window. She loved living here. They had great neighbors and her best friend, Heather, lived at the end of the street with her daughter, Tiffany. Heather's ex, Derek, had moved out almost two years ago now. While Travis missed his friend, Taylor certainly didn't miss the drama that came with him.

Heather had been her first friend in Myrtle Beach, and Taylor liked to think that she was the one who knew her best. But the truth was that, here, nobody really knew her at all. But that was the whole point of moving, wasn't it? To get away from her past?

She wanted to hide from the stares she might have gotten back in California and live a normal life where her name wouldn't come up in almost every conversation.

Mrs. Murphy waved as she passed their house, walking their beagle, Freckles. Taylor waved back and then froze when she realized that Mrs. Murphy was waving at Travis, who was working out in the garage. Taylor smirked. Travis certainly had a way with the older ladies. Not in a flirty way, he just knew how to make people feel safe—like they, in that moment, were the only thing that mattered. It was a special gift of which she was envious. Taylor had been through too much in her life and she now shied away from personal questions and opening up to anyone and everyone who asked too many of them. She constantly diverted conversation to the present; she had changed from the Taylor of the past.

Taylor broke out of her daze when she saw Hazel walk out her front door and march across the street toward Eliza Murphy and Travis, who were now chatting at the end of the driveway. Hazel was in a pink bathrobe, her hair already done like she was going to the country club for brunch, and she had on bright white tennis shoes.

The sight of Hazel made Taylor feel bad about dismissing her so quickly and easily. Hazel was just trying to get to know her neighbors, and because of Taylor's insecurities about her past, her first instinct was to head for the hills. But Taylor's fears weren't fair to Hazel.

Making her decision, Taylor got up and started to collect ingredients to make Hazel and Frank some muffins. She would drop them off today and ask to meet Hazel's husband. She'd ask them questions about their life, their move, and his sickness.

She'd channel her inner Travis.

Taylor wondered if she would ever get to the point of being able to answer questions about her life without having her heart race, afraid to answer. Where did you grow up? Do you have any other family? Hey, you look familiar. Aren't you the girl who was locked up for the disappearance of her boyfriend?

Taylor heard a door slam behind her and she dropped the egg carton at her feet in shock. She took in a sharp breath as she turned to see Travis walking in from the garage.

"Morning, love." He gave her a quick kiss on her cheek, keeping his distance, knowing that Taylor didn't like his post-workout sweaty hugs. "Are you okay?" He stepped back and took in the sight of her, as though he could see her thoughts in her expression. "Tay, what's going on?" He put a hand on her shoulder, rubbing it gently with his thumb.

Taylor couldn't do anything but break eye contact and stare at the mess of broken eggs on her slippers. Egg whites, yolks, and shells covered them, and shame washed over her. Not from the broken eggs, which was disappointing in itself, but because of the secrets she was keeping from Travis.

He was the one who had saved her from a past she was running from all those years ago, and he didn't even know the truth about that time in her life. Her secret was buried deep within her, and she'd thought it was locked away—for good.

How foolish she was for thinking she could run and hide from her past when, in reality, she carried that burden everywhere she went.

Taylor put her hands on the kitchen counter and leaned forward. She started laughing out of sheer nerves and Travis gave her a confused smile.

"Am I missing something, Tay?" Travis took out the roll of paper towels they kept under the kitchen sink and bent down, starting to pick up the broken shells piece by piece.

Taylor shook her head, still laughing at the ridiculousness of her situation. How was she supposed to tell her husband what was swirling around in her head? *Well, Travis, I was just thinking of how I think Hazel knows who I really am, and surprise! You don't know anything about it!* The whole situation was crazy.

"No," she finally managed to get out as she started to wipe her eyes, her laughs now turning into sobs. The realization of the mess she'd made of her emotional life—on top of the damage it would cause her marriage if this was to ever get out—was all too much to think about right now.

"Here." Travis put his hand on Taylor's ankle, slowly guiding her foot out of her slippers that were sticky from the egg whites. "Let's get these off, and you go upstairs. Have a shower and take all the time you need. I'll finish up down here. Okay?"

Taylor nodded, taking one foot out and then the other, looking down at her husband and feeling so much love for him among her many other emotions.

Travis didn't deserve this.

Taylor looked at the top of her husband's head as he cleaned her feet—he certainly didn't ask for a life built on a lie, or a wife who had convinced everyone around her that she was a sane and normal person who didn't have this secret past looming over her. He also definitely didn't deserve the emotional toll and the ramifications that Taylor was silly enough to think wouldn't come back to haunt her.

"Okay." Travis stood up and wiped a tear off her cheek. "You're all set. Now go." He pointed up the stairs where Taylor could take all the time she needed.

"Thank you." Taylor's voice was shaky as she put her hand on his shoulder, giving it a squeeze before walking upstairs.

In the shower, she willingly let her mind drift and linger on her past, and for the first time in almost twenty years, she let her emotions take over. More than thirty minutes later, there were no more tears left to cry. She grabbed her towel that hung over the shower door and got out. Rubbing the steam away from the mirror, she looked at herself. Her eyes were red and puffy, and her face was blotchy. She vowed that this was the last time she would cry over the James of her past, over her parents who had practically disowned her, and over a life that could have been.

As she was getting dressed, Taylor heard the boys get up and use the bathroom they shared just down the hall. She listened to them laughing and then fighting and heard the occasional "Ow!" She could only assume which brother was smacking the other brother up the side of his head. She knew how boys could be, but she *did* have to talk to Jake about bullying his brothers just because he could. She just hoped that was where it ended and his behavior didn't carry over to school, too.

Once dressed and downstairs, she saw all four of her boys eating cereal at the kitchen table. Jamie was talking with a mouthful of Cheerios about what he and Dylan were going to do today while Travis and Taylor took the two older boys to their basketball game.

"You like her." Jake's voice was flat and mean between bites.

"I do not!" Jamie screamed as he stood up, pounding his fists on the table, causing his cereal to go flying all over Travis and the floor.

"Jacob!" Taylor scolded as Travis yelled "Jamie!" at the same time.

Jake didn't flinch and his eyes didn't even look up from his phone as he shoveled another bite into his mouth.

Taylor was appalled. Her sweet firstborn boy was acting like a total monster, and she was struggling to get a handle her *own* emotions, let alone her teenager's as well.

"Jacob Hector, go to your room right now." Taylor's voice was now calm and steady. Her eyes would stare directly into his soul if they could.

Jake just looked up at her. "Or what?"

"Or *what*?" Taylor couldn't say anything else. The shock of his tone rendered her speechless.

"No basketball," Travis cut in, standing up from picking Jamie's spoon and cereal bowl up off the floor. "You will not be playing today, Jake."

Jake stood up, arms in the air. "Dad, are you kidding me? You can't—"

"I'm not kidding, and I just did." Travis raised his voice and Taylor had never seen him so angry at Jacob before.

Those two were so close, like-minded in almost everything. Taylor was shocked by this exchange, but thankful to her husband for stepping in when she felt ill-equipped.

Travis pointed a finger at Jake. "And the next time you speak to your mother that way, I'm pulling you from the team for good. Now get to your room."

He and Jake stood there, breathing heavily and staring at each other. Finally, Jake threw his spoon onto the counter, hitting the sink, but the force caused the spoon to bounce right out and hit him on his back as he turned to walk away.

Taylor's hand flew up to her mouth in an attempt to stifle the laugh that was about to burst forth, but it was no use. Jake only looked back to scowl at her before marching up to his room and slamming his door.

The kitchen was silent. This was so out of character for Jake that no one had any words. Taylor looked at Travis, who was still staring at the top of the stairs, his jawline sharp from clenching his teeth.

Josh eventually broke the silence as he took another bite, starting to chew his cereal loudly, clearly happy to see his older brother finally getting in trouble. Jamie ran to the kitchen sink to grab the dish towel, sputtering a trail of *I'm sorry*s along the way.

Travis finally looked at Taylor, eyes softening as Taylor mouthed *thank you*. Travis mouthed *I love you* back, giving a sad smile.

At the high school, Taylor scanned the bleachers for Heather, who was waving frantically from the top bleacher. Taylor took the steps two at a time until she reached her friend. Despite their heated text message exchange, they couldn't stay mad at each other. It just wasn't the kind of friendship they had.

"Where's Tiff?" Taylor set her purse down and crossed her legs, trying not to kick the back of the man in front of her.

Heather's daughter, Tiffany, came to the boys' games primarily for Jake. She was the same age as Josh, but she and Jake had always harbored secret feelings for each other that were actually not so secret, but painfully obvious to everyone every time they were around each other. They were constantly sneaking glances, sitting next to each other but not *too* close, always wanting to do the same things, go the same places, and ride in the same car. Everyone who knew them could see what was happening but chose not to say anything out of respect. Taylor and Heather always just gave each other a knowing smile.

"She's with her *boyfriend*." Heather rolled her eyes.

"Wait, her *boyfriend*?" There was not much Heather could have said to shock Taylor, but there she sat, shocked, and questions started to spill out of her. "So, the friend *was* a boy? Who is he? Do I know him?" She grabbed her purse from underneath her seat in the bleachers to pull out her lip gloss. When she looked up, she saw that Heather was scrolling on her phone.

"At first, I thought he was some tourist she'd met at the beach last weekend, but I guess he just moved here. Here." Heather held her phone up to show Taylor a picture. "Look."

Taylor was taking a sip of coffee when his picture came into view. Shocked at the sight of him, Taylor choked, and coffee came out of her nose.

"Tay!" Heather grabbed a pack of tissues from her purse and started pulling them out one by one, handing them to Taylor. "Are you okay?"

She was still coughing, her nose was burning, and tears stung the back of her eyes, so she squeezed them shut.

Who did I just see?

"Can I—" She coughed again and took another tissue to clean her nose. "Can I see the picture again?"

Heather handed the phone back to Taylor, who glanced down, steeling herself from showing any emotion over the picture. Despite preparing herself, her breath still caught in her throat. Tiffany's boyfriend was the spitting image of James. The James of her past, her high school sweetheart who had disappeared all those years ago. But it couldn't be him. It just wasn't possible.

"Tay?" Heather gently took her phone back. "Is everything okay?"

Taylor smiled, but it didn't reach her eyes, and she nodded slightly. She was too consumed with the image and the memories of James to verbalize an answer.

Despite her shock, her eyes widened with realization, and she turned to face her friend, grabbing her arm with her free hand.

"Heather! *This* is why! This makes all the sense in the world now!" Taylor threw her free hand up in the air and got a few looks from others around her.

Heather's face was confused but supportive. "What makes sense?" Her tone was slow and even, like she was talking to a toddler about a story that jumped plot lines and only made sense in whatever world toddlers' brains lived in.

Taylor laughed and shook her head, turning back to the court where the visiting players had started filing out of the locker rooms ready to warm-up to Usher's "Yeah!"

"It was …" Taylor paused, not knowing how much to say. "It was a tough morning with Jake." She remembered his outburst and anger and nonchalance about, well, everything—until Travis had stepped in. Her mama's heart hurt for her son, but if it had anything to do with Tiffany, his recent behavior made a bit more sense.

"Jake hasn't been himself lately. I mean, you saw what happened last week. And then he and Trav got into it today, and long story short, he's grounded from today's game."

"Wait, *what*?" Heather's long blonde ponytail whipped around as her head did. "You mean he's not playing today?" Heather looked more concerned about his absence from the game than about the fact that there was actually cause for being grounded.

Taylor just shook her head. "Nope. Travis stayed home with him today to make sure he doesn't bolt. I dropped Jamie off at Dylan's this morning and only came with Josh." She shrugged and then, hearing the home team's warm-up song, she started cheering as Josh and the other players made their way out of their locker room and onto the court, starting to take practice shots.

Heather was still staring at Taylor with her mouth open in disbelief. "Jake is *grounded*?"

Not looking back at Heather, Taylor just nodded through a tight-lipped smile.

"How did Travis feel about you keeping him home? Can't imagine that went well."

Taylor laughed. "Oh, that's the best part." She looked at her sideways. "I wasn't the one who grounded him."

"No!" Heather's voice was so loud that even spectators three rows in front of them turned to look at her. "Travis did?"

"He certainly did!" Taylor's voice was delighted.

Heather started laughing, then raised her hands in the air to dance to the warm-up songs. Heather was always up for a party.

They heard the whistle and then the boys lined up, taking their positions, ready to start the game. Taylor looked at the starting players, thinking it was weird not seeing Jake out there, and then, her stomach did a flip. There, at center court, was Josh. Josh was taking over Jake's place as a starter. She could hardly believe it.

Heather put her hand on Taylor's arm. "Taylor, look!" She pointed to Josh and then started clapping and cheering his name.

"I know!" Taylor squealed in delight like she was back in high school herself and clapped and cheered right alongside her best friend. Josh was a good distraction from the image of Tiffany's boyfriend that was now burned into her mind.

And the game was a nail-biter. It was obvious that Jake was missing, but the team was still able to keep up, only falling behind by two to five points the whole game. They usually always won by at least twenty, but that was with Jake starting.

Taylor was proud of Josh. He was playing well and even if the team lost, she would be happy for him. She watched him play his heart out, be a leader on the court, and give the game all he had. She had never seen this side of Josh before, and she wondered if it was because he was always seen as Jake's little brother who constantly lived in his shadow. But today, he was a shining star. Maybe she and Travis were wrong about keeping them together. They talked about splitting them up into different teams, but because of the convenience of having the same practice and game times, they'd ended up keeping them together.

There was only a minute left in the game, and it was tied at forty-seven. Taylor's voice was raw from screaming. She couldn't remember a game that was more intense than this one.

She held her breath as the visiting team took the ball down the court, passing it back and forth as the home team pressured them. It all happened fast, and the next thing they saw was Josh stealing the pass and breaking away toward the opposite net. The crowd was on their feet and Taylor held her breath as the clock counted down.

There were seven seconds left. Six. Five. Four …

Josh went up for an easy layup. The ball circled the rim, once, then twice, and then sank in the net just as the final buzzer blared throughout the gymnasium.

Josh fell to his knees in relief as all his teammates jumped up and ran toward him. They surrounded him, taking turns patting his back or rubbing his sweaty brown hair.

Heather threw her arms around Taylor as they both jumped up and down, screaming. Taylor grabbed Heather's arms, still wound tight around her own, and laughed out of joy for her son. She couldn't wait to tell Travis all about the game, and that they would maybe have to re-think the boys' basketball futures.

She grabbed her purse and empty coffee cup from under the bleachers to head down to congratulate her son, but when she took her phone out to call Travis, she saw that she had seven missed calls from Anna Davis, Dylan's mom.

Worry took over and she swiped her screen to call Anna back. It only rang once before Anna picked up.

"You coming, Tay?" Heather called from over her shoulder as she walked down the bleachers, then turned around when Taylor didn't answer.

Anna's voice was frantic and out of breath. "Taylor? Oh, Taylor I've been trying to reach you ... It's ..." Her breath became heavy as a sob escaped through the phone. "It's Jamie ..."

Taylor's head started spinning at Anna's words and she grabbed onto Heather, who came running back up the steps at the sight of Taylor's pale face.

"Taylor ..." Anna sniffed into the phone before she uttered the words that would send Taylor back to her worst nightmare. "We can't find Jamie ... He's gone."

CHAPTER NINE

Then

May 29, 1995—Orange, California

Taylor wanted to be back in her bed and in the safety of her room. Instead, she was sitting on a stiff plastic chair at St. Peter's Behavioral Health Hospital while her parents sat on either side of her, fidgeting, waiting for the doctor.

The room was plain—a few framed degrees were hanging on white walls above a large wooden bookcase that held blue books with gold lettering. They reminded her of the encyclopedias in her school's library. Taylor noticed that there were no personal pictures and wondered if that said more about the doctor or the patients he saw in his office.

"Tay ..." Her mother cleared her throat. "I need you to talk to the doctor today. *Please.*" Nina's voice was soft but pleading.

Taylor stared at the empty chair behind the bulky wood desk and wondered who this guy even was. She hadn't uttered a word since Callum had left her house on Friday. She didn't know how to formulate any words after what she'd heard. How could she tell her parents, or the doctor, that James was forty-eight years old?

Taylor decided to choose silence over truth. Whatever the truth was.

"Did you hear me, baby?" Nina put her hand on Taylor's shoulder, but Taylor didn't look at her mom.

She felt betrayed by her. In her biggest moment of need, her mom didn't believe her. She had even laughed at her.

Taylor felt alone.

There was a knock on the door, making her parents jump up from their chairs in enthusiastic greeting.

"Mr. and Mrs. Brown," Taylor heard the doctor say from behind her, but she didn't bother to stand up like her parents did. She didn't even turn around to give a smile.

She didn't want to be here. She would endure today's visit so that she could go home and start doing some research of her own. Knowing that James had gone to visit Callum meant that Taylor could, too. She would go home and call him so they could try to figure this out.

Together.

Taylor didn't care how crazy these thoughts were. She'd seen the truth in Callum's eyes. He wasn't playing games with her. What he was telling her was real and Taylor needed someone in her life who believed her, who actually wanted to help her, and that person wasn't this doctor.

The doctor's voice broke through her thoughts. "And this must be Taylor."

She finally raised her eyes to see a large man in a white coat come around the desk. He placed a folder in front of his chair and put his hand out toward her. His eyes clearly demanded respect. Her only movement was to slowly look down at his hand, then back up to stare at him in defiance.

She could tell by looking into his eyes that he wasn't a kind man. He wasn't here to help her; she couldn't trust him.

Taylor felt a nudge on her left side by her mom's elbow that basically meant she was appalled by her actions. *I raised you better than that*, she mentally heard Nina's voice as she felt her mom's eyes drill into the side of her head.

The doctor just nodded and put his hand back down to rest on the file in front of him. "I'm Dr. Michael Green."

Taylor didn't take her eyes off him, which she could tell bothered him a great deal. And she liked that.

She didn't move other than to blink when she needed to. She wouldn't let this man make her uncomfortable.

"What brings you in today?" Dr. Green only broke eye contact to open the file and scan its information.

"We're here by recommendation—the Newport Beach Police Department thought she may need to see someone based on …" Jerry placed a reassuring hand on Taylor's leg, not needing to finish the sentence.

But Nina helped him finish. "Taylor has been through a lot over the past few days, after her boyfriend disappeared on Thursday, and she's just not quite herself." She spewed these facts like they were everyday occurrences.

If Taylor didn't have her heart set on leveling the playing field with Dr. Green, she would have rolled her eyes at her mom. Why was Nina so adamant about making Taylor look good?

You took me to a mental hospital, Mom. They know I'm not okay.

"I see." Dr. Green ran his tongue over his top teeth and narrowed his eyes in concentration at the information he was reading. "So, your boyfriend—"

"James." Nina couldn't stay silent when she was uncomfortable and always talked more than she should, often giving away information that wasn't relevant to the conversation.

Taylor hoped this wasn't one of those times.

"Right. *James.*" Dr. Green leaned forward to get closer to Taylor, which wasn't possible given the size of his desk and his belly. "So … you say he …" He looked up from the file. His eyes were wide in either disbelief or mocking. "He disappeared?" His eyebrows shot up and he dared Taylor to agree with him.

She didn't break. She stared back at him, and although she had never had thoughts of wanting to hurt anyone before, she wondered what it would be like to grab his pen and stab him in the side of his neck. Her eyes dropped slightly to see the point where she would stick it. Would he even feel anything before he collapsed on his desk? Would he try to stop her? He didn't seem like the athletic type to be quick enough to.

"Well, that's only what it *seemed* like …" Nina laughed nervously. "I mean, Taylor doesn't *really* think that he disappeared!" She rubbed Taylor's back while continuing to laugh. "I'm pretty sure that the officer taking her statement just heard her wrong …"

"But it says here that *you* told them that, Mrs. Brown." Dr. Green leaned back in his chair, put the opened folder back on his desk, and clasped his hands in front of his mouth to hide a smirk.

Taylor took her eyes off the doctor for a second just to see her mom's mouth go wide, unable to formulate words.

Dr. Green put his elbows on the arms of his chair with his palms up, shaking his head. "I have to be honest. I'm not sure why Taylor was recommended to come see me, other than to help sort out her thoughts of what happened on Thursday." He let out an exasperated breath as though they were wasting his time.

Taylor looked at the pen. It was just out of reach. She balled her hands on her lap in an effort to control her raging thoughts about him, although she was glad he was easily dismissing them. She couldn't get out of here soon enough.

"She hasn't spoken a word, doctor. Not one word since Dr. Carter came to see her on Friday night." Jerry sounded desperate and Taylor was shocked both at this, and that he'd brought up Callum, whom Dr. Green knew nothing about and about whom her dad didn't know the truth.

She held her breath, waiting for Dr. Green's response, but he only glanced up, his brow giving away his confusion. His silence giving away his pride. She could tell that he didn't want to admit he didn't know what Jerry was talking about. Taylor was thankful, but swiftly slipped into her own confusion. She thought they were simply here to comply with the police, not because her parents actually wanted her here.

"*Please*, doctor." Jerry squeezed Taylor's knee, and Taylor clenched her jaw, refusing to look anywhere else but at the open file with all of her information about what had happened this weekend. "We want our daughter back. We were told you could help us."

Taylor focused on keeping her breath steady, trying to fight back the tears stinging her eyes. What did they mean *they were told*? Who had they really been talking to and what did they say about her? *Breathe, Taylor, breathe. In and out. In and out.*

Dr. Green looked down and nodded sympathetically. He rubbed his chin with his left hand, picking the file back up with his other hand, and read it over again, still nodding.

Taylor's body went stiff. What was happening? Why were her parents so adamant about her being "fixed"? She didn't need fixing. She needed to get James back. She needed to go home and get Callum's phone number, and start making a plan to find her boyfriend.

"I could keep her overnight and do an assessment, some blood work, and a few sessions to gauge what might be rendering her mute. We could meet again tomorrow to discuss the best course of action."

Nina let out a relieved sigh and Taylor's mind started racing as her head spun. *No, no, no, no.*

Jerry stood up, putting his hand out to shake Dr. Green's. "We would really appreciate that, doctor. Thank you."

Dr. Green stood up and took Jerry's hand. "We'll make sure to get your daughter the care she needs to get her mind back in working order."

Nina put her arms around Taylor's rigid body. "Did you hear that, Honey Bear? You're going to be okay," Nina whispered into Taylor's ear, but she stayed stiff, jaw tight, a tear escaping down her cheek.

No, she wasn't going to be okay. Taylor didn't know what to think as she watched her parents smile and give reassuring glances and nods at each other. This had nothing to do with Taylor; this was all about them not wanting to lose another daughter. They wanted her to act normal; they didn't really want to help her. They were helping themselves. Would this prove to the world that she was crazy, after all? That way if anything got out, they could really say it was all in her mind? Or were they hoping for this outcome so that she wasn't accused of something that would land her in jail?

How did this escalate so quickly?

Taylor vaguely heard Dr. Green ask her parents if they wanted to escort her to her room. She felt her dad's hand take her arm to pull her up, and she only obliged because she was in a fog.

Taylor felt like she was floating down the white sterile hall. They went through stainless-steel double doors that only opened when Dr. Green showed his badge to the camera. There was a buzz as the doors unlocked, and they all went through as he waved at the camera above in thanks.

Nina and Jerry were on either side of her, grinning thankful smiles much to Taylor's confusion.

She'd thought that this was how they would be taking her to college for the first time: walking down the dormitory halls to her room to meet her roommate, setting up her new clear plastic phone in her room to call James immediately (who was already there and set up because he had a water polo scholarship and had started practices a week prior). He would come over and help them set up while telling Nina and Jerry all there was to do there. He'd talk about his coach and teammates and who they'd play their first match against, and that yes, he would in fact take very good care of their daughter and see them at Thanksgiving when he would drive her home.

But this wasn't college. This was a behavioral health hospital where her parents were leaving her.

It was more like they were abandoning her.

They all turned a corner and saw a nurse in light blue scrubs with a key fob, waiting outside a door. She had the fob in her hand, and when Dr. Green verified Taylor's identity, date of birth, and reason for being there, the nurse unlocked the door and led the way inside. He put his arm out, gesturing for Nina and Jerry to follow.

"Thank you!" Nina sounded like she was being led into a suite at the Four Seasons.

"It's so bright in here." Jerry walked over to the window, looking out with his hand on his hips. "Look at the view of the foothills, Nina!"

Taylor watched her mother walk over to join her father at the window and stared at them in disbelief. How were they happy about this? She wanted to scream. She wanted to take them by their shoulders and shake them, demanding that they stop this act and see her hurt and pain. *Why are you leaving me here?* she wanted to shout. *You think this is the best thing for me?*

Nina turned, her face beaming at Taylor. "You'll get a perfect view of the sunrise, Honey Bear!" She turned back and placed her hand on the window in awe.

Taylor's ears started pulsing from the force of the blood rushing through her veins. She watched the nurse explain something to her parents while Dr. Green stood back and nodded his agreement. She watched her parents shake the nurse's hand and then turn to smile at the doctor.

Taylor felt detached from her body. This must be someone else's life. This couldn't be hers.

Nina came over and hugged Taylor, but Taylor didn't move, her arms floppy at her side. Jerry put his arm around her while Nina kissed the top of Taylor's head.

Taylor squeezed her eyes shut. She would not let them see her cry. She refused.

They let go and Taylor stayed in place, staring straight ahead out the window. She didn't turn when she heard the door open. She didn't turn when she heard her parents' voices say her name followed by *I love you.* She didn't turn around when she heard the door shut behind them.

She didn't turn around even though she was alone. She stood there in shock, tears flowing silently down her cheeks.

She only turned around when she felt something, or someone. She looked through the tiny glass window in the hospital door to see a figure walk away. She walked closer and looked out. She only saw a tall man with a white coat and graying blond hair walk away from her room and down the hall.

Taylor let out a shaky breath and knew for certain that she was now definitely alone.

She vowed that after she got out of here tomorrow, she would do things differently. She wouldn't rely on anyone. She made up her mind to get the help she really needed. And that help wasn't in this hospital.

It was wherever Callum was.

CHAPTER TEN

Now

July 2, 2016—Myrtle Beach, South Carolina

He's gone.

Taylor couldn't breathe.

"Where was the last place you saw him?" the police officer asked Anna, who had her arm in Taylor's, rubbing her hand while Taylor stared blankly out at the ocean, stuck in a fog and clouded by her own fears.

The voices in her head were loud and started to drown out the real voices all around her. This couldn't happen, again. It just couldn't. It was a dream. No. It was a nightmare. And it *was* happening.

Again.

Heather had taken Josh home from his game so Taylor could go straight to the Davis' house. Travis and Jake had met her there, Jake refusing to be left home, and they were now showing pictures of Jamie to anyone and everyone who passed by. The Davis' summer home was on the beach, half a mile from the main strip. Their back deck stepped down onto the white sand, making it a perfect ten-minute walk to local grocery stores, restaurants, and souvenir shops.

Anna was talking fast as the officer furiously wrote down the information she was given.

"I gave the kids money to walk and get ice cream, which they normally do." Anna turned to nod at Taylor for reassurance in her decision, but Taylor gave none, so Anna looked back at the officer. "But Dylan came running home alone." She let out another soft sob. "She was so afraid."

"Where is Dylan now?" The officer looked up from writing notes as she asked questions.

"She's in her room. Do you need me to go get her?"

The officer nodded. "That would be helpful. The more information we can get, the better chance we have of finding him."

Taylor had heard these words before.

But even after all the information the police had years ago, they still never found James—for reasons she couldn't share with anyone. Would she really have to relive all of that again? The agony she felt inside must have been painfully evident on the outside because Travis came up to help her stay standing. Anna then brought a chair over so Taylor could sit, and Taylor collapsed into it, leaning forward and breathing heavily.

"I think I'm going to be sick," she whispered between her legs to the deck below her.

"Stay with her?" she heard Travis ask Anna as he walked back down the steps to the beach. "I'm going to run the route the kids took and show his picture …" His voice was getting further away as the wind carried the rest away.

Did the wind carry Jamie away, too? Just like it had with James?

"Hi, Dylan. I'm Officer Hayes."

Taylor lifted her nauseous head to look at Dylan. The little girl had been hiding in her room, crying and scared, and Taylor hadn't seen her since she arrived. Dylan's eyes and nose were red, and she had a bunched-up tissue in her hand that she played with. As the officer asked more questions, she replied, "After I paid, I turned back to Jamie but … he wasn't there anymore. I didn't see him leave."

Taylor wanted to reach out and hold the precious girl. Dylan was the one there when Jamie had disappeared. Would Taylor have to talk to her about what she had experienced all those years ago? Would Dylan's life be altered forever, too?

The thought was too much to take in. Nausea overwhelmed her again and she hugged her knees, her stomach threatening to empty its contents of everything she'd eaten today. She felt a hand rub her back but had no clue whose it was.

At that moment, she didn't care. There was a familiar peace, right then, that overtook her. She couldn't explain it, but her head became clearer and more determined than ever to do anything to try to find Jamie.

God, she thought, *please bring Jamie home.* Taylor had prayed when James went missing. Her prayer wasn't answered, and she'd never talked to God again. Until now.

She sat up and looked around. Officer Hayes and Dylan were now on the beach, and Dylan was pointing in the direction of the ice cream store.

She turned and looked up to see who her comforter was, but there was no one there. She saw an older man walking down the beach and thought that it looked like Frank. But it couldn't be him, could it? She turned her gaze to the house to see another officer in the kitchen, talking with Dylan's dad, Tony.

It must have been Officer Hayes. It definitely wouldn't have been Tony. He was nice and all, but Taylor rarely saw him. He was always cooped up in his office working, or pacing the beach while he was on the phone, making obscene hand gestures as he aggressively spoke. Anna was always out with the kids on the beach, out for dinner, or riding bikes down the strip while Tony sat at the computer with his Bluetooth speaker in his ear while he was on the phone talking to yet another client.

He was not the back-rubbing type.

"Taylor!" She heard her name being called but couldn't make out by whom. "Taylor!"

Someone was shouting now, and an unknown force propelled Taylor up and out of the chair to lean against the deck's wooden railing. She saw Dylan race down the beach and looked in the direction she was running. Taylor squinted and was able to make out Travis, hand in hand with ...

"Jamie!" Taylor cried and hurled herself down the stairs and onto the beach, her lungs protesting the effort, but her mind and legs had a different agenda. "Jamie!" she called out again as they got closer.

Through her eyes, blurry with tears, there was Jamie, running right to her. He broke away from Travis just as he reached Taylor, throwing his arms around her neck.

"Jamie ..." Taylor silently sobbed into his neck. She held him close and breathed him in.

"I'm okay, Mom. Really! Look!" He backed away from her, holding out his arms like he was showing her a new outfit.

"I see that!" Taylor laughed and wiped her nose on her sleeve.

Travis came up behind Jamie. When she stood up, he put his arm around his shoulder. "I went around to Thrifty's to show them Jamie's picture, and there he comes, walking around the corner without a care in the world. He had no idea anyone was looking for him at all." Travis shook his head in disbelief. "He thought he saw Frank and ended up chasing him for a block before realizing it wasn't him." Travis and Taylor exchanged a look, but the truth was everyone was too happy to see him to be angry at him.

Except for Dylan. She walked forward and hit Jamie on the arm.

"Ow!" He looked at her, stunned. "What was that for?" Jamie rubbed his arm, completely offended, but Anna, Taylor, and Travis all laughed.

"You scared me!" She was still crying. "Don't ever do that again. *Ever!*" Dylan screamed at him before running back to her house.

Jamie looked at Anna, then at Taylor, and finally down at his bare feet. "I'm sorry. I didn't mean to—"

"I know." Anna leaned down and side-hugged him, kissing the top of his head. "But you're Dylan's best friend and today, well, she was scared that she lost you."

For the first time, Jamie looked sad about the situation. His eyes met Taylor's and she saw that they were full of tears.

"Did you think that too, Mom?"

Taylor shut her eyes while memories of twenty years earlier came rushing back to her. When she opened them, she got on her knees in front of him, eye-to-eye. She put her hands on either side of his face and told him the truth.

"Yes, Jamie. I was so scared. I actually *prayed.* I prayed that we'd find you." She smiled at him and hugged him tight again.

"God answered your prayer, Mom." Jamie's voice in her ear made her cry all over again.

"He certainly did, love." And she kissed her son on the top of his head.

Later that night, Taylor said goodnight to her boys before joining Travis on the couch with a glass of wine. She put her feet on his lap, and he rubbed one of them as he watched Josh's game on his laptop.

Coach Chad always taped the game for replays and uploaded the games to YouTube so parents and players could re-watch, also.

"I can't believe I missed *this* game." Travis took another sip of his wine. "And out of all the games to miss, too. I'm so dang proud of Josh!" Travis put down his glass and shut the laptop.

"I can't believe that you actually made Jake stay home." Taylor poked Travis in the ribs with her free foot. "I didn't think you had it in you."

Travis looked hurt. "What does that mean?"

"It means," Taylor said and reclaimed both feet, tucking them in underneath her, "that you favor Jake. It's pretty clear he's your favorite."

"He is not!" Travis was defensive, but then smiled and gave it right back to her. "Just like Jamie's yours?"

Taylor put her hand on her heart and gasped. "Do you really think that?"

"I think it in the same way that you think Jake's mine."

That silenced Taylor. He wasn't wrong, but it wasn't for the reasons he thought.

Jamie was born on the tenth anniversary of James's disappearance, May 25, 2005, arriving three weeks early. Every anniversary of James's disappearance was hard, and she always suffered in silence while trying to suppress the memory.

But this one hit different. It marked a full decade without him. When a nurse announced that she and Travis had another son, she'd placed Taylor's newborn baby on her chest and Taylor had cried.

"James," she'd said over and over, weeping over her third boy. "James."

Travis had walked over and kissed her on her forehead. "James it is."

Taylor had been stunned into silence. She hadn't realized that she was saying his name out loud, but Travis had seemed at peace with the name.

They'd had two names picked out months ago, sticking to "J" names—Julia for a girl, and Justin for a boy. But even knowing this, Travis hadn't flinched at the change.

But who would argue with a tired and emotional mom who had just delivered a baby? He was a smart man.

Taylor had hugged her newborn son even closer, not realizing how much this meant to her. She'd had no idea how hard it would be for her in the future. James Brooks had been hard enough to forget, but now she'd have a son named after him and a birthday to celebrate instead of a loss to mourn.

Jamie, as he would later be called, was definitely a standout among her boys for these reasons, but he wasn't her favorite. She didn't have a favorite. She couldn't tell Travis any of this, and her mind raced for something to say. But nothing came. She just stayed silent.

Travis took her silence as an admission and stood with his hands in the air. "I rest my case." He started walking upstairs. "I have a few emails to send, and then I'll take the trash out."

"Okay." Taylor watched him walk upstairs, forgetting entirely about trash day, and still stunned that he'd actually admitted to Jake being his favorite. She'd have to bring this up another time when she had an actual defense for her argument.

She had thought about it for only a moment longer when she heard a crash outside. She got up and looked out the bay window across the street. Hazel's husband, Frank, was taking the garbage out, and one of the bins had tipped over, scattering its contents all over the street. Without hesitating, Taylor put on her flip-flops and went outside to help.

"Hi there!" Taylor tried to make her voice sound light, but it came out aggressive, even to her own ears.

He looked up and froze.

"Can I, uh …" Feeling uncomfortable under his stare, she started second-guessing this decision. "Can I help you?"

He just nodded. He looked significantly older than Hazel, who was still youthful, lively, and energetic. He was wearing sunglasses, even though the sun had set almost an hour ago. His cheeks were sunken in, his head bald. He looked down and picked up a banana peel with shaking hands.

"Here," Taylor said and took it from him, "let me help you." Standing up, she took the handle of the trash bin that had turned on its side and lifted it to its rightful position then put the peel in. "I'm happy to clean this up for you." Taylor nodded in earnest.

He just stared right back at her.

Taylor put her hand out. "I'm Taylor." She smiled, feeling like she was talking to a shy child; she wanted to be gentle with each word and movement.

He gently took her hand, letting her do the rest.

"Frank." His voice was thick and raspy. He cleared his throat and tried again. "I'm Frank." The corners of his mouth went up into what Taylor assumed was a smile.

"It's a pleasure to meet you, Frank." She let go of his hand. "Is Hazel home tonight?"

Frank shook his head. Taylor realized that might be all that she was getting from him.

"Well, seriously, please go inside and rest. I'm honestly happy to clean this up for you. I was actually going to bake you and Hazel muffins today, and then I dropped my whole carton of eggs and the boys had basketball and I didn't get around to picking something up for you on the way home because my youngest son got lost at the beach and the whole day just got turned upside down so …" She stopped short, but not short enough, now mortified that she was rambling without the slightest clue as to why.

"Did you find him?" Frank coughed into his jacket's sleeve, and Taylor wondered if talking was an effort for him.

She smiled and put her hand on her chest. "Yes!" She laughed nervously. "Yes, he was found. Thank God!"

Frank smiled again, or at least he did what Taylor thought was smiling. "Praise God, indeed."

Taylor stilled. James's parents used to say that about everything. It left a funny feeling in her stomach. The weather was nice? *Praise God!* James got a good grade, again? *Praise God!* The horrendous neighbors with the overgrown bushes are moving? *Praise God!* The only things they seemed to "praise" Him for was their selfishness, and it was why she was always so reluctant to trust Christians. They used God when they felt like it and praised Him when life was going well. Did they praise Him when James had disappeared, though? No. All she'd seen was anger and hatred toward her, with them throwing accusations around, claiming that it was her fault. She hadn't seen them praise God in those last moments.

Taylor's words caught in her throat, trying to respond to Frank. She cleared her throat and gave a weak attempt at a smile.

"Indeed."

Frank looked at her for a beat, then turned and walked back into the house, raising his hand in a wave that Taylor took as a thank you.

She bent down to start cleaning up when she remembered the man on the beach.

"Hey, Frank?" she called out to ask him, but when she looked up, it was just in time to see the front door close behind him. Sighing, she turned back to the task at hand.

It only took her about ten minutes, but she was able to pick up the trash bags, paper, and coffee filters as best she could. After Taylor got back home, she showered and got into her pajamas.

Travis was now on the phone and motioned to Taylor that he was going to be a while. She gave him a quick kiss goodnight and settled into bed. She was happy that Travis got promoted, but it was taking up a lot of his time.

She was too exhausted to wait up for him after the emotional toll that today had taken on her, and she drifted easily into sleep.

"Taylor?" someone was saying, gently shaking her awake. "Tay, wake up. I have a surprise for you."

"Hmm?" She rubbed her eyes, slowly opening them.

"I'll be right back." The voice got further away down the hall.

"How Sweet It Is (To Be Loved by You)" was playing. Her heart skipped. She hadn't heard this song, or any of James Taylor's songs, for a very long time.

On purpose.

Who was playing it and why? She sat up in bed and looked around. The morning light was shining through her window and there was a vase of flowers on her nightstand. Except, they hadn't been there the night before.

She heard footsteps down the hall, and someone humming to the music. It was coming closer and sounded so familiar. Too familiar.

Time stood still as James Brooks walked into her bedroom. He had a tray in his hands with breakfast laid out, the sun caught his golden-blond hair, and his bright blue eyes were radiant.

"I missed you, Tay."

He looked exactly the same as when she'd last seen him at eighteen years old.

"How did you ..." She rubbed her eyes as he came to sit on the end of the bed.

He leaned over and kissed her on the cheek.

She wanted to reach up and touch her cheek where his lips left warmth, but she couldn't move. Taylor stayed frozen except for her eyes, which darted to look at the door. What if Travis walked in? Or one of her boys? How would she explain any of this?

"How is this ... happening?"

"Shh." He put his finger over her lips. "Now's not the time to explain. Here." He grabbed a strawberry and fed it to her. "All you need to know is I'm here. I'm watching you, Tay." He took another strawberry and she tried to ask another question, but he put it in her mouth before she could speak.

He stood up and grabbed the vase of flowers, smelling them.

"From what I remember, lilies are your favorite." He winked.

"Taylor?" Travis called, his footsteps coming up the stairs. "I'm home!"

Taylor's heart was about to leap out of her chest, and she and James both looked in the direction of the bedroom door.

No, no, no, this isn't real.

She shut her eyes, but when she opened them, James was still standing there.

He smiled again. "I'm watching you." Then he winked.

As Travis walked into the bedroom, James disappeared and the vase of flowers he was holding came crashing down.

Taylor shot up in bed, covered in sweat, her bedroom still dark.

"Taylor? What's wrong?" Travis was in bed next to her, rubbing her back.

"I uh ..." She caught her breath and looked around. The clock read 3:03 a.m. "It was so real. It was all *so* real." Her breath was shaky and she shook her hands, willing the adrenaline out of them.

"What was, love? What was so real?"

Before she could think about it, she blurted out, "James is here. He's ... right here." Realizing her mistake, she covered her mouth with her hand, eyes wide.

"Oh, Tay." Travis rolled over and hugged her. "It was scary for all of us today. But he *is* here. He's safe, love. He's home."

Of course. Travis thought she meant their son. He knew nothing of her past James.

"Yes." She breathed out, steadying her breath. "Yes, you're right. He's home."

She lay back down, pulling the covers up to her chin. She wondered if Jamie's scare today was the reason that James had crept back into her head, starting to invade her thoughts, and now ... her dreams.

And she wondered how she was ever going to get him out before he ruined her life. Again.

CHAPTER ELEVEN

Then

June 5, 1995—Orange, California

One night at the hospital turned into one week and now, to Taylor's horror, one week had just turned into "indefinitely."

Taylor watched her dad leave her room, hearing his fast-paced footsteps squeaking down the sterile white corridor.

She felt depleted. There were no more tears left to cry. Her mom hadn't even bothered to show up today. Her dad wasn't the happy man she knew him to be, and he certainly wasn't the optimistic parent he'd been when he'd first dropped her off.

But why would he be?

Taylor hadn't been very cooperative since she'd been there and was the first to admit that. She hated Dr. Green and refused to utter a single word while under his care. He was fishing for something and seemed to want to get a reaction out of her. She wasn't playing his game and it angered him. And while that made her happy, it was also probably the reason why she wasn't going home anytime soon.

He seemed to have it in for her. Taylor wasn't sure whether she was a conquest that he alone had to win, or if she was a pawn in his sad little game.

She was playing her own game back.

"Can I get you more water?" Abby was the new nurse who had been assigned to her. She picked up the jug of water, lifting the lid to examine how full it was.

Taylor, sitting on her bed, went from staring at the door to staring blankly at Abby. It wasn't Abby's fault that she was in here. But she refused to break. Abby seemed friendly enough and had a soft, kind face. She looked young, and Taylor felt bad that she was stuck with a patient like her.

Abby set down the empty jug, wrote something in her file and tucked it under her arm before turning to look at Taylor.

"I'll go ahead and take this since you're finished. Press the button if you need any more." She smiled politely but it didn't reach her eyes.

Was that pity Taylor saw in them?

Without breaking eye contact, Taylor reached over, and pressed the red button for help that reached the nurse's station.

Abby's lips pressed into a tight line, and she slowly nodded in under-standing. Her eyes narrowed as if to say, *So it'll be like this, will it?*

"I'll be right back, Taylor." She grabbed the empty water jug, turned on the heels of what looked to be brand-new white Reebok sneakers and left the room.

Taylor grinned. *Poor Abby. Caught in the middle of this.* But then her mouth turned down as she contemplated getting Abby on her side—would she even help her if Taylor asked? There was only one way to find out.

Taylor's initial goal had been to get out of here as quickly as possible. But now she didn't quite know what her endgame was.

She knew she didn't want to go home. What was there waiting for her other than her disappointed parents who had brought her here hoping they'd get a shiny new daughter back? There was no James to turn to, and she hadn't talked to any of her friends since that Thursday at school.

She knew that she and James were all over the news. Mr. and Mrs. Brooks were making sure of it. Taylor heard her dad apologize to Dr. Green for being late because news vans were parked outside their house waiting for a sighting and hoping for a comment. She could only imagine how difficult it was to leave their house.

After only a week, it was hard to imagine life outside this hospital. The outside world already seemed a lot different to her. She needed to re-strategize.

Taylor looked out the window, watching an airplane disappear into the clouds, wondering what she would do if she were at home. *I would call Callum.* But now, without his number, how? Taylor needed a computer.

There was no clock in her room to tell what time it was, but judging by her dad's one p.m. appointment with Dr. Green, and given that her dad had been late, the meeting had lasted maybe twenty minutes, and it must have been about fifteen minutes since he'd left and Abby had brought her water … so Taylor guessed it was around two o'clock now. She was usually escorted out for a walk around the grounds at two-thirty, and then she had another session with a counselor at three. Then, back to her room until it was time for dinner.

Taylor now had a plan, and that plan involved Abby.

She lay down on her bed, counting the planes out her window until she heard her door unlock again.

Abby came in and put her keys back in her pocket. But then a loud voice came in from behind Abby.

"I didn't ask you to get her water; I asked you to take her outside." Dr. Green was standing in the doorway staring at Abby, who looked like a puppy who just got in trouble.

"Her water needed refilling, sir—"

"*Doctor.*" Dr. Green's eyes were angry, and his voice sent shivers down Taylor's spine.

Abby stammered. "Yes, Doctor. Sorry. She needed water, so I—"

Dr. Green pointed a finger at Abby. "So, *you* thought you'd get her what she needs because you can read her mind now? Because she certainly can't speak." He shot a look to Taylor, who was still lying in her bed, also frozen from this interaction.

Just because she was choosing silence, people apparently also thought her stupid. Taylor's plan was now shifting in favor of her new nurse.

Abby stood still, unsure of what to say under these accusations, the jug of water shaking in her hand. Assessing the situation, Taylor leaned over and pressed the red button again, making Abby and Dr. Green look at her. When she'd first pressed it, it was for the sole purpose of making Abby mad, for which Taylor now felt shame. Abby was just doing her job and Taylor had taken out all of her frustration over this situation on her.

But now, as they both looked at her. Taylor's eyes implored Abby to stand up for herself.

"Dr. Green." Abby's voice was now steady and sure, looking at him with clarity. "This patient pushed her call button for water. I am now bringing her that water so she will be ready to go outside." Abby's chest didn't rise or fall, and Taylor knew she was holding her breath.

Dr. Green only stared at Abby, sizing her up, before finally saying, "Fine." He shook his head. "But next time, remember this is a hospital. Not a hotel." And with that, he turned abruptly and slammed the door behind him.

Both Abby and Taylor remained still, watching the door bounce on its hinges from the force, Taylor's eyes blinking shut from the sound carrying down the halls.

Abby let out a long and shaky breath before composing herself again and facing Taylor.

"Ready for your walk, Tay?"

Abby still didn't look at her as she walked around the other side of the bed and lifted the covers for Taylor to get out.

Abby had just called her Tay. Only her friends and family called her that. Taylor's heart softened and she knew what she needed to do.

Taylor's voice let out a scratchy, whispered, "Yes."

Abby stilled, her eyes wide, but other than that, she gave no indication that she was shocked. She simply nodded, and as Taylor swung her feet out from under the covers and placed them on the floor, Abby spoke quietly, "Cheryl won."

Taylor gave Abby a confused look. She didn't know a Cheryl or what she had to do with anything.

Abby smirked, then bent down to grab Taylor's shoes. "We placed bets." Abby slipped them on Taylor's feet. "Cheryl guessed you'd speak one week after getting here. She won." Abby shrugged, then held out her hand.

Taylor took it and stood up.

"What did you guess?" Taylor's curiosity got the best of her, but her voice was still dry and raspy, and a coughing fit followed.

Abby poured water from the jug into the cup and handed it to Taylor, who drank it like she hadn't had water in a year. Her throat felt like sandpaper now that words were trying to make their way out.

Abby just chuckled. "I thought it would at least be two months."

Taylor couldn't resist asking, "Did Dr. Green guess?"

Abby laughed and Taylor smiled at its sound. "He was the one who started it!" Abby shook her head, still laughing. "He bragged to everyone that he'd have you talking after your first night here." She smirked at Taylor. "That's probably why he's mad at the world right now."

Taylor snorted a laugh. She looked down at Abby sliding her shoes on her feet and knew she made the right decision. She and Abby would get along perfectly.

And Taylor's plan would, too.

Taylor changed the subject. "Are there any computers here?" She coughed again, then reached for her cup and took another sip.

Abby looked confused. "In the hospital?"

Taylor nodded, still drinking, letting the water settle in her throat before taking a long and painful swallow.

"Yes, there are. For the doctors to use," Abby added.

Taylor knew she had to tread lightly. She'd only just started speaking, and she couldn't play her hand all at once or she'd raise suspicion. But she had to know.

"What about for us?" She raised her eyes to Abby's.

Abby just shook her head. "None for patients. We have one in the nurse's station to access our email, though."

Taylor could work with that. She'd just have to get on Abby's good side.

For the first time since James had disappeared, she felt hopeful.

They stood up, heading out of the room and into the courtyard shared with the rest of the ward, now walking in silence. She had used up all her words for the day and she didn't think her throat could take another cough.

Abby asked her questions, to which Taylor only nodded "yes" or shook her head "no." Abby was patient with Taylor, and as they sat on a bench under a tree. Then, Abby broke the silence again.

"I was sent here to look after you."

She looked away from Taylor and up into the tree's branches above them. Then she leaned forward and put her elbows on her knees.

Taylor's breath caught and all she could do was stare at the nurse's profile. What was Abby talking about? And why specifically her?

Abby took a breath. "I was transferred here from up north ..." She took a sideways glance at Taylor before continuing. "I was sent here by a Dr. Carter? I don't know him ... you seem really important to him, though."

Taylor didn't understand at first, and then realization dawned on her. She took in a short breath as her mind raced to when Callum had first come to their house. *This is Dr. Carter,*" her dad had said as he'd introduced her to Callum. Was this a coincidence? Was this a joke?

Taylor searched Abby's eyes. She didn't look confident in what she was saying but kept talking anyway.

She sat up and put her hands on her knees to help herself up off the bench. Abby turned to Taylor. "He got me a job here once I got my nursing license. Sent a letter of recommendation and everything."

Taylor looked up at her, processing this, and Abby held out her hand to help her up. *Time to head back, I guess.* She took it and although they walked in silence, Taylor's mind loud with possibilities. How did Callum know Abby? And why didn't she know him? Why did he want to get her in here? Was it for her? To help her escape? The questions flooding Taylor's mind were too much to take and she felt herself getting dizzy. She stopped and steadied herself against the rail leading back up to the hospital.

"Are you okay?" asked Abby. "Do you need to sit down?"

Taylor shook her head. She wasn't okay and she didn't need to sit down. She needed to take action.

She needed a computer. She needed to find Callum.

"I know I shocked you, Taylor. And I know it doesn't make sense; it doesn't even make sense to me, but—" Abby was interrupted as another nurse came to relieve her for her break. "I can take my break after I take my patient back to her room." Abby was adamant and wasn't ready to leave this conversation.

The other nurse shook her head. "You'll be too close to getting overtime hours and you know how *he* will respond to that." Taylor assumed the "he" in question was Dr. Green.

Abby sighed, then gave Taylor an apologetic look. "I'll see you after dinner, okay, Tay?"

Taylor nodded, and looked longingly after her as Abby walked away, turning around every so often with eyes telling her that this conversation definitely was not over.

Taylor nodded at her in understanding before Abby smiled, winked, and walked around the corner of the brick hospital.

CHAPTER TWELVE

Now

July 3, 2016—Myrtle Beach, South Carolina

Taylor flipped the French toast and felt little arms around her waist. She smiled and put her free hand on top of Jamie's.

"I love you, Mom." His voice was muffled against her back, but she turned her head to look at the top of his.

"I love you too, buddy."

Taylor still felt drained from yesterday's events. She'd gone from being elated for Josh at his basketball game to hitting rock bottom thinking that Jamie was gone. She had already gone through it once, and even though she knew her son was home and not gone, like all her fears had led her to believe, it would still take her a while to get over.

Yet again.

"Ready for breakfast?" Taylor let go of Jamie's arm, lifting a corner of the toast to make sure she hadn't burned the final side. It was perfect.

She piled the last of the French toast on a plastic pineapple platter that they usually used for summer barbecues. It was already out in preparation for tomorrow's Fourth of July block party, so Taylor took advantage, loaded it up and placed it in the center of the kitchen table.

"Something smells good!" Travis came downstairs, still wearing the basketball shorts he slept in and his old university shirt, and kissed Taylor on her cheek.

Taylor didn't respond like she otherwise would have. She stiffened, remembering her dream last night. She had a guilty feeling, like she had betrayed Travis somehow. But that was silly because she knew she hadn't. She only had a dream that brought up old and unresolved feelings that she thought she had buried years ago. That wasn't a betrayal, right?

"Someone *looks* good!" Taylor cringed at her overcompensation for feeling like she'd cheated on her husband in her dream the night before. When Travis raised an eyebrow, reading her like a book, she cleared her throat and said, "Can you grab the syrup?"

Travis walked over to Taylor, opened the cupboard and, without taking his eyes off her, he reached up with a sly smile and grabbed the syrup. "Someone *looks* good?" Travis gave her a smile that caused Taylor to shrink inside herself.

Why was she awkwardly flirting with her own husband? What was wrong with her?

Travis walked away and back to the kitchen table, strutting like he was on a runway. Taylor burst out laughing, then rolled her eyes.

Jamie, oblivious to what was happening in the kitchen, had a mouthful of food that splattered all over when he asked, "Dad, can we ride bikes today?"

"Yeah we can, buddy!" He ruffled Jamie's hair. "Oh, that reminds me, Tay," Travis casually wiped the food spit off the table with the table runner and Taylor winced. "I have a last-minute work dinner with Stan and our new clients tonight."

Taylor tried to remain calm as she walked over to the kitchen table, set his plate down, and gathered up the table runner to put it in the wash.

Travis poured a tiny bit of syrup on his plate just to taste. "But I was thinking, maybe you could go out with Heather tonight. Jake's still grounded, so, you know, he'll be home to stay with Josh and Jamie."

"Hmm." Taylor thought out loud. It wasn't a bad idea. She could use a girls' night but didn't want to leave Jamie after almost losing him only yesterday.

"Just do it." Travis cut into the toast, stacked a pile onto his fork, and put it in his mouth. "I feel bad leaving you, and I'd feel better if I knew you were out having fun." Taylor didn't have to wonder where Jamie got his messy eating habit from as a piece of food flew out of Travis's mouth, landing in front of him.

"Just like you'll be having fun?" she teased. She knew he struggled with Stan, his overbearing boss who wasn't the easiest to work for. Stan was probably only bringing Travis because he was the only employee who took Stan's put-downs without complaint. He constantly did this in front of others just to make himself look better. Why Travis took it, she would never understand. Her husband was a good, good man.

"I don't want you going just to be Stan's punching bag all night." Taylor stole a bite of Travis's French toast. "And who has a work dinner on the night before the Fourth?"

Travis shrugged. "I'm the new District Manager. I *should* be there and trust me—Stan only makes himself look bad by how he acts. I'll be fine." He stood up with his now-empty plate to put it in the sink. "He wanted it to be a breakfast meeting tomorrow morning of all days, but no one could make it." Travis grabbed his keys off the counter and headed to the garage door. "I'm going to head to the grocery store—text me your shopping list?" he called over his shoulder, then disappeared, the garage door slamming behind him.

Taylor heard a faint "Love you!" from the garage. She chuckled and picked up her phone to text Travis: *Love you too!*

Taylor watched his car back out of the garage, and then he waved to Hazel and Frank, who looked like they were on their way to church. Hazel was wearing a short-sleeved sundress with a large white barrette in her hair, tying up one side of her silver locks, and Frank had on a blue tie that matched her dress.

Despite her being wary of them, they were seriously the cutest couple she'd ever seen.

After she watched them drive away, she sent a text to Heather.

Margaritas? Tonight? Blue's?

Taylor had barely put her phone down before she heard it chime. She laughed when she saw Heather's response: *I'll pick you up at seven* was followed by the dancing woman emoji.

Taylor sent back the party popper emoji and then slipped the phone into her back pocket with a renewed sense of energy. She was excited about a night out with her best friend.

The day went by quickly, and she was pleased she didn't have a negative reaction when Jake found out that he was on babysitting duty for his younger two brothers. Taylor wondered about bringing up Tiffany as she stood in the doorway of his room but wanted his mood to remain *not* sucky. She didn't know what reaction she would get from him if he found out that his mom knew the real reason for his recent outbursts. Taylor wondered if he would be embarrassed, or if he would come clean, happy to talk about it. But that was for a later conversation.

She quickly showered and blow-dried her hair before finishing her makeup. Then Taylor picked out her nicest dark-wash jeans with the frayed cuffs, her white fitted v-neck T-shirt, and matched it with her fitted green army jacket and black flats. She put on her gold chain necklace and bangles, popped in her hoop earrings, and headed downstairs to wait for Heather.

"I'll miss you, Mom." Jamie hugged Taylor from behind and she reached around to hug him back.

"I'll miss *you*!" She let go to turn around and face him, bending down to kiss the top of his head. "Call me if you boys need anything. I'll just be at Blue's and can be home in five minutes."

Josh didn't turn around from the couch, where he was watching a baseball game. "Is there any pizza left?"

Taylor saw the headlights before Heather's car pulled up in front of her house.

"I put the rest of it in the fridge, buddy." She walked to the bottom of the stairs and put her hand on the handrail. "Jake!" she called up to her son. "I'm leaving!"

"K!" she heard him shout from behind his closed door, but it was good enough.

At least he'd answered. It was a step in the right direction.

"Josh, promise me you'll call if anything happens." Not getting an answer, she walked around to the front of the couch, blocking his line of sight to the TV. "Josh?"

"I'll call, Mom. Promise." He still didn't take his eyes off the TV, moving his body to look around Taylor, then shot up, pumping his fist. "Yes! Home run, baby!"

Taylor laughed. "Thank you. Love you guys."

"Bye, Mom!" Jamie ran to give her another hug, then climbed back on his stool at the kitchen island with his pen and notebook, writing something furiously fast.

"Bye, sweets." She gave a wave and locked the front door behind her.

Heather was waiting in her car, waving her hands in the air and singing along to Justin Bieber's "Sorry."

"Girls' night!" Heather screamed over the beat when Taylor got in.

They sang and danced in the car all the way to Blue's, their favorite Mexican restaurant for chips, tacos, and margaritas.

They sat down and immediately ordered their usual. They never needed the menu—a taco salad for Heather and the chicken enchiladas with red sauce for Taylor.

Heather turned to her friend with raised eyebrows. "So, I finally met him."

"Met who?" Taylor turned her body in the half-moon booth to look at her.

"Tiffany's boyfriend, Andrew!" Heather swatted her arm like she should have known. "She brought him over today."

"And?" Taylor wanted to know her friend's exact thoughts.

In her mind, she saw the picture Heather showed her at the basketball game and wondered if he really did look like James, or if that was only because of recent events? Between that and the dream she'd had last night, James was stuck in her head.

Heather shrugged. "I like him!" She smiled at her confession and then looked up at the waitress who brought their chips and salsa and refilled their waters.

"Drinks will be out soon, ladies!" The waitress grinned and grabbed the menus that were left untouched at the edge of the table.

"Thanks!" Taylor smiled at her, then turned her attention back to Heather. "Well, I'm happy for her." She took another sip of water.

"He's really sweet, and super handsome, and I guess he's living here for good now. His parents just got divorced, and he and his mom came here to be closer to his grandparents." Heather shoved a salsa-slathered chip in her mouth, then wiped her lips with the paper napkin her water was on. "His grandpa has cancer and doesn't have much longer, I guess."

Taylor's narrowed her eyes as her mind went to the DeLucas.

"What's his last name?" Taylor tried to sound casual, but it came out urgent.

"Stafford. Why?" Heather ate another chip as her eyes scanned the restaurant. At first Taylor assumed she was looking for their margaritas but, knowing Heather, she was probably scanning for eligible guys.

Ever since Heather's divorce was final last year, she'd turned into the teenager Taylor had known when they'd first met—always wanting to go out for drinks, go to parties or concerts, and make friends with absolutely anyone and everyone while also flirting with anyone and everyone.

Heather's eyes were locked in on something, and Taylor followed her eyes to the bar where a new, young bartender was working. She looked back and forth between the bartender, who was looking at Heather, and Heather, who was looking back at him.

Taylor rolled her eyes and smiled but continued anyway. "Well, you know Hazel's husband, Frank, is sick and we haven't found out their whole story yet. I just thought there was a chance it might be them."

Heather nodded, turning her attention back to Taylor. "You're right! I've met Hazel but not Frank. What's their last name, again?"

"DeLuca."

"DeLuca," Heather repeated, eyes drifting again.

Taylor laughed out loud. "So, am I your wing-woman tonight or did you actually want to hang out with me?"

"What? No! I just ..." Heather stammered over her words as the waitress approached with their drinks.

"Ladies, these are on the house." She put the first margarita in front of Heather, then set Taylor's down on the table. "Enjoy!"

And with no other explanation, the waitress walked away.

"On the house!" Taylor repeated and raised her glass to the bartender, who'd undoubtedly sent them. He smiled back, raising his water glass in response. "Well," she continued, "if my best friend wants to flirt with Marty McFree-drinks over there instead of hanging out with me, then at least I got a free drink out of it." She took a sip and shut her eyes. "Oh! Does he make a good spicy cucumber margarita or what?" Taylor shivered in response to tasting the alcohol. "I approve." She clinked her glass to Heather's, breaking her out of her bartender-staring trance.

Heather turned and looked offended. "No, it's not that ... I just ..."

"Just what?" Taylor challenged.

"Ugh, okay." Heather sighed and gestured toward to bar. "I met him yesterday while I was running on the beach and we got talking, and I knew he was young but I honestly didn't think I'd see him again, let alone think that he *worked* here, and now I'm slightly mortified because I kind of maybe was a little *too* flirty with him, but honestly, Taylor, I was just having a little fun and he made me feel good and confident and I liked having someone young and sexy think that I'm young and sexy too, and ..." Heather's ramblings stopped short when she looked somewhere over Taylor's left shoulder.

The look on her face could only mean one thing. Derek.

"Heather?" Taylor's mind raced, knowing her best friend's look all too well. "Is it—"

"Yes," she cut Taylor off, already knowing the question.

"And is he with—"

"Yes." Heather's color drained from her face.

Taylor put her hand on Heather's leg and slowly turned around to see Derek, Heather's ex-husband, with his new wife, Sheri, who was twelve years younger than he was.

Taylor turned back and took Heather's chin in her right hand. "Heather. Don't do this. You don't love him. He's a bully who made you feel bad about yourself, and I bet he's making Sheri feel bad about herself, too. He will never change, and you just need to take a good look at them and be glad that that's not *you* anymore. Okay?"

Tears sprouted in Heather's eyes as she looked over Taylor's shoulder again.

"Okay?" Taylor jerked Heather's chin back toward her, so they were making eye contact again, then let go.

A tight line replaced Heather's quivering lips to fight back the tears, and she looked down and nodded. "Okay," she whispered.

"Now, let's drink our free margaritas and cheers to the fact that a young and sexy bartender has the hots for you."

Heather let out a laugh and used her napkin to dab her eyes. "Thank you, Tay. Now, *please* tell me something to take my mind off all of this." She grabbed her drink and held it up to Taylor's glass.

Taylor clinked hers with Heather's and they both finished their drinks in one long gulp, then flagged down their waitress for a refill.

Taylor told her about Travis's new position at work. They talked about when basketball tryouts were for high school, and if Josh would play varsity next year after what had happened in yesterday's game. She also got more information about Tiffany's boyfriend and what that meant for her and Jake.

After finishing their meals, their third round of margaritas arrived and Heather asked how Taylor was feeling after everything with Jamie that had happened the day before.

"I can't imagine the emotional toll it must have taken on you, Tay."

Taylor sighed, taking another sip of her way-too-delicious margarita. She had a sudden and overwhelming sensation of wanting to be seen, to be heard and truly known for the first time in her entire adult life.

Taylor let out a steady breath and mentally crossed her fingers for what she was about to do—unleash her past.

"This isn't the first time that happened, you know." Taylor looked down at the folded napkin on her lap.

Heather pushed her empty plate away from her and to the edge of the table for the waitress. "The first time what happened?" She looked confused. "That you got free drinks? 'Cause I doubt that, hottie." Heather laughed, clearly feeling the buzz.

Taylor shook her head. "No, no. But thanks for the compliment." She nudged Heather's arm. Was she actually going to do this? Now? After all these years? Although she knew she was feeling bold because of the drinks, she was excited to share now. "This isn't the first time one of my James's has gone missing."

"*One* of your James's? One?" Heather was picking something out of her teeth and looking at Taylor. "How many do you have, Tay? Or is this a riddle? Because I don't get it."

Taylor laughed nervously. "No, not a riddle." She pushed a cucumber around in her margarita with her straw, not wanting to make eye contact. "I had a boyfriend … in high school …" Taylor started but immediately felt regret about even thinking that this was remotely close to being a good idea.

But just by opening her mouth, she was in too deep now to take it back. This door of information that she'd worked her whole adult life to keep buried was officially opened. She wanted this, though, didn't she?

"Wait," Heather said and put her hands up, "is Taylor *finally* telling something about her past?" She picked up Taylor's margarita and stared into the bottom of the glass. "Is this a margarita or a truth serum?" She looked up then winked.

"I'm pretty sure it's both." Taylor dropped her head on the table, resigned to continuing what she couldn't undo—her full confession.

Bottled inside of her was this huge secret, and for years it had been bubbling at the surface just waiting to get out.

Apparently, thanks to a lot of alcohol, now was the time.

"Out with it." Heather was leaning forward, eyes wide with expectation like she was about to hear the gossip of the century.

She probably was.

Taylor took a breath and looked up at her friend. She could trust Heather with anything, right? But was this a smart idea? Or foolish?

Foolish, Taylor decided. Definitely foolish.

Letting out her breath, Taylor started talking.

She told her all about James Brooks—when and how they'd met and started dating. And then she told her about her graduation night.

Heather's hands were waving in the air. "Wait, wait, wait. Taylor—" She slapped her hands on the table and leaned in closer. "What do you mean he disappeared? Did he drown?"

Taylor shook her head as another margarita came. Her fourth. She took a sip, and then she just said it.

"Heather. He literally disappeared. Like, just vanished." Her fingers danced in the air as if it would make this muddied story any clearer. "Literally into thin air." She rolled her eyes, then mimicked the cop in a whiney voice like when they had questioned her at the station, *"Like a magic trick."*

Heather's eyes narrowed at Taylor, but she didn't notice. The words just kept coming, and the more she drank, the easier the words were to say.

She told Heather about the cops, James's parents, and then Heather's eyes were wide when Taylor told her about St. Peter's Hospital. "You got locked up?"

"Uh-huh!" Taylor raised her glass as if she were proud of that fact. Like it was some esteemed school she'd been accepted into instead of feeling like a lunatic for speaking the truth.

She told her about Callum coming to her house and his time travel theory and then she confessed that finding him was the real reason she'd moved to Myrtle Beach in the first place.

Even though Heather went silent, her eyes growing wider and mouth hanging open, Taylor didn't stop talking. It was somewhere between the alcohol taking control of her mind, through the hiccups, and then her spurts of laughter that she started to wonder how this all sounded to Heather, who was now looking more concerned than amused.

But Taylor, now being four margaritas deep, couldn't take the silence.

"So now ..." *hiccup* "I have a son who's named after my ..." *hiccup* "missing ex-boyfriend." She started to laugh like a hyena, and she leaned on

Heather's shoulder as the room started to spin around her. "And my husband has absolutely no …" *hiccup* "idea!" She started laughing again.

Taylor saw Heather take out her phone and text someone, and then Marty McFree-drinks came over and took hold of Taylor's arm, pulling her out of the booth as Heather pushed her out from the other side.

The bartender put his arms around Taylor's waist to hold her up.

"Ooooooh … your boyfriend's getting *fresh* with me." Taylor threw her head back laughing, but stopped abruptly when it made her feel nauseous. She squeezed her eyes shut, trying to make everything stop moving around her.

A familiar voice stung Taylor's ears. "Your boyfriend?"

Taylor opened her eyes to see Derek. She tried to focus on him while he stood right in front of Heather, who was holding Taylor up.

"Yes, Derek. Now is the perfect time to come up and make nice. Thank you for your *impeccable* timing," Heather snapped, walking right by him, dragging Taylor behind her.

"Did your wife order from the kids' menu tonight?" Taylor grinned at her own sloppy joke, then tried to turn as Marty McFree-drinks and Heather pulled her toward the front entrance, but she couldn't focus on which of the three Derek's to look at. "*Derek* …" was all she could get out before leaning forward to puke all over the hostess stand.

Taylor was relieved that she felt slightly better, but she still wasn't in a place to feel shame over what had just happened. Her body just swayed back and forth as she stared at her enchiladas in regurgitated-acid form.

"Well, shoot," Taylor said, starting to laugh all over again. "That sucks."

Heather brought a napkin to Taylor's face to wipe her chin.

Taylor put her head on Heather's shoulder. "Aw … You're the sweetest best friend."

Then she turned to try to focus on the bartender.

Taylor pointed at Heather. "She's a keeper," Taylor sang like she was a Disney princess. "Hey!" Taylor dug her feet into the ground as she tried to stop them from leading her outside. "I wasn't finished with my margarita!" *Hiccup.* She poked the bartender in the chest.

"Okay, Taylor, let's get you outside." Marty McFree-drinks slung her arm over his shoulder and held her up by her waist, taking her outside with Heather leading the way to her car.

He all but threw her in, not so gracefully, and Taylor felt her seat recline and heard the window get rolled down. Then she saw Derek, the bartender, and Heather in front of the car and briefly thought she heard yelling. But instead of being concerned with what was happening outside of the car, she closed her eyes in a desperate attempt to feel stable and not all floaty and nauseous inside of the car.

When she opened her eyes next, she was in bed. Except, it wasn't her bed.

Her hair was in a bun at the top of her head, and she was wearing an oversized gray T-shirt and no pants. Just her underwear. She rolled over to see a glass of water on the bedside table and she knew instantly that she was in Heather's guest room.

Oh, Heather, I love you.

After chugging the whole glass of water, she flopped back on the pillow, thankful that she could trust Heather with her secret.

She fell back to sleep easily, not knowing the chaos that she was about to wake up to in the morning.

All because of what she'd confessed tonight.

CHAPTER THIRTEEN

Then

April 22, 1996—Orange, California

Taylor couldn't believe that today was the day. After eleven months, or forty-seven weeks, or 329 days, (but who's counting) she was finally going home.

It felt surreal, and she was sincerely sad about saying goodbye to Abby, who came into her room as Taylor was putting her shoes on.

"Ready to go, Tay?" She dropped a white note on the floor on the other side of the bed where Taylor was sitting.

Taylor smiled. She was already bending, putting it in her shoes in the process, so picking up the note wasn't obvious to Dr. Green as he lurked in the doorway—like he often did.

Over the course of the almost eleven months, or forty-seven weeks, or 329 days (but who's counting?) since Taylor had been at St. Peter's Hospital, Abby and Taylor had mastered the art of note-passing, slipping them into pockets, meals, and bedsheets.

The two had become fast friends. Dr. Green didn't treat Abby, or anyone else for that matter, particularly kindly and Taylor had decided early on that she would only speak to Abby. For the first few months, Abby didn't even tell the doctor that Taylor was speaking, as per Taylor's request. When it finally came out, and after the haughty doctor got angry and threatened Abby's career, she'd looked him in the eye, saying that she had recorded every detail in the chart, and he'd had every opportunity to read it. He was, after all, the doctor in charge. Abby had almost lost her job for standing up to him, but "Dr.

Carter" had been able to talk Dr. Green off the ledge. Abby had been taken off Taylor's service, but when Taylor had refused to speak to anyone else, Dr. Green had had no choice but to put Abby back on.

That's when the plan was put into action.

Taylor looked over her shoulder at the doorway to see Dr. Green standing there, looking smug. She felt the note in her shoe like a burning sensation, excited to read it but also afraid to be found out.

Taylor stood up after her laces were tied and smiled at Abby, who handed her a duffle bag with the few belongings Taylor had had on her when she arrived.

"I'm going to miss you." Abby leaned in for a hug.

"You too," Taylor whispered in her ear.

She still never wanted to speak out loud in the doctor's presence out of principle, but she knew that she wouldn't be alone with Abby again, and Abby deserved her voice. She was Taylor's saving grace at the hospital, sneaking her information and newspaper clippings about James, while also helping her try to track down Callum.

Abby couldn't do it at the hospital, as all of the internet activity was tracked, but would go to the library and write down any and all information that Taylor might need on tiny pieces of paper like a spy.

Taylor nodded at Dr. Green, who let her out of her room and followed her and Abby down the hall to the visitors' area where her parents were waiting to take her home.

Surprisingly, she wasn't looking forward to seeing them—she was nervous. They weren't regular visitors and, save for a few awkward phone calls when Taylor started speaking, she hadn't even talked to them.

Taylor still couldn't believe how her life had changed so abruptly over the course of that one fated weekend.

Now, she turned the corner to see her dad sitting on a chair in the tiny visitor's room. Jerry grinned and stood up to take her in his arms. Taylor fell into them and felt her dad's chest stifle a silent sob. Her eyes teared up in response, and neither one was in a rush to let go.

"Mr. Brown," Dr. Green entered the room, not respecting this moment between father and daughter. "There is just some paperwork that you need to sign before we let Taylor go. Standard protocol."

They broke away and Taylor looked around the room.

"Is mom in the car?" Taylor's voice was quiet, and she wasn't sure if she really wanted to ask the question for fear of the answer.

Jerry walked over to the table where the doctor was sitting and sorted through the papers, signing where needed.

Without looking up, he just shook his head. "No, sweetie."

Taylor stared at the back of her dad's head, where his bald spot was quite a bit larger than it had been when she last saw him. Her eyes narrowed, waiting for more information, but none was given.

As she waited for her dad and Dr. Green to go over the discharge papers, Taylor felt like she was a business transaction instead of a patient.

She stared at her shoes. All she wanted was to get that note out and read it, but she couldn't risk it now. Maybe she could take a quick trip to the bathroom while they were going through the paperwork. Taylor stood up, ready to ask, but as she did, so did her dad, and Dr. Green put his hand out to shake Jerry's.

"Thank you again for everything you did for her, Doctor." Jerry's smile was tired but wide, and he turned to look at Taylor, who didn't return his smile. "I can't wait to take her home."

Dr. Green also looked at Taylor now. "I'm just thankful that we could provide the help she needed." He gave a weary smile and narrowed his eyes as he said, "I hear that our nurses were *very* accommodating to your daughter."

Taylor froze. Did he know?

Would Abby get into trouble if he did? Part of her "recovery" was to have no contact with the world outside so she wouldn't be traumatized by events that could potentially cause her to backslide in her mindset. But was it really that bad to know what was happening? It was her life, after all.

Jerry squeezed Taylor's shoulder. "Well, her mom and I are very thankful to all those who helped care for our daughter. I just wish there were a way to thank them for their kindness."

Still looking at Taylor, Dr. Green gave a knowing smile. "Oh, don't worry. We will make sure they get *exactly* what they deserve." He put his hands in his white coat's pockets, rocking back on his heels.

"Oh good!" Jerry took his arm off Taylor's shoulders, and picked up her bag that was sitting on the chair next to her. "Ready to head home, Honey Bear?"

Taylor didn't respond. She was getting angry again but didn't want to show it in case the past year turned out to be for nothing.

Taylor smiled up at her dad and nodded. "Ready."

He put his hand on her back, and they walked out of the room together, toward the front doors. Taylor didn't offer a goodbye to Dr. Green. She was too afraid to even turn around and look at him. His words kept circling in her mind, and she couldn't quite make sense of it all. She wasn't sure if she'd made it all up in her head, or if he'd intentionally left her with that to mull over. She knew in her heart that it was definitely the latter.

Once at the car, Jerry put her bag in the backseat and opened the passenger door for her to get in.

"Why didn't Mom come?" Taylor wanted to know now before they get home so she could mentally prepare herself on the ride home.

She had to move Burger King wrappers and paper bags off her seat before getting in, which was odd to her. Her parents never ate fast food. She sat and swung her legs in the car. Before he shut the door, Jerry's eyes looked pleadingly at hers to understand. But Taylor didn't get it. What was there to understand?

Jerry sighed and turned on the engine in the same car they'd had since Taylor could remember. They bought a second car when Kimberly learned how to drive but, after her accident, refused to replace it. They've had this old Subaru since it was brand new in 1983.

Jerry stayed silent as they left the parking lot of the hospital, and while Taylor should have been elated to be free, she felt a sense of dread overtake her. Something was wrong and she didn't know what.

"Is Mom ..." She didn't know how to finish.

Is she what? Excited to see Taylor or dreading it? Still a loving mother? Still alive? Taylor let the end of the question float in the air, letting her dad do with it what he wanted to.

Jerry flipped the radio to a classical station and gripped the steering wheel with both hands.

"She, uh ..." He cleared his throat and Taylor wondered why he was so nervous. "She wanted to stay home and get your room ready."

He grabbed the Burger King cup in the center cup holder and took a long sip, keeping his eyes on the road as they merged onto the I-5 south.

Why would her mom want to get her room ready? It hadn't been slept in for almost a year. Maybe Nina was washing her sheets, or getting rid of anything that would remind Taylor of James. She'd literally had eleven months to do it, so why was it a big deal today, of all days?

They'd be home in twenty or so minutes. Taylor would find out soon enough.

She and Jerry settled into a comfortable silence listening to music, and Taylor imagined what her life would look like now that she was going home. Maybe she'd reach out to Ashley and try to resume a normal routine again. She'd been given strict orders to not go out to find work, but to do jobs around the house and look for a local college she could attend in the fall, all while still living at home. They'd told her she needed the stability of home in case she had another episode of trauma forcing her into her silent spells. If they only knew that those "silent spells" were by choice, and nothing to do with her state of mind, but she was happy to oblige.

Taylor watched the sign for the I-55 south entrance pass them and she sat up, looking behind her.

"Dad. You just missed the 55."

A grim expression was plastered on Jerry's face, and he didn't make an effort to look at Taylor. They both just sat there in awkward silence until Taylor couldn't take the lack of response or confusion anymore.

"Dad?" She let her voice hang in the air until he barely turned and gave her a sideways glance. "Dad, where are we going?"

She saw his expression turn from grim to fearful.

His voice was just above a whisper. "Home." Then he took another long sip of Coke, placed it back in the cup holder, and grabbed the wheel with both hands again.

"But ... we just passed home."

She watched her dad's jaw muscles tighten. "We moved."

Taylor's head shook involuntarily in response. "We ... what?" Her voice was sharp, and it surprised even her.

"We moved," he repeated, as though Taylor hadn't heard him the first time.

"Okay, but where?" Taylor's body was now fully turned to face her dad, her mouth open in disbelief, waiting for a response that she didn't even let come before she started speaking again, her voice tight with fury. "You and Mom *moved* and didn't tell me this? When did you move? And *why*?" Taylor let her arms fly in the air. She might have gone into the hospital not speaking, but now? The words were endless. "I mean, your only daughter is stuck in a hospital but it's totally fine. She doesn't need to know what's going on with her *own family.*"

She sat back in the seat with force and crossed her arms. She knew she was acting like a child, but this was so unfair.

Jerry stayed silent and Taylor only slightly regretted her outburst.

She spoke more softly now, thinking that a kinder tone might erase what she'd said. "Where did we … uh, you … move to?"

Jerry grabbed his Coke and finished it with a slurp and a slight shake of the ice cubes. He looked in his cup and seemed more concerned with its emptiness than he did with Taylor's question.

"San Diego."

"San Diego?" Taylor spat it out as though she were about to catch him in a lie.

That couldn't be right. *They moved to San Diego?* What about her friends? Her memories? Her life?

Her dad seemed to read her mind. "It got to be too much for your mom and me. She couldn't take the questions about everything that happened, and I was having a hard time talking her off the ledge from the questions. We were getting calls every day, Taylor, and multiple times a day from reporters wanting more on the story, and—"

Her dad looked over his right shoulder as he put the blinker on to get to the next exit off the freeway and then pulled into a gas station like he hadn't just cut the conversation short. Wordlessly, he got out and started pumping gas.

He opened the door a crack and leaned his head in. "Do you need a water or a snack? Are you hungry?"

Taylor shook her head and watched her dad go into the gas station.

She didn't have too much time to fume over the sudden change in her life before she remembered the note. Taylor reached down and took off her shoe, grabbing the note after it fell out onto the car's floor. She didn't know why she was so nervous to read it. It was doubtful that her dad would report back to Dr. Green about this, but the cautious behavior she'd had in the hospital was hard to break.

With shaking fingers, she opened the note and found an address written on it, and the words "University of Charleston" underlined twice. Her heart skipped. This is what they had been searching for. Callum's address, and maybe where he worked? How had Abby gotten it? She memorized his address, which she was used to doing by now. She had to dispose of every note that she got from Abby so there was no evidence. She had Abby's phone number and email engraved in the depths of her mind so she could let her know how she was doing and give her any updates. They had planned to meet up, but now that Taylor was living in San Diego, she thought it unlikely.

Taylor jumped when the car door abruptly opened, and her dad put a Diet Coke and a water in the cupholders between them.

"I got you popcorn. Just in case." He smiled at no one in particular, then held the bag of Smartfood between them until Taylor reluctantly took it from him.

"Thank you." She forced a smile and was grateful that her dad had remembered her favorite snack. She hadn't had it since being in the hospital and felt a rush of sympathy for her father. This wasn't his fault. None of this was. She was unfairly taking out her feelings about a situation, which was out of everyone's control, on him.

Maybe they'd all be okay after all.

She tucked the note into her shirt sleeve and went through the address in her mind again. Callum lived in Forestbrook, wherever that was.

They drove the rest of the way to San Diego in silence. There were too many questions swirling around in her head about the past year and what had happened with her parents. Her dad had opened up a bit about it, and it was obvious that something had drastically changed with her parents, but she didn't want to push. She knew that she didn't feel as safe as she once had, and assumed that he might not, either.

Just over an hour later, Jerry finally pulled off the freeway and almost directly into a residential neighborhood. Taylor wiped her hands on her jeans as she looked out the window, forgetting how much cheese would be layered on her fingers from eating an entire bag of Smartfood.

He stopped in front of a tiny, two-story faded blue house with run-down concrete steps leading to the front door. The house looked old and unloved but could be cute with a new paint job, wooden shutters, and a canopy over the front door. The house should have been the first indication that something wasn't right. Nina always made a house a home quickly, starting with a flowerbed or window boxes.

Taylor didn't realize that her dad had gotten out of the car until he opened her door for her, her bag in hand. This was her home now. She was about to step into her new normal and she wasn't sure what to expect.

Walking slowly and tentatively, she walked up the front steps, then inside—it looked completely different from their old home. She didn't know what to anticipate, though—maybe the same furniture at least. But it was like this house belonged to someone she didn't know.

"Nina?" Jerry called out, coming in behind Taylor.

He put her duffle bag at the bottom of the stairs that were right at the front door.

Taylor heard footsteps above her, and she looked up at the ceiling as if she could see her mom through it. Taylor's heart was pounding because she knew something wasn't right. Taylor had thought her mom would run down the stairs and throw her arms around her, holding on tight and whispering *I missed you* and *I love you* over and over again in her ear.

But that didn't happen.

Instead, Nina's footsteps got to the top of the stairs, then stopped. Finally, her mother slowly made her way down as though she had a fear of falling.

As Nina came into view, Taylor tried to hide how taken aback she was at the sight of her.

Her mother's long, graying hair was now cut into a short, uneven, grayer bob, and there were dark circles under eyes that didn't even look at Taylor—they looked right through her.

"Hi, Mom," Taylor finally managed to get out, trying to steady her voice.

Nina stopped halfway down when she heard Taylor's voice, the corners of her mouth turned down. "Your stuff is in the garage," was her only response.

There was a brief silence, both unsure what to make of that greeting. Then, Nina turned and headed back upstairs.

Taylor stayed frozen, staring at the top of the stairs.

She heard her dad sigh. "I'm sorry, Tay." He put his arm around her shoulders, giving her a tight squeeze. "It's been ..." His voice caught and Taylor looked up to see unfallen tears in his eyes. He sniffed and rubbed his eyes with his free hand. "It's been rough for her."

But it hasn't been rough for me, Dad?

He let go of Taylor and grabbed her duffle bag. "Come on, I'll show you to your room. You can get settled or go through your box in the garage and bring up anything you want to make it feel like home."

To make it feel like home.

And that's just what it was. Taylor felt like she was an intruder now—an unwelcome houseguest who was forced to live with these people against their will. None of this was like the homecoming she'd expected.

She followed her dad up the wooden stairs and into a tiny yellow room. It had a small wooden bed with white-and-yellow flowered sheets and matching curtains.

"The house came furnished," Jerry offered as a way of explanation for the dirty and outdated room.

Taylor nodded, and her dad came over and kissed the top of her head. Her eyes squeezed shut, not realizing how much she needed to feel this love from him.

"I'm so sorry, Tay." His voice was quiet, and then he left without another word, shutting the door behind him.

After staring at the back of the door for a minute, Taylor slowly made her way to the bed. Her mom didn't stay home to get her room ready. This room was anything but ready for her. She looked at the cleanest area of the dusty sheets and sat down, wondering what to do next. She was thirsty but didn't feel like going to the kitchen. She was afraid of running into her mom who looked like she was medicated.. Taylor put her hand to her mouth as she thought of her mom's appearance and her curt greeting—if you could even call it a greeting. What had happened to her?

Wiping her eyes, she decided to risk going down to the garage to look through her things, except Taylor didn't know where the garage was. Once downstairs, she opened a few doors before finally finding it. It wasn't a big house, after all, and she now knew where the bathroom, the closet, and hot water tank were.

The garage was empty save for a few boxes. It didn't seem like her parents had brought a lot of personal items from the old house, if any.

She saw one with her name on it right away and rushed over to open it. It was a disaster inside and she pictured her parents just throwing in random things from her room, not taking care of what they'd put in or how they'd put it in. She knew there was a whole story about how they'd left their old home and why they'd left in such a hurry, but right now she didn't know, and she would try to give her mom grace in the process.

Taylor began sorting through journals, pictures, medals, and her wallet among other things, but she stopped short when she pulled out an unopened letter with her name on it.

It was in James's handwriting.

How had she missed a letter from him? She'd read every letter James had ever written her and pretty much knew them all by heart. But this one looked different somehow.

She opened it with shaking hands.

Tay,

I love you.
I'm safe.
And how sweet it is, to be loved by you.

J

Taylor felt dizzy.

She read this letter over and over again, convincing herself of the one thing she knew she had to do. It was what she *must* do—she couldn't stay in this house. She needed to find out where Forestbrook was, and she needed to find Callum.

Taylor stood up with James's letter in her hand and grabbed her wallet from the box. She knew that by finding Callum, she'd also find James, and time was running out.

CHAPTER FOURTEEN

Now

July 4, 2016—Myrtle Beach, South Carolina

Taylor woke up in a fog.

Bits and pieces of last night's events ran around her head like an unattended toddler hopped up on chocolate. She let out an audible groan.

When she rolled over, the cup of water on the nightstand was full again. She drank it so fast that water spilled from either side of the cup, around her mouth, and down her chin.

Taylor sat up, wiping her chin with her arm, and looked around for her phone. She needed to call Travis and tell him where she was. He must be so worried.

She saw that her clothes were neatly folded on the dusty rose chair in the corner of the guest room, along with her purse and shoes on the ground beside it. She pulled off the covers and not so gracefully swung her legs to the ground. Getting out of bed took more effort than she'd thought it would, and her head pounded in protest.

Taylor stood and found her phone in her purse. Taking it out, she saw five missed calls and seven unread texts. They were all from Travis and the timing ranged from 11:32 last night to only five minutes ago. Taylor sighed and swiped to unlock her phone to call him back. She was so embarrassed. She couldn't remember ever drinking this much.

Ever.

She always wanted to be in control, or else her tongue was loose, and she felt trusting and—oh no.

Did she *really* tell Heather all about James last night?

"Oh, I did."

Taylor groaned and sat back down on the bed, listening to her phone ring. As Travis answered, she put her head on her knees, wondering what exactly to tell her husband—if he already didn't already know.

"I'm almost at Heather's," was his only greeting. And did she detect disapproval in his voice?

"Oh, okay. I'll see you—"

Then he hung up on her. He just … hung up.

"—soon." She breathed out, barely audible.

Sitting on the edge of Heather's guest bed, Taylor stared blankly at her clothes in front of her. It looked like Heather had even washed them for her. She dropped her phone to the floor and hugged the back of her head, remembering the reason why Heather had needed to wash her clothes in the first place. This was not good. And she could never show her face at Blue's again.

Taylor had two incredible people in her life that she'd probably just shattered because she had been stupid enough to tell her secret. The secret she'd vowed she'd *never* share with anyone. The secret that had ruined her life once and now had just blown up all over again.

Why did she feel like telling Heather *everything* yesterday? Did she really tell her everything, though?

Yes, Taylor. Yes, you did.

She groaned out loud again and flopped backward on the bed, grabbing her hair in frustration over her lack of discretion.

Taylor jumped when she heard a knock at her door, then grabbed a pillow to put over her face.

"Morning, Tay," Heather's voice floated in through the inch that was opened. "Are you decent?"

"When have you ever cared about my decency?" Taylor spoke into the pillow, not wanting to look Heather in the eye. She didn't want to see her pity.

She already knew she was pitiful.

"True." Heather walked in and stood on the other side of her bed. "Travis just came over."

"Okay." Taylor took the pillow off her face and sat up. "Tell him I'll be down in five."

Heather shook her head. "No, he's not coming to pick you up. He left already."

Taylor was confused. "Then, why did he—"

"He's leaving to take the boys to his parents' house for a few days," Heather cut Taylor off, walking over to squeeze her shoulder. "He just wanted you to know that he'll be home around four or five tonight." Heather smiled kindly.

Travis's parents lived in Charleston; it was a two-and-a-half-hour drive with no traffic.

"On the Fourth of July? I didn't know about these plans. And why without me ..."

Taylor let her question trail off when she looked up at Heather. Heather's expression said it all. But she was afraid to ask the question she needed the answer to.

"Did you ..." She searched Heather's eyes that were now looking right back at her. "Did you tell him?"

Heather nodded. "Yes, Taylor. I did. I had to." She sat down next to Taylor on the end of the bed. "Do you not remember what happened last night? Anything about it?"

Taylor closed her eyes, trying to remember anything that had happened after being dragged out of Blue's by the bartender, but shook her head. She didn't remember a thing.

"Do you remember what you told me?" Heather looked over at Taylor, who nodded in agony over the memory. "I brought you home last night, to *your* house, and you went right upstairs to try and find the news articles of what happened. You woke Josh up when you went into his room to use his computer to google it. I had to call Travis at his work dinner to let him know that I'd brought you to my house before the boys saw you like that." Heather rubbed Taylor's leg as Taylor threw her head back in emotional agony.

"I did that?" Taylor's mind seemed to give up trying to remember as she pictured Heather divulging to Travis all that was said at Blue's.

"Yes, you did." Heather squeezed her knee before breaking away and heading back to the door. "Are you hungry?" She put her hand on the door-knob, ready to make her exit.

Taylor just shook her head. The thought of food made her nauseous.

"Okay, stay as long as you need. You can shower if you want. I put another pot of coffee on if you want a cup." Heather smiled and added, "I'd try to get home before the Fourth of July celebrations really start, though." Then she headed out the door and down the hall to her kitchen.

Taylor knew she was right. Kids and families would be out in the cul-de-sac soon to start the day's celebrations and she wasn't prepared for the walk of shame in front of her entire neighborhood. She didn't even want them to know she wasn't spending it with her family.

She felt tears coming, and all she wanted to do was go home. She wanted her own shower and her own bed—she wanted privacy and to not be under anyone's scrutiny.

Taylor was mortified by how she'd acted last night. How many people were at Blue's whom she knew? Were they all talking about her now? The thought made her want to disappear.

Taylor pulled on her jeans from last night and then threw her jacket over the gray T-shirt that she'd wore to bed, slipped on her shoes, and grabbed her purse. She smelled the coffee as she walked down the hall, but it wasn't at all appealing to her this morning. She needed to brush her teeth to get the cottony feeling out of her mouth, take Advil for her head, and drink a gallon or two of water to keep the nausea at bay.

Heather held up a mug, eyebrows raised in question.

Taylor shook her head. "No, thank you. I think I just need to head home."

Heather nodded and smiled. "Of course. You let me know if you need anything today. Okay?"

"I will." Taylor smiled back and turned to the front door. "Heather?" Taylor turned her head to look back at her. "I'm really sorry."

Heather's smile disappeared. "For what?"

Her eyes pierced Taylor's. Heather knew that there was a lot to be sorry about. Taylor would have to be more specific.

"I'm just … sorry." *For everything*, she mentally added.

"You've gotten me out of situations much worse," Heather reminded Taylor.

"But you're Heather, and I'm …"

Heather smiled. "You're Taylor. The calm, cool, and collected one who treads lightly in every situation."

Taylor sighed. Heather was right. Taylor never let herself get out of control and it was all out of fear.

"Thank you," Taylor whispered before she walked out the front door.

It was less than a minute later when Taylor reached her front door. She only passed one neighbor who was putting out his bright green plastic pylon of a fake child holding a flag to remind cars to slow down. People drove way too fast on this road, despite the fact that it wasn't even a through-street.

She heard the front door open to the DeLucas' house across the street, and the fear of them seeing her in her present state gave her hives. She turned her doorknob and pushed.

"Ow!" Taylor grunted, realization hitting her like a mac truck. "No!" she whined to the door.

It was locked. She closed her eyes and took in a breath, then frantically fumbled in her purse for her keys before dropping them on the ground.

"Taylor?"

Taylor heard his voice behind her. Her eyes shot open, realizing that she was just standing in front of her locked door looking like a lunatic. *Well, if the shoe fits …*

Taylor turned to see Frank. He was wearing his sunglasses and a fishing hat. She was glad she couldn't see his eyes; they were probably judging her. And he had a right to—she was looking quite questionable at the moment.

"Hi." Taylor gave a weary smile, then narrowed her eyes, wondering why he was here and if he was okay. Maybe she should ask.

Before she could, Frank bent down to pick up her keychain, then extended his hand to give it to her. Taylor just stared at it.

"Umm …" was all she could manage out of her embarrassment.

Frank cleared his throat. "It looks as though you could use some help." His voice was hoarse, as though he hadn't spoken in a while.

"Oh." Taylor was mortified. "Well, thank you." Taylor smiled and nodded at Frank, reaching out and taking her keys from his hand, careful not to touch him, as if he were too frail and would break.

"Your … Jamie …" Franked coughed again and Taylor wished he would stop speaking. It seemed painful for him. "He's quite the boy," he finally finished.

For the first time that morning, Taylor genuinely smiled. "He really is."

Frank stared for a beat too long and Taylor wondered if there was something that she'd missed, or if he was waiting for an offer of some kind.

"Oh, umm …" She held up the key. "Thanks again." She smiled looking down at it. "It's not my finest moment."

"You're just fine." Frank sounded strong and sure.

She looked up at him, trying to hide the shock that she felt upon hearing his voice. His real voice. Not the sick, raspy voice she had only heard until now. A familiarity rang in her head like a sweet song, and she felt dizzy. She must still be drunk.

Frank took a step forward and put his hand on her arm to steady her. "Are you okay?"

His scratchy voice was back, and Taylor thought she'd imagined what she'd heard. Her mind was playing tricks on her, and she needed this day to be over.

And it had only just begun.

"Yes. Thank you again, Frank." She smiled as politely as she could, then turned to unlock her front door, desperately wanting to get inside and away from prying eyes. Knowing that Frank was making no attempt to go home made her move faster than she otherwise would have in her state. But she was too embarrassed to face him again. She'd basically swooned over his voice right in front of him and she didn't want to know what he really thought. She wanted to push the interaction far from her mind. But she couldn't.

Taylor walked in the front door and her breath caught in her chest. There was a box sitting on the kitchen island.

The box.

"How did he find this?" Taylor wondered out loud as she slowly walked toward it, knowing what was inside but afraid all the same.

Her heart sank as she saw old letters, articles, and pictures littered all over the counter.

Taylor put her hands to her mouth. She started to cry, letting herself unleash every emotion she'd held in over the past twenty years. She dropped her purse and sank to her knees, letting out a sob that she didn't know she had in her. She let her mind drift back to the love that she and James had shared that she never really let go of. How would she explain all of this to Travis? It made her question why she had hidden it all from him in the first place.

She thought about everything that she'd told him when they'd first met. Everything about her past, her parents, and her reason for coming to South Carolina. None of it was true. None of it was real, and she was stupid for thinking she could get away with any of it.

She was lying on the kitchen floor, hands over her face, when her phone vibrated next to her. She slowly opened her eyes, blurry and swollen from crying, and squinted to see the screen.

A text from an unknown number.

She pushed herself up and tucked her feet under her. Sitting on her knees, she held her phone in her hand, wiping her eyes with her other.

Hi Taylor. I was at Blue's last night.

I'd like to talk with you. Maybe have coffee?

Hazel

Taylor inhaled and tilted her head back in exasperation. *This day couldn't get any worse.* She felt claustrophobic. Like everyone was coming in to attack her from all sides. Resigned, she got up, poured herself a glass of orange juice, added ice, then headed upstairs to shower.

Once clean and in her comfiest sweats, she crawled into bed. It was the only thing she could think to do. It was now 11:42 in the morning, and she could hear the street in full-blown party mode.

She thought about her boys and how sad they must be to miss the Fourth of July celebration on their street with their friends.

They adored their Lita and Lito and Taylor knew they'd have a great time with them, but the Fourth of July on Adler Lane was definitely something to be desired. Taylor couldn't believe that her own Perez family would not be present this year. But she didn't think about it for too long before Taylor drifted off quickly, letting go of her thoughts when she closed her eyes.

When Taylor opened them again, it was almost dark, and she could hear fireworks going off in the distance. She groggily rolled over, feeling for her phone on her nightstand to look at the time. It was 8:16 p.m.

Taylor stared at the time as though it were playing a trick on her. She didn't understand how she'd just slept the day away. Did she just have an eight-hour sleep in the middle of the day? Her body must have needed it because she felt as though it was only five minutes ago that she'd fallen asleep.

The memory of everything that had happened came flooding back to her and she sank further into her bed. How long would it be until she stopped feeling like this every time she woke up? It made her want to go back to sleep, where the weight of her reality wasn't so heavy. Then Taylor heard the front door shut.

Travis is home.

She sat up and swung her feet out of bed. She knew she needed to face him, and seemed to be feeling better enough to do so. She dreaded the conversation she also knew they'd had to have. Not only was she not ready to have it, but would she ever really be ready to tell her husband about the first love of her life, about the lies she'd told, about the lies she'd *lived out* the entirety of their relationship, their *marriage*?

Dragging herself out of bed, she found her slippers and headed out the bedroom door before fear got the best of her. What she really wanted to do was to hide under her covers like she had when she was a teenager all those years ago. But she wasn't that teenager anymore; she was a grown, married adult who needed to come face-to-face with the truth for once in her life. So, she turned on the hall lights on her way down, as if announcing her entrance into the world as this new, confident person.

The downstairs bathroom door shut as Taylor walked into the kitchen. Her stomach grumbled; she hadn't eaten anything today. She hadn't been hungry earlier, but she sure was now. She grabbed the least brown banana from the counter, the peel already coming off, and took a tentative bite, not knowing how it was going to go down. The first bite proved just how hungry she actually was, and then she hurriedly ate the rest. Still hungry, she opened the fridge and saw the pizza box she'd gotten for the boys last night. *Pizza works.*

It wasn't until she grabbed a plate out of the cupboard that she saw a pair of shoes at the front door that she didn't recognize. Hand still on the plate, she heard the toilet flush. Her heart sped up and she felt like she couldn't move.

Who was in her house if it wasn't Travis?

Putting the plate down on the counter, Taylor walked to the shoes as though a closer look would reveal their owner. But it didn't. She had never seen those shoes in her life.

She looked up and noticed a purse on the kitchen table. Her mind raced as she pictured all the female friends in her life to see if the purse looked at all familiar to her, but it didn't. Taylor heard the bathroom door open and she started backing up. Did she remember to lock the door behind her when she came in today? She'd been so rattled by Frank and seeing the box that she couldn't remember if she did. But what type of intruder would take off their shoes at the door and use the bathroom?

She saw a woman walk around the corner, and upon seeing Taylor, she gave a warm smile.

But Taylor froze like a deer in headlights.

The woman was slender, pretty, had a sleek gray bob, and wore a touch of mascara. She was classy and elegant, wearing slim-fitting black pants and a jean jacket over a floral blouse.

Taylor thought she was seeing a ghost.

The woman's eyes squinted as she smiled, and her mouth was moving, saying something that Taylor couldn't hear through the thudding of her heartbeat in her ears.

Taylor shook her head in disbelief over what she was seeing.

The woman took a step closer to Taylor.

"Hey, Honey Bear. Are you okay?" She looked genuinely concerned for Taylor's well-being.

Honey Bear. Only two people called her that, and one of them was dead.

The woman put her arms out in front of her, beckoning Taylor to come toward her.

"Come here, Tay. Mama missed you."

CHAPTER FIFTEEN

Then

April 27, 1996—Myrtle Beach, South Carolina

Taylor stepped off the air-conditioned bus at the station in Myrtle Beach, and the humidity hit her like an oven. It made her miss the cool breeze off the ocean on the West Coast.

Not knowing what to do next, she headed over to a bench to put her bag down. She didn't want to sit, but rather to stretch her legs out after sitting for the better part of the thirty-eight hours. She was tired, she was hungry, and she was disoriented.

But she was here, and she had an address.

What was she going to do now? Taylor had the past few days to sit and stew on the bus, hoping to figure it all out, but every plan she'd come up with seemed ridiculous.

This whole situation was ridiculous.

Was James really gone? Did she really just spend the better part of a year in a behavioral health center because her parents thought she was crazy and needed fixing? Did she really just leave their house in the middle of the night—without a word—taking money from her dad's wallet to get on a Greyhound bus only 30 minutes after finding out where she needed to go?

Yes, she did.

One thing was certain, she was definitely not the same person she'd been before James disappeared.

Taylor slipped the now-worn piece of paper out of her jeans pocket and stared at the address one more time. She kept it close to her, which seemed silly as she had it memorized now, but looking at it made it real.

She opened her wallet and counted the bills and coins. After paying her bus fare and getting food at the bus terminals they'd stopped at along the way, she had $182.76 left.

She looked up at the people around her getting taxis, walking down the street, and hugging friends and family members who came to pick them up.

Taylor's heart ached as she watched a mother and daughter embrace. Her mom hadn't even touched her when she'd come home. She started to mourn a relationship that was once strong, yet somewhere along the line had turned brittle, eventually crumbling under pressure.

Taylor looked away, refusing to shed another tear over her broken relationships. Not only were she and James supposed to be finishing their first year of college together, but she officially started her adult life surrounded by nurses and other patients. In the moment, Taylor forgot about her milestone birthday that she should be celebrating with her friends and family that she no longer had.

With a renewed sense of determination, she picked up her backpack, heavy with clothes, shoes, and a few keepsakes that she couldn't bear to leave behind, and started walking down Seventh Street. She was here to find answers and would make a new life for herself if she had to. She passed hotels, restaurants, and a car dealership. Then, she heard it before she saw it.

The ocean.

There was a pier at the end of a parking lot, and before she knew what she was doing, she started toward it. It was a magnificent sight and for some reason it made her feel closer to James. She wondered why this wasn't discouraging to her. For the first time since she'd left the hospital, she had a renewed sense of hope.

The last time she'd been at the ocean, James had disappeared and her world had shattered. Now, seeing it was life-giving. Its vastness was like wave after wave of possibilities for her. She dropped her backpack, took off her shoes, rolled up her jeans, and ran across the soft, white sand. She needed to feel it. The ocean was warmer than the Pacific, and as she stared at the horizon, the salty air giving her a rush of energy as a peace washed over her, she knew what to do.

Taylor didn't put her shoes on after she ran out of the water, just grabbed them and her backpack and headed toward the street again.

She hailed a taxi and gave the driver the memorized address. After a four-minute drive during which she put her shoes back on, she was standing at the end of a gravel driveway. As the taxi drove away, leaving her alone, she stared at a white house with dark green shutters that was surrounded by trees. The house was old but beautiful and very well kept—and it looked like there was an apartment over its two-car garage.

Her sandy feet in her shoes started to itch and she was about to reach down to wipe her feet off, until she saw movement in the upstairs window.

She'd been spotted. *I might as well knock.*

Walking up the brick walkway off the driveway, her heart pounded.

Taylor was having doubts about everything. She didn't even know for sure this was Callum's house. What was she going to say? She'd been so confident at the beach, knowing that without a doubt she *had* to come here. There was something she needed to see, someone she had to meet, information she had to get.

It was now or never.

So, she knocked.

Taylor heard movement inside followed by voices. She heard a man's voice, and then a woman's. All of a sudden, it went silent. Should she knock again? Maybe they didn't hear her the first time.

She raised her hand to knock again when the door swung open. A girl with wavy dirty-blonde hair and blue eyes, who looked a few years older than her, stood just past the threshold, staring at her. The girl didn't say hello. She just smiled.

Taylor opened her mouth to say something, but the girl spoke first.

"Hi?" She sounded confused. "Can I help you with something?"

"Uh, ya, I …" Taylor stopped and cleared her throat when she heard how tired she sounded. It was almost four p.m. and her voice sounded like she had just woken up. "I am looking for a man named Callum?" Taylor regretted not sounding more sure of herself.

The girl looked confused at first, but then her face fell into understanding.

"Oh! Are you one of his students?" Her head tilted to one side, waiting for an answer.

"No. I'm not." Taylor shook her head. "But, does he live here?" Her eyes tried to look past the girl and into the house, as if it would provide answers.

The girl shook her head. "No, he doesn't." She turned away from Taylor to call her mom, and in the process opened the door a little wider.

Taylor looked in and saw a living room with navy-blue-and-white plaid couches, a dark wood coffee table and matching hutch in the corner by the fireplace full of old china. On the fireplace, there was a family picture. Taylor squinted to try to see it better, but it was too far away. She knew that they were a family of three, though. Just like Taylor had been.

"Mom?" The girl's voice was sweet. "Can you come to the door? There's a girl here looking for Uncle Cal."

Uncle Cal?

Taylor's heart sped up, knowing she was on the right track. Even if he didn't live here, they could help her. But how far would Taylor go to tell them what was going on? Did they know his theories? Did they have a good relationship, or did they think he was crazy? Taylor wondered if the mom was coming to tell Taylor to stop wasting time looking for him.

A petite woman came into view. The woman was pretty with long blonde hair. Taylor was in awe of how she could make jeans and a T-shirt look so classy. In that moment, she felt painfully aware of how she herself looked, or worse, how she smelled.

"Hi, dear! You're looking for Callum? How do you know him?" The woman's smile lit up and made Taylor feel safe, even though she had no answers.

She decided to go with the truth, or at least a version of the truth.

"He uh, helped me," Taylor started. When the mom and daughter duo looked at her, waiting for more, she continued hesitantly. "It was about a year ago. With a ..." She hesitated, not knowing what to say. The two were looking expectantly at Taylor when it came to her. "He helped me with a project I was working on. I just ...wanted to thank him." Her voice went quieter as she finished, wondering if they would read between the lines, ask more questions, or think she wasn't being truthful.

Her fingers fiddled with one another, not knowing what else to do.

"He was in California a year ago, wasn't he?" the woman chirped. "Is that where you're from?"

Taylor nodded, her head now the only part of her body that was moving out of fear of being caught as the runaway that she was. She realized that she was acting suspiciously, and decided to put a smile on her face, hoping what she was feeling inside wasn't evident on the outside.

"Well, right now I think he's still in California. He's helping write a course for quantum mechanics at UCLA. But he'll be back in July. He teaches at the University of Charleston. It's a couple of hours away, but he's coming to stay with us for my husband's birthday weekend. How long are you in town for? If you're still here, you should come by!"

Taylor wanted to hug this woman. She did want to come, but that was still months away. She had nowhere to stay, and she definitely didn't have enough money to stay in a hotel until then, or even buy a bus ticket back home if she wanted to.

"Thank you," was all she could say in response.

"Well, any friend of Cal's is a friend of ours." The woman smiled warmly. "We'll plan to have dinner around five on July 6, so come any time after four." She smiled, turned on her heels and walked toward the kitchen that Taylor saw was to the right of the living room. "Which reminds me! I should start planning his birthday meal!" She opened drawers, grabbing paper and a pen and started writing.

"I'm Emily, by the way." The girl smiled. "It'll be a nice treat to have someone my age here for dinner."

"I'm Taylor." She smiled back, feeling the warmth of being included. "Nice to meet you."

She wanted to tell Emily how lucky she was to have a loving family. To have a mom who was excited to invite complete strangers to dinner and a nice house that was full of love and joy. Then, Taylor saw a sign on the wall.

"Do everything in love."
1 Corinthians 16:14

Taylor stared at the sign, remembering one just like it in James's parents' house. If Emily's family was Christian, then they were the good kind. Not the kind who did everything in love only when things were going their way.

"Well ..." Emily looked over her shoulder, following Taylor's gaze, then back. "I'll see you soon?"

A little embarrassed at being caught peeking in her house, Taylor smiled bigger than she should have. "Yes!" Her voice was also more emphatic than it should have been, and she now sounded psychotic.

But how did they know she *wasn't* psychotic? What if they knew where she'd just been released from, and the type of the hospital it was, and what she was being accused of back in California? They definitely wouldn't have invited her over. Taylor briefly wondered if she should have given them a different name. What if they tried to look up a Taylor from California on AltaVista? Would they see her picture and know for sure it was the same girl who had randomly knocked on their door? They'd lock their doors once they learned, pretending not to be home. Maybe she should change her appearance. But then she'd show up looking completely different and that might scare them off, too.

"Okay." Emily stared at her. "See you then." She started closing the door, giving a wry smile, probably seeing the confusion on Taylor's face and not at all understanding the inner crisis Taylor had just experienced.

"See you then." Taylor backed away, her foot slipping off the first step, and she stumbled backward.

"Are you okay?" Emily opened the door again, stepping out.

Taylor saw movement in the window again and looked up.

Emily followed her gaze. "That's my dad. Weird he didn't come down." She shrugged and turned back inside. "When you meet him, you'll love him—everyone does!"

"What should I bring?" Taylor realized that, if she would be celebrating her dad's birthday, she shouldn't come empty-handed, although she wasn't sure how much money she'd have left, if any, for a gift by mid-summer.

Emily thought for a moment, and then her eyes lit up. "He loves sweets, so really anything chocolate." She rolled her eyes like there was a story there that she wasn't sharing. "He also plays golf, he reads a ton, and he plays the guitar."

Emily's dad sounded really cool. Taylor's thoughts went back to her own dad whose only hobbies included *Law and Order* and *I Love Lucy*.

"Thanks. That's really helpful." Taylor lifted up a hand to wave goodbye.

"Oh!" Emily looked hurried to add something before shutting the door. "And he pretty much only listens to James Taylor."

Taylor's eyes went wide with shock as her breath caught in her throat.

Oblivious, Emily continued, "Which is funny because your name is Taylor. I'm actually surprised that's not my name." She shrugged and then waved back. "See you soon, Taylor."

And with that, she shut the door.

Except Taylor couldn't move.

She looked back up at the window, which showed no signs of movement. Out of fear of being seen lingering outside their home, Taylor slowly turned away and walked back down the walkway. The taxi had dropped her off, but then left. How would she get back? And back to where, exactly?

With no plan, she started walking down their street, trying to remember the turns the taxi had taken before dropping her off.

As she walked, her mind went back to Emily's mom—she was really kind and Taylor was comfortable around them. They seemed like really great people. And was Callum really an uncle? Or just a good family friend? And was James Taylor just a coincidence? She knew many people her parents' age loved his music. She willed herself not to dwell on it or she'd go crazy.

Her thoughts brought her back to the weight of her current reality. She had no family to help her, no friends to turn to, and next to no money left.

A cop car drove right past her and she became worried—she didn't even know if her parents were trying to look for her. Was her picture circulating? Were they asking people to help find her? Was she now a missing person too? Despite the heat, she put on her hoodie, just in case.

Taylor wasn't sure how long she'd been walking, but she finally came to a plaza with a Food Lion. She went in and bought a few apples, crackers, and some water, then sat on a bench, relishing every bite of her apple. She opened the crackers and ate a few, looking around for the first time at her surroundings. There was a bulletin board on the wall outside the grocery store next to the front doors. Taking her belongings, she walked over to look at it.

There were signs posted for lost pets, summer camps, and outdoor concerts at the local church. Then she saw job postings to the right. She scanned the jobs, mentally noting which ones needed little to no experience or qualifications, when her eyes landed on one in particular.

Sea Dunne's Oceanfront Employment Opportunities
Housekeeper—$4.75/hour

Taylor didn't continue to read. She ripped off the advertisement and folded it before putting it in her backpack. She turned to look for a payphone. There was one on the other side of the doors and she rushed over to call a taxi.

While her life was up in the air, she knew what her immediate next steps should be.

Right now, her only mission was to get a job and stay in South Carolina for as long as it took to get answers. She needed a place to stay, but right now, she needed to get herself to the Sea Dunne's Hotel and do whatever she needed to get that job.

CHAPTER SIXTEEN

Now

July 4, 2016—Myrtle Beach, South Carolina

Taylor stared at her mom in disbelief.

Time stood still as her brain tried to keep up with what her eyes were taking in. Taylor hadn't seen her mom since the night she'd left San Diego in 1996 without a word of goodbye. While she was looking directly at her mom, almost certain that it was her, she felt as if a lifetime had passed but also like no time had passed at all. The woman standing in front of her was confident and happy. Her short, gray bob was perfectly combed. In a floral blouse and jean jacket, she looked put-together and healthy.

The last time they'd spoken was when her dad had passed away of a heart attack six years earlier. Nina had sounded bitter and angry. It had been a horrible conversation that had gotten worse by the second, and Taylor had ended up hanging up on her and then taking a long, hot shower just to cry in peace.

The world seemed like it was caving in on her as realization dawned. Travis didn't even know her mom was still alive. When they'd first met, Taylor had told him she didn't have parents anymore. She couldn't bring herself to tell him the truth, and after so much time had passed, their death had *become* her truth.

And now, the truth smacked her in the face in the form of her mom standing in front of her in her kitchen.

"How did you get in?" It was all Taylor could think to ask.

Nina gave her a sly smile and pointed to the door, not seeming to be offended by the question. "Your front door was unlocked, sweetie. I just let myself in." Then she walked over to the kitchen island where Taylor's box was still opened, with its contents scattered all over the counter. She picked up a picture of Taylor and James.

"Hmm ..." Nina shook her head, looking sad. "Honey Bear, you really should let go of him. This obsession with your past is getting quite out of hand—it's simply not healthy."

Obsession with my past?

Taylor stared at her mom. It was quite the opposite. She'd done everything she could do to *forget* her past.

There was a knock on the door.

"Oh!" Nina put her hands in the air. "She's here!" She floated her way over to the front door to open it to her guest. *Her Guest.*

"Who's here?" Taylor breathed out in a whisper, and Nina, clearly not hearing her daughter's question, opened the front door and shouted, "Darling!" Then she leaned in to kiss someone on each side of their cheek.

Taylor couldn't see who it was from where she was standing, and wondered who was coming over at eight-thirty at night.

"Please, come in!" Nina didn't sound like herself.

Taylor found herself questioning if this was really her mom after all.

"Why, thank you!" came another sing-song voice that made the hairs on Taylor's arms stand up.

It couldn't be.

But it was.

James's mother, Lydia Brooks, stepped over the threshold and into Taylor's house.

"Hello, Taylor," Lydia Brooks spat her name out, then grinned. Her smile only revealed her potentially evil motive.

Taylor backed up as thoughts of the police station all those years ago came flooding into her mind—Lydia pointing a narrow finger with perfectly manicured fingernails while yelling at her, asking her what she'd done to her son. She had watched her turn around to tell the police that she'd never trusted Taylor to begin with and knew something was off about the whole story. Lydia had demanded imprisonment.

Taylor started to shrink inside as both women slowly approached her now. She tried to steady her breath and clutched the counter behind her as she looked from one mom to the next, afraid of what was coming. Why were they here?

"You *know* what we should do, Nina?" Lydia gave her a sideways glance.

"I'm intrigued!" Nina turned to look at Lydia. "What did you have in mind?" She turned back to look at Taylor as if she were a piece of furniture in need of reupholstering, sizing her up and down.

Lydia leaned in, raising her hand to point at Taylor, and Taylor's heart rate sped up, the drumming in her ears becoming so intense that she brought her hands up to cover them, hoping to drown out its deafening sound.

"We should let Taylor know *exactly* what we think of her."

Then, as if on cue, Lydia and Nina both lunged at Taylor, who shot up in bed in a cold sweat. Her body was shaking so hard that she had to grab onto the side of the bed to try to calm herself down.

She breathed hard, looking around the dark room for her phone, it was 8:21, eerily close to her nightmare.

But it had all been so real.

Still shaking, she slowly brought her feet out from under the covers, and down to the floor. Her mind was spinning as she tried to determine fact from fiction. She jumped and stopped breathing at the sound of something downstairs.

No.

It was just a dream. Her mom wasn't really downstairs in her house, right?

Bang!

Taylor froze, listening for anything else that might give away who was in her house. Light illuminated the hallway, streaming under the bedroom door, and she heard footsteps coming up the stairs.

Visions of her mom and Lydia were so fierce in Taylor's mind that she was surprised when Travis opened the bedroom door, stopping in the doorway, choosing not to come in.

His words were quiet and slow. "How are you feeling?"

His face remained kind, but something was different in how he looked at her.

Taylor was instantly taken back to the previous night when she'd laid it all bare for Heather, who had then told Travis all of her secrets.

Once again, Taylor felt alone.

It had started with her parents, and now, it was her husband *and* her best friend. She felt betrayed but knew deep down that she had been the one to betray him. It hurt so much that Taylor leaned back in bed and covered her face with her hand, starting to cry in lieu of words.

Travis didn't come over to comfort her. He didn't even offer any words of encouragement. He just stood there, watching her.

Taylor wiped away her tears. She took a few deep breaths, and then sat back up, pushing herself off the mattress with a bit of trouble. Her muscles ached, as though she had worked out every single part of her body.

Travis still made no move to help her. He looked tired and wary himself.

She considered her husband, a hurt expression on his face, and she wondered what it was like, in this very moment, to be in his shoes.

He just found out that he had a deceitful wife. Knowing that she had lived out this lie and that it had only come out because of a horribly drunken mistake must have been downright devastating for him.

She felt tears stinging her eyes, not from the shame of lying, and not from being caught—she felt genuine sadness about the thought of losing *him*. He'd saved her—in more ways than one, and at a critical time in her life. Except he didn't even know the half of it.

Or maybe he did now.

Would he still have loved her if he'd known the truth from the beginning? Or would he have thought she was crazy just like her parents and everyone back home did? Would he have treated her differently? The same? Would he have even wanted to get to know her after finding out the truth?

All of these questions flooded her mind as the tears now streamed down her face.

Travis, Taylor saw, was crying, too.

Did they both know their marriage was over? Had Taylor broken them both beyond repair, all because she'd lived her life based on the fears and pain from her past?

Travis wiped his eyes, but before shutting the door again, he whispered, "I brought you home Nora's."

And with that, she was left alone in her dark bedroom again.

He brought me Nora's.

Her heart fluttered with hope. It meant he'd thought about her today. Well, she knew that he definitely would have thought about her, but not like this. Not enough to do something *nice* for her, even after the pain she'd caused.

Nora's was a pizzeria by his parents' house with the best pizza Taylor had ever had. Every time they went to visit Hector and Iva Perez, they *had* to stop there—even if it was just to grab the infamous prosciutto and goat cheese pizza to go. Then, she would spend the first part of the car ride home shoving the pizza in her mouth as if it were her last meal, burning her palate in the process. That pizza was worth every bite.

Taylor flipped on her bedside table lamp and found her sweater on the corner chair. She put it on, taking hold of her hair and sliding it out of the back, fastening it into a ponytail with the elastic that lived on her right wrist.

She headed downstairs, not knowing what to expect. Did an apology even make sense right now? If she was really and truly sorry, she would have confessed all of this long ago instead of hiding it her whole adult life and lying about it.

Was she really sorry or just sorry that she'd gotten caught?

Taylor walked down the hall, hearing Travis talking, she assumed on the phone.

"Yeah, I just got home."

Taylor stopped at the top of the stairs, listening and wondering whom he was talking to.

"No, Mami, I haven't told her yet. I'm not sure when ..." Travis spotted Taylor and he turned around, his back to her, head bent down. "Mom, I gotta' go. Love you. Thanks." And with that, he hung up.

Turning around, he had the pizza box in his hands, holding it up a few inches higher as if Taylor couldn't see it before. "Are you hungry?" He had a tired smile on his face.

She nodded, and started walking down the stairs, not making eye contact, but staring at her feet like she was going to trip any moment.

"It's probably not hot anymore, though. Can I heat it up for you?" He opened the pizza box, its smell wafting out, making Taylor instantly at ease with its familiar aroma.

"No, thank you, though." She took a slice from the plate that Travis handed her, and he leaned against the counter opposite Taylor with a plate of his own.

They ate in silence, save for the chewing sounds that usually made Taylor cringe inside. She was too tired or nervous to care now, though.

Was *she* the one who was going to start talking? Would she just open her mouth and start telling him what he already knew and heard from Heather? Or was he going to confront her, demanding it from her?

Other than the fireworks in the distance, it was utterly quiet. Not being able to take the silence anymore, she blurted out the burning questions on her mind. "How much do you know?"

Travis stopped chewing and looked up at her for a beat. He swallowed what was in his mouth and took a breath in. He was nervous. She could tell.

That wasn't a good sign.

"Well …" he started but stopped, his eyes staring at the box laid out before them, blinking rapidly.

Taylor wondered if he was thinking about where he should start. She debated even having this conversation right now. What was once a burning question now turned into a fear of what she would hear. She wanted to run back upstairs, shut herself in their room and sleep for another eight hours.

Travis stood up straight and ran his hands through his hair. "I know what Heather told me last night, and from there I …" He stopped running his hands through his hair and looked at Taylor. "Well, after looking at everything in this box, I Googled you." He let out a breath and put his hands back on the counter. "I wasn't sure what to expect, but nothing much came up until …"

Taylor swallowed her bite and cleared her throat. "Until what?"

Travis shook his head and rubbed his eyes. When he looked up, they glistened with tears. "Until I saw a picture of you at your homecoming."

Taylor's heart fell and she knew exactly what picture he was talking about.

"I clicked on the name of the guy in the picture with you, and …" Travis shrugged. "A lot came up about James Brooks." His voice was soft, almost scared to say his name out loud.

Taylor locked eyes with her husband, and without saying another word, she knew the hurt he felt. She could see it in him. She knew what he'd found when he'd Googled James's name. The picture of her and James at homecoming was the one that had circulated the most. It was still so vivid in her mind—how bright their smiles were and how happy they'd both looked at the start of their senior year. All the possibilities for their lives after they graduated from high school came back to her every time she saw that picture.

"And then," Travis said and walked over to the kitchen island, "I went to get changed and saw this box on the floor of our closet."

Taylor's eyes went to the box. She hadn't questioned why it was here until now. But it was all coming back to her.

When Heather wouldn't let her use Josh's computer, she'd gone into her closet and started climbing the shoe rack to get to the attic. She'd pulled the string and climbed right up despite Heather's protests, and then the box had come hurling down.

She didn't remember what had happened next, but she assumed that it was simply left there because Heather had dragged her back to her own house instead of waking up the boys.

This was turning into a nightmare of a situation and was exactly why she wanted her past and James to be kept *far* from her mind. But now, it was all out in the open and she couldn't ignore it anymore. Travis and Heather knew, and from what it sounded like, her in-laws knew as well. Then she recalled the texts that Hazel had sent, wondering what she'd seen, or what she'd heard.

Taylor groaned and put her head down on the cold countertop. It was all catching up with her. They'd all think that she was insane and that this was going to get out to everyone they knew. Why would Travis ever let her see her boys again after finding out about her past? Maybe fears would creep into his mind that she was still crazy or that she actually *did* have something to do with James's disappearance. Either way, she was screwed.

She felt a hand on her back, and she realized she was having a panic attack. Her breaths were short and fast, and she heard her husband tell her that everything was going to be okay, to just breathe.

But *would* it all be okay? Maybe he didn't know as much as he was letting on. She certainly didn't want to find out. Maybe the hurt from not knowing about James was enough for him to stop going down the rabbit hole of information that Google easily allowed one to do for literally hours on end.

She heard a glass get put down beside her. "Drink some water, Tay."

She lifted her head, took the glass, and started to chug. She didn't realize how thirsty she was until right now. Putting it back on the counter and wiping the corners of her mouth with her sleeve, she looked up at Travis, whose expression hadn't changed.

"Thanks." She smiled slightly, not sure if it was the right thing to do.

He nodded and took her empty glass, placing it in the sink. "You can go back to bed if you want." His back was still to her and he opened the dishwasher, starting to load it. "We'll leave at about nine-thirty tomorrow morning to get the boys."

Taylor nodded, even though Travis couldn't see her. "Okay," she let out softly. Then she remembered what Heather had told her. "Wait, I thought they were going to be there for a few days?"

Travis shut the dishwasher and walked past her without making eye contact. "That was the plan at first, but you know my mom." He finally looked at her and shrugged. "She wants to take care of you." He gave her a smile that quickly disappeared when he looked right past her and at the contents of the box that were still littered all over the kitchen island. "Can you put all of this away before you head upstairs?"

Taylor looked around at the mess, and although she knew exactly what it was, she was seeing it all through Travis's eyes as though it were the first time.

She was staring at the truth.

And now, Travis knew the truth.

"I'm not sure I can handle seeing it all." He vaguely gestured at the whole counter, then his lips pressed tightly together, and he looked away from her and the box, and headed upstairs.

Taylor watched him go, then turned to the island again, looking at all the newspaper clippings, letters from James, pictures of the two of them, and copious notes she'd taken when she had been at the height of her search for him. There had been a period of time when she would stop at absolutely nothing to find James and get him back.

It wasn't until that horrible day when everything, once again, had turned her life upside down.

The day she'd found out that Callum had died, and along with his death, the truth about James's new life that had left her shattered.

It was the day that she had let herself fall in love with Travis.

CHAPTER SEVENTEEN

Then

April 27, 1996—Myrtle Beach, South Carolina

T aylor stood at the front of Sea Dunne's Oceanfront Hotel. It was a simple but clean three-story boxy-looking hotel with green railings on the outside of each room's balcony. She wasn't sure what to do with her backpack, thinking it was pretty obvious everything she owned was with her right now, but she couldn't afford to leave it hidden in the bushes to the right of the entrance, which had been her initial thought.

She decided to own her circumstances, and walked confidently into the lobby, letting the man—or boy she realized as she was getting closer to the front desk—know that she was interested in the housekeeping position and wondered if she could fill out an application.

He looked happy with her request and proceeded to pick up his phone and call a Mrs. Garcia, who came hurriedly out of a back office to meet Taylor.

Mrs. Garcia was a sizable woman with dark hair that was starting to go gray around her temples. She wore a tan button-up dress with a white apron and had white running shoes that were scuffed on all sides. Mrs. Garcia explained that she had recently lost her three housekeepers, who happened to be sisters because they'd moved to Florida with their parents in the middle of the night two weeks ago with no explanation or warning.

Mrs. Garcia seemed more concerned over her lack of help and the fact that she had not had a single day off in those two weeks than she was with the sisters' circumstances. She made it clear to Taylor that she'd only had one resume that had been dropped off for the position, and the applicant didn't even call her back when they'd called her to schedule an interview, so Taylor better be serious about this position before she filled it out.

Little did Mrs. Garcia know, Taylor was *more* than serious. She was ready to start *now* and told her as much. Taylor didn't have too much time to feel sad for the sisters because, to her delight, she was offered the job on the spot. She didn't even hesitate before accepting, even though she couldn't give her a phone number or address.

"Are you able to start tomorrow morning?" Mrs. Garcia had asked Taylor, who was now busy filling out the application just so they had something official on file.

"Yes, I am!" Taylor nodded enthusiastically, not believing her luck.

"Good." Mrs. Garcia gave one firm nod. "Come to my office at seven sharp and we'll clean a few rooms together so you can see what we do. I'd take you through now, but it's well past the time housekeeping can go in and most of our rooms are already full."

"Thank you, Mrs. Garcia," Taylor said to her back as the woman walked away into her office just as fast as she had come out of it.

Taylor smiled at the young man, passing her application back to him. He gave it a once-over, then put it back down on the counter next to the bell, pointing at the missing information.

"We just need a phone number and an address, then we're all set." He smiled, pushed the application back, and passed her the pen, finally taking a call that had been ringing almost the whole time she was standing there.

"Sea Dunne's Oceanfront. This is Justin. How can I help you?"

Taylor listened to his *mm-hmm*s as she stared at the missing information that they expected her to fill in. She looked around the small lobby and saw a stack of pamphlets with local attractions and restaurants. They all had the same area code on them. She decided to use the common area code and make up a number, hoping that there would be no need to call her between now and tomorrow morning. But an address? Only one came to mind. She held her breath and wrote down Emily's address that she had committed to memory. When she was finished, she hesitantly slid the application back to Justin, who didn't look up before grabbing it from her.

"Thanks," he mouthed before rolling his chair back, still holding the phone and answering all of the questions he was being asked, then slipped the application into a file folder on a table behind him next to a large printer.

Taylor looked at the folder, wondering if it was a mistake to use her real name, but she'd put her social security number on it, and it had to match. She wanted to be paid, after all.

Maybe she could request that her paycheck was handed to her instead of having it mailed to her. It also just occurred to her that she had no checking account here. Would they agree to pay her in cash? Taylor doubted it. Her dad had gone with her the first time to open up her account at home, but she hadn't really paid attention. Could she do it on her own? Maybe she'd be lucky enough that her Credit Union would have a sister branch in Myrtle Beach. Her mind swirled with what-ifs until Justin cleared his throat.

"Can I help you with anything else, Miss Brown?"

Taylor was frozen in place and wasn't sure how long she'd been standing there worrying while Justin just watched her. His smile wasn't super friendly, and Taylor took that as her cue to let it go.

She shook her head. "No. Thank you." She gave an awkward wave before turning around when a pamphlet stood out to her. It was for the University of Charleston. Remembering what Emily's mom had said, she grabbed it before giving another small wave, and walking out the front doors.

Once she was in the parking lot, she looked around, not entirely sure what to do next. Regardless, Taylor smiled to herself, not believing that she'd actually just gotten a job. This was her first-ever *real* job. And she'd gotten it all by herself.

Back home, she'd had an occasional job cleaning her parents' friends' houses, or babysitting, but they'd always paid her in cash, sometimes a personal check. But this, her housekeeping job, was entirely different. This wasn't her parents telling her where to go once she got home from school. This job was *hers.*

She thought about the job she was supposed to have last summer. Even though it was technically her first real job, she couldn't count it. She'd never had the chance to start. It was also the only one her parents would let her get because it was close to home, working with a family they knew and trusted so that she didn't have to drive, and she could work in the mornings and be home before it was dark.

She questioned what her parents would think if they could see her right now. Her mind tried to picture their reaction, but she genuinely couldn't. Were they worried about her? Were they trying to find her, or were they upset, even? She still wasn't sure if they were distraught over her absence when she was in the hospital, or if was just the turmoil it had caused in their lives. She shook her head, demanding she stop dwelling on them.

Right now, she was all on her own, and she was doing okay.

That is until her stomach growled. She was reminded that she needed food and a place to stay, but not knowing the area or even where to start looking hindered her motivation. She started walking down the street parallel to the beach, looking for a place to eat. She felt more comfortable spending a bit of money now that she had a job.

She had only walked a block when she saw a diner and she checked her watch. It was almost five and her stomach was telling her that it was definitely dinner time.

Walking up, she saw only three cars in the parking lot. Stepping inside, the bell hanging on the door chimed and the few customers who were inside looked up at her.

"Sit anywhere!" she heard a voice call out to her left.

Taylor looked at a pretty waitress about her age who was cleaning a table. The girl stood up straight, balancing a tray of dirty dishes and napkins on one hand and picking up the bill and the tip with the other. "Anywhere." She smiled and nodded at Taylor, then gave the restaurant a sweep with her eyes as if to reinforce that literally anywhere was open for her to sit.

Taylor turned and saw a booth in the corner by a window. She walked over and put her backpack down on one side of the booth, then walked over to sit on the other. But *everything* she owned was in that bag, so she got back out of the booth, picked up her bag, and brought it back around to her side of the booth, tucking it between her and the window. She wasn't sure who would run into a restaurant, see a bag, grab it, then run out again. Chances were slim—but slim or not, Taylor couldn't afford to take any chances. She turned and unzipped the front pouch of her bag and grabbed her wallet, recounting the leftover bills. She sighed, her heart at ease knowing she would start getting paid in a few weeks, but wondering how much she would have to skimp until her first paycheck—especially if she had to put a down payment on a place to live.

The waitress came over with a glass and a pitcher of water. Putting the cup down and filling it up, she smiled warmly at Taylor. "I'll be right back with a menu."

"Thank you." Taylor smiled back, but the waitress had already turned and was walking to the hostess stand to grab a menu, thanking a family who had finished their meal and was walking out at the same time.

Taylor watched as the family headed out the doors and to their car. She felt a pang in her chest, and the world seemed to crash in on her as she thought about her own life. She, for all intents and purposes, had *no* family. Her parents had pretty much deserted her after she was admitted to St. Peter's Hospital. She had no siblings, aunts, uncles, or cousins whom she knew about. Her parents were both only children. Unless they'd spent their whole lives lying to their only living daughter, there also were no grandparents to speak of.

While she'd once taken this as truth, she now thought of it as extremely odd. They came from somewhere, didn't they? But there was no one to talk about, no one to get together with at Christmas time or have Thanksgiving dinner with. After her sister died, it was *always* just the three of them.

The waitress came back with a menu. "My favorite is the grilled cheese and tomato soup combo." She set it in front of Taylor, opening it up and pointing to the item. "And I add bacon to the grilled cheese, if that's something you're into." Her finger moved to a different section. "The chicken salad sandwich is also a favorite here, but we're known for our fish and chips."

She took out a notepad and her pencil, and Taylor glanced at her nametag. *Anita.*

"Thanks, Anita." She smiled shyly at the waitress, hoping she didn't just cross a personal line, but if she was being honest with herself, she was desperate to know someone here.

Anita stared at her without saying a word and Taylor's fears came flooding in. Did she just make herself recognizable? Was she sizing Taylor up, or would she ask another waitress to take her table? But when Anita sat down opposite her, Taylor felt herself relax a little.

"What's your deal?" Anita asked, resting her chin on her fist with her elbow on the table. It wasn't in a judgmental way, just in a "I want to know your story" way.

It caught Taylor off-guard.

Anita pointed to her backpack. "Do you have a place to put that?"

Taylor looked at her backpack and knew that Anita saw her for what she was right now.

Homeless. She was homeless.

With her face burning red from shame and embarrassment, she lowered her head, not looking up from her bag, tears threating to spill at any given moment. She was tired, she was hungry, and she was scared.

There was a silence from the other side of the table, and then, "Do you need a coffee? Iced tea?"

Taylor looked up. "Could I have an orange juice?"

"You got it." Anita stood up and started walking away, but then turned back. Her face looked like she was mentally weighing something. She opened her mouth and breathed in. "And my name's not Anita. This is my coworker's apron." She looked down at her uniform, which was quite large on her. "That's what happens when you forget to do laundry, I guess." She gave a chuckle and then shrugged. "I'm Heather."

Taylor smiled, feeling seen. "I'm Taylor."

"Nice meeting you, Taylor. I'll be right back with your orange juice." And with that, Heather walked away, leaving Taylor feeling like she had made her first friend.

She spent the rest of Heather's shift in the corner booth by the window, nibbling on the bottomless french fries that Heather kept bringing out even though Taylor knew were not bottomless.

"Ready?" Heather said at the end of her shift and smiled with a twinkle in her eye like she was up to no good.

Since Taylor had been at the diner, Heather had offered her free food and a place to stay. Taylor's mood was the lightest it has been since James had disappeared, and now she grabbed her backpack, actually excited for what was ahead of her.

"Ready!" Taylor echoed and bounded out of the booth.

"Bye, Joe!" Heather waved at the cook, who winked back at her, then Taylor followed her out of the front doors.

"It's not too far from here." Heather pointed up the road that led away from the beach. "But it's still like a twenty-minute walk." She shrugged. "You okay with that?"

Taylor couldn't help but laugh. "Heather! You just offered me a place to stay! I'd walk an hour if I had to!"

"Okay, okay! Just checking!" Heather put her hands up in defense. "Just don't expect much. I've lived on my own since ..." she trailed off, shaking her head. "Oh gosh, has it been two years already?" Her face scrunched up as if she couldn't believe it herself. "I guess so. My parents divorced in the summer of 1992, my dad lives somewhere in Europe and makes no attempt at having a relationship with me, and my mom died about two years ago now, so … yeah."

Taylor didn't know what to do with that information. She felt sorry for Heather, but at the same time also felt a twinge of jealousy.

But why? Why would Taylor be jealous about Heather's estranged dad and dead mom?

"What about you?" Heather broke Taylor out of her thoughts. "Why did you move out here if you didn't know anyone?" She was walking slowly to keep at Taylor's pace.

"Well, I do. Kind of." Taylor's mind raced with what to say and how best to say it. She'd been vague in the booth at the diner, telling Heather she needed a place to stay now that she'd gotten a job, and was here to look for someone—although she wasn't sure how long it would take.

"Right. The person you're trying to find." Heather nodded. "Which is, who? Exactly?"

"He's a professor. At University of Charleston?" Taylor didn't mean to sound like she was asking a question, and gave Heather a sideways glance, not knowing what her response would be.

"And you need to find him, why?" Heather sideways glanced right back, and Taylor felt herself shrink inside. Not because of *how* Heather asked, but because she actually *did* ask. She knew this would happen at some point, and all of a sudden here it was. Was she supposed to tell her the truth, as crazy as it was, and deal with its consequences? She'd surely be out of a place to stay, and then would she even be able to keep her job? Would her reputation go before her and everything she did to get to this point be lost?

Realizing her silence was also incriminating her—for what, she wasn't sure—she just blurted out the first thing that came to her mind.

"He was friends with my dad, and …" Taylor took a deep breath. "I don't really have any parents, either."

"Oh, Taylor, I'm so sorry!" Heather put an arm around her shoulder as they walked, giving it a gentle squeeze. "Since when?"

Knowing that Heather had made a huge assumption, Taylor felt better knowing she didn't outright lie to her. Yes, Heather had assumed it, but Taylor had let her. At what moment did she feel like she really lost them? Was it at the police station? When they admitted her to St. Peter's? Or was it when her dad picked her up just last week and everything about them had changed?

Taylor shook her head. "May. Of last year." She decided to go with a date that would be forever ingrained into her memory that had unequivocally changed the course of her life.

The night James disappeared.

"Well, you have me now." Heather put her head on Taylor's shoulder, and they walked down Oak Street.

Taylor held back the urge to cry, not even realizing how true that was.

She was *here* and she was doing what she'd set out to do. This was the reason she had endured Dr. Green and all of her therapy sessions and treatments. She'd severed ties from her friends and family back home, if she could still call it home. Or did they sever ties with her first?

Right now, it didn't matter. She was so close to finding Callum. She had a job, a place to stay, and now, she also had a friend.

Everything was going to be okay.

CHAPTER EIGHTEEN

Now

July 5, 2016—Charleston, South Carolina

Travis and Taylor were in their Yukon, heading down US-17 south on their way to pick up the boys from his parents' house, the radio playing softly in the background.

The last time she'd been on such an awkward car ride was when her dad had picked her up from St. Peter's Hospital and taken her to their new house in San Diego.

This felt like that, only worse.

She was like that eighteen-year-old girl with an uncertain future. And now that her past had caught up with her, she was in the same uncertain situation. Her heart sped up at the thought.

Taylor had so many questions for Travis but was afraid to ask even a single one right now. For starters, how much of what was in her box did he really see? She assumed that he'd looked through it, but what other information did he know other than what Heather had told him, or what he'd Googled? She wanted to know, but was also too scared to find out. How could she be pulled in so many directions?

Thinking about all she had to lose had her feeling claustrophobic. She couldn't run from it this time. She was married, she had three boys to take care of, and she had a life that she absolutely treasured. She started feeling dizzy, and after a few breaths in through her nose and out through her mouth, she decided to close her eyes and rest her head on the seat, facing the side window.

Travis was usually the one to fill the silences, but now he made no attempt to talk or even turn the radio up, and it paralyzed her. She spent the majority of the two-hour car ride debating if she should be the one to say something, grab his hand, or man the radio, but she was too mentally exhausted to attempt anything. Taylor had finally relinquished the thought that Travis would talk to her, but then she heard his quiet question: "What do you want me to tell my parents?"

Her eyes opened and she turned to look at her husband, taking in the question.

"You mean, you didn't tell them?" She searched his side profile for the answer.

She assumed that when he'd dropped the boys off, they would have known *for sure*. But he just shook his head, silently giving her the answer.

"I just told them you had a rough night after being with Heather and needed a day to recover." He didn't turn his head to look at Taylor, keeping his eyes on the road instead.

Taylor looked back out the window. It was a gloomy day, which was rare for this time of year, but it fit her mood.

"I guess I assumed that you told them." She spoke quietly to the window, more verbalizing her astonishment out loud than responding to him.

Travis was silent for a moment. "I think my mom knows something's up. I guess it's up to you what you want to share with them."

Taylor spent the rest of the car ride contemplating what to say. Would she apologize for pretending to be someone she wasn't? Would she explain herself away again, or would she outright tell them everything like she had with Heather on Saturday night?

Taylor adored Travis's parents. The thought of hurting them or giving them any reason to distrust her made her physically ill. Hector and Iva were kids of Cuban immigrants, and they'd married in Florida in 1972. Hector had started his dental career by going to University of Florida, then gotten his first job working under a dentist in Charleston in 1977. Travis was only two years old when they moved, and he'd spent his entire childhood and young adult life there. At least, until the point he'd seen Taylor for the first time. He always said that, for him, it was love at first sight and he'd wanted to spend every moment he could that summer in Myrtle Beach.

It only took Taylor a devastating loss to learn to trust and give in to Travis.

Taylor could go back to that moment again and again, wishing the outcome to change, willing the past to correct itself so she could be honest with him from the get-go. If he loved her as much as he said he did, her theories wouldn't matter to him, right? What would have happened if, instead of letting everyone assume her parents had died, she was forthright? Maybe if he had known, he would have encouraged her to reconnect with them. Her boys would have had a chance to know her dad before he passed away. But she couldn't go back, and now she was living with the consequences and dragging everyone through the mud in the process.

Thirty minutes later, they pulled into the Pérezes' neighborhood. The massive two-story, six-bedroom white house with navy blue shutters and a long, tree-lined driveway always made Taylor feel as though she belonged to something greater than she was. She felt like it was an honor to be considered part of this family.

It's why she didn't want to mess it up.

But she worried she already had—she didn't know how much but had a sinking feeling that she was about to find out.

Travis pulled up the drive, parking on the left side of the detached garage.

Taylor slowly opened the car door, her nerves dissolving as she heard her youngest son call out to her as he ran down the front porch steps.

"Mommy!" Jamie ran into her arms, almost knocking her down. He was still wet from being in the pool.

Taylor laughed, hugging him tight and not at all caring that his bathing suit was soaking her jeans through.

"I missed you," she whispered into his neck, his wet hair sticking to her forehead.

Jamie pushed away from her, either not hearing or not caring what she said. His eyes were wide with the anticipation of relaying his next story.

"Me and Tito won chicken! Against Jake and Josh!"

"That's amazing, bud!" Taylor lifted her hand, which Jamie immediately high-fived.

It was all she could say in response before Jamie ran away from her and toward the house, yelling behind him, "Lita is making sandwiches for lunch!"

Taylor pushed herself up off the ground, dusting off her knees from the gravel driveway, and followed Travis into the house.

The kitchen was quiet, save for Iva standing at the kitchen island slicing bread. Only her mother-in-law would make sandwiches from a loaf of freshly baked bread. The smell was intoxicating, taking Taylor back to the first time Travis had brought her home to meet them. It had truly been the second-worst weekend of her life but she had been embraced, loved, and cared for through it all, which turned it into the best weekend. Since Taylor had met Hector and Iva, there hadn't been a sour moment between them.

Now, the fear of everything changing turned Taylor's stomach once again, and now the smell of the freshly baked bread now made her want to run to the powder room and vomit. Or maybe it was from the margaritas. She still felt like she hadn't recovered from last night.

Iva looked up once they entered the kitchen and smiled. "Mija!" She put her knife down and walked around the island to wrap her arms around Taylor. "How are you feeling?"

Taylor squeezed her back, breathing in her floral scent, and not wanting to let go. She wanted to tell Iva the truth but didn't know where to start. Instead, a cascade of tears flowed. Iva only held her tighter.

Travis, silently watching the exchange, knocked on the kitchen counter as though that were a code, allowing him to leave. "I'll go see Papi."

If Iva noticed her son was there, she didn't acknowledge him. Instead, she held onto Taylor's shoulders at arm's length to look into her eyes. "Tell me, mija. What's going on?"

Only Iva could be so direct and so loving at the same time.

Taylor hung her head and shook it slightly. Iva had always filled a void in her life where her own mom had abandoned her. That piece of her heart that left her feeling depleted had been filled by her mother-in-law's love for her. Taylor knew that she could trust Iva, but to what extent?

"Taylor?" Iva lifted Taylor's head, putting her finger under her chin, forcing her to look up and into her big brown eyes. "I know a lot more than you think I do."

Iva nodded, and in that nod, Taylor felt seen—as though all of her secrets had already been let out. For some strange reason, Taylor was comforted by that.

She nodded back, asking something she never thought that she'd ask, or never thought she'd *want* to know the answer to.

"What do you know?" Taylor's voice came out as a whisper.

Iva gathered her close again. "Everything."

Taylor froze hearing that one word in her ear.

She was mulling it over when she heard the back door open and Hector's welcoming voice: "Taylor!"

Iva turned around to greet her husband, keeping one arm around Taylor. "She is finally here and looking well, don't you think?"

Taylor knew that she looked like death warmed over but let Hector kindly scrutinize her while he nodded.

"You are *always* a vision, mija." His smile was warm, and he came close to kiss her on her cheek. "You have never looked better. I'm happy to see you, my love." Then he squeezed her shoulder before walking down the hall and into the bathroom.

Taylor remained in place. She certainly *had* looked better, and she may be a vision but not in a good way. Baffled, she didn't know if she should continue to look down the empty hall or turn and gape at her mother-in-law, who had just let out that she already knew the biggest secret of her life. Taylor was the one who was supposed to have secrets, not the other way around.

"Are you hungry?" Iva asked while gathering condiments, not looking up. "I have mayo, mustard, cheese, lettuce, tomatoes, and pickles—bread and butter for Travis, and dill for you."

Iva was making light of the situation, and Taylor didn't know if she should be thankful or annoyed. She felt both emotions at once, but *all* of her emotions were all over the place at the moment and she wasn't sure what was right anymore.

Taylor watched as Iva started to slice the bread as though this were an everyday conversation, and her mind spun with questions. How could Iva know everything? And what *was* everything anyway? Surely, she only *thought* she knew ... right?

The sound of yelling came through the screen door at the back of the kitchen and Taylor glanced out the window. She could see the pool, where Jamie was on Travis's shoulders, trying to push Josh, who was on Jake's. They all looked so happy and brotherly, like they should be.

Hector came out of the bathroom and was now taking a video of them on his phone while walking through the screen door and into the backyard cheering Jamie on, whose face looked as though he was giving everything he had in him to win again.

Taylor found herself smiling. She loved her boys. *All* of them. She didn't know what she'd do without them and certainly didn't want to wish them away.

Is that what Travis thought she was doing? Pining over her high school boyfriend, and wishing that her life was different than it currently was? A wave of guilt settled in at the thought and she started to cry.

Iva took her arm and led her over to the kitchen chair. Taylor slumped in it and let her head fall in her hands. She felt Iva rub her back.

"It's okay, mija ... It really is okay."

Taylor looked up to see her mother-in-law look at her with nothing but love. It only made her cry harder.

"Taylor, love, go upstairs to your room. I have something I want to show you." Iva turned and walked out the back door, putting her hands on either side of her mouth. "Hector! Lunch is ready!"

Hector just waved from the side of the pool, laughing as Jamie came up for air, clearly just having been knocked off first. Josh was pumping his fists in the air before Jake fell backward, submerging Josh with a yelp.

Taylor wiped her eyes, smiling despite her pain, and then headed upstairs.

This house was beyond a doubt the most idyllic and comforting home Taylor had ever seen. She still couldn't believe this was her family. Running her hand up the wood banister as she walked, she turned to the wall, taking each step slowly to gaze at the family pictures that had accumulated over the years. Taylor felt like she was seeing them all through a new lens.

There were Iva and Hector on their wedding day. Iva was in a simple white dress and veil, standing next to a young and handsome man whose big bright smile was the spitting image of Travis's. There was a picture of Travis as a baby at his christening, and a family picture when Travis was six years old, standing in front of the gates at Disney World. Up a few more steps, there was a picture of Taylor and Travis. It was their very first picture together. They were standing on the boardwalk on the Fourth of July with the SkyWheel behind them. They weren't even dating then. They had only just met that day.

Taylor touched that picture, remembering every minute of it. That had been such a confusing day for her because she'd known how Travis felt about her, but it hadn't been until the next week that Taylor had really let herself feel for him. She was brought back to that time in her life when she was so confused with James gone and this new boy in her life. It felt like a betrayal to

James to even contemplate having feelings for anyone else. She remembered that when the depression had set in, Travis, quite literally, had pulled her out of it.

Taylor moved up the stairs, looking at their first family picture with Jacob. Travis was wearing his white button-up that Taylor had loved him in. She was sitting on the front porch of Iva and Hector's home holding a two-week-old Jake. It was difficult not to smile back at the proud and happy faces of the new family of three.

She looked at each picture on the wall that Iva had treasured over the years, framing them and making them part of this house's permanent memory vault. Iva and Hector had made a special life despite their hardships, and always focused on the here and now, concerning themselves with who was in front of them and remembering not to take *any* moment for granted.

Taylor had learned so much from them, and yet she had never really put any of it into practice. If they knew her mom was still alive, would they urge her to reconnect with Nina? Or would they validate her reasons for staying away? Did Iva already know Nina was out there … somewhere? What would Nina even think of her life now?

Taylor smiled at all the pictures she passed on her way up the stairs, eyes darting from one to the next. She had wiped her parents' memory out of her life, but now, seeing the years of history on this wall, Taylor wasn't sure she'd made the right choice. It was too late for her dad, but she could still try with her mom, couldn't she? But did she want to?

Taking the final step, Taylor turned right and down the hall to her room. There were now four guest rooms in the Pérezes' six-bedroom home. There was Iva and Hector's bedroom with its en suite at the back of the house, overlooking their backyard with a sliver of an ocean view. Travis's younger sister, Rachel, had her room still. Although Rachel had just graduated from college and was off working her first job as a nanny in Virginia, her parents had refused to touch her room or let anyone stay in it out of respect for their daughter, hoping that Rachel would one day come back home. It had taken five years of Taylor and Travis's marriage for Iva to even consider changing Travis's childhood bedroom. They had a wonderful relationship with Rachel, but she wasn't the homebody that Travis was. She wanted to spread her wings and see the world, to live her life without being tied down. Taylor had always loved her sister-in-law but sometimes wanted to shake her.

Don't you know how lucky you are to have parents who love you no matter what?

Taylor would have killed for her parents to remain strong for her, for *both* of them be there to greet her with arms wide open after she left the hospital, excited to be reunited with her after the horrendous ordeal, and vow that they would be a family no matter what and tell her that they'd love her forever regardless.

Maybe that's why Iva had always made her feel welcome in this family. She told Taylor that she knew *everything*, and yet she still loved her.

Although Taylor still wasn't sure how Iva came about the knowledge, her mother-in-law still loved her, knowing that Taylor harbored a secret love for her high school sweetheart. She still loved her even though Taylor was keeping secrets from Travis. She still loved Taylor even though she'd been found out and now had to confess what Iva already knew.

Yet Iva still loved her.

Walking into her room, Taylor flopped face first onto her bed. When Iva had been told almost twenty years ago that Taylor had no parents, she'd insisted that this room was now hers. Taylor wondered what Iva thought as she'd made up her room. Did she know then that Taylor was lying? Or did Iva find out later?

A knock interrupted her thoughts and Taylor sat up, embarrassed over feeling like a teenager waiting for her mom to come in and scold her.

Iva poked her head around the door as she slowly opened it.

As she walked in, Taylor saw a photo album tucked under her arm. Iva held it up, giving her a weary smile.

"I have kept these through the years ..." Iva started as she looked down at the worn pages, and some loose page corners sticking out of the sides. "But I wasn't sure when to tell you," Iva shrugged, "or when to show you." She inhaled and stepped closer to the bed, setting the photo album down beside Taylor. "But I think now is the time, mija. And please, take as much time as you need." There was no hint of sadness or condemnation in Iva's smile. It was a smile of pure love.

Iva was so warm and genuine that Taylor instinctively reached her hand out to touch her arm. Iva put her hand over Taylor's, giving it a squeeze before letting go and walking out the door.

Not having the energy to cry anymore, Taylor put her palm on the album and closing her eyes, as if that would tell her all she needed to know about the information this book held between its pages.

Taylor couldn't see all the secrets, pictures, and memories it held right away, but she mentally prepared herself for them regardless. Taking a deep breath, she opened her eyes, staring at the album's cover and slowly opened the book, diving into the past she'd so desperately tried to cover up. Staring at the first page, she wondered how Iva got her hands on this information to begin with.

CHAPTER NINETEEN

Then

July 4, 1996—Myrtle Beach, South Carolina

Taylor looked at the bathing suits and outfits that Heather had laid out on her bed. She was not looking forward to celebrating her first real Fourth of July without James. But she didn't want to tell that to Heather.

Her first Fourth of July without him had been in the horrid hospital and, save for a few nurses wearing their patriotic scrubs and bows, Taylor wouldn't have known what day it was.

She wished she hadn't.

Living with Heather over the past few months had been the best thing for Taylor. She had someone to come home to and make dinner with. She was learning how to live on her own without the trial and error of trying to do it by herself and had someone to come to if she was having a bad day. Heather never needed to know the details of her bad day or why it was so hard. Maybe that would bother some people but to Taylor, she was just a steady comfort in her life. Heather was tough—very little got under her skin and this independent life seemed to suit her. She couldn't imagine Heather living with parents. She felt as though she were a parent enough for herself.

"Wear the red bikini!" Heather called out from the bathroom. "And your ripped jean shorts. That'll look so cute!"

Taylor wasn't in the mood to be cute. She was in the mood to crawl back into bed like she'd wanted to do since she'd opened her eyes this morning and dreamed about her last Independence Day with James.

He had picked her up in his dad's car and they'd driven to Ashley's house for her family's annual BBQ and pool party. James's and Taylor's parents had been content to let them go alone, knowing there would be plenty of adult supervision. Mr. and Mrs. Brooks were going to a BBQ at their church, and Jerry and Nina always spent the Fourth together, sometimes with a few families on their street who invited them over, and that seem to satisfy them. Taylor had never minded this because she had James. She had her forever plus-one; he was her security blanket. She was more confident when she was with him, but also more confident *because* of him. He brought something out in her that she didn't know she had, a happiness she'd never known before. That's not to say she wasn't happy when she wasn't with him, but a certain joy exuded from her very being since the day she'd found out that he liked her, and it was obvious.

It was a joy that couldn't be contained.

But now, a full two years after that party, Taylor had to play the role of a teenage girl with no ambiguous past of mental illness or disappearing boyfriend.

Taylor wasn't sure if she was up for it.

Heather stood in the doorway of Taylor's room and took off the towel that was wrapped around her head, throwing it at Taylor, snapping her out of her memories.

"What's going on with you, Tay? You seem different today ..." Heather let the end of her sentence linger in the air.

Taylor gritted her teeth and picked up the towel off the floor. She looked up at Heather and threw the towel right back at her, deciding to try out the part she'd have to play.

"Are you kidding? I'm so excited!" Taylor faked a laughed. "Now let me get into my little red bikini." She winked at Heather and did a little booty shake before shutting the door.

Then she broke down in tears.

Today was going to be harder than she'd thought.

She crawled back into bed, covering her head with her blankets. Thinking about wearing that bikini and hating the thought, she let her mind drift to the year at the Hanks'.

Her last-ever Fourth of July with James ...

"You look ..." James ran his eyes up and down Taylor's body as she sported her new red-and-white-striped bikini, "amazing," he said breathlessly.

Taylor laughed and danced in front of him, oblivious that almost twenty others were also poolside when she had taken off her sun dress, uncovering the new purchase she had made specifically for that day.

"Ready to swim?" Taylor's eyes twinkled with mischief as she darted away from his outstretched hands and dove into the pool instead.

She came up, surprised to see that James had already jumped in right after her, eager to get his hands on her. He put his hands around her waist and drew her in for a kiss. Taylor forgot for a moment where they were, getting lost with James until she heard a sharp whistle.

"No making out in the pool." Ashley's dad, Mr. Hanks, was standing on the side of the pool wearing his grill master apron, pointing his spatula at them with a grin on his face.

Ashley's dad was the coolest, but in a mature sort of way. He never made Ashley or her friends feel embarrassed for being teenagers, but he kept the boundaries quite clear.

James laughed and took his hands off Taylor's waist, throwing his hands in the air in surrender, while Taylor's face grew hot with embarrassment. "Yes, sir!"

Still laughing, James swam to the side of the pool and held on, looking back at Taylor with his hand out, offering help to the side. Taylor gladly took it, smiling in thanks.

After Mr. Hanks walked away, James leaned in close. "You're the most beautiful girl I've ever seen, ya' know." He kissed her on the cheek before hoisting himself out of the pool.

James grabbed his towel and lay back down on the lounge chairs they had claimed with their bags when they'd first arrived.

Only to you, Taylor thought.

One of the reasons she was so confident in her relationship with James was the fact that Taylor knew she wasn't the prettiest. Ashley, for starters, was way prettier than she was. With her long, golden-blonde hair, perfect cheekbones, and full lips, guys were always after Ashley. Taylor felt that she was always in her shadow and often wondered what James saw in her. But there he was, looking perfect in the sun with his athletic swimmer's body. She knew girls whispered. She saw where their eyes drifted, and knew they flirted with him when she wasn't around. She'd been jealous at first. But James was so real, so genuine, and so honest that it didn't take her long to embrace his love and affection for her and fall in step with it, not looking back, and definitely not overthinking it. She knew that she had nothing to worry about.

She got out of the pool when he caught her looking at him and walked over to grab her towel.

"It's okay to admit it." He smirked at her.

"Admit what?" She put her towel down and sat on her chair, making a point not to make eye contact.

She wasn't sure why she was so embarrassed talking like this with him.

"Oh, come on …" James grabbed her towel and hit her leg with it.

Taylor put her hand to her chest with her mouth open. "James Brooks! Whatever do you mean?" She feigned shock, knowing full well where this conversation was going.

James balled his fists up and started flexing all the muscles in his arms and shoulders. Taylor laughed and threw the towel back at him.

"Gross, James!" Ashley's voice was clear across the other side of the pool and Taylor laughed out loud.

"Taylor, we're starting bocce ball. And guess what?" Ashley jumped in the air with excitement. "We're on the same team!"

The Hanks always had a bocce ball tournament in their backyard, but everyone who wanted to play had to write their name down and put it in the bowl on the table as soon as they walked in. Mrs. Hanks pulled names out of the bowl, making teams of two in random order. Taylor couldn't believe that she and Ashley were *actually* paired, and she squealed back in excitement, jumping up from her chair and clapping wildly.

Taylor now smiled at the memory and wiped away her tears from under her blankets. She sat up and stared at the red bikini Heather had put on her bed to borrow for today and decided to go out and have fun.

She deserved to, didn't she?

She looked out the window and saw families outside on the street, throwing footballs, playing badminton, and kids throwing water balloons at their moms, who laughed before yelling at them to go get their dads instead.

Taylor had always wanted a family, and she thought that family would have been with James. She couldn't imagine meeting anyone else.

A black pickup truck drove into their driveway, but the angle of the house from her bedroom window prevented her from seeing the driver get out.

A knock at the door made her jump.

"Tay? The guys are here. Ready?"

Heather had said they were being picked up by friends and heading to the beach, something they did every Fourth of July. But Taylor had assumed the friends would be girls.

"Okay." Taylor was apprehensive now. "Be out in five!"

She glanced at her reflection in the mirror, wondering if it was obvious that she had been crying. Dabbing a bit of concealer under her eyes, she did a quick swipe of mascara before looking in the mirror and unfairly judging herself. She decided that her hair could use a quick brush after being air-dried, then grabbed her lip gloss and flip-flops, and opened her bedroom door.

She heard voices down the hall, and then Heather looked at her from the kitchen and let out a low whistle.

"Gentlemen, I'd like to introduce you to … my roommate." Heather put her arms out in dramatic fashion and Taylor felt her face flush.

There were two guys sitting on the couch, and when Taylor walked out from the hall and into view, the boy sitting with his back to her stood up to say hi.

He locked eyes with Taylor, and once she realized she was awkwardly staring back, she quickly tore her gaze away from his. He was tall, his dark, shaggy hair swept to one side, and his olive skin contrasting against his white Billabong T-shirt. His eyes were dark and piercing, and she was embarrassed by how immediately attracted to him she was.

"Guys, this is Taylor. Taylor, this is Derek, and that's Travis."

Taylor just gave a little smile and a wave, not trusting herself to say anything that would seem cool right now. Heather bent down to grab her bag that was overflowing with towels, water, snacks, and a book that was about to fall out.

"You actually plan to read?" Derek walked over to Heather and picked up the book, holding it out as if he had never seen one in his life.

"Umm … actually, yeah. I do." Heather snatched the book back, and Derek laughed, putting his hands in the air.

"Okay, okay!" He looked at Taylor. "Did you bring a book, too? Or are you the fun roommate?" He winked at her, and she opened her mouth to respond, although she wasn't exactly sure how to.

Travis hit Derek on the arm. "Come on, man. Let's get going." He turned and smiled at Taylor, who was still working out what to say.

Instead, she gave a sheepish smile back as a thank you.

Taylor grabbed her purse, her hands a little shaky from nerves, and they headed out to the truck. She held her breath when she heard Heather yell "Shotgun!" before climbing into the front passenger seat.

So that's how today was going to go, was it? Taylor hadn't seen this coming, but she wasn't surprised. Heather was full of surprises.

Travis opened the half door to the back seat and pointed inside, looking at Taylor. "After you." And when he smiled at her, she felt like she was going to melt.

She put her head down and pretended not to notice Travis's hand that he held out for her to take, grabbing onto the seat for support instead. She crawled over to sit behind Derek on the driver's side and then stared at Heather's side profile, willing her to turn around so she could show her exactly what she thought of this situation. Instead, Heather just gave googly eyes to Derek, putting her hand on his arm, throwing her head back and laughing at something super unfunny that he had just said.

That was Heather.

Taylor literally wanted to be anywhere else right now.

She looked longingly at their house and wondered if it was too late to back out of today.

Travis got in and shut the door behind him. After he buckled himself in, he turned and looked at Taylor. "So, how long have you been living with Heather?"

She looked down at her hands, clutching her purse as though it were going to be snatched away from her. "Uh ..." She did a mental calculation, but she was so anxious over the situation that the numbers in her head didn't make sense and the right answer wasn't coming to her. "Since the end of April?"

Taylor wasn't sure why she made it sound like she was asking him, as if he'd know. He was asking her. She started scratching her arms, which was definitely *not* a nervous habit, and she couldn't for the life of her figure out why she was so fidgety and uncomfortable right now.

But here she was. Twitching, scratching, acting super weird, and not making eye contact with this super-hot guy. Instead, she was acting super dodgy, like she was a serial killer.

The truth was she *did* have something to hide, and any question made her anxious. She hated lying, but still had a lot to get over and a lot more to find out before she could start sharing the truth.

Derek backed out of the driveway and sped down their street at a pace that was way too fast. With all the kids and families playing on the street, Taylor's eyes grew wide, wondering if she was the only one in the car genuinely fearful that his truck was going to collide with a human. Then her heart felt a twinge of remorse that she was leaving the comfort and safety of her room. It was definitely too late to say anything now. She sighed in resignation, knowing that today was going to be hard.

She snuck a glance at Travis, who was still looking at her, one eyebrow raised. She smiled by tightening her lips and raising the corner of her mouth slightly. Somehow, she was going to have to act normal if she wanted these questions to stop, so she took a deep breath.

"I came out here to visit a friend, and then … I didn't leave." She shrugged, hoping this would satisfy his curiosity.

It seemed to.

Travis nodded. Then he looked out the window.

It was Taylor's turn to look at Travis. He looked older than she was by a few years and had a similar build to James. But where James was blond and fair, Travis was dark and tanned. She looked at Travis's arms, resting on his thighs, hands clasped in front of him.

"Earth to *Taylor!*"

She jumped when she heard her name being yelled at her, and looked at Heather, who was turned all the way around in the front seat, wide eyes staring back at her, then at Travis. Heather gave her a sly smile and a nod in approval.

"Derek was asking you what it was like to live with me, but—"

"Not just *with* you!" Derek rolled down his window and waved at a group of boys walking down the street barefoot, heading away from the beach. They all called out his name, one ran into the middle of the street before being honked at, then ran back to the sidewalk, giving Derek an obscene gesture with a specific finger.

Derek gave it right back, then turned his attention back to the conversation, looking in his rearview mirror at Taylor in the backseat. "Taylor, what's it *really* like living with someone who is so self-absorbed that—Ow!"

Heather hit him on his arm. "Derek! Don't be rude!"

"All I'm saying is that you love staring at yourself in the mirror. I wanted to know if you actually talk to your roommate?"

"You caught me doing that once, Derek. *Once!*"

Derek slowly shook his head back and forth, mouth open. "And once is all I needed to know everything about you."

Heather hit him on the arm again. "Oh, please. Like I haven't caught you doing the same thing." She started flexing her arms, mocking a guy who clearly looked as though he spent most, if not all, of his time at the gym working out.

Taylor found herself laughing in the backseat while Heather and Derek made fun of each other. The happiness she felt in this moment caught her off-guard. She hadn't felt this light in a long time. She felt herself relax a little, and for the first time this summer she was excited about the day ahead. Maybe it wouldn't be all that bad.

Derek pulled into a crowded parking lot, and after he parked quite illegally in a fire lane, they all jumped out. This time, Taylor took Travis up on the offer of his hand, letting him help her out of the backseat. Taylor got down, then grabbed the beach bag and her purse, and she and Travis walked behind Heather, who was getting a piggy-back ride from Derek.

They listened to Heather and Derek flirt with each other right in front of them, Taylor feeling a little like a child next to Travis—small and shy.

"Can I carry that for you?" Travis asked but didn't wait for a response. He just took the beach bag from her.

Taylor didn't protest, though. That bag was getting heavy.

"Thanks." She offered a smile as for penance for how she acted toward him earlier.

They walked down the crowded boardwalk, dodging rollerbladers, strollers, and people who had already had way too much to drink, even though it was only eleven in the morning.

Heather jumped off Derek's back and ran to Taylor, leaning in to whisper in her ear, "I saw you ogling Travis in the back." Heather giggled, then let go of Taylor's hand.

"I wasn't!" Taylor protested, but realized that yes, yes, she had been.

But not for the reasons Heather thought.

"Don't even try to deny it." Heather wasn't whispering now, and Taylor couldn't look at Travis out of fear that he'd heard everything.

How could Taylor tell her that she wasn't really ogling, only judging, and comparing him to James, whom Heather knew nothing about.

"He's hot, Taylor! You should go for him!" Heather swatted her arm and Taylor reached up, grabbing the arm that was hit on impulse. What was with Heather and hitting people today?

Taylor shook her head, then looked up only to make eye contact with Travis. This time, she didn't immediately look away. She let herself stare at him as he stared right back at her, and she wondered if she could let someone else into her life after all ...

She couldn't let that thought fester, though. Until she knew exactly where James was, Travis couldn't be a thought in her mind.

Heather grabbed something out of the beach bag, and before Taylor could protest, Heather held up her digital camera, demanding Taylor and Travis smile because they were right in front of the SkyWheel.

Taylor snuck a fearful glance at him, but he was at her side in an instant, putting an arm around her shoulder. She stood still, secretly relishing this feeling and giving a smile that she thought just might have been genuine.

She could give in to this, just for today. Couldn't she?

Yes, she decided. Yes, she could.

CHAPTER TWENTY

Now

July 5, 2016—Charleston, South Carolina

Taylor's mind spun with the news laid out before her.

News clippings of different disappearances across the United States had been cut out and fixed under the clear plastic of the old photo album. At first, she couldn't make out what all this was until she got to the back of the album where there were clippings about James.

Taylor's heart fluttered at the sight of his face and his bright smile.

Iva truly did know everything.

Taylor's hand went to her mouth, trying to suppress the sobs that uncontrollably came up. She touched the picture of James, then turned the page to the picture of Taylor and James at Homecoming. This was the article that haunted her. The article that hung over her head, making her think that she should have changed her name. It was the article that had driven her mom mad and her father to pull away from her.

Taylor inhaled, and then forced herself to reread the words that had propelled her life into a completely different direction.

May 27, 1995

Star Water Polo Player "Vanished"
By: Mary Tannehill

What was supposed to be a romantic night at the beach for two high school sweethearts took a drastic turn as Taylor Brown, 17, claimed that her boyfriend, James Brooks, 18, vanished before her very eyes. It was Thursday evening at Crystal Cove State Park when the two set out to celebrate the end of their high school career, but the celebration turned into a missing person case in the blink of an eye. Brown didn't alert authorities, instead heading home after the night had ended. Brooks' mother, Lydia Brooks, claimed that she had to call the Brown residence, and then the police station, to get any answers as to why her son never came home. Lydia Brooks said that Brown's bad influence on her son had led to this and demanded that the police look into foul play. An investigation has opened up and the Newport Beach Police Department is urging anyone who knows anything about James Brooks to call the department. In the meantime, the chief of police has given a statement: "James was last seen at Crystal Cove State Beach. He was wearing white-and-blue board shorts. He is 6'3" with blond hair and blue eyes. Any information as to his whereabouts should be reported to the Newport Beach Police Department." James's family is pleading for anyone who knows anything to please come forward with information. Taylor Brown's family has yet to give a statement.

Taylor put the album down. She was mentally and physically exhausted from reliving all of this again. She heard shuffling at the doorway and looked up to see Travis leaning against the doorframe, arms folded. His eyes were soft. How he wasn't looking at her with the anger she deserved, she'd never know.

"I loved you the moment I laid eyes on you, you know." His voice was shaky, coming out like a whisper.

Taylor's eyes welled up again and she didn't look away from him. She simply nodded, blinking, and letting a few tears fall.

Travis walked over and sat on the bed next to her, one strong arm wrapped around her shoulders, rubbing her arm gently. Taylor rested her head on his shoulder.

"How can you still love me after all of this?" She wiped her nose with her sweater's sleeve, and he stopped rubbing her arm at the question.

Taylor stiffened, thinking that maybe he didn't love her anymore and she only assumed that he still did. He'd only told her *when* he'd fallen in love with her, not that he was *still* in love with her. Maybe this was it for them, and even though he was being kind, he was figuring out a way to let her down gently.

"Taylor, I'm hurt. But …" He sighed. "Being hurt doesn't erase how I feel about you." He turned and kissed the top of her head, then pulled away, lifting her face to look at his. "I had my own feelings to sort through. I was confused and angry at first. I felt betrayed by you …" He trailed off, shaking his head. "But it took me less than a day to think about it. It didn't even take a whole day to know for sure."

Taylor looked up at him. He wasn't looking at her anymore, but instead out the door and down the hall, eyes not focused on anything in particular.

"Do you know what I thought last night?" He looked down at Taylor now, one eyebrow raised.

Taylor shook her head.

He smiled and took her face in his hands. "I thought that it was torture spending that day without you. As mad as I was, and as hurt as I felt, I didn't want to spend another moment away from you."

His eyes searched hers until she squeezed them shut, too ashamed to look at him.

"Tay …" His thumbs caressed her cheeks until she opened her eyes again. "I love you—and throughout all of this, I realized that there isn't much you could do to change that. You're stuck with me." He planted a gentle kiss on her forehead. "And even after knowing all of this …" He let go of her face and gestured to the album that was still on her lap, "it gives me an appreciation for how strong you are." He gave a lopsided smile and looked down at his hands that were clasped in front of him. "You're a lot stronger than I am."

Taylor shook her head. "Travis, I *lied* to you." She stood up, now standing over him.

Why she was trying to convince him she wasn't worth his love, she didn't know, but she couldn't stop. Whether out of disbelief in Travis's words or revenge on herself, she kept talking.

"And it wasn't just a little white 'I told you that I liked my eggs scrambled but I actually like them over-easy' kind of lie. We *met* on a lie. We got *married* on a lie. We even lived out our *whole marriage* based on a lie!" Taylor threw her arms in the air out of exasperation and turned away from him. "I am a *liar*, Travis."

"You are *not* a liar!" He stood and walked around her to face her. "I refuse to let you believe that!"

"Travis! You can't just excuse what I did to you. What I did to our boys!" She was no longer crying now, but intent on letting Travis see the real her for once. "You basically don't even know me." Her eyes were wide as she shook her head. "You don't." She raised her shoulders, then let them fall with her arms at her side, like she was giving up. "Did you know that my mom's still alive?"

His head shook slowly from side to side as he took in her words. And then, she said what she was afraid to say. "You might not love the real me after you know everything ... What if you don't even *like* the real me?" She whispered, "What then?"

Travis dropped his arms to his side and looked over at the album sitting on the bed. He walked over and picked it up, flipping to the last page. There was an article there that Taylor hadn't seen before. She walked over, reading the headline over his shoulder.

Teens Mourn Friends' Loss
By: Mary Tannehill

"This," Travis said, pointing to the article. "Mami showed me this before coming upstairs to give it to you. And this proves that I do know who you are, Tay." He sighed, then looked over at Taylor, who was trying to skim the article, confused as to what it was or who it was about. "I already know the real you because you haven't changed."

Taylor took the album from him, now wanting to read this article in its entirety, wondering why she'd never seen it before.

It was dated Tuesday, April 24,1996. She knew why she hadn't seen it before. Taylor had only gotten out of the hospital two days before. She had already left for Myrtle Beach on a bus and had no access to a computer or the internet at that time.

Travis came up behind her, starting to read out loud for her.

Friends of James Brooks and Taylor Brown gathered together on the shores of Crystal Cove State Beach in Newport
Beach last night. They were there to remember the life of
James Brooks, then 18, who disappeared the night of May
25, 1995. Taylor Brown, now 18, was hospitalized due to
trauma over the disappearance of her high school boyfriend.
Upon her release, she fled in the middle of night on April
22, with no trace or clue as to where she was going. Brown's
friend, Ashley Hanks, commented, 'She was my best friend.
I've never met anyone so selfless, kind, and generous. She
made us all laugh and I can't imagine my life without her.'
Hanks finished her statement by talking directly to Brown.
'Taylor, if you read this, please come home. We don't care
what happened. We really miss you. I love you, Tay.' The
teens from Anderson High School finished the night off by
lighting candles and singing James Taylor songs late into the
night, as tribute.

Taylor looked up at her husband. There were tears in his eyes and Travis
wiped them away before they could fall.

He took a step closer to her, his forehead touching hers as he spoke soft
and slow. "Tay ... when you hurt, so does my heart. When you're in pain, I
want to heal you. When you feel lonely, I want to comfort you. When you
laugh, I laugh. And now ... now that you feel vulnerable and exposed?" His
eyes bounce back and forth between hers. "I want to protect you."

Taylor's knees buckled, and she turned and sat on the bed, her head dizzy.
She didn't feel like she deserved any of this. She didn't. She didn't deserve to
be comforted, loved, and protected by him. All she had known in her life was
rejection and shame.

Why wasn't Travis treating her like he was ashamed of her, too?

He got on his knees before her, taking her hands in his.

"Taylor, when I said, 'I do,' I meant it. I meant it when I vowed to love
you through thick and thin. I meant it when I told you that I want to live out
my days with *you* by my side. I meant every single word." He shook his head,
and Taylor saw a fresh trickle of tears run down his face.

She reached to wipe them away, now crying along with him. He cupped her hand on his face and looked up into her eyes. Pleading.

"This doesn't change anything." He shrugged. "But it does mean that I have some catching up to do …" They both let out a nervous chuckle.

Taylor wiped her nose on her sleeve again, then brought her hand back to holding onto his.

"I have truly never known a love like yours." Taylor's voice was soft. She couldn't believe she was uttering those words.

She'd spent her entire adult life secretly pining over a love that was lost. She hadn't given herself *fully* to Travis because a part of her heart really was with someone else.

Taylor knew that Travis loved her. He did such a good job of showing her—every day. Taylor wasn't nearly as good at it, and now, able to look back over the course of their marriage with new eyes, she knew she had a lot of making up to do. She had always held back a little bit of her love out of fear, yet he still loved her.

Travis was a good man.

"Let's have some lunch, then head home?"

Taylor smiled at her husband and nodded. "I'd like that."

He took her hand, and they walked out of the bedroom and down the hall.

Taylor felt like she was floating. Her marriage felt stronger than ever, and she vowed to herself that she would never tell Travis another lie.

Ever again.

CHAPTER TWENTY-ONE

Then

July 11, 1996—Charleston, South Carolina

T aylor sat nervously in the front seat of Travis's car, having taken him up on his offer of a ride to the University of Charleston.

They'd left at five-thirty in the morning to beat traffic, knowing that a storm was rolling in. Hurricane Bertha had already swept through Puerto Rico and the Bahamas, but there had not been a hurricane warning issued for their area yet. Taylor was determined to meet Callum before the storm, and Travis's parents had offered to let her stay at their home for the night if the weather took a turn.

Disappointment had surged through her when she'd shown up to Emily's dark and quiet house on Saturday, a birthday gift of various chocolates for Emily's dad in hand, only for there to be no answer when Taylor had knocked.

Four times.

She'd questioned if she had gotten the time wrong, or the day confused. But she knew she hadn't. She'd had it engraved in her mind and had been able to think of little until then. But the fear that they weren't answering because they'd found out who she was had caused her to back away from the door, knowing that she wouldn't try to reach out to them again. She'd find another way to get to Callum, and Taylor had only agreed to the ride from Travis because she was so determined to find him and get the answers she was after.

Callum was why she'd come to Myrtle Beach, after all. He was finally back from California, and although he never actually responded to her emails, she'd found out this information from his answering machine message when she'd tried to call him at work.

"You've reached Dr. Callum Decker. I'm currently out of the office but will return on July 5. If you must get ahold of me sooner, please send an email. Thank you."

Taylor had listened to this recording over and over, if only just to hear his voice, wondering how it would sound when he told her that he'd be able to tell her how to find James. She had so many questions for him, but now that she was on her way, she didn't know where to start.

All of Taylor's senses were acutely heightened as she sat next to Travis. He had made it clear at the beach on the Fourth of July that he was interested in getting to know her, but she wasn't in a place to be known. She didn't want to let anyone in. How could she? If her own parents didn't believe her, then why would anyone else see her as anything *but* crazy?

"So, who are you going to see, again?" Travis finally spoke after a few minutes of silence.

Taylor had learned a lot about Travis early on in the car. Like, for instance, he was quite uncomfortable with silence and tended to fill the void with questions.

And this was one she didn't want to answer.

Travis was good at asking questions. Which made it easy for Taylor to deflect the ones she didn't want to answer. All she had to do was ask the same question back when she gave a short and vague answer. By doing that, she found out that Travis was living with his parents for the summer and would return to college as a junior at Liberty University in the fall, where he was studying Business Management. His parents were from Cuba and had moved to Florida with their families when they were both teenagers. He had a younger sister who was only three, his dad was a dentist, and he'd lived in the same house in Charleston since he was four.

Travis turned his head slightly to look at her with an eyebrow raised, waiting for an answer.

"Umm ..." Her mind raced and she was mad at herself for not being prepared with a story to tell him. "Just a friend of my parents." She settled on the same thing she'd told Heather in case they somehow cross-checked her answers with each other. She let him think that her parents *had* in fact died, just as Heather had also assumed.

Travis was nodding and Taylor wanted to turn the conversation back on him, but this was a question she couldn't ask him back. He didn't seem to mind, though, switching hands on the steering wheel as she changed the radio station.

Taylor turned to look out the window. She hadn't been south of Myrtle Beach since she'd arrived, and she was stunned by its beauty. It was so green here. California was, too, but it was a different green. It wasn't as lush as it was here. She felt comfortable in it, like she was enveloped by nature, safe and not exposed.

The song changed and her heart skipped as she heard the guitar starting James Taylor's "Fire and Rain." She held her breath as James's face flooded her mind and then tears flooded her eyes. Everything in her wanted to make this stop. She wasn't sure if she could endure hearing him sing—it was too painful. She glanced at the controls and found the knob to turn the station but couldn't move. What would Travis think of her outburst?

Taylor started really listening to the words that she has heard a million times with James—whether singing along while they were lying on the beach, driving in the car, or in the background while she did her homework.

The lyrics rendered her frozen. Her breath became shaky, and she did a quick swipe of her eyes, fearful that tears might escape without her permission.

The longer the song went on, the more anxious she got. She wondered if this was a sign, and then, surprising herself and Travis, Taylor leaned forward with a jolt, her hand finding the volume knob, turning it all the way down.

She sat back in her seat, aware that Travis was looking at her, eyes wide with shock.

"I'm … I'm sorry," she stammered not knowing what else to say.

Travis shook his head, sneaking glances at her and then quickly back to the road. "It's okay." Both of his hands were on the steering wheel, and he seemed like his guard was now up. "Are you …" He cleared his throat, then swallowed. "Are you okay?" He glanced at her sideways again.

Taylor sat rigid, hands on her thighs, and she stared at the road in front of her, trying to keep her breath steady. She couldn't find the strength to speak, so she simply nodded in response.

Deep down, she knew that Travis didn't believe her. That nod was just another lie piled on top of all the other ones she'd been telling.

Travis didn't make any movement, and Taylor shut her eyes, mortified by her random panic attack over a song. She'd had no idea that James Taylor's voice and that melody would provoke her in the way it had. She knew she couldn't escape hearing him forever, but she was determined to try.

From now on, she'd listen to what she could control—cassette tapes and CDs.

"We're about five minutes away." Travis pulled off the freeway, entering residential streets of pastel-colored buildings and flowerbeds. She wished she could spend more time here, to wander the streets to explore the city's beauty, but this wasn't a leisure trip.

Taylor was on a mission.

She was determined to get to the bottom of what had happened to James. For months her head had spun with possibilities.

She imagined running into Callum in the halls, that he would be delighted to see her because there was just *so much* that he needed to tell her. He would apologize for not getting back to her email because he was so busy with work— "But please come into my office so I can tell you *everything*," he'd say.

Taylor smiled at the possibility, and then the butterflies in her stomach got the best of her as Travis pulled into one of the many parking lots at the university. She stared at all the buildings around her, for a moment forgetting why she was there, but her nerves brought her back to reality.

She pulled out a map of the university that she'd got from the front lobby of Sand Dunne's Hotel and found the building she needed. It was in the middle of the campus.

Getting out of the car, she spun a full 360, looking all around her, then back at the map.

"What time do you want me to come back and get you?" It was the first thing Travis had said since the t-minus-five-minutes announcement.

Taylor looked at her watch. It was just past eight a.m. She mentally calculated how much time she thought she'd need.

"Maybe eleven?" She shrugged and looked at him. "Unless it's not convenient—then I can just walk around campus."

"Yeah, that works." He smiled, but it didn't reach his eyes. Instead, they were narrowed right back at Taylor's.

"But what?" Taylor knew something else was on his mind, and she just wanted him to say it.

Was this a bad idea? Did he know something she didn't? What was he not telling her? Insecurities rose in her as she watched him look at his feet.

His eyes came back and locked on hers, his dark eyes soft and imploring. "Are you sure you don't just want me to stay?"

Taylor felt something just then. A feeling of sadness that those eyes weren't James's eyes, as well as overwhelming gratitude for Travis and the fact that he was in her life. He had a protective nature over her that she couldn't understand.

But she welcomed it.

She did, in fact, want him to stay. But that would mean letting him in on why she'd really come here. She couldn't risk being looked at by him the same way all the others looked at her back in California.

Like she was crazy.

She wanted his eyes to always be this kind toward her, to see her in this very light, the way that he was looking at her in this moment.

Making her decision, she shook her head. "No, but thank you."

She smiled sadly, wishing she could make a different choice, but deep down knowing she couldn't.

Travis looked down again and shook his keys. "Okay." He nodded, then opened his car door. "I'll be right here. At eleven." He looked up and gave her a tight-lipped smile.

She smiled back. "Thank you, Travis. I really do appreciate this."

She had a strong urge to walk over and hug him, but she wasn't there yet.

He nodded, and without a word, got into his car. Taylor watched as he started the car, then backed up. He gave a little wave before driving away, and Taylor stared at his car until it disappeared out of the parking lot and behind campus buildings.

She let out a breath she didn't know she was holding, and turned to look up at the building that Callum was in.

Her feet, like lead, wouldn't move.

Taylor, you are not fearful, she gave herself a mental pep talk. *This is why you came here. Move! Find Callum. Find James!*

She found herself finally putting one foot in front of the other, and the next thing she knew, she was at the front doors. She pulled them open, entering a large lobby. There were only a few students walking around, one sitting on a bench with headphones on, nodding to whatever beat his Discman was playing, and another rushing to the staircase, clearly in a hurry.

She looked around, trying to find a directory of some sort telling her where to go, like in a medical office building. She wasn't even sure if that was a thing in college. She found herself taking short breaths, worry overtaking her, thinking that she had gotten herself in too deep. What if finding Callum was like finding a needle in a haystack?

Suddenly she wanted Travis to come back.

Then a quiet voice came from behind her: "Taylor?"

Hearing her name, Taylor turned, finding herself face-to-face with Emily. She hadn't seen her since being at her house months earlier, and she was stunned into silence.

Emily's eyes were red, her blonde hair pulled into a messy bun at the top of her head in a scrunchy, and she was holding an empty box.

Emily seemed to find her voice first, as Taylor couldn't summon any words to say by way of explanation. "What are you doing here?" Her voice grew louder and sounded hurt. "Are you here to pick up your letter?"

Taylor had no idea what she was talking about. She opened her mouth to say something, ready to confess this fact, when she heard a man's voice from above them.

"Em, is everything—" Then, as if on cue, Emily and Taylor looked up at the same time to see a man drop a box, full of papers that were now flying all over the place, some sliding down the stairs. The sound of the fallen box echoed loudly throughout the nearly empty lobby.

Taylor wasn't sure where to look—at the mess that was still cascading down the stairs, or at the man, who she assumed was Emily's dad, who had turned to run down the hall.

Taylor instinctively started after him for no other reason than something nagging at her heart, telling her she needed to talk to him. She bounded up the stairs, ignoring the mess she was passing, willing her feet to catch up with him.

"Taylor!" she heard Emily call up the stairs, but she ignored her.

Her only mission was to see Emily's dad. To look at his face.

It couldn't be him. Could it?

Breathing heavily and slowing her run, she walked down the hall she thought he'd turned down, trying to listen for movement. She peeked in classrooms and offices as she passed, steadying her breath as though it would help her hear him—wherever he had gone.

Was it in her mind that she'd seen those eyes and known them? But how was it possible that they were on an older man? Callum's words came back to her, and she felt in her heart that it really was him. She'd found James.

She finally reached the end of the hall. There was one more office, but the door wasn't labeled.

There was a window at the end of the hall that overlooked the parking lot where Travis had dropped her off. She looked down at the spot where she'd stood with him just minutes before and found herself hoping to see Travis's car. But it wasn't there.

Taylor had, after all, told him she didn't need him. Why would he come back after that? She wondered what he was doing at this moment, if he had any idea what she was doing or if he even cared. What would he think of her if he were to find out the truth? She didn't want to know.

Hearing a noise to her left, she looked up as Emily came into view. She was no longer holding the box, and her eyes were less red now but more inquisitive as she narrowed them at Taylor.

"What just happened?" Emily's eyes drove into Taylor's.

Taylor shrank back at her stare and stammered, "I ... uh ..." She swallowed but there was nothing to swallow. Her mouth was dry, feeling like this was an interrogation, not a friend genuinely asking. "I thought I saw ... someone." Taylor's eyes darted back and forth between Emily's eyes, and she felt unwelcome here.

"Like ... my dad?" Emily didn't break her gaze as she backed up into the doorway of the office that was missing a name plate.

Taylor looked at Emily, at the space where the name plate should have been on the door, and then at the back of Emily's head, who had finally turned away to walk into that office.

Taylor looked just past her, and inside. It was full of boxes, empty bookshelves, and frames that were stacked together leaning against the wall. Emily picked up an empty box and put it on the desk, starting to fill it with papers and books that were sitting on a chair to the right of the desk.

Taylor stepped inside, and Emily didn't break away from what she was doing. If she cared that Taylor was there, she didn't show it.

"Is this Callum's office?" Taylor looked at a degree from the University of Southern California leaning against the wall. It had Callum's name on it.

Taylor sighed and closed her eyes, feeling small, like she'd just asked the dumbest question ever. *Of course* it was his office. Emily didn't respond. Instead, she continued piling up the papers, then moving them to one side of the box to put a few books upright on the other side.

Taylor wasn't sure what was going on. She was fearful to ask another dumb question, then remembered what Emily had asked her in the lobby downstairs.

There was a letter for her.

Taylor took a step closer to Emily's back. "What letter were you talking about?"

Emily stopped what she was doing, then turned to look at the desk. Watching her side profile, Taylor could see that Emily's expression had changed from a frown to genuine confusion, then continued to search the desk.

"It was just here." Emily looked confused, then turned around, looking on the ground.

Taylor did the same, assuming she was looking for an envelope, but not entirely sure that was the case.

Emily walked over to a closet and bent down to pick up a folded piece of paper. She opened it, reading the top, then turned it over, seeming to read the last part. She looked up, her eyes full of sorrow and wonder. "Here." She slowly folded it back up and held it out for Taylor to take.

Stepping closer to Emily, Taylor took the paper. "Thank you," she said in a whisper.

"Don't read it here." Emily's voice was stern, and her face matched her voice. "Please."

Taylor was confused over this Emily versus the sweet Emily who had answered the door back in April. Not knowing the reason, she just nodded in response, taking the folded letter and putting it in her pocket.

They both stood there for a second in awkward silence and Taylor grew anxious, feeling like she was imposing. But she was here to find Callum and she didn't want to back down just because of an awkward encounter with Emily.

She steeled herself to ask when she heard footsteps coming down the hall. "Emily? Are you up here?"

Taylor turned her head to the sound of the voice and then let out a gasp when she saw who walked in.

"Taylor!" Abby couldn't hide her shock and excitement as she rushed over and took Taylor in her arms, hugging her tightly. "I can't believe you're here!" she said in Taylor's ear, then let her go to look at her. "You look good!" She smiled brightly, but she had been crying, too. "How are you? What are you doing here?"

Taylor blinked. She couldn't believe her eyes. Abby was right in front of her. The Abby who had helped her get through those long months at the hospital, who had endured Dr. Green, and had slipped her information to help find Callum.

Taylor laughed as tears streamed down her face, now. It was so refreshing to see someone who knew her—who *really* knew her and not only didn't judge her, but who had come alongside her to *help* her.

"Me? What are *you* doing here?" Taylor couldn't help but ask back.

Emily stood there, staring at them in turn, mouth open in apparent shock.

"I'm here to help Emily and her dad sort through Callum's things." Abby took her hands off Taylor's arms, her voice now somber, and crossed them in front of her chest. "I'm going to take some of it back to California with me."

Taylor narrowed her eyes at her. "Why do you need to sort through his things?"

There was a silence in the room and Taylor knew what was coming before it was even said. She shook her head, as if that would change the outcome, but seeing the look that passed between the two girls, and then the look that Abby gave her confirmed what she had not yet been told.

"Taylor …" Abby stepped forward, putting her hand on Taylor's shoulder. "Callum passed away."

Taylor's vision narrowed and she felt unsteady on her feet.

Abby's voice seemed far away even though she was right in front of Taylor. "He had a heart attack five days ago …"

This couldn't be happening. Five days. Wasn't five days ago Saturday? The Saturday of Emily's dad's birthday dinner. Is that why there was no one was home?

She was so close. This wasn't real. She put her hands on either side of her head as the room started to spin. She breathed hard but couldn't get enough air in her lungs.

"No," she breathed out. Then, everything went black.

CHAPTER TWENTY-TWO

Now

August 15, 2016—Myrtle Beach, South Carolina

The boys' basketball league was over and they were, of course, outside playing basketball. Taylor was inside, going through the boys' school supplies and checking them off her list. She couldn't believe they were starting school again in just three weeks.

She heard her phone chime and looked at the screen. It was Heather asking about the time, place, and headcount for the back-to-school brunch. It was a tradition that all the moms on Adler Lane had every year: they dropped their kids off on the first day of school, then headed off to have brunch, with mimosas, in celebration.

Taylor loved this tradition, and she was happy to be in a good place and able to help plan. She shook her head slowly, thinking over this past summer and all that had happened, including the colossal mess she'd made of everything, almost ruining her marriage and her friendship with her best friend. She was thankful to have such supportive people in her life.

"Mom!" Jamie bounded down the stairs, Josh not too far behind him. "Hazel invited us over to meet Andrew!"

Taylor's eyebrows raised in curiosity. She thought back to the picture that Heather had shown her at the basketball game, which seemed like a lifetime ago now. The boy in the picture, at the time, had looked like the spitting image of James. But that was impossible. Taylor had gotten so caught up in her past and her fears about being found out that imagined she saw his face everywhere, including in her dreams. Those dreams had stopped once everything was out in the open, and she was still amazed by the grace and understanding that had been given to her by Travis and Heather. Although she didn't dive into why Iva knew everything, or even how she knew, Taylor understood that there was time to get answers.

And for Taylor, that meant little by little, as her heart was just now truly beginning to heal.

Her two youngest boys were standing next to her at the kitchen table, picking up pencils and notebooks, binders and folders, examining them until Taylor swatted at their hands to put the stationery down.

"Boys, stop! I have them in piles, and I need to keep them there to know what belongs to whom."

Josh saluted her and put down a pack of dividers. "Yes, ma'am!"

Jamie laughed and mimicked Josh with his own salute. "But seriously, can we go over now?" He looked at Taylor expectantly.

She nodded. "Yes."

They both turned on their heels and started running to the front door.

"Wait, wait, wait!" Taylor got up, walking awkwardly to the kitchen counter. Her legs were stiff from sitting cross-legged for way too long, poring over the checklists. She picked up a basket of muffins and handed them to Josh. "These are for Hazel and Frank. Please thank her for having you two over, and please …" she pointed to Josh, then at Jamie, "mind your manners." She narrowed her eyes at each of them. "Got it?"

Jamie waved his hand at her. "Mom, when have you ever known me not to mind my manners?"

Taylor laughed because she knew it was true. She didn't have to worry about either one of them; she just thought it was something she should say as a mom.

"You're right." She smiled at them. "Have fun."

Turning back to the door with a chorus of *thank you*s and *we will*s, the two boys ran out the door, slamming it behind them. Taylor watched them run across the road and huffed over the fact that Jamie didn't look either way before he crossed the street. She made a mental note to talk to him about it when he got home. It was such a bad habit, and she hated it.

They knocked on the DeLucas' door, and as Taylor saw it open, Hazel looked over the boys' heads in her direction at the kitchen window and gave a wave. Not knowing if Hazel could actually see her, Taylor smiled and waved back. The last thing she saw was Jamie hand Hazel the basket full of muffins as his mouth moved a mile a minute. Taylor could only imagine what story he was telling her.

She laughed to herself, wondering what Hazel would think of them, and then sat back down, determined to finish organizing the piles of back-to-school supplies.

She was lost in her world of checklists when she felt a hand on her shoulder. "I'm almost done, love," she said, assuming it was Travis. "Want to grab lunch after?"

She jumped when she heard her oldest son's voice: "Mom, can we talk?"

She looked up at him, surprised for a few reasons. She didn't realize how much he looked like Travis until he'd gotten older—he was positively the spitting image of his father, with his dark hair and eyes, looking more and more like the boy she'd met all those years ago. It also surprised her that Jake was willingly coming to her, actually wanting to talk about something. From the look on his face, it was something important.

She nodded and pulled out a chair, patting the seat as he came around her and sat down. He put his elbows on his knees and clutched his hands together.

Taylor could see his nerves and she wanted desperately to know what was going on but knew to give him space. She felt torn between prying and being patient.

She stared at the top of his head as he looked down, avoiding eye contact as he started to speak. "I overheard Lita and Dad talking ... a while ago." He looked up, briefly making eye contact before looking away again and leaning back in the chair. "When Dad dropped us off a few weeks ago."

"Okay ..." Taylor started and could only imagine what would have been said that he'd overheard. Her heart raced as she questioned herself about what to tell him. She'd promised to never lie to Travis, but she hadn't thought about her kids. She assumed that they would learn what happened *one* day, but she wasn't ready for today to be that day. "What did you hear?"

His eyes darted around the room before they settled back on his fingers that were still clasped together.

"I heard that you lost someone ... You know ..." His eyes met hers. "Before you met Dad."

Taylor stared back into her son's eyes that were searching her own for answers. She could handle that, if that's as far as it went. She breathed out a sigh and leaned forward. Putting her hands on his, she rubbed the top of his hand with her thumbs and bent a little lower to look up at her son, whose head was bowed.

"I did," she agreed, deciding that she would be honest with her sons, too.

Who knew she would be talking to her son about James? But here they were.

"Over a year before I met your dad ..." Taylor trailed off, not wanting to get into the details of exactly what had happened and hoping that he wasn't coming to her to ask about them either.

"So, how did you get over it? I mean ..." Jake sat up straighter in his chair, running his hands through his dark hair. "How did you move on?"

"Are you asking how I could move on and fall in love with someone else?" Taylor let go of his hand and sat up in her chair to match his posture.

Jake nodded and Taylor's heart lightened. For once, she felt like she could talk about her feelings through the loss, instead of feeling interrogated about the details of it. She closed her eyes and smiled.

This was what moving on looked like.

"Your dad made it easy for me to love him." She smiled at the memory of that summer in 1996. "But I can tell you right now, I didn't make it easy on him."

"You didn't?" Josh looked confused but smiled, clearly wanting to know more. "But Dad said it was love at first sight."

Taylor nodded. "It was for him. But for me ..." She shrugged and glanced at Jake, who was taking in everything she said, seemingly not breathing for fear of missing something. "For me, I was still healing. Your dad gave me space to heal, while at the same time making it clear he wasn't going anywhere."

She wondered why he was asking and decided to turn it around. A risky move, but if she'd learned anything from this, it was to be honest about situations. Taylor wanted to know her son and his truth.

"Jake, does this have anything to do with Tiffany?" she asked with an eyebrow raised as she studied her son's very uncomfortable reaction to this question. He'd been fine when they were talking about her, but now that the heat was on him, he was squirming in his seat.

Instead of being mad or frustrated though, he bit his bottom lip, as though admitting the truth, before finally nodding.

Taylor's heart filled with love for her son. This was a breakthrough moment for them, but she had to conceal her emotions or Jake might not come to her again. So, instead of smiling her face off and hugging him senseless like she wanted to, she remained calm and followed it up with another obvious question.

"And is that why you seemed so angry all summer?" She finished her question more softly than she'd started, knowing this was a sore spot for him.

Jake nodded again, not looking up.

Taylor's eyes filled with tears, and for once she let them fall, not caring if her son saw her cry. In fact, she thought he needed to see her cry. She had been hiding her feelings and emotions for too long out of fear of really being seen and it had gotten her in a world of trouble. She wanted to set an example for her boys, to teach them that honesty and vulnerability were attributes worth showing. And when done in a safe space, like with family, it was life-giving and made everyone stronger.

She wiped her eyes as Jake looked up at her, registering what was happening.

"Mom, are you okay? I didn't mean to …" His eyes were full of sadness, as though he'd done something wrong.

Taylor waved her hand as if to shoo away those thoughts mid-air. "No, no, Jake. You did nothing wrong." She reached over, squeezing his arm to reassure him. "My heart doesn't hurt for him anymore, but it still remembers the hurt. And now …" She shook her head, closing her eyes. "Watching *you* hurt just stirs all that up again." She opened her eyes and smiled. "I don't like seeing you hurt, bud."

Jake breathed out, watching his mom go through different emotions, and processing it all. "I guess I just don't know how to move past it, though." He rubbed his cheek where a little stubble was starting to show. Taylor wasn't sure how she'd blinked and all of a sudden, her little boy was almost man, with grownup feelings and an almost-beard. "I like her, Mom. Like, a *lot*." He shrugged. "And I thought she did, too, but … she likes someone else."

Taylor's heart sank for him. How hard must it be to watch your crush start falling for someone else, someone new. And right in front of you.

"Oh, Jake." She couldn't take it anymore.

She stood up and walked around his chair, putting her arms around her son, letting his shoulders rise and fall as he started to cry. "It's okay to hurt, bud. It's okay to cry." She rubbed his arms but didn't let go, and Jake made no move to get away from her grasp. Instead, he found her hands with his and held on for dear life.

She let him hold onto her as long as he needed, although her back was getting sore from leaning forward, and she straightened her legs in an attempt to stretch. Jake must have known because he let go, turning around in his chair to face her.

"Thank you." He wiped his eyes, then stood up just as the front door flew open.

Jamie came running in. "Mom! I need—" He stopped short when he saw his brother. "Jake, what's wrong?"

"Nothing." Jake turned away from him and walked over to the fridge, opening it in an attempt to hide his face.

Jamie wasn't letting it go. "But it looks like you're crying."

Jake spun around, slamming the fridge door, making Taylor wince.

"I'm not crying, dummy," he barked at him, then stormed past Taylor and Jamie, up the stairs.

Taylor frowned after him. The moment they'd shared had vanished in the blink of an eye and he was back to his normal, hormonal, teenage self. She turned back to Jamie, still perturbed by Jake's sudden change of heart, and sad that Jamie had to be at the receiving end of his foul mood.

She knelt down to be on his level. "What do you need, love?"

Jamie, still looking at the top of the stairs after Jake, finally broke his gaze, and a look of confusion crossed his face. "I don't remember." He spoke softly, eyes now staring blankly but not seeing anything.

Taylor knew her son was racking his brain to try to remember, and remember he would. He had an excellent memory; he was just a little bit distracted by his brother's outburst.

She stood up, making her way over to the school supplies yet again, ready to check the last few items off the list.

"I'm missing something …" she said to no one in particular, but scanned the list again, and then the table, for the third box of highlighters.

She looked under boxes, folders, and bags and then finally under the table. They were on the floor on other side of the table, almost underneath the bench. Taylor assumed they'd gotten pushed off when the boys were looking through all their things before Taylor had snapped at them to stop.

Taylor stood up and went over to the other side of the table, getting down on her knees to crawl under and retrieve the highlighters. She was determined, stretching her fingertips, wishing they were longer, and confused as to how something right there was so hard to get to. Also, how could highlighters be the bane of her existence right now?

"I remembered!" Jamie's voice rang through the kitchen and Taylor jumped, briefly forgetting he was still there and hitting the back of her head on the bottom of the kitchen table as she was getting up.

"Ow," Taylor muttered, holding her head with one hand, and pushing herself up with the other while grasping the box. "You did?"

"Yeah!" Jamie was jumping up and down. "I do! Do you have jewelry cleaner?"

"You ran back home to ask for jewelry cleaner?" She raised an eyebrow. "That was your question?"

"Well, *I* don't. But Andrew does!" Jamie's smile was mischievous, and it raised many questions in Taylor's mind.

"And why does Andrew need jewelry cleaner?" Taylor crossed her arms, not letting Jamie get away without sharing what was going on.

Jamie raised his arms in exasperation as if Taylor's questions were causing him physical pain. "Mom!" He bent over at the waist and then stood up, putting his hand on his hips.

Taylor laughed at the sight and wondered how she'd given birth to an old man.

"Because ..." He drew out the word for three whole seconds before spilling the rest of his story. "Andrew found a necklace and was thinking of giving it to Tiffany because, you know, she's his girlfriend, but it looks kind of dirty, so I said that you probably had something to clean it with, so ... do you?"

Taylor was holding her breath and didn't let it out as she continued to stare at her son. She refused to project this situation onto herself as if it were her past life. Because that's all it was. A projection of a story in her past.

But how could Andrew look exactly like James did, and where exactly did he find this necklace?

"Jamie ..." Taylor started, but then thought better of it.

"Yeah, Mom?" He stood there, waiting for what she was going to say.

But she couldn't say what she wanted to. She couldn't ask the question burning in her mind. For one, it was inconsequential. It was not the same necklace—how could it be? And two, James wasn't the first person in the history of the world to give a necklace as a gift. It was a common and popular gift to give.

She decided to drop it.

"Mom?"

Taylor smiled at Jamie. She loved how invested he was in this sweet gift that Andrew wanted to give Tiffany. "I don't have cleaner, but you can tell him that I clean all my special pieces in hot water and vinegar." She gave one nod in finality and Jamie's face lit up.

"Thanks, Mom! I will!" He jumped up and started out the door.

Taylor laughed to herself, her heart swelling out of love for him.

Then she thought back to the first time they'd run over to the DeLucas' and how Jamie hadn't stopped to look and hadn't cared about the road or the cars that might be on it. She pictured him running across the street and she started walking to the door, ready to call out to him to look both ways when she heard it.

Her worst fears were coming to life and she stood frozen as she heard tires screeching to a halt before people called for help.

"Mom!" Jake's voice was behind her but then he was out the door in a flash. "Mom, *hurry*!" His voice trailed off as he ran down the drive.

It seemed like it happened in slow motion. She didn't know how, but she finally made her way to the door, only to see Jamie sprawled out on the road.

She was too late. She hadn't told him when she should have and now it was too late.

"Jamie!" Taylor cried, and with a pounding heart and shaky legs, she ran toward her son.

CHAPTER TWENTY-THREE

Then

July 11, 1996—Charleston, South Carolina

Taylor wasn't sure how much time had passed, but she was in someone's arms and she heard a deep voice above her. "Pull up the chair." She heard shuffling, and then the arms placed her in a chair before pulling away.

"Dad? Where are you going?" she heard Emily call out. "We need help! Dad!"

Taylor groaned.

"She's waking up, Em."

Taylor heard Abby and felt her stroke her hair. She was used to this feeling in the hospital and for the briefest of moments, Taylor wondered why she was back there. Abby was her comforter and Taylor was instantly transported to the only good memories she had at St. Peter's. Taylor was able to keep her focus and mental well-being because of Abby's encouragement and willingness to help her. But right now, regardless of where she was, she wanted to keep sleeping. She happily let herself drift away again.

She was back on the beach with James. He ran back from the water, fastening her necklace before kissing her neck once it was secured.

Taylor giggled and touched the pearl. "I absolutely love it." She spun around to face him, putting her arms around his neck, kissing his salty lips.

"And I absolutely love you." He kissed her back.

"Taylor!"

Taylor looked around down the beach at who was calling out to her but there was no one in sight. "James, did you hear some—" She turned to face him again, but James was gone.

She was standing alone on the beach.

"Taylor!" she heard someone call out again.

She looked to the right and saw a figure running down the beach toward her. She squinted, putting her hand up to stop the glare from the sun.

"Travis?" she murmured, not understanding what she was seeing.

"I'm here …" His voice was closer.

There was a pain on her head, and she felt the side of it. There was a bump. She didn't remember hitting her head.

She stood on the beach, not remembering how she'd gotten there. But James was just here, and now he wasn't.

Travis was.

The beach blurred as she heard more voices.

"How long has she been out?"

"Maybe seven minutes?"

"Her vitals are good."

Abby's voice was clear, and that's when it all came back to her. She wasn't on the beach at all. She was in Charleston. She'd tried to find Callum, but she'd failed. He'd died before she'd gotten her answers.

"Taylor." Travis's voice was right next to her ear. "Can you hear me?"

She could, but couldn't summon the energy to respond. Her willpower was gone. She felt a hand in hers. It was large. It couldn't be Abby or Emily's. It had to have been Travis's.

She squeezed back.

She felt a head touch hers. "Tay …" His voice was so soft and tender.

It all flooded back. Everything she'd done to try to find answers was all for nothing. Her dream of finding James had died with Callum.

Keeping her eyes closed, Taylor started to cry. "He's gone," she breathed out, softly sobbing. "He's gone."

"Who's gone, Taylor?" Travis asked.

She heard Abby answer: "She just found out that Professor Decker …" then trailed off.

Taylor wondered if Abby mouthed the rest, or gestured, sparing Taylor from hearing those painful words again.

Callum had died.

"Oh no ..." Travis put his arms around Taylor, who was curled up in a leather desk chair. "Tay. I'm so, so sorry." He hugged her tighter.

It only made Taylor cry harder. Why was he being so kind to her?

"Does she have a place to stay?" Emily sounded like she was on the other side of the room. "Because I certainly can't bring her back to my house ..." She sounded panicked, and Taylor was too caught up in her grief to wonder why.

"My hotel is close by," Abby offered. "She can stay with me, but I leave to go back home tomorrow afternoon."

"It's okay, my parents already said she can stay the night." Travis sounded determined and proud. "I'll take her back."

Taylor heard a rustling of papers and then Abby went back into full nurse mode. "Here's my phone number and address back home. *Please* give me any updates, and give this to Taylor, too. I want to make sure she's okay."

"I will," Travis promised. "I'll give you mine, too. The storm is rolling in—you might not be able to leave tomorrow."

The storm. Taylor had forgotten all about it.

"Hurricane Bertha," he responded to someone, flatly, although Taylor had missed the question. "Hopefully it misses us, but it's heading our way."

Taylor heard a gasp, and assumed it was Abby. Being born and raised in California, Taylor wasn't sure about preparing for a hurricane. A drought maybe, or an earthquake, but not a storm.

Emily sounded closer. "You should stay with us tonight, Abby. You shouldn't be alone tonight." There was a silence. Taylor wondered if looks were being passed between them. "To be safe," she quietly added.

"Are you sure, Em? You just said that there was no room for—"

"It's hard to explain," Emily cut Abby off. "But *you* can stay."

And then there was more silence.

Taylor's fingers found Travis's arm and she held onto him. She needed to know he was real. She wasn't ready to open her eyes and face this world yet. The world where her only lead to James was gone. The world in which she had to face the reality that she would never see him again.

She just wasn't ready for it.

She kept her eyes closed, holding onto Travis while Abby told him to come say goodbye before he left with her, saying they had to finish clearing out Callum's office.

Travis promised to but didn't move from holding onto Taylor. She wasn't sure how long they stayed that way, but she slowly started to open her eyes to her new reality.

The reality without James.

She felt Travis move his arms out from under her. "Can I take you back, now?" He stood up and put his hand out to her.

Taylor stared at it, then slowly put her hand in his and let him pull her up. She nodded, and without saying another word, he hugged her. He wrapped his arms around her, his voice was quiet and sad.

"I'm sorry, Tay. I'm so sorry you lost someone else."

He didn't even know the half of it, but Taylor buried her face in his chest. When she finally let him go, she wiped her eyes as they walked out of the office. Travis had his arm protectively around Taylor while they walked down the stairs, her mind becoming clearer about the events that had happened once she'd arrived here.

What had she seen in Emily's dad that had made her run after him? And where did he go after that? Was he running away from her?

Taylor felt the letter in her pocket and knew that it was still there, but she didn't want to read it in front of Travis. She saw Emily's face after telling her about it and decided that she'd wait until she got to his parents' house to open it.

They said their goodbyes to the girls who were still in the lobby. Emily's was cold and she made no eye contact, but Abby's hug made Taylor start sobbing all over again. After reluctantly letting go, Taylor followed Travis back to his car, and nervously picked at her fingernails as they drove away from the university.

When Travis entered his parents' neighborhood, she sat in awe. Her eyes were wide and her mouth hung open seeing the houses as they passed by, each one more beautiful than the last. The trees that lined the streets and the gates across the driveways were otherworldly to her.

Travis turned right into a driveway that led to a stunning two-story, white-brick house with navy blue shutters. He pulled up next to a detached two-car garage and Taylor slowly unbuckled her seat belt, almost as if she were awaiting permission to get out of the car. She felt as though she didn't belong there.

She opened her car door a second before Travis got there, but he still pulled it open the rest of the way for her. She was getting embarrassed over the fact that he felt he had to take care of her, constantly putting his hand out for her, keeping her upright by putting his arm around her, and asking her if she was all right or in pain.

She *was* in pain and in need of help, but she refused to let him help again. She wanted to be stronger than she felt and was embarrassed because she wasn't usually so fragile. She hated that Travis was seeing her like this, but was thankful for his presence. Was it possible to feel both humiliation and gratitude at the same time?

She wished that Travis had known her when she wasn't so weak and confused and that she could be the Taylor who made him laugh and joked with him. But she was *this* Taylor, and despite the difference a year had made, he seemed to like her for it.

As they neared the house, the front door swung open, and the most beautiful woman Taylor had ever seen was standing on the front steps.

Her arms were held out to Travis, and she had a huge smile on her bright red lips. "Mijo!"

Travis broke away from Taylor to give his mother a hug. "Mami, this is Taylor." He turned to Taylor with a smile on his face that Taylor hadn't seen yet. She really liked that smile.

His mom put her hand on Taylor's shoulders. "I have heard so much about you, Taylor. It is a pleasure to meet you." And with that, she brought Taylor into a hug that was warm and inviting.

Taylor swallowed hard, trying to suppress tears that were on the verge of escaping. She'd just met the most wonderful woman who had heard who-knew-what about her, and Taylor wasn't about to ruin it by crying all over her pristine white blouse.

Taylor smiled back at her when she broke away from the hug. "Thank you, Mrs. Perez." She glanced at Travis to gauge his reaction. His eyes were on her, and it made Taylor feel safe, somehow. "And thank you for letting me stay tonight."

Travis's mom waved her hand in the air. "Please, Taylor, call me Iva. And I wouldn't dream of sending you away." She put an arm around Taylor, bringing her into the house. "Any friend of Travis is like family to us." She turned and pointed at Travis, all of a sudden getting very serious. "Mijo, bring her bag up to the white guest room."

And then Iva led Taylor up the stairs, stopping on every step to show her all the family pictures that filled the wall.

Taylor was mesmerized, not only by all they had done as a family, but by how close they were. A pang of sadness filled her, and Iva must have sensed it, because she ushered her up the stairs and to the right, into the white room.

Taylor understood its name as soon as she walked in.

The bedspread was a white eyelet coverlet on a white iron bed frame. White lace curtains lined the windows, and white wallpaper with faint rustic roses covered the walls.

She had never seen anything more serene.

"This is your room." Iva smiled at her and sat on the bed, patting the seat next to her.

Taylor obeyed the motion and sat next to her. Iva put both arms around her and Taylor melted into them. She truly didn't know how much she had been craving this touch and affection until it was offered to her. She didn't want Iva to let her go.

"Travis told me about your parents." Iva's voice was soft, but Taylor went stiff.

Taylor's lie was now catching up to her, even reaching this sweet woman who was opening up her heart and home to her. She once again broke down in sobs.

"I'm so sorry, mija. I'm so sorry," Iva said over and over again.

If only Iva knew the real reason for her tears. Taylor wasn't crying over the supposed loss of her parents—not in the way Iva thought, anyway. She was mourning her story that had led her here. A very different kind of loss.

Here she sat, in a perfect bedroom with this wonderful woman, and Taylor was deceiving all of them. Who was she that she felt like it was okay to do this to them? To anyone? She should just come clean now before they found out—because she was sure they eventually would.

Iva was rubbing Taylor's back as her sobs subsided. She wiped her eyes and Iva leaned over her to grab the box of tissues on the white wooden bed-side table.

"Take these, mija. And know that I will always be here for you."

Once again, Taylor obeyed, taking one tissue and folding it in half before wiping her eyes and then her nose.

"Thank you, Iva." Taylor's voice squeaked and she cleared her throat before asking again, louder, as if it would make up for the squeak.

Iva nodded. "Of course."

There was a knock on the door, and Taylor and Iva both looked up to see Travis holding Taylor's backpack. He held it out. "Where would you like me to put it?" He studied Taylor tentatively, as though a look might break her.

Iva stood up and took the bag from her son. "I'll take that, Mijo. Will you see if your father needs help? He's in the back putting away the patio furniture." She looked over her shoulder at Taylor. "The storm is coming, and we never know what it will look like. We *always* have to prepare for the worst!" She clicked her tongue. "Remember last summer? That was a doozy!" She gave Travis a knowing look, and he just rolled his eyes before laughing.

"Not this again, Mami."

But he poked his mother with his elbow and Taylor knew this was in jest.

Iva laughed along with Travis and then looked at Taylor. "I made my boys board up our windows, cover the pool, put every piece of furniture and flowerpot away because of the horrible storm that was coming—"

Travis laughed, then interrupted her: "After almost five hours of work, we only got a few drops of rain and mild wind."

He patted his mom on her back. She was almost as tall as Travis was. Iva barely had to look up at him, but when she did, Taylor could see the love in her eyes. A mother's love for her child.

"And my sweet boys …" Iva shook her head laughing. "They then had to undo it all! Not letting out one complaint." She smiled at Travis, who put his arm around his mother.

"Anything for you, Mami." Travis gave her a squeeze, then Iva left them alone, heading back downstairs to start making lunch.

Taylor's heart longed to be included in the love that she was witnessing— she ached for Iva to look at her the way she looked at Travis. She wanted Iva to be the mom in her life that her own mother couldn't be through all of their trials. Would she ever see her parents again? Would she ever tell Travis or his family the truth about her past?

Taylor couldn't handle another rejection. She decided to keep this to herself.

For now.

"Okay," Travis started, breaking Taylor's train of thought. "I'm going to go help my dad. Will you be okay?" He didn't move from his spot at the door.

Taylor smiled and nodded. She was actually anxious to be alone. She wanted to read the letter from Callum.

Travis gave a sheepish smile, then looked down at the floor. "I'd hug you right now, but, uh … I'm not allowed in." He looked back up at Taylor and shrugged. "House rules."

"I get it." Taylor's voice was a whisper. She crossed her two index fingers in front of her. "No boys allowed."

Travis chuckled. "Exactly." He stood there for a beat longer, his gaze on Taylor, which gave her butterflies, and she didn't break his stare.

What was happening?

Her stomach told her that she was welcoming this attention, but her heart was still broken. She looked down at her hands.

"Come down to the kitchen when you're ready." Travis started to turn away. "We'll eat at twelve-thirty, but feel free to take your time." He started walking down the hall to the top of the stairs and pointed to his right. "That's the bathroom, and there are clean towels in your closet if you need to shower." He turned back to the staircase, putting his hand on the top of the railing, and smiled at Taylor, who was still sitting on the bed, watching him. "I'm glad you're here."

"I am, too."

Then Travis tapped the railing, smiled, and started down the stairs.

Taylor breathed out, then stood up, looking around the room. She finally walked over to the door, shutting it slowly and quietly. She turned back, taking in the bed, before looking down at what she was wearing. She was afraid that if she laid down, she'd get dirt on it like she was five years old again and had just come in from playing at the park. Maybe she *should* take a shower, or at the very least change.

But first, the letter.

She took it out of her pocket and started reading, not hesitating or over-thinking what might be in there, though she knew it would inevitably break her heart.

Once she finished, she reread it, her breath taken from her each time. This couldn't be true. Callum's words simply could not be.

Her head spun and she laid down on the bed, burying her face in the pillow to muffle the sobs that came in uncontrollable waves.

The room was dark when she opened her eyes, and after remembering Callum's words to her, she had no energy to keep them open. She gave in to her exhaustion and fell into a deep sleep.

Taylor was still sleeping when Iva knocked on the door and poked her head in. She'd didn't make a fuss when Taylor skipped lunch but brought up a dinner tray after Taylor again hadn't come down to eat with them. Iva noticed that Taylor wasn't even under the covers. She set the tray down on the desk across from the bed and pulled a quilt out from the chest that was at the foot of the bed. She covered Taylor, then noticed the letter that was still in her limp grasp.

Hesitating for only a moment, she took the paper out of her hand, making sure Taylor was really sleeping. Only then, did Iva start reading.

Dear Taylor,

I'm sorry that I'm writing you instead of meeting with you, like you requested in your previous emails. I went back and forth, wondering if I should. If it was wise. In truth, I haven't had the words to tell you what I know I must.

I wanted to first apologize. I should not have come to your house the night he traveled. I know that I told you he was safe and that he was alive. And he is. But there is so much more to that.

My apology comes only because I know I gave you hope. A hope that I could reunite you with him, that you could find him again, find him in the same time that you knew him. But that was always impossible to do.

I have devoted my life to researching everything there is to know about time travel, and this I now know for sure. I shouldn't have meddled. I shouldn't have come to find you. I knew better and he did, too, but his emotions overtook him, Taylor—and it was either him, or me. I had to beat him to it, or else both of your lives would have been destroyed.

I know that you think yours already has been, but you have your whole life ahead of you. You have the opportunity to create something beautiful from this. I know he didn't believe it then, but he does now, Taylor.

James would want you to move on and live your life. He would want you to meet someone who will love you for

211

you—despite your past. I know openness and honesty will be difficult in light of the truth. There are so many people who will write you off, but remember this, Taylor—they react out of fear of the unknown. It is not personal.

Open yourself up to opportunities that you otherwise wouldn't.

You already took a big step of faith coming out to Myrtle Beach. You, Taylor, are a lot stronger and braver than you realize.

When James talked about you—and he did often—he lit up. He lit up from your memory, the way one would remember a beautiful dream, desperately trying to hold on to the details. To him, you were that dream.

Taylor, there is no easy way to say this. I know that this information will be hard to read, but read you must, if only to help you let go of the chase.

Yes, James traveled back in time. Significantly. And because of this, he has relived a whole life, a different one than the one you knew, plus many more years on top of that. James got married and they had a daughter. A beautiful daughter. In a different life, I firmly believe that you and she would have been friends. Great friends, even.

But regretfully, I must share with you that the James you knew is no longer here. I can't risk giving you details of how or why, and I implore you to understand the reasoning for this.

I have known him for almost thirty years now. We became friends. He trusted me, he confided in me, and I'm not sure if there is anyone else on this planet who knows more about him than I do. It is because of this that I can write confidently to you, asking you to let him go.

None of this is easy to write, and I can only imagine the immense difficulty with which you will read this, even process this.

Taylor, you will bounce back. You will live a wonderful life, and you will always look back and think with only fondness of that time in your life. This will shape you into a stronger woman and you will be better because of it.

Please believe this about yourself because James would want nothing more for you than this.

I hope to see you again one day, Taylor. Until then, enjoy every one of your days now that you know the truth. Have peace in every moment, knowing that James lived a truly great life. His wife never replaced the spot in his heart that you held, and no one will be able to fill the void in your heart.

If nothing else, take comfort in that.

All my best,
Callum

CHAPTER TWENTY-FOUR

Now

August 15, 2016—Myrtle Beach, South Carolina

Taylor's legs couldn't move fast enough as she hurled herself toward Jamie, his body lying at an unnatural angle on the side of the street. A black car was sitting sideways in the middle of the road. She heard screams as neighbors were now making their way out of their homes to see the scene.

"Mom …" she heard someone call but didn't register who was speaking or if she was the mom they were referring to.

She threw herself down beside Jamie, too scared to touch him, but also wanting to scoop him up and hold him like she used to. Seeing an open cut on his forehead, she decided to leave him on the ground. As painful as it was for her to not have him close, safe in his mom's arms, she didn't want to do any more damage to his little body.

"Call 911!" Taylor heard from the crowd that was now beginning to form around the scene.

Taylor held her breath as she leaned in toward her son and rested her lips on his cheek. "Jamie …" she breathed out in a whisper. "Baby, please wake up. *Please.*"

Tears fell freely, without a sob or a cry, onto Jamie's cheek, and Taylor didn't move to wipe them away. She took his hands gently and squeezed them. She waited for a squeeze back, a movement, or a breath … only to be met with absolutely anything.

"Jamie," Taylor started to cry out, over and over again. "Jamie." She put her hands on each side of his face, kissing the cheek closest to her. "Jamie ..." She shut her eyes, praying this wasn't real. "Please no ... God. *Please!*" She started sobbing in his neck, refusing to let go of his face.

She thought about his lively spirit, his contagious laugh, and how just moments ago he had been so concerned about the interests of someone else over his own. She pictured his face light up as he ran into the kitchen asking for jewelry cleaner.

Did he get hit by a car because of jewelry cleaner?

She felt anger rise up in her but had to check herself. No one could have known this was going to happen. She reached down and squeezed Jamie's hand tight, as if that would help her not lash out at someone innocent in all of this.

It was Jamie who had run across the road without looking.

It was she who had failed to warn him time and time again about the dangers of running across the road without looking.

She squeezed his hand harder.

Why did someone need to go that fast down this road when it wasn't even a through-street?

No one should have been driving that fast.

She squeezed his hand harder.

Who was the driver?

She squeezed his hand harder.

"Mom?" She opened her eyes to see Jamie's eyes looking right back at her.

Taylor let in a sharp breath, eyes bouncing back and forth between his as if she couldn't believe it.

"Mom, that hurts." He looked down at his hands, his fingers white and squished together by her grasp.

"Oh!" Taylor let go his hand, bringing her hands to her mouth. "Jamie, I'm sorry!"

She started to cry, putting her hands back on either side of his face, feeling his breath on hers.

"Jamie," she said again, knowing that he could hear her, she wanted to say his name over and over again. "Jamie, I love you so much. I was so scared." She opened her eyes again, and her face fell as she tried to read his expression.

Taylor sat up straight, alarms going off in her head. Something was still not right.

"Jamie, what's wrong. Can you move? The ambulance should be here soon …"

Jamie shook his head and then tried to sit up. "I need to see if he's all right." He grabbed Taylor's arms to steady himself, clearly dizzy from hitting his head.

"No, don't." Taylor gently brought him back down, then took off her sweater and put it under his head so he wasn't laying on the road's hard pavement.

"Mom, he's hurt, I have to see him." His eyes were begging hers and Taylor gave him a confused look.

"Who's hurt, Jamie." Taylor's question came out like a statement, and she looked up for the first time and scanned the crowd for her sons.

She didn't see them, but she saw another group of bystanders huddled on the other side of the car. She looked back at Jamie, frantic now. Taylor was afraid to ask, but knew she had to.

"Jamie? Who's hurt?"

Jamie started to cry. "Frank is." He grabbed her hands. "Frank pushed me out of the way, and I think he's really hurt, Mom … I need to go see him."

He started to sit up again, and against her better judgment, she helped him to his feet. She put her arms under his and together they slowly walked over to where the others were gathered. She stopped short when she saw blood, and as her eyes wandered up, she saw Hazel, kneeling beside her husband.

"Jamie!"

She heard Jake come up behind them and she turned to see him bend down and give Jamie a hug. Jamie's little arms wrapped around his brother's neck and they both cried.

"Jamie!" Josh ran up to his brothers, who were still holding each other, and without completely letting go, Jake brought Josh into the hug and the three of them stayed that way. A mixture of tears, *I love you*s, and don't ever do that agains filled their intimate circle.

Taylor vowed to not take them for granted—even through the fighting, disciplining, messy bedrooms, and crumbs all over her kitchen, she would always remember this moment and their true brotherly love for one another.

She glanced over at Hazel, still by Frank's side. Her heart sank and she stood frozen for a moment as she thought about what to do. She wanted to give them space, but she also wanted to thank Frank ... And if he wasn't here anymore, she wanted to comfort Hazel.

Taylor put her hand over her chest in an attempt to steady her heart, which felt as if it were going to leap out of her chest at any moment.

She tapped Jake's shoulder and he looked up, eyes red from crying, and she nodded over at Frank. "I'm going to go over, but can you ..." She trailed off and looked at the back of Jamie's head.

Jake nodded in understanding and Taylor smiled in thanks. She didn't want Jamie to see this, and she especially didn't want his first experience of death to be this way. She wasn't sure what she wanted his memories of Frank to be, but it wasn't this. They shared a bond that was unexpected, to say the least.

Taylor chastised herself for how she'd reacted to the DeLucas when they'd first moved in—how dismissive she had been when they were just trying to be friendly neighbors. She was thankful that they'd been persistent and now, as her feet slowly took her over to Frank, she promised herself something else. She would take care of Hazel.

As if reading her mind, Hazel looked up and smiled at Taylor.

"It's your turn, dear." Hazel stood up and walked around Frank to hug Taylor.

Confusion washed over Taylor, and her first thought was wondering why Hazel had just left her husband's side. Nothing was usual or natural about this situation.

Hazel walked away and toward Jamie, ready for her turn for his hug. Taylor found herself watching her and was jolted back by hearing sirens in the distance. The ambulance was on its way.

She looked at Frank, still laying on the ground, a blanket over him and blood underneath his head. She took a few baby steps toward him, not sure how to proceed.

She knew that if he was still alive, she had to thank him. She needed and wanted to. But how to thank someone for giving their life for someone else's? No words she could think of sufficed.

"Tay ..." she heard from below her and looked at Frank, who slowly turned his hand toward her.

She just shook her head and rushed to his side. "No. No, Frank, please. Don't move."

He coughed and brought his hand to his mouth.

"The ambulance is almost here. Just … just hang on. Okay?" She took hold of his hand, wanting to comfort him, but she started crying all over again. She absolutely didn't want him to die. She wanted to thank him every minute of every day for taking Jamie's place.

"Tay …" he repeated and looked into her eyes, his expression at peace and knowing.

Taylor took a sharp breath in at the sight. His sunglasses were no longer on, and she looked into his blue eyes. His piercing blue eyes.

She'd know those blue eyes anywhere.

She fumbled over words that got stuck in her throat and ended up choking out, "Frank?"

He shook his head slowly … and she knew why.

He wasn't Frank at all.

"*James?*"

Realization dawned as the world around her got smaller, voices drifted far away, and the only thing real in that moment was his frail hand in hers. Even with its frailty, it was still so very familiar.

She vaguely registered the paramedics gently taking her away from him, and reluctantly letting go of that hand that she'd fought for so many years to find, then even more years to forget.

"No—" She reached back out to grab it again, but Hazel was swiftly by her side, holding her back.

She watched helplessly as they put him on the stretcher. Then, she saw a figure running down the street, and she knew for certain that this must be a dream.

"Mom!" the woman cried.

Hazel turned to the voice and her brave face melted away as she let go of Taylor.

"Emily!" Hazel cried and ran toward her daughter.

Emily was Hazel's daughter? That meant that Frank was … Emily's dad?

Memories swept over Taylor's mind like a tidal wave—meeting Emily for the first time when she'd knocked on their door looking for Callum, seeing her when she'd finally made it to the university to talk to Callum, and then … seeing Emily's dad at the top of the stairs rush off in a panic.

It was Frank.

Frank was James.

He had seen Taylor and just … ran off.

Hazel and Emily were standing in front of Taylor now, breaking her out of a daze. Emily wiped her cheeks and offered Taylor a small smile.

"Emily," Taylor choked out, because now, knowing exactly who she was, she saw James in her.

Her blonde hair, blue eyes, and her smile. She should have seen it all along, but either she'd refused to believe the truth, or she'd been so caught up in her own grief and despair that she couldn't plainly see what was right in front of her.

"It's good to see you again." Emily's voice was quiet, her eyes not smiling, and they didn't have to say that it sucked seeing each other under these circumstances.

Would Emily blame Taylor if her dad died?

A paramedic came up to the three women who were all expectant for news. "He's asking for … Taylor?" Her raised eyebrows and voice questioned which one of the women was Taylor, and Emily's glare was enough to kill Taylor on the spot.

Hazel shot her daughter a look and something passed between them. A look Taylor didn't understand.

"I'm Taylor." Her voice cracked under the pressure and embarrassment of the moment. But she put her head down and followed the young woman to where Frank … or James … was.

He was laying on the stretcher, raised to her height, with buckles tucking him and the blankets securely in place, save for his arms, which were lying at his sides, an IV already in one arm and a pulse monitor on the other one.

Taylor approached him warily, now that she knew who it was that she was speaking to. She hesitated just for a moment, but then slowly put both her hands in his.

His eyes never left hers. "I wanted to tell you."

She just nodded. "I understand why you didn't."

She let out a soft laugh and he smiled back at her.

They were quiet, James looking at Taylor, and Taylor staring down at their hands. After all this time, she had a million questions, but it seemed like an unspoken agreement that they couldn't talk about it now, when anyone could hear and knowing that no one would understand.

She was having a hard time understanding herself.

What must people around them be thinking right now? Neighbors who weren't that close were now eavesdropping on this private moment before he was swept away by the ambulance. Would this be the last time she'd see him? Alive?

Her eyes made their way back up to his tear-filled ones. Did he know this would be the last time, too?

Taylor shook her head, and despite the glances, she rested her head on his chest. "You can't just come back into my life to leave it …" A sob cut her off as she felt his hand on her head, stroking her hair, and she wanted to stay like this for as long as she could.

He coughed, and when he got his breath back, he was able to speak again. "I'm an old man, Tay, and I'm sick."

Taylor lifted her head to look at him again. Her eyes were so full of sorrow. She'd known he was sick and had done nothing about it. Now, she'd give anything to go back and be there for him, even if it meant that she'd never find out who he really was. Instead, she'd just left him sick and alone. She was so mad at her thoughts and actions toward him. "I'm so sorry I did nothing to help. I'm so …" She sobbed again. "I'm so sorry." She let go of James's hand with one of hers to wipe her nose, then reached for him again.

James stared back at Taylor with a look that Taylor had never seen in him before.

"I lived a good life, Taylor." He smiled, and Taylor wondered what memories were whirling through his head right now. "And trust me when I say, Jamie did enough … for both of you."

She looked over at Jamie, who was staring back, eyes full of hope. Then, at Hazel and Emily, who were both watching at a distance.

"I need to know everything, James…but—" She looked back at him, whose eyes were now closed. "James?" He didn't open them. "James?" she said louder.

She shook her head and looked at the heart rate monitor, just as a paramedic came.

"We have to go, now!" The paramedic's voice was rushed and, without looking behind her, she called out, "You can follow us to the hospital."

"No, not yet … I'm not ready." Taylor tried to grab James's hand, but the paramedics lifted the gurney into the ambulance. *"Please!"*

After her ignored plea, Taylor could only stand there, stunned. Was this it?

"Dad!" she heard Emily's pained voice followed by Hazel's firm and steady one.

"Em, let's go. We'll take your car."

They both ran past Taylor, who was rendered silent, watching the ambulance speed down the street, lights and sirens blazing.

She wondered if she just had lost James, again.

CHAPTER TWENTY-FIVE

Then

July 12, 1996—Charleston, South Carolina

A noise outside startled Taylor and she opened her eyes.

It was dark in the guestroom, and when she looked at the clock, it was 6:32 a.m. The wind howled outside, and she heard rain on the window. She wondered if they were officially on hurricane watch. She heard voices outside and knew that Travis was helping his dad get ready for the storm. As much as Taylor wanted to help them, after yesterday she had no strength to even stay awake.

She remembered Callum's letter and, turning her head back toward the nightstand, she saw it folded up on the edge. His words came right back to her.

James was married. He had a child. But he's gone. Forever.

She closed her eyes, not wanting to be in or live in a world where she couldn't have him. He had someone else. He *loved* someone else. He was probably happy with his new life, regardless of how it had started, and it pained Taylor's heart. She wasn't sure how she was going to move on.

She stayed in bed, dwelling over James's new life and mourning the loss of hers. Thinking an hour had passed, she looked back at the time—only twenty-two minutes had gone by. Today was going to be a long day; she wasn't sure her heart could take it.

Sitting up, she looked around for her backpack. It was empty and folded up in the corner chair.

Looking around the room again, she wondered where her clothes were. She got up and opened the drawers of the small white dresser. She saw her clothes, neatly folded in piles, separating her pants and shirts. Opening another drawer, she shuddered as she saw her bras and underwear folded in their tidy little piles, and she knew that Iva must have done it, as Travis was not allowed in her room.

She groaned out of embarrassment over the fact that the most stunning woman she had ever met had seen her tattered and colorless undergarments, Taylor still smiled out of thanks. She was being taken care of by a mom. It didn't matter that it wasn't her own; Iva was a loving mother and Taylor's heart swelled with gratitude for the kindness she was being shown.

But the guilt she had over lying to them, to everyone, was unbearable.

Despite the humidity of the tropical storm, Taylor pulled out a pair of sweatpants and a sweatshirt, put on her socks, and prepared for the day that she knew she had to face. She listened for noise outside her bedroom door before slowly opening it. Taking a minute to gauge where everyone was, she took a few baby steps out of her door and tip-toed down the hall, making sure that no one could hear her.

She stood at the top of the stairs, heart pounding, afraid of being caught, but she had to leave. She had to get out of here. Her anxiety was so great that she didn't care what she left behind—her things, or Travis.

She held onto the railing, taking one step at a time, ignoring the pictures smiling back at her from the seemingly perfect Perez family, and stayed the course. Once she reached the bottom, she heard voices coming from the kitchen, and knew her only option was to leave through the front door.

"I'm going to make eggs before we lose power, but what kind should I make? What do you think Taylor likes? And do you think she likes toast with her eggs?" Iva's voice was soft and loving in her perfect Cuban accent.

It made Taylor want to change her mind, turn the other way, and run down the hall into the kitchen, saying, *Yes! I love toast with my eggs, and I like my eggs soft boiled so I can dip my toast in the yolk!* Instead, she let a silent tear fall, knowing she'd miss Iva so much.

She readied herself and crept toward the front door, jumping when she heard Hector's voice behind her.

"Good morning, Taylor! We were just talking about you!"

Like a deer caught in headlights, she didn't smile back, but remained frozen in place. Hector's brows furrowed as he studied her.

"Are you looking for Travis?" Now one eyebrow was raised.

Taylor nodded.

Hector smiled. "He's finishing up outside for me. Can you tell him to come in for breakfast and to get warm before we have no power?"

Taylor nodded again, smiling back, still not able to find her voice.

"Thank you. He must be soaked to the bone by now." Hector looked at the newspaper that was still in his hand and grunted in amusement over something he had just read. Opening it up to the full page, he walked away from her and down the hall toward the kitchen again.

She let out a breath she had been holding, assuming that she was in the clear, but now she'd have to get by Travis outside.

Taylor opened the front door, not afraid of being caught now that she had an excuse to leave the house. She heard Iva say something to Hector in Spanish, and without another thought, she shut the door behind her.

The wind and rain hit Taylor's face and she wondered if this was the right decision, but she felt like she had no other choice. She pulled up her hood to shield her face from the rain and started running down the driveway, the gates already opened and locked in placed so as to not get damaged in the wind.

She didn't think twice or turn around. She just continued to run. She ran in the general direction of the university, but slowed down after about a mile or so, catching her breath and taking in her surroundings.

There was no one in sight. No cars on the road, no other people walking around. Some houses were boarded up, and some front lawns were already littered with broken pots, flowers, and mud from not putting them away in time.

The wind was vicious, and she turned her back to it. As she turned, she saw a pathway between two houses. Unsure of what was propelling her, she started walking toward the path. Once she saw that it led to the ocean, she started running again until her feet hit the sand.

Taylor stood, panting, not caring that the rain was hitting her face. She watched the waves come crashing down as the tide crept up on the beach, higher and higher while washing away all traces of the soft, white beach that was in its path.

Taylor stared at the ocean and the waves, feeling the wind and rain, and becoming so overwhelmed that she dropped to her knees. She screamed into the noise that roared above her.

"Why?" Her voice was hoarse, but she yelled again: "Why?"

There was no one there and she was given no reply.

"Why did you leave me?" She breathed hard, actually anticipating a response.

The last time she'd yelled at the ocean, nothing happened. Why would she think it would be any different this time? But she didn't care. She didn't care who saw her, who heard her, or if anyone thought she was crazy. She came here to get answers and she wasn't happy with the ones she got. She felt like she had no other option than to get mad at what had initially taken him away.

The ocean.

Maybe if she got close enough, she could be taken, too. Taken to wherever James was, because a life without James was a life she didn't want to live.

She didn't even want to think about trying. She stood up and took a step closer to the waves.

"Did you even *try*?" she screamed. Her sobs now muffled her words. "Did you even try to get back to me?"

She took another step closer.

"Do you even *care* that I'm broken right now?"

The next thing she knew, the ocean had responded with a rogue wave coming in and crashing down around her, sweeping her out to sea.

She clung to the sand that was slipping through her fingers as she got farther and farther away from shore. The warm water turned cold the farther away she got, taking her breath away and leaving her with no air in her lungs to scream.

She was up long enough to see the shore in the distance, houses close enough that maybe, just maybe someone would hear her if she screamed loud enough.

She opened her mouth to inhale the air she would need to save her life before another wave hit her from behind—this one tumbling her underwater, leaving her shocked and disoriented. She wanted to swim and get up for air but wasn't sure which way was up.

Panicked, she opened her mouth, hoping for air, but instead, more water filled her, and she got tumbled again, this time smashing into the sand, sending a sharp pain through her shoulder.

The pain rendered her rigid, the cold ocean water lowering her body temperature, and the weight of her soaked sweats left her immobilized, carrying her lower and farther out into the vast, dark, and angry waters.

She gave in to the weight of the water and the tiredness she felt, letting out her breath underwater in pain before everything went black.

"Taylor! Come on!" James happily shouted at her from the beach, but she couldn't move in the water.

She was just floating along, taking in James's face, smiling back at her. She felt joy in her heart knowing that he loved her and had chosen her. She wanted to stare at him all day.

"Taylor!" He cupped his hands over his mouth, trying to make his voice reach her. "It's time to come in! We have to go home!"

Taylor stayed in the water, and felt like even if she wanted to, she couldn't move on her own. She looked around her, confused. Nothing was keeping her here, so why couldn't she get out?

"Fine!" James raised his hand in surrender. "I'll have to come in and get you."

Taylor laughed as James ran in the ocean toward her, splashing and making a scene before diving underwater. When he didn't resurface, Taylor tried to call out for him, but she sputtered water instead. Taylor went under, opening her eyes which were stinging from the salt, but still not able to see him.

She came back up as two strong arms grabbed her from behind and started pulling her to shore.

She let her body rest into his and smiled. The one she loved, and the one who loved her, had come to rescue her. But from what? Why was she stuck and why couldn't she move?

"I've got you, Tay. Hang on." A voice that wasn't James's voice was in her ear. Taylor suddenly felt cold. "We're almost there. Hang on, Taylor. Please."

The pain in her shoulder brought her back, followed by a tightness in her chest. Her eyes sprung open just in time to see a wave coming down and she let out a gasp before it washed over her once again.

But this time, the two arms brought her back up. She didn't tumble around, and instead of hitting the ocean's floor with force, the ocean floor was now under her heels, and she was being dragged to safety.

She let herself stay limp, not having the energy to help with the rescue.

Taylor felt herself being laid down, and then the arms went from being under hers, to around her back and under her knees. She coughed as she was being picked up and jostled around, as she was carried away from the beach and into a nearby home.

Then she was settled on the couch and the voice was close to her face.

"Taylor. I'm here. You're safe. Taylor, open your eyes, *please*." She felt a kiss on her forehead. "Don't leave me, Taylor."

It was Travis.

Travis had come, but how had he known where she was? Did he see her run down his driveway? Did he hear her as she violently screamed at the ocean?

Her tired and cold body was shaking as she felt her wet and heavy sweatpants being taken off and a warm blanket put on her as a replacement.

"Sit her up," a woman directed.

She felt Travis cradle her neck and head as her sweatshirt was taken off and he laid her back down on the couch.

The blanket was so warm.

"Is she okay?" There was so much concern in Travis's voice which brought Taylor comfort.

She didn't want him to be worried, though. She wanted to open her eyes and smile and thank him, but her body physically wouldn't let her.

She felt a warm soft hand on her neck that didn't leave.

"She has a steady pulse, but it's stringy." The woman sounded kind.

"Is there an ambulance coming?" Travis spoke fast. "Or should we take her to the hospital?"

The woman sighed in frustration. "No, I already called, and they won't be here for a bit. They're all out on a lot of other calls this morning."

"Then what do we do? What happens if she—"

The woman cut him off. "She won't."

There was silence and Taylor assumed that they were looking at each other, unspoken words between them. She pictured Travis's face and how worried he had been when she'd fainted in Callum's office. Taylor bet that was exactly how his face looked now.

She finally opened her eyes to look at Travis, and she was right. She put her hand up to his cheek.

"Thank you," was all she managed, before she closed her eyes, letting herself give in to her body's weakness.

CHAPTER TWENTY-SIX

Now

August 23, 2016—Myrtle Beach, South Carolina

The funeral for Frank—or James—was confusing for Taylor. She could tell that it was for Travis, too. She was there mourning the loss of two men, and while her husband was supportive, he was also more quiet than usual. But nothing about this situation was usual and she knew that she and Travis had their own road to recovery.

She clutched both Jamie's and Travis's hands as they listened to stories from his life. Stories that she couldn't believe had happened to James. Some stories made her laugh, but most made her cry. Not because they were sad; they were all meant to be happy reminders of a life well-lived. But they made her cry because she wasn't part of any of them. He'd had this whole life and she knew nothing about it.

But, he'd also lived a different life that only *she* knew about, and Taylor wondered if Hazel or Emily would ever want to hear stories about him from her one day. Would she tell them about his parents, the Brooks, or their high school, or James's best friend, Mark? About his water polo scholarship, surfing competitions, or how they met?

Right now, she couldn't think about that because he wasn't James. He was Frank.

But he was still the boy she'd fallen in love with, the boy who had turned into a man before her eyes, and then had turned into someone old and wise without her knowing.

The pictures she saw of him throughout the service were shocking to her at first, because she was staring at the very boy she had once loved. He and Hazel on their wedding day was hard to see, but Taylor squeezed Travis's hand a little harder as a reminder that this was where she belonged.

With Travis.

Taylor couldn't get past the fact that James had gotten married, had a baby, and had taken a family trip to Disney World all before Taylor was even born.

There was a part of her that wanted to know every single detail about what had happened to him. She wished they'd had longer at the end, so she could ask him all the questions that she now had for him.

But they'd had no time.

All those questions were left unanswered, and Taylor had to accept it.

She knew that sometimes it would be hard to accept—but she had Travis and Heather, who knew everything now, to turn to for strength and support. She had people who loved her to talk to about how she was feeling. She could ask and wonder and cry and share without fear of judgment.

And Taylor felt lighter because of it.

She promised herself, and mentally promised James, that she would start living her life the way he had. Embracing the love of people nearest her, accepting it as truth, and not running away from it, as though something else were out there.

At one point, after Hazel had called Taylor from the hospital, letting her know that Frank had passed away during the night, Taylor had cried out of anger—anger at James, who had been alive this whole time and had never come to find her. He hadn't bothered letting her know where he was, or that he missed her or that he'd tried to reconnect with her again.

She knew they could never have had the same relationship they'd once shared, but it could have looked different, and Taylor thought that she would have been fine with that, as long as she knew he was happy and safe.

But that's not what had happened. Instead, she'd fought every minute either to find him, or to forget him. Either way, all that fighting was exhausting, and she was tired of being exhausted.

The minister leading the service introduced Jamie, who was set to speak next.

Taylor reassuringly squeezed his hand, and then let go as Jamie made his way to the stage. Hazel had asked if Jamie could say a few words and he hadn't hesitated to agree.

As much as Taylor wanted to read his speech, Jamie wouldn't let her. He'd worked over at Hazel's house for two days straight, and when Taylor had questioned her about it, Hazel had only waved her hand.

"Nonsense!" Hazel had cried. "I am loving telling Jamie all about him. I'll miss him and our time together once this is all over." She'd given Taylor a sad smile to which Taylor had nodded her thanks.

Now, Jamie stood on a stool to reach the podium and flattened out his paper. He cleared his throat, which prompted a ripple of respectful laughter throughout the church, and then he started.

"Ladies and gentlemen, we are all here today to celebrate the life of one extraordinary man."

Taylor reached over and took Travis's hand. He let it go, switching hands, and placed his arm around Taylor that she didn't hesitate to sink into.

Jamie smiled, then looked down at his speech. "Frank was not only our neighbor ..." He paused, staring at his words. He took a breath before continuing, "Frank was also my best friend."

Taylor stilled, taking in every word of what her son was saying. Was she so absent over the past few months that she didn't see this sweet relationship forming right before her eyes?

"He listened to me, he told me stories, he made me laugh, and he made me feel like I was the most important person when I was with him." Jamie looked up, found his mom, and smiled.

Taylor smiled back, proud that this was her son up there. Jamie spoke about the first time they'd met and then made everyone laugh as he told a story about the first time he got caught sneaking into their house to raid their fridge.

"I was hungry, and old people always have treats in their house for young neighbors like me."

Taylor looked over at Hazel, who was wiping her eyes, laughing along with everyone else at the memory, then nodded, and pointed at Jamie. "You were right!" she said and made everyone laugh again.

"And that's why I kept coming back." Jamie was beaming on stage. He had everyone in the palm of his hand and Taylor didn't think her heart could swell any bigger than it already was with the pride she had for her youngest son.

This was *her* son.

What if she did live a life with James? She wouldn't dream of wishing her sons away; she wouldn't dream of Travis not being in her life.

She loved her life. She was thankful for her life and *all* the people in it. She was thankful for her in-laws who took the place of a mother and father in her life when she didn't have her own to turn to and look up to.

Heather had been there for her when Taylor had first come out to Myrtle Beach, giving her a place to live and providing her with a true friendship. Travis had literally saved her life when she was at her lowest, and because of them, she was living *this* amazing life. She had been given a second chance, and she'd almost ruined it. Her heart hurt to even think about it, making her that much more grateful for the people around her.

Taylor focused her attention back on Jamie and his speech.

"I knew that Frank was my best friend when I went over to their house after I was mad at my mom one day ..." Jamie froze and looked at Taylor with a shrug. The place was silent, save for a few nervous laughs scatter around the church. "Sorry, Mom."

Taylor smiled, then winked at Jamie, giving him a thumbs-up to encourage him to keep going.

"So, when I finished complaining about how *awful* she was ..." He froze again, finding Taylor's curious stare, then continued. "Frank told me exactly what I needed to hear. Which was that my mom was not awful at all. He said that my mom loves me *so much* that she had to do something that was really hard to do, but she did it because it was the best thing for me. Frank said that when we love someone, it means we do the *right* thing over the *easy* thing."

Taylor took in a shaky breath as she let his words sink in. She knew that Frank hadn't just been talking about her parenting. He'd been talking about what he'd done to her ... or better yet ... *for* her.

Everyone erupted in applause as Jamie concluded, and even though Taylor wasn't sure it was appropriate to applaud at a funeral, she clapped along with everyone else, beaming at her son as he made his way down the stage and into their row. Jake and Josh patted Jamie on his back as he passed them and slid into his seat beside Taylor. He put his arms around her waist, and she brought him in close, kissing the top of his head.

"I love you so much," she whispered in his hair.

"I love you, too, Mom."

The minister was back on the stage, thanking Jamie, and then asking everyone to turn in their hymnals to page 321, to sing a song that was near and dear to Frank's heart— "Amazing Grace." In unison, everyone shuffled to their feet and, after a rustling of pages, the organ started and they all started to sing.

Taylor was struck by how this song settled differently in her heart now, and she was brought to tears with how it stirred her. She watched as Hazel sang with her eyes closed and a dainty hand raised in the air, making Taylor even more drawn to her. She wanted to talk to Hazel about her unwavering faith once everything settled down.

After the service, they all headed to the church basement for refreshments. Hazel found Taylor and asked her to take a seat.

"It was a lovely service, Hazel." Taylor smiled and gave her a quick hug. "How are you holding up?"

Hazel looked down at the tissues in her hand and nodded with pursed lips. "I'm doing okay." She looked up at Taylor with a weary expression. "But I needed to talk to you about something …" She started looking around her purse, then pulled out an envelope. She held on tight, staring down at it on her lap.

Taylor stayed silent, knowing that, whatever this was, it was hard for Hazel to do.

Finally, Hazel held it out for Taylor to take.

"What is this?" Taylor managed to get out, as she gently took it from Hazel's grasp.

Inhaling, Hazel looked up. "Taylor, I've known who you are," she smiled sadly "for quite some time now." Taylor was taken back. She'd assumed there would have to be some kind of explanation for Frank's wanting Taylor while his wife and daughter had looked on, but Hazel already knew?

"How? When?" Taylor shook her head, wondering how Hazel could have been so kind to her if she knew all this time.

"Right after Cal died." She let out a shaky breath. "I came home early from a prayer meeting at our church that night, to see Frank sitting on his recliner in the living room. His face looked like …" Hazel had a faraway look, as if she were reliving that day. "He looked as if he had seen a ghost."

Taylor, not sure where this was going, asked, "Did he?"

Hazel chuckled and nodded. "He kind of did."

Taylor gave her a puzzled expression before Hazel explained.

"Taylor, he saw you." She put her hand on Taylor's knee. "You came to find Callum at the university, remember?"

Taylor nodded. "I do remember."

"Well, Emily had found, and read, the letter Cal wrote you." She chuckled. "Frank was already in deep water with her all day for it. No pun intended." Hazel winked at Taylor, who grinned and looked down at the envelope now in her lap, remembering Callum's words to her. "He told me everything that night, Taylor. It was …" Hazel drifted off as she politely smiled at friends walking past "it was hard to take."

Taylor had never imagined Hazel's perspective of finding out. Or even Emily's. No wonder Emily was so cold to her that day at the university.

Hazel played with her wedding band. "I knew it was you when we first met out on the street, too." She chuckled. "I couldn't believe it was, and to know you had a family! And then, when you helped him clean up the trash outside our house when we first moved in …" Hazel stared down at the ring, twisting on her finger. "Did you know it was him?" Hazel looked up, as though she were afraid to know the answer.

Taylor earnestly shook her head. "No, I … I didn't know."

Hazel sighed. "I didn't think so, but it left Frank at a standstill. He went from being an independent, outgoing man, who was friends with all the neighbors, to a man afraid to leave his own house."

Taylor narrowed her eyes. "Because of me?"

"Yes." Hazel started to play with the strap of her purse. "All because he was afraid to face you. He never thought he'd see you again, let alone randomly move in across from you … I mean, what are the odds?" Hazel's awkward laugh and deep sigh revealed all Taylor needed to know. She was still in disbelief. "He didn't want to be known by you in the state he was in, and he certainly couldn't believe how you'd ended up in his life again." Hazel's smile was genuine, but sad.

"I wish I knew, Hazel."

"He had said there must be a reason for it…" Hazel sniffed and wiped her nose.

Hearing that gave Taylor a funny feeling in her stomach. He couldn't have thought it was to give his life for Jamie's, was it?

Taylor looked down at the envelope in her hand, afraid to know what was in it. She decided to give it back. "I'm not sure whatever this is … will do me any good." Taylor looked up at Hazel, who had a bewildered expression on her face.

"Oh no, this is nonnegotiable." Hazel pushed Taylor's hand back. "You have to take it. This doesn't belong to me, and *I promised* him I would!" Hazel, eyes wide, pleaded with Taylor to take it. "Don't do it for me." She tilted her head to the side "Do it for … James," she finally let out.

Hearing his name on Hazel's lips shocked Taylor, so much so that she didn't fight her on it, and she let Hazel stand up and walk away.

She watched Hazel go to Emily's side, who was standing next to Andrew. James' grandson, was in fact, the spitting image of James. Taylor was thankful that it wasn't all in her head, although she wasn't sure how seeing him in her daily life was going to pan out.

Taylor sat there for a few minutes, watching her family talk to friends and neighbors, eating the tiny sandwiches on the table in the center of the room, and saw Emily take a few glances her way but make no move to come over and talk.

Knowing that Emily knew, too, Taylor found herself wondering if they'd be able to have any sort of a friendship. She hoped they could. She would love to get to know James's daughter, just like he'd been able to get to know her son.

Taylor fiddled with the envelope from Hazel and, taking a breath, she slowly opened it.

A gasp escaped her lips as the necklace fell into her hands. After all this time, she was holding it. The pearl was a lot smaller than she remembered and the gold chain was not gold at all but looked brassy and was turning green from age. Taylor couldn't help but smile at the distant memory of it. Placing it back in the envelope, she took out the folded piece of paper and began to open it as she held her breath.

She was confused at first.

She was looking at an email address. It was her name, but it wasn't an email address she had ever seen before.

Taytay_brown@hotmail.com and a password with various letters, numbers, and special characters was written underneath it.

She stared at it, processing what this meant, but once she realized, she smiled down at the paper. Folding it back up, she put it in her purse and stood up. She would eventually prepare herself to read his words that had been written for her eyes only, but first, she joined Travis. She slipped her hand in his and together, they talked with their friends on Adler Lane about the incredible life of the man, Frank DeLuca.

CHAPTER TWENTY-SEVEN

Now

December 4, 2016—Myrtle Beach, South Carolina

J ust over three months had passed since Frank's funeral.

Taylor had decided to refer to him as Frank, and leave James a distant, but happy memory. One from her past—just like a dream, as Callum had said James did with her.

But now, she sat at the desk in their home office, fingers hovering over the keyboard, ready to type in "hotmail.com" which ended up taking her to Outlook.

Her boys were at school, and Travis was at work. She had told Travis about this secret email account the day she'd received it, and not only did he not seem intimidated, but he actually encouraged her to read whatever it was that James had wanted her to know. He even asked if she wanted him there when she read it. Although she refused, she couldn't believe how supportive he was through it all.

At first, there had been the initial shock of finding out the truth of who Frank was, and Travis had had the same questions Taylor had when she'd first learned, but then he was quiet, silently processing this news. He and his mom had had long conversations over the phone, and he'd let Taylor grieve in the way she needed to.

But Taylor truly felt at peace now, and she knew she *had* to be at peace with her life—past and present—in order to move on with her future. If she was going to read these emails, whatever was in them, she knew the state of mind she had to be in because she wasn't going to allow his words to throw her off in any way.

Getting to Outlooks' home page, she unfolded the paper, now worn at the edges from being held, carried around, and anxiously played with. She typed in the email followed by the password she was given, and held her breath as she pushed "enter."

A page popped up with a blue and white screen. A total of five emails were in there, all from one email address: jbroman_78@hotmail.com.

They were all from James, dates ranging from 1996 until 2016, a month before he passed away.

Taylor took a breath, and then clicked on the first email.

Date: July 4, 1996
To: taytay_brown@hotmail.com
From: jbroman_78@hotmail.com
Subject: Another Fourth Gone By ...

Taylor,

I have been waiting for this day for almost thirty years. That sounds wild, doesn't it? Thirty years. And I want to get to that—I do. I have so much to tell you, but first I need you to know that I actually can imagine what today must be like for you. It is the second Fourth of July we haven't spent together, for you at least. Today is not my second one, and I can't even count how many I've now spent without you, but I remember exactly what it was like for me at first.

So entirely different in so many ways.

It will always hold a special place in my heart, no matter how many years go by, and I wish I could tell you that in person. But, for obvious reasons, I'm unable to. Just like I'm not sure if you'll ever read these emails. How could I get the login and password info to you? And then expect you to carry on with your life as though this is a completely normal situation? It's not like people get sucked into a different time every day, and how is it not an actual mind-blowingly big deal?

So, if nothing else, it's therapeutic for me, writing things down even if no one sees them. I've read all about what happened to you and, Tay, I am so sorry. I made a friend, Callum Decker, and I asked him to go to you to make sure things were okay. Actually, I'm pretty sure that I begged him at one point. My heart broke when I found out just how bad things were for you, and I even hired lawyers after I found out what my parents put you through. I can tell you right now that they will never bother, or look for, you again. I promise because, Taylor, I can honestly say that I am heartbroken over their words, actions, and accusations. You deserved none of what happened to you, what was said to you, or where they sent you.

I have Callum to thank for the idea of sending someone in there to help you. She was one of my students—I became a high school history teacher—and Abby was my eyes and ears while you were in there. I only kept in touch with her because she and my daughter were close friends in high school, and then they kept in touch through college. When she graduated from nursing school, I did what I could to get her a job there. With help from Cal, we were able to get her in as close as we could to you.

While Abby didn't know the backstory, or that I was even involved, she was more than willing to help "Dr. Carter." I asked her to use Cal's pseudonym, instead of my own, only because it would have made more sense to you. For starters, why would an old man named Frank have any interest in you whatsoever? But you already knew a Dr. Carter, even though he didn't really exist.

I was happy to hear you kept your sense of humor. Abby emailed updates to "Dr. Carter" and shared stories of all you said that made her laugh. They made me laugh, too. And then I saw you, Taylor. You came to my house, and I didn't know it then, but she unknowingly gave you my home address. My daughter answered the door, and I remained upstairs, frozen in place at the sight of you. I was so shocked that you looked exactly the same. I had to keep reminding myself that I was not the same person that I was when you knew me, but you … you were beautiful. I lost sight of you when Emily opened the door, and then I raced to the top of the stairs to listen. I needed to hear your voice.

I was a forty-eight-year-old man completely taken back in time by you. I felt giddy and excited, and then I heard my wife's voice inviting you to my birthday dinner, and it brought me back to my reality.

I felt ashamed. I knew you couldn't come. It would have been too dangerous. But we had no way to get ahold of you and I couldn't tell them why I didn't want you there. They don't know anything about my past, and I was unable to explain my behavior and my sudden reasons for not wanting guests. But something in me sparked to life when I saw you. A flame re-lit and I couldn't ignore it. It was one thing to know you were out there somewhere, but it was quite another to see your physical being with you having no knowledge that it was me, right upstairs.

I would have given anything to run down those stairs and hug you, to tell you that everything was okay, and it would be okay. I hope you understand why I didn't. Why I couldn't.

It's weird, going back in time. To know what's coming without letting on what you know is actually a strength I never thought I'd possess. But here I am, knowing that today, of all days, launched the first day of independent email (I'd like to thank Mrs. Lynch for all of the random facts she gave us in high school History 201 … am I right?)

I actually came on here wanting to tell you what happened to me. Where I ended up and how I got to where I am, but that will have to wait for another day because, right now, I'm exhausted. Reliving all of this is emotionally draining. I hope you understand and have patience with me as I try to get through this piece by piece.

So today, on the Fourth of July, I truly hope you are out enjoying yourself. That you have found friends and are out partying like an eighteen-year-old should be. I hope that you can put me in your past so you can move on. Emily told me you were looking for Callum, and I know you're excited to see him again at my birthday if only for the sole purpose of finding me, or maybe to try to bring me back, as I was, to you again. I'm still stressing over how to handle that, but I know it'll work out as it should. And Taylor, please believe me when I say that you deserve nothing more than to live your life to its fullest, and to embrace those who are currently in your life, instead of holding onto the ones who are only a memory of your past.

I love you, Taylor.
I always will.
James xoxo

Taylor swiped at her eyes, unsure of what to make of this. It didn't sound anything like James. She felt that she could see his heart in it, and he knew exactly what to say, but why didn't it *sound* like him?

There was the memory about Mrs. Lynch, and it brought a smile to Taylor. She sat beside James in that history class. They'd pass notes, share a Dr. Pepper that James had bought at the vending machine right before class, and laugh over all the random tidbits of information she'd come up with as though she were a vault of useless but amazing facts. Mrs. Lynch was the best.

And James ... or Frank ... knew about her.

Taylor slammed the laptop closed and covered her eyes, breathing heavily into the cuffs of her sweater. She shouldn't have read this. It was already bringing up so many old emotions that she wasn't ready to uncover.

She marched to the kitchen. It was only nine-thirty in the morning. She had all day, but she needed fuel. It was too early to have a drink, although, if she wanted to, she could ask Heather, who would be over with mimosas in two seconds flat. Taylor seriously contemplated it before making another pot of coffee instead. She leaned against the counter, biting her thumbnail, and bouncing her foot while she waited for it to drip, added a splash of vanilla soy creamer to her coffee when it was ready, then raced back to the office. She needed to keep going, or else the anticipation would consume her day.

Sitting back down, she steeled herself against what else she was about to read. Would he tell her about meeting Hazel? Although she knew, she wasn't sure her heart could handle reading about it. There was only one way to find out.

She opened the laptop again, set her coffee down, and entered the password to the laptop. Her Hotmail session had expired, so she re-entered her login information, clicking on the next email.

Date: July 12, 1996
To: taytay_brown@hotmail.com
From: jbroman_78@hotmail.com
Subject: Goodbye, Tay

My Tay,

I expected to write you earlier to tell you everything about what it was like for me, to go to a different time, but I couldn't find the words. And then we found out that Cal had died. His death was such a shock, a huge loss for me and others like me.

I know that you weren't waiting for the next email. You haven't even read my first one. But something happened today, Taylor.

The world almost lost you.

Yesterday, I saw you again. A day I never thought would happen. I don't know how, but there you were in the lobby at the University of Charleston, no doubt to find Callum once again. I was bringing down another box from his office, clearing away files that I knew he'd want in safekeeping, and I heard Emily talking to someone. When I heard her voice and knew she was upset, I rushed over to see what was going on.

And then I saw you—and I understood.

You and Emily both turned toward me and, without thinking, I dropped the box and bolted down the hall. Did you even see me?

I heard fast footsteps and the only place I could go was into the office. I tried to hide, but other than the tiny closet, there was nowhere to go.

I'm too large of a man to be hiding in the office closet, but there I was, feeling like a child. And then I remembered the letter to you, from Callum. I'd brought it there as I was clearing things out, knowing it had to get to you. But I didn't know how, hoping his department would send it to you ... somehow.

Then, seeing you put me in a frenzy that I wasn't equipped to handle. I didn't want you to find it and read it like this, not with me in there watching. I tried to beat you to it, grabbing the envelope and sneaking it back into the closet. Instead, when I grabbed the envelope to bring it with me, the letter fell out. I reached to pick it up but paused when you walked right past the open office door, staring straight ahead and out the window in the hall. I watched you for a millisecond before realizing that you could turn your head at any moment and see me. Once again, flustered, I buried myself into the depths of Cal's closet. The letter was sitting a foot away from the door with no chance of me retrieving it before you and Emily entered.

Emily's behavior toward you was inexcusable, and for that I'm truly sorry. She is the most wonderful girl. She is kind, strong, fiercely loyal, and stubborn just like her mother, but she found the letter too, Tay. He had given it to me when he came back from California and I stupidly left it out at home. He wanted me to read it, to make sure he was doing and saying the right thing.

Then we changed my birthday plans. Cal was supposed to come early for my birthday dinner and help me explain everything to them, then wait at my house for you to arrive while Emily, Hazel, and I went out to dinner, but then ... he was gone. That night, Emily confronted me about the letter ... I had to explain everything to her. She gave me the silent treatment until I finally told Hazel only yesterday, after I saw you at the University.

To say things aren't good between Hazel and I would be an understatement. Trust has been broken and she legitimately questions my mental health—it's giving me a completely new perspective on what you went through, but it's also giving me a new sense of awe for you. You went through that, too, and not only were you resilient through it, but you came out on the other side stronger and more determined than before.

I was jealous of Travis when he took care of you in the office, because holding you in my arms again made me feel like I was back in high school and he was taking my girlfriend away. Then I saw my wedding ring and the gray hairs on my arms reminding me that you aren't mine anymore. It was hard but, in my heart, I knew you'd be okay. That boy sure likes you a lot. At first it was hard for me to watch, but if it couldn't be me, then I wanted it to be him. With all my heart, I want that for you.

How he looked at you, Taylor, is how I once looked at you, too, and I want a man to look at my daughter the same way. Once I realized that, I knew that I was ready to let you go. I just needed to see you through a different lens.

When June 16, 1978 came, I was elated knowing that this was the day Taylor Brown was going to be born and I would finally live in a world that you were in again. But seeing you in daily life is something else entirely. It's a situation I didn't expect I'd have to deal with and it's one that I hope makes me stronger.

I hope that it makes my marriage with Hazel stronger, too. And Emily? Well ... she's still young and processing this life-changing information. It took me years to accept what happened. How can I expect her to be okay with it in a few short weeks? This morning I went out for a walk, regardless of the weather, because in all honesty, it was hard to be in the same house with Hazel, just as it must have been tough for her to be in the same house with me. She couldn't even look at me after my betrayal of her trust and I didn't blame her one bit.

So, I walked out into the rain, turning down streets and paths with no specific destination in mind until I saw you—you were walking out to the ocean. I tried to call to you, but the wind drowned out my voice. I saw it when it was too late—the wave that took you—and my heart stopped. I started running to you, calling out your name, but then he came. Travis came running and jumped in the waves trying to find you. I stood on the shore, watching, praying. He had to find you. I held my breath for I don't know how long until I saw him emerge with you in his arms. I burst into tears and ran to the nearest house, banging on the back door until a woman answered. I asked her to call an ambulance and pointed to Travis coming out of the water with you, limp in his arms. She ran to put blankets in the dryer before running out to meet Travis and you to bring you in. I stood back, watching. I couldn't tell what was rain and what were my tears, but I was drenched.

I cried out of fear of losing you, even though I didn't have you. I cried out of joy that you were safe, and I cried out of sadness that I wasn't the one to save you. And then, Taylor, it hit me. I knew what I had to do, and it's what you need to do, too.

I walked away.

You are no longer mine to save. You're not mine to comfort, or even mine to love. I have to walk away and let you go, Taylor. I have to run back home to my wife and my daughter and hold them and love them and work hard at keeping them safe every minute of every day as long as I live.

And right now, I take comfort in knowing that you are safe with him.

That's all I can ask for.

I'm happy you're safe, Taylor.
James xoxo

Tears streamed down her face. Taylor hadn't anticipated the emotions that would come with reliving that day. To think that James had been there the whole time … Most of that day was a blur to Taylor and one that she and Travis rarely spoke of. Taylor had never admitted to Travis the reason for walking out there or the reason that she'd gotten mad and eventually given up. But now that he knew, she could open up about it.

And she would.

She blew her nose, then took another sip of coffee, staring at the date of the next email, scrolling to see other dates, thinking there were a few that she missed. But there were none between them. The next one was dated January 14, 2014.

Taylor wondered why he let eighteen years go by, but then she knew that he honestly had let her go. Without hesitating, she clicked on the email.

To: taytay_brown@hotmail.com
From: jbroman_78@hotmail.com
Subject: News

Taylor,

I told myself I wasn't going to email you again. How could I let you go if I was still writing to you? And while I know it's not really keeping in contact with you if you have no knowledge that these emails even exist, I was still holding onto you in my heart by the words I hoped you'd one day read. I couldn't do that to Hazel, or to Emily.

But right now, I'm breaking that promise to myself.

I have undergone many tests for abnormalities in my blood, and today I was officially diagnosed with non-Hodgkin's Lymphoma.

For some reason, I needed to tell you, Taylor. It's part of my acceptance of it, telling those I love.

I can't accept this news unless I share it with you.

I truly hope you're well and living an amazing life.

James

Taylor stared at the words he wrote. Eighteen years has passed, and he'd felt the need to tell her this life-altering news.

She smiled in understanding.

In high school, he would call Taylor at home just to tell her that he'd had the most unbelievable burger with Mark and that he *had* to take her there so she could experience it for herself.

That's who he was. A sharer of information, and her heart swelled knowing that even in the absence of the emails she didn't know existed, he was still thinking of her.

She felt a surge of excitement clicking on the next email.

Date: March 7, 2016
To: taytay_brown@hotmail.com
From: jbroman_78@hotmail.com
Subject: none

Taylor,

These past two years have been hard. The combination of chemo treatments and surgeries have worn me out. The cancer is not only refusing to leave my body, but it is rapidly spreading.

Hazel and I have made the decision to stop treatment and for the two of us to live out the rest of my days back in Myrtle Beach. Our daughter, Emily, is recently divorced and desires to move back to where she was raised, with her son, Andrew.

I hesitate even writing these words because I'm not sure if you're still there. Both Hazel and I have fears of running into you, although Hazel assures me that, even if we did, you wouldn't know who I am. She and I are fearful for two very different reasons, and I'm ashamed to admit that Hazel is the stronger of the two of us. She was very easily able to move past what happened all those years ago, deciding that it would be best to move away from our home so we could move on and grow together. We went back to California where I could see my parents from a distance.

Although I didn't make it a habit to say hello to familiar faces, the familiar faces helped remind me of the life I once lived, and it helped Hazel and Emily get to know me more—it was part of our healing together, letting them in to who I once was, and they loved experiencing it alongside me. It gave me a sense of peace, and I was able to make new memories with my family.

I took them to our cove, once. Only once. Not that it was too difficult to be there—I cherished the memories you and I made, and I genuinely looked forward to making new ones—but I was too afraid to go to the water. I know I don't have to remind you of the last time I did. I ended up at the same place in a completely different time. I looked around for you, necklace still in my hand, but you weren't there. The confusion lasted almost a week before I resigned myself to what had happened and was forced to survive in a world that I knew nothing about.

I laugh now and, Taylor, if you could have only seen the look on people's faces as I walked the streets of Newport Beach in my boardshorts that were quite literally something from the future. I was tempted to start calling myself Marty McFly, but I knew that no one would know who he was.

I was a scared, and half naked eighteen-year-old boy, alone in a world I knew, but in a time I didn't.

I couldn't do that to my family again, and while Cal told me that the reality of a time warp occurring in the exact same place is pretty much impossible, I couldn't take the chance again. So, we found ourselves a new favorite beach spot—Thirty-Second Street on the Peninsula. Remember where Mark's grandparents had a house? Well, they gave it to Mark after they had passed away about three years ago.

I see Mark there with his sons on the beach every so often. He married Ashley and they look really happy together, Taylor.

At first, I thought we couldn't go back. If I kept seeing them, I thought that I would always see them and mourn the friendship we had, and what we could have had with them. I abruptly got up to leave and Hazel took my hand, asking who I was watching. She knew they meant something to me. So I told her everything, I didn't keep this from her either.

Hazel has been my rock and helped immensely with my healing. I'm so ashamed that I didn't let her in sooner.

I pray that Travis is your rock, and that you let him in just like I did with Hazel. You deserve that, Taylor. I want that for you.

So, it is with a heavy heart that I sign off, for what might possibly be the last time. I'm still debating whether or not to try to get these to you. Only time will tell.

And if not, thank you, Taylor. Thank you for being who I needed in a time of my life when I needed you. And thank you for being a memory of my dreams. If it weren't for the memories I had of you, I wouldn't have kept fighting. I didn't want to live in a world without you, but you kept me going as long as I could, until I met Hazel. I was able to love two amazing women who shaped my life in two incredibly different ways.

I will always be thankful for you.
Until we meet again,
James

Taylor smiled. She knew what he meant, and she was thankful for his words. Even though there was one more email, she had read enough for today's emotional capacity—she even debated whether or not she'd read the last one.

She closed the laptop and picked up her phone to text Travis.

Date night?

She smiled when he immediately texted her again, not needing to wait for a reply.

I already made reservations.

Taylor hugged her phone to her chest.

For the first time in twenty years, Taylor felt a sense of absolute peace about her life that she hadn't experienced before. She knew that she had been given a new lease on her life and she wasn't going to take a single moment for granted.

EPILOGUE

Date: July 2, 2016
To: taytay_brown@hotmail.com
From: jbroman_78@hotmail.com
Subject: My Story

Taylor,

When I ended my previous email, I thought that was it. I thought I might see you in my afterlife, in heaven one day, and even through my fears, or maybe even in my dreams of seeing you here. I sincerely never imagined that I'd live across the street from you. You rendered me speechless at the garbage cans tonight and I'm embarrassed that I was so tongue-tied. Hazel was correct in assuming that you wouldn't recognize me. I'm thankful for that. Although while sometimes I'd imagine our reunion, it never looked like this. But that's not the reason for this email. Seeing you tonight made me realize that I truly owe you my story.

My whole story.

I'm not even sure you want to hear it, but maybe hearing it will bring you clarity and peace. If I can do anything for you in my life, I pray that this is it.

So, Taylor, if you want to proceed in reading these words, this is what happened to me, all those years ago.

You already know the beginning when I ran to the water to clean off your necklace. And then, to you, I was gone. For me, a wave of dizziness and nausea overtook me. I leaned forward thinking I might throw up, but I didn't. I regained my balance and when I looked up, the ocean was there, but the sail boats were no longer visible. I had briefly wondered if there was an earthquake, but when I turned to ask if you had noticed, you weren't there either. Our blanket and picnic basket, even the pathway leading up to the car was gone, overgrown by brush. There was a family down the way, and they all looked at me as though I were an alien when I asked if they saw the direction in which you'd headed. They hadn't seen you.

I walked up and down the beach, calling your name, swimming up and down the coast in case something had happened to you. I had no explanation other than perhaps a wave came, taking you and all of our beach things along with it. The overgrown path and the fact that my car wasn't there wasn't a rational thought in my mind—it didn't occur to me that I may need to reassess my surroundings or even stop to think it odd that everything looked different.

I was more concerned about finding you.

It wasn't until I was walking up and down Main Street that I felt like I was on a movie set. Everyone was dressed differently, and Ruby's had a "Now Open!" sign in the window. Taylor, it was brand-new. Just built. In my confusion, I ran home, only to see that my neighborhood was under construction. There were only three homes finished on our street and my house was just a lot that had yet to be sold. I ran to the same liquor store on the corner of Fifth and Main that's still there today and grabbed a newspaper. It was May 25, 1965.

I thought I was in a dream.

I ran back to the beach, thinking that this was an elaborate prank, but it was the same as I'd left it, and on top of it all, it was starting to get dark.

I slept on the beach that night. I was cold, I was scared, and I was still convinced all would be right in the morning.

Except it wasn't. I woke up soaking wet due to the high tide. The sun was just starting to come up and you still weren't there.

I needed somewhere to go. I made the trek back up the overgrown path and headed back into town. I ended up going into the first church I saw, St. John's Presbyterian Church. I walked in, barefoot, shirtless and covered in sand. There was an older lady whose jaw dropped as she took in the sight of me. She didn't even greet me but ran away and down the hall instead. I thought initially that I had scared her and was on my way out of the church when I heard a man's voice.

She had run to get the pastor. He brought me to the church's lost and found, dressed me, then took me out for breakfast. He told me I could work as a custodian at their church in exchange for a bit of money and, more importantly, a place to stay. So, I lived with the pastor and his wife in a room over their garage on Magnolia Street.

I thought I was going crazy, and I didn't end up telling him right away what had happened. Taylor, I couldn't tell anyone. I was alone and knew that no one would believe me. But Pastor Jerry was so kind. He prayed with me and for me, and I knew that he was someone I could trust. So, over mid-morning coffee at the church about a week later, I told him everything.

If he was shocked by my story, he didn't show it. But instead, without a word, he walked away. I sat there feeling so stupid and even started questioning my own story. But he came back, showing me a sheet of paper.

It was for the draft.

I was resigned to only being good enough in this life to go fight for my country and lose my life. But honestly, Taylor, I was fine with it. I didn't think that I had a life here without you. I didn't want one. I had no family, no friends, no ID, and so I jumped at the chance to go somewhere that I was needed, and even maybe wanted.

Pastor Jerry's words stayed with me as he handed me the form. "Son, no matter where you are in life, or in time, be the man God created you to be."

It gave me a boost of confidence that propelled me to fight for what I wanted and needed.

Except, I had no ID.

So, I went to the office to see if there was anything I could do without being drafted and without having identification. There was a boy out front. He was only a boy. He had his draft card and ID and was crying. He was standing there, frozen in place as boys walked in and out around him. I stood next to him, asking if he was all right. He didn't register my presence until about the third time I asked. He looked right through me as though I were a ghost. At least I now blended in with my new, or old, clothes.

He shook his head and told me he didn't want to go in. He had just gotten engaged, and he didn't want to lose his life. He didn't want to fight.

I asked him to sit on the bench by the sidewalk with me. I'm not sure what prompted me to do this, but I did. We sat in silence for a few moments, and then I asked him about his fiancée. Taylor, his face lit up like a Christmas tree as he spoke of her, and an idea came to mind. I told him about you, but obviously not everything about you. I didn't mention the tiny detail that you weren't even born yet, but I *did* tell him that I'd lost you.

So, without hesitation, I asked him if he wanted me to take his place. His bewildered eyes took me in, and I thought he was going to say no. But instead, he asked why I, a complete and utter stranger to him, would want to take his place in a war that I probably would not come back from. And the truth spilled out of me.

I told him that I'd already lost someone I loved, and if I couldn't have my happily-ever-after, I wanted to make sure that a couple who was so clearly in love would have theirs—a chance to grow old together.

He cried, then hugged me so tight and for so long, sobbing into my shoulder. He all but shoved his draft card and ID into my hands, thanking me profusely, and then told me that he had to go tell Marilyn the good news.

I sat on that bench, not able to hold back the smile over this man's joy, and then looked down at the ID.

I was now Frank Roger DeLuca.

I confidently walked into the office, and the next day I was on an airplane to Vietnam with fifty other soldiers, ready to fight.

And fight we did.

Remember in Mrs. Lynch's history class when she made us watch that one scene in Forest Gump when Tom Hanks keeps running back in to grab all the wounded soldiers as he looks for Bubba?

It was nothing like that, Taylor. It was much worse.

I don't know if there's one single movie that accurately depicts all the emotions that come with being in the middle of a war. The noises, the fears, the body parts not attached to their owners which became something of a norm that should never be considered normal. I was there for six weeks fighting, then losing friends I had just met the day before. I was cold, I was wet, and eventually, I was sick.

I had a fever from gangrene in my foot that started causing delusions and I was sent to the hospital where I was in a fever-induced coma for almost a week. When I woke up, I had lost my right leg from the knee down, and my nurse sat on the edge of the bed and let me cry.

I had no shame in my tears. I told her over and over again that I wished I had lost my life instead. I asked her why she didn't just let me die. And she took my face in her hands and spoke to me like a mother speaking to her child.

She was adamant in telling me that she was not about to let them win by taking the best men away from us—this was her way of fighting back, and under her watch, she would do everything in her power to raise up a healthy army that could do just that.

Fight back.

So, I stopped crying. I willed myself to heal and, in the meantime, I worked alongside her in the only capacity that I could, given my condition. I helped clean and sterilize instruments, I took account of the beds, and I sat and prayed with other soldiers who came in wounded and wanting to die just like I had. I helped their resolve as I showed them my leg, and together, the nurse and I made sure that these men left the hospital with determined spirits that would help us all get through our time in Vietnam, together.

Taylor, that nurse was Hazel.

She saved my life in more ways than one. It seems like our romance happened fast, but facing the times and trials that we did, we were forced to lean and depend on each other in a way I had never known before. I fell in love with her while working side-by-side, not that I ever fell out of love with you, but I also knew that I would never get back to you.

I knew that, even if I did see you again, I'd be an old man.

I gave in to a love that I needed in that moment, and I was so afraid that you would find out. As if I were betraying you, even though you didn't exist yet.

When we got home from the war, we moved to South Carolina where Hazel grew up, and while we were there, I met Callum. He started teaching as a young professor at the university in quantum physics and I had made a meeting with him, telling him that I was interested in getting his opinion on time travel. That first meeting lasted almost three hours and we ended up meeting every week to talk about theories and possibilities.

I told him my story, albeit hesitantly, and after about a month of meetings, I had never felt more seen. He not only believed me, but he introduced me to another man who traveled in the same manner that I had. He went eleven years

THAT TIME I LOVED YOU

into the future, and it was like an out-of-body experience showing someone my true self and talking openly about it.

This was in 1967, and there were still quite a few years to go before you were born. But when you were, on the actual day of your birth, I couldn't stop smiling and crying—because I now lived in a world where you were in it, once again.

Emily was three when you were born, and I took her to get ice cream, without Hazel's knowledge, and together we celebrated you.

Then the day was coming when I traveled. I debated whether or not to show up on the beach, to tell you everything and let you know that I was okay. Callum convinced me not to. He explained that you seeing me would hinder my life as Frank, and that you would be a seventeen-year-old girl who had just lost her love and would do everything you could to be in my life again.

I still hadn't told Hazel the truth, and I realized that he was, in fact, correct. I wrote you a note that I was able to give him, which he reluctantly took for me. I didn't ask if he ever gave it to you, though.

The weekend of May 25, 1995 pained me, Taylor, so much that I went away that weekend so I could be in my sorrow and personal despair in peace. I didn't want my daughter or Hazel to see the turmoil that day would bring.

Every May 25 brings so many emotions, but to relive that day, knowing exactly what you would be going through, made me feel like less of a man somehow. I felt helpless knowing that I couldn't be there for you.

Cal was my rock during that summer. He had traveled for work on and off, and I didn't know that he was going to see you that very night. Part of me was so glad that he let you know I was safe, but I know he did it against his better judgment—he did it for me. I heard stories and read the paper about what was happening, and I got involved when my parents blamed you for everything that was happening. I paid a lawyer to silence them, and I never told them who

I was. I just needed you to be left alone. I needed you to be okay. When I heard that you had been sent to the behavioral hospital, I broke down. I couldn't imagine all that you were going through.

I'm still so thankful that Abby was able to get so close to you. She was a true blessing as she sent emails updating "Dr. Carter" about how you were doing.

I didn't know the extent that she had helped you and that she had given you our home address.

I came to see you in there. I'm not sure what prompted it, but I needed eyes on you, to know that, despite the situation, you were at least okay. I spoke to Dr. Green while I was there. He wanted a reference for Abby, and I decided to give one in person.

I didn't like that man one bit, and I'm happy to tell you that after what I heard from Abby about how he treated you, we were able to get testimonials from other nurses and staff members. Eventually, he was "welcomed to not work there anymore." At least I think that's the term he prefers to use now.

There's not much more to the story, as now, you know most everything else. Seeing you tonight though, after all these years, stirred something up in me. It reminded me how much I wanted to tell you everything that happened to me. How much you deserved to know.

But now that I know exactly where you are, I'm not sure I can face seeing you every day. I have to be honest, though, and tell you that I am quite enjoying seeing your sons. Seeing an extension of you is mesmerizing.

I sometimes watch them out my window from my chair, playing basketball with Travis, or riding bikes with their friends. I see you washing dishes at the kitchen sink, and out of fear of sounding like a stalker, I see when Travis comes up and kisses you. It stung the first time I saw. It shouldn't have, but it did.

And there you have it. This old man's dying confessions.

I know your story. I was there for a lot of it back home, and now seeing how you ended up … well, it gives me peace. Peace knowing that you are being taken care of, that you have moved on, and even through all of your hardships, I have peace seeing you come out stronger. And I have peace that I am in your life, again, for a reason. Although I'm not sure of that reason quite yet, I know only time will tell. But I hope that, after all these years, all that we've both gone through, and all you have yet to face, we didn't go through all of this without a purpose for it happening.

I'm determined that there is a reason for all of this, Taylor.

You don't know it yet, but I feel it deep inside me.

Thank you again for helping me with my trash bins tonight. I was in a lot of pain, and Hazel was at our church's bingo night. I know you're wary of me, and I hope I can change that. I hope I can get past the shock of you being in my life again, and I hope that this reunion is fate.

You are an amazing, beautiful, and kind woman, Tay.

My forever with you might have been lost to time … but I will make sure that time is well spent. I will *always* remember that time I loved you.

Until my dying breath.

James xoxo

ACKNOWLEDGEMENTS

Sitting down to write this and thinking about everyone I want to thank is so overwhelming because so many very important people had a hand in this book.

But first, my husband. Ryan, Thank you first and foremost for believing in me. Walking around Balboa Island and dreaming about book ideas will always be one of my favorite pre-kid memories with you. Thank you for allowing me time to write in our, now, crazy family of six schedules and being my biggest cheerleader! I could have never done this without you. I love you!

To my kids, for being so excited for me, even wanting to be my early editors, and asking for the rights to its screenplay. (Jackson…it's still yours!)

To my parents, for covering me in prayer every step of the way.

To my first ever readers—Colby Moore, Kaley Brandon, Andrew Hoffman, Lisa Collier, Julie Dunbar, Tracy Walker, Sheryl Gunderson (my mother-in-law), and my dad, Rob Hayes. Your comments, suggestions, encouragement, and excitement over this book are truly as invaluable as your friendship to me! Love you all!

Thank you to everyone at hope*books for providing this opportunity to publish my book in a publishing world that I have zero clue about how to navigate. I have learned so much through this process and will forever be thankful for the guidance and ease of each and every step!

And finally, to Stephanie Mack. The one who went before me, the author of two books, and my writing bestie. From our Nashville writing conference to hiding out in Pasadena as we wrote all weekend, this book will forever be laced with memories of writing *with* you, laughing, sharing, and occasionally looking up from our laptops to grab a snack! My head might not be on my shoulders if you weren't listening to all my Marco Polo's, giving advice, building me up and motivating me to keep going when I didn't feel like writing, and for being the best friend that I needed when I felt as though I couldn't finish this marathon. You, my friend, are a treasure, and I am honored to write alongside you!